*LAMB IN HIS BOSOM*

# LAMB
# IN HIS BOSOM

## Caroline Miller

*Afterword by Elizabeth Fox-Genovese*

PEACHTREE PUBLISHERS LTD.
*Atlanta*

Published by
PEACHTREE PUBLISHERS LTD.
494 Armour Circle, NE
Atlanta, Georgia 30324

*Jacket/cover design: Candace J. Magee*
*Jacket/cover illustration: Geo Sipp*

MANUFACTURED IN THE UNITED STATES OF AMERICA

10  9  8  7  6  5  4  3  2  1

This book was originally published in 1933 by Harper & Brothers Publishers

**Library of Congress Cataloging-in-Publication Data**

Miller, Caroline Pafford, 1903-
        Lamb in his bosom / Caroline Miller ; afterword by
Elizabeth Fox-Genovese.
            p.      cm. — (Modern southern classics series)
        ISBN 1-56145-074-X
        1. Frontier and pioneer life—Georgia—Fiction.
2. Georgia—History—Fiction.    I. Title.    II. Series.
PS3525.I517L3    1993
813'.52—dc20
                                                                    92-38286
                                                                    CIP

*For*
*Wi'D and little Bill and Nip 'n' Tuck*

*LAMB IN HIS BOSOM*

# Chapter 1

CEAN turned and lifted her hand briefly in farewell as she rode away beside Lonzo in the ox-cart. Her mother and father and Jasper and Lias stood in front of the house, watching her go. The old elder who had married Cean to Lonzo was in the house somewhere, leaving the members of the family to themselves in their leave-taking of Cean. But the youngest of the family, Jake, was not there; he had fled away, his thin face hard with grief. He had laid his deepest curse on Lonzo Smith's head. Now he lay on his face under a budding willow on a sandbank of the river that ran two miles from his father's place. He hoped, with a fiendish hope that was a curse, that hairy, red worms would find out the holes in Lonzo Smith's ears, that they would crawl in and grow horny heads and furry tails, and eat out Lonzo's in'ards. But Cean would hate that; she would brew all kinds of yerb teas for him to drink. There wasn't anything to do. Cean had gone and done it; she had made her bed; now let her lie in it. She wouldn't ever know he cared, neither. She wasn't his sister any more; she was all Lonzo's. Now she would sleep in Lonzo's bed instead of Jake's. At this thought, misery almost suffocated the child; he found it hard to draw his breath out of his lungs. For he could shut his eyes and feel her body warming his body under the covers. She had a way of rounding his head into her shoulder, of catching his legs up against her with her strong, lean hand, and they would sleep so, their bodies fitted one to the other. In the night they might turn, and then his thin body would fit in a protecting curve along her back.

He opened his eyes, and there was the white sand against his face, magnified into little hills and valleys before his eyes. There were the budding willow branches above him, rising and falling in lifts of wind that ran down the river. He blew on a hill of sand close beside his mouth, and it fluttered down. He'd go on back and bring up the calves. They'd think that's where he was.

Cean's and Lonzo's bodies jounced gently in the slow motion of the wooden-wheeled cart. The way to their new home lay across the woods, close around the edge of the great swamp of cypress, through a little creek, and across a rise where there were huckleberries and rattlesnakes in hot weather. Farther on there were tall timbers and fine grazing; and there, six miles to the west of her mother's home, Lonzo had set up Cean's house with its broad clay-stuck chimney. There was a spring at the side under a smother of elder bushes and sweet bays; a new-set fig bush and Seven Sisters rose cuttings and a bed of pinks were beginning to take root by Cean's back door where her mother had set them. Lonzo had cut down every tree for the house, and Cean's brothers had helped him to notch them and lock them into the sturdy walls, and to line the walls with heavy planks riven from heart-pine. They had split the rails for the cow-pen, and Betsey was there now with her little pied-ed calf close against her. Lonzo would set up a spring-house for Cean, for the milk and butter, when he had his seed in the ground; and in the late summer, Cean's brothers would help him with the crib for the corn that he would raise in the new ground, corn for meal and grits, corn for feed for the ox. Pumpkins, peas, potatoes, melons—they would raise fields full of them; they would fare fine. Cean would water and tend such things. Her mother had told her that a woman must see to things like that—fruit, a garden-patch, milk and butter and the children; men must raise and butcher the meat and make and gather in the crops.

Cean's new bonnet was hot about her neck. She slipped

it back off her head, tied the strings together under her chin, and let it swing free down her back. Her face was brown and full and bright; her mouth was wide and closed firmly over her teeth. Her hair blowsed over her temples from where it was parted in the middle. Her bright brown eyes went shyly about, seeking gentle satisfaction in the soft air, the sunshine, the thick plodding of the hooves of the ox on the slick brown pine-needles and soft sand. Her happy glance slipped shyly to Lonzo's bearded face. His neck, browned by sunlight, was moist in fine beads of sweat. Her glance moved upward to his coarse black hair that came down from under the fine hat he had bargained for last fall on the Coast. She saw the set of his large head, the set of his strong shoulders, then her eyes hurried away, a little frightened by that nearness, by the coarse black hair, the strong male shoulders, the sturdy silence of the man beside her who was her husband.

Now she was married. The elder that came through twice a year had said the marriage words over them: "Do you take this woman, Tillitha Cean Carver . . . ? . . ." After that, she belonged to him, to cook his victuals and to wash his clothes. After that, she belonged to herself, too. Now she was a woman and would churn her own butter, scald her own milk-crocks and set them in the sun to make them smell sweet and clean; now she would own and tend her little patch of herbs and melons, drop corn behind her own man, and watch it grow, and hoe the grass out from around the sharp, clean blades cutting through the earth. She would have her own corn, her own man, her own way of living from now on, but her eyes hurried away from his strong, sinewy neck going down into his shirt, his strong, sinewy body wet with fine-beaded new sweat.

The trail hugged the edge of the swamp, and the undergrowth pressed in close about them. It was cool and sweet here. The air was wet from the swamp water and the black, spongy bogs. Yellow jessamine sprawled high on the trees and swarms of its sweet-smelling bright blooms burst out through the green. The cypresses were new-feathered on their pale high trunks. All the swamp seemed stirred into sweet unease. In the summer it lay sluggish and fevered in muck; alligators drowsed in the mud and moccasins slipped through the water. In winter the swamp was dismal and forbidding, with the beasts screaming in the cold, and the water black and still. But now, on Cean's marriage day, yellow jessamine smothered the tops of the pine trees, maples burned aloft in the cool gloom, and all the little saplings and all the giant pines lifted the candles of their wax-colored leaf-buds, white candles on the tip of every tree, on the end of every limb, burning with slow fire into new growth. Orioles chittered carelessly. A cardinal stitched a bar of song over and over, reiterating spring. Close about them Cean heard the stealthy, hurrying feet of little creatures escaping from their path; bushes rustled in brief panic, then stilled. Coveys of partridges whirred away in sudden, frantic haste; Lonzo would trap them when the crops were laid by. And there were turkeys in the swamp and squirrels and fish—all manner of meat. Oh, they would fare fine!

Cean drew her legs closer to herself so that her skirt might escape the bamboo's little thorns that came over the cart's side to pluck at her. Her leg under her heavy skirts pressed close against Lonzo's right leg along the seat beside her. The road to the creek bore sharply to the left, and she pressed hard on Lonzo, leaning against her will. Fear moved through her as she felt herself so close upon him. She tried to move back from him, but could not, for the incline was more than a little steep. Her breathing came and went close against his shoulder. The ox halted and lowered his head in the little stream to drink. Bright-brown water flowed beneath them; bay leaves shone green above them. A creeper of bamboo swam on the current. Here the afternoon light was stifled to clear, pale green. Cean saw the sandy bottom of the stream worn into little ruffles by the water's slow flowing. A little way down the branch, she heard squirrels bark and swing through the tree-tops. For the first time since they had started their journey Lonzo turned his black eyes on her. He said:

"Gittin' tired?"

She flushed and looked far down the little stream.

"No, I ain't a-tired."

There was silence as his eyes went after hers down the stream. She had a feeling that his thoughts were close on the trail of her thoughts. She was too shy now to move farther from him. She said:

"This is a first-rate place fer yore hogs to waller in when hit's hot."

His voice was proud:

"Our hogs, ye'd better say."

Cean's eyes clouded over with shyness. She was miserable under the glance of his eyes and the tone of his voice. He said:

"The hogs'll help keep out snakes fer ye . . . if ye're scared of 'em."

"I ain't a-scared. . . ."

His black eyes shone.

"Ye ain't a-scared of nothin', air ye?"

She shook her head and dropped her eyes miserably. He watched her for a moment and spoke heavily and sweetly:

"Little un!"

He turned his head quickly and chucked to the ox; the three of them moved up to the bank where the sand was washed white, and on up the rise where the palmettos whispered in clumps, where new leaves of the scrub oaks were pale yellow and green, where pines soughed aloft on their great rough trunks and grass was springing, heavy and green in the open spaces, where Cean's cow would graze.

Smoke from Lonzo's slow-burning stumps in the new ground drifted far across the swamp. Cean saw it—a thin fog in the lowlands. And off there she saw her house, bright-yellow as the sun, new in the sun, the logs fresh from the bark, the chimney fresh from the clay in Lonzo's hands. At the back the bright new fence rails held in her cow and calf. Far and wide about the house, holes where the stumps had been were smoking in the still air. The undergrowth had been grubbed out, the labor leaving Lonzo's hands horny and hard, and his heavy shoulders a little stooped. The ground was broken into dark clods, ready for the seeds, yellow, black, white, to burst into bright green down the furrows. Cean could think of the house as almost hidden from sight by rows and rows of rough, rustling corn. There would be cotton at the back, and a patch of tobacco for Lonzo to dry and twist for his own taste. She would root a grape vine to spread across her back yard on posts, and tomorrow she would drop the little handful of sunflower seeds to grow for the hens and rooster her mother had given her.

The ox plodded on across the rising ground and struck into the new ground. The cart jolted them roughly as it went over the uneven plowed ground, making the first road to the door of their house. The house came nearer to Cean, the logs of it golden in the afternoon sunlight, the roof of it sloping sharply down to thwart the soaking rains, the doors and shutters tightly chinked to shut out the sharpest wind of winter.

Finally, there was the yard, cleared but with the soil unturned by the plow. And there was the clean, new block that led from the ground into the house. The chickens scurried past the door, feeling strange away from the great flock that was Cean's mother's. The cow lowed lonesomely down in the pen. Lonzo lifted one of his long legs over the side of the cart and jumped to the ground. He turned back to Cean, and his lips spread a little, almost disclosing his teeth in his soft, thick beard. A little shyly he held out his arms to Cean, saying:

"Come, little un!" And she gave her weight to his arms and slipped through them to the ground.

She went into the house where the floor of split logs had never been scrubbed and yet was clean, where Lonzo had set the bedplace in the corner with its depth of dry corn-shucks soaked and softened in water, and dried again in recent suns. Over these shucks, that would rustle softly with the turn of their bodies, was spread the thick mattress of soft new cotton, caught between its homespun ticking with strong thread in the hands of Cean's mother. Atop the cotton mattress lay Cean's feather bed, the feathers saved from every goose for years gone. Atop this were homespun sheets and Cean's quilts, one of them the bright and dark scraps of the Widow's Trouble pattern, sewn by Cean's fingers through her girlhood. She had two other quilts—Star of the East, and Maiden's Tear—that she had pieced herself. That would be more than enough cover for these bright, cool nights, and before winter came again she would make other quilts. Lonzo's mother had promised wool for two comforts when the sheep should be sheared in April.

Before the deep fireplace were set the well-built chairs that Lonzo had made, the wood bright and new, the cow-hide bottoms only lately stretched and cured. There was a low, wide chest along the wall, for quilts or any such thing. Across the hearth were set the iron pots and the big hoecake spider. From the rafters hung the sides of meat their parents had given them, and there was a keg of shelled corn in the corner; and a grist-mill was to be found in the yard to grind their corn, if Cean would but swing the rock around. From the Smiths or the Carvers, Lonzo could have as many more cartloads of corn as they should need until the crops were made and gathered in. Cean could go to her mother's any day for greens, and her own patch would soon be sown, and green in a month.

The house was ready for living. Cean's mother had made the bed and set out the pots on the fireplace. Betsey would give no milk tonight, because the calf had not been parted off, but after today Cean would be milking.

Cean unrolled the bundle of clothing she had brought with her, and placed it in the chest. She hung her bonnet on a wooden peg by the head of the bed alongside Lonzo's new hat and old coonskin cap. She took off her fine new shoes, brushed the thin dust from them, and set them in the chest. The floor was cool to her feet as she walked about.

It was near dark. Lonzo brought firewood and set fire for cooking. Then he went out again to the cow-pen. Her mother had sent along plenty of cold food for supper, but Cean would cook on her own fireplace this first night in her new home. She sliced meat, and mixed meal and water and salt for cornbread. A song pushed up in her throat as she worked, but she held still because she was afraid Lonzo might notice. When the meal was spread on the eating-table, she called him briefly:

"Supper's done."

He came, and they ate, their glances dropping away, each from the other's, to their victuals, their hands clumsy at breaking the bread and sopping the meat grease.

As night fell the fire on the fireplace was built up and filled the room with soft, pulsing light. Cean cleared the table and brought water to wash her feet.

Lonzo went to the bed and, stooping, brought out a roll of goods. He brought them to Cean's chair by the fire, and spread them on the floor for her to see:

"I thought ye mought like somethin' sorter fer ye-self."

There was a clean-washed rug of sheepskin. There was a

little chest of cherrywood not a foot high, with carved knobs and rings across the lid, and a little catch with a piece of wood no bigger than your little finger to slip in and hold it shut. There was a pearly trinket carved from a cow's horn. There were six hairpins of cedar wood. And there were two knitting-needles of cedar, polished and shining.

Cean handled the things, each to itself. She could not decide which pleased her most. Lonzo had a turn with his hands. He could make 'most anything.

She moved the slender needles of cedar in the motions of knitting. The wood slipped, cool and quick, through her fingers. She spoke shyly:

"I'll be knittin' ye stockin's 'fore cold weather."

He watched her hands in stubborn embarrassment:

"Better knit ye some, ye own self. . . ."

She said:

"I wasn't askin' fer no pretty things such as these, Lonzo."

He explained, simply:

"I jes' give 'em to ye, to be a-givin', little un."

She laid the pretty things in the chest, and spread the rug beside the bed. She washed her feet before the fire; going to the shadows by the bed, she dropped her dress about her feet and slipped a shift that her mother's hands had woven over her head and down her body. She slid beneath the cover while the soft shucks whispered huskily, and turned her face to the wall until Lonzo should come.

When Cean moved from the fire into the shadows by the bed, Lonzo left the house and walked through the dark to the cow-pen. The night was a thin and gauzy blackness, not dark and heavy as are moonless nights. There was not much of a moon, though, only a little one, cool and high, that foretold rain in the open, downward swing of its curved blade. Before it was full, that moon would empty itself of rain, soaking the new ground. Lonzo must put in his seed. He must spread a shelter for Betsey and her calf in the near

[9]

side of the cow-pen. The cow was used to rain, doubtless, but the little pied-ed feller might not like it, and a lean-to would keep rain off of Cean at milking-time.

Lonzo walked to the rough rails of the cow-pen, and leaned upon them. Betsey, hearing his footsteps, came to the fence and answered his low-spoken "Coa" with a plaintive moo. He fingered her ear, roughing the short, coarse hair with his finger nail. He moved his hand down across the bony sockets of her eyes. Always the feel of a cow's forehead reminded him of the sightless stare of bleached skulls that he sometimes saw far from any clearing, where critters had wandered off to die. Dumb things don't like to die with others looking on. They'll drag off by a branch somewhere, and lie down, and nobody will ever know until you see the buzzards circling lower and lower above some thin cypress, or sitting in solemn black rows along dead limbs, glossing their greasy-black feathers, one by one. There beneath, if you have a mind to, you can find a hide ripped open, and lank bones picked clean.

Lonzo could hear the little calf nuzzling his mother's bag. He wasn't hungry; but he'd better suck while he could. Tomorrow he'd be shut up while his mother went to crop grass on the slope toward the swamp.

Lonzo turned and faced his fields, leaning his weight upon his elbows on the fence. His eyes went through the thin darkness and saw his land ready for planting—through the thin dark, and saw the crops leaning heavy above the soil. The corn would go in there, and the cotton across yonder, and a pea-patch close beyond the cow-pen. Peas would bring partridges in the fall. He'd have to fix a garden-patch for Cean's seeds, and a washing-shed by the spring. He'd have to clear out some of the brush; a moccasin will slip up on you if you give him a chance. He must fix Cean a cypress wash-block like his mother's, and a dug-out wash-trough with a soap-rack. He had the tree picked out;

all there was to do was to strip it and dig it out and set it up on four legs. He had enough to do to keep him busy till frost, what with Cean's little jobs. And there was the land to fence, once and for all, with no tellin' how many rails to be split.

The little moon hung lonesome in the early night, unwearied in fulling and shrinking over woods and waters. Lonzo found it over his left shoulder through space clear of tree or cloud; it meant good luck—rain and good luck. He walked back to the house with slow eagerness. He would put the old brood sow's pen on the other side of the spring; she'd rake straw in another month. He walked heavily across the back yard, and pushed in the back door with unwanted roughness. He'd get a hound-puppy or two to chase rabbits and to keep the house from seeming so still.

Cean heard his coming, and her lashes quivered on her cheeks. Hidden under the thin white coverlids with their soft fringe of lashes, her eyes were warm and bright.

# Chapter 2

BY THE time the moon was new once more, eight pigs were squealing in the pen by the little stream that ran away from the spring's head. Their mother, heavy with milk and content, nosed sleepily through the rails; the pigs plunged about the boggy pen after her, pulling greedily on her dugs. There were five boars and three gilts. In his mind, Lonzo could see the smokehouse already built, could see the sides and hams swinging by their palmetto thongs, and the soft, white lard in kegs newly carved from soft white juniper wood. The first tree toward the smokehouse was not felled, but the pigs fell about over their mother's body bogged in the mud.

Cean's sunflowers were a foot high; the pinks were sprawling out, and here and there was a small striped bloom for Cean to stoop and see; the greens would soon be ready to crap. Her father had brought her a new churn with fancy-carved handles; he had made it himself and dressed it down to smooth, pale yellow. Cean liked to churn on the block by the back door, because from there she could seek out Lonzo's figure across the furrows—Lonzo and the ox. Now the corn was high as your hand. The rows of cotton came almost to the back door, dark-green plants that would grow and blossom into fleece for warm clothes and quilts and bartering at the Coast.

The day was clear and hot. Cean set her churn on the ground by the back step and poured in a crockful of clabber covered in thick cream. She sat in the door, and her arm moved swiftly and easily up and down, plunging the dasher against the churn's bottom. She had fitted a white rag about the neck of the churn to hold in the flecks of white that the dasher might scatter. Her eyes sought across the field for Lonzo where he worked.

She had dropped every last yellow grain of corn into the earth—like that! Walking in Lonzo's tracks, she had counted four grains to a hill—one for the cutworm, one for the crow, one to rot, and one to grow. Four times she had soaked his and her clothes in the wash-trough, had battled them free of dirt on the block, had boiled them white and rinsed them through the spring water, had hung them out on the elder bushes to dry. Together in the water, she had washed their clothes—his long, sweaty shirts and britches, her short shimmies and full-skirted homespun dresses of pale natural color, and of the soft blue of indigo, and of mingled colors patterned on the loom. One dress that she had brought with her from her mother's was brown mingled-y, and that dress had not been washed. It lay folded in the chest beside her soft shoes of tanned calfskin. She liked the brown dress best, for she was married in it. A dark color is likelier for a grown woman. She would not wash the brown dress; goods is never so pretty after it is washed, though it be rubbed ever so gently, and ironed ever so carefully with the hot smoothing-irons while it is damp.

Her mother had brought her three settings of eggs—one of geese, long and white; one of guineas, small, speckled, curious-looking, like bird eggs; and one of chickens. Already Cean's red hen was huddled over the twenty guinea eggs in a nest of pine straw under the house by the chimney. Cean would set the goose eggs under the hen that was laying under the dead log by the wash-trough. The chicken eggs could go into the nest under the back step. Soon her yard would be full of little things running about. She would stir up meal and water for them, and Lonzo must set up a tall pole and bring gourds from his Ma's so that the martins could nest in the little swinging houses and keep off the hawks. And Lonzo must find some hound-puppies to keep off the 'possums.

Cean's hand did not loose the dasher, nor her arm slow its motion. She watched the flakes of clabber at the top of the churn; the butter would come presently.

She lifted the top of the churn and stirred the milk about; gold globes swam all through the white. She churned on, and the butter gathered in a soft, loose lump. She lifted the churn across the room to the eating-table, took out the butter, kneaded the water from it, salted it, and molded it in a wooden mold from the shelf where she kept her milk things. It would be ready for dinner, for Lonzo's cornbread. She took down a jug from the shelf, filled it with buttermilk, closed the doors and shutters of the house against the flies and chickens, and went with the buttermilk down the furrows to find Lonzo.

The sun was hot this morning. There had been days of rain when Lonzo had stayed by the fireplace, whittling on a set of wooden crocks—a large-sized one for salt, and smaller ones for spices. Cean had no spices now, but Lonzo would go to the Coast in the fall, and he would barter and trade and bring back many things in the bottom of his cart in place of the things he would carry away. Maybe Cean would have something to send by Lonzo to barter for pretties—maybe some of the frying-sized chickens to be hatched, or goose feathers, or flower seeds tied in little white rags.

Cean had never been to the Coast. It was no place for womenfolks, Pa said, with men full of rum going about, and fist and skull fights at every turn. No womenfolks ever went. Cean's mother had never gone. But she had come through Dublin when they came from Carolina to settle in the piny woods. She had got down from inside the covered wagon to walk about a little bit; Cean had often heard her tell of the wide road with the houses on each side, and dwelling-houses every which way. There were people all up and down the road, going about the houses busily. Cean's mother had seen an Israelite standing in the door of his storehouse, the only Israelite ever she saw. He was shorter than our kind of men, and darker complected. Cean's father had traded with him for a packet of fine sewing-needles with gold eyes, and a gold thimble for Cean's mother's finger. She had the thimble and some of the needles now; they should be Cean's when her mother died. Cean's father grumbled at his wife's wanting fine trinkets. "You can trade off a herd of cows and bring home a pearl hair-comb and some little shears," he said. He had always begrudged his wife's love for trinkets; maybe it was because she would always rather sew than chop cotton. She was a home body, loving slow women's work by the fireplace, hating hard labor in the field. She would mull a week over something that had angered her, over as small a matter as the calling of her name. She hated the way her husband called her name. "Seen" he called it, when any fool knew that it spelled "Cean." When this girl-child of hers was born, she chided Vince Carver: "Now take yore time in sayin' hit. Her name is 'Ce-an'." Cean had heard tell that her father did not like her to be called by that outlandish name of her mother's. He wanted her named for his mother, Tillitha. And her mother had named her Tillitha Cean, but ever she was called Cean.

Cean's toes spread into the warm, moist earth of the cornfield. She walked with sturdy, vibrant strength moving her legs. She carried the jug of buttermilk on her hip. The corn was trying itself growing. She had dropped every last grain out of her hand, like that, and there it was growing in long rows far as you could see. That was her part, to drop the seeds and help with the hoeing, if Lonzo needed her. Ma had never liked to work in the field, but Cean wouldn't mind. Like Pa said, crops had to be made, if folks wore rags and tatters, and Pa was right; let first things come first; Ma was a good woman, but she wasn't in the right to sull over her loom as she did. Ma was happy at her loom, or when she was spinning, the long hum of the wheel filling the house, or when she was dyeing, mixing her likkers of indigo with maple bark or poplar, or this or that or the other root she had dug to see what color it would make. She would souse the hanks of cotton or worsted yarn into the pot, pushing them gently under the bubbling, swirling surface. She would take them out, and dry them on a leaning bush, and the colors would be softly blent through the threads, set with the lye of the green-oak ashes. She used the juice of the poke-berries for short lengths of red for bright bibs and tuckers. But that color would run in the washing, and it was a pity.

Cean would try new dyes herself when she made cloth. Lonzo would set her up a loom when the cotton was in. He was working at her spinning-wheel now by the firelight of nights. The wood squeaked softly under the blade of his knife where he rounded off a corner or settled a spoke into place. Cean would make all her frocks straight blue or yaller, or block her colors together as she wove them. She would have a frock of blue with flounces of yaller across the bottom.

Her eyes swam away to the horizon with soft blue sky set behind it, and soft yellow sunlight falling across it. Blue and yaller, that would be a purty way to make a frock, and a bonnet to match.

She went down the furrow to where Lonzo had whoaed the ox, waiting for her at the end of the row. She might have waited for him at the upper end next to the cotton, but she hadn't thought about it.

She handed the jug to Lonzo.

"I thought you mought like some fresh-churned buttermilk."

He took the jug and pushed back the brim of his old hat and wiped his face on his sleeve:

"Yeah. This sun's hot."

Cean waited in silence while he drank. The ox stood stolidly under the wooden yoke; his bleary eyes were closed; his lower jaw worked sideways as he chewed on his cud; his head swayed a little in contented weariness; his forelegs were planted stiffly in the earth.

Lonzo was tilting the jug to his mouth again, swigging down the buttermilk. His shirt was open and the bright-brown skin of his upturned neck ran with sweat. His Adam's apple worked in gulps as the milk went down—down to where black curly hairs crawled on his chest, down farther to his stomach and liver and lights under the sweaty white skin she could see through the front of his shirt. She watched his skin working with his breathing; it made her think of maggots in a mislaid piece of beef. The little fat, round worms heaved themselves up and down like that little round fat roll of white flesh on Lonzo's belly. Before she knew what she was doing, her stomach was heaving and the breakfast she had eaten lay there in the furrow and Lonzo was holding her by the shoulders. It was sudden and unforeseen. She was all right now; with a shamed face she said:

"Well, I don't know as I ever done that in broad-open daylight—pukin' like a dog in the grass."

Lonzo backed away from her. His eyes were troubled and his shaggy brows met in dumb anxiety.

Cean's shamed eyes watched her big toe furrow the soft earth that lay between their feet.

He stared at her face that was flushed red by her sweet shame, and said:

"Ye'd better go on back to the house out o' the hot sun."

When she had gone, he took the lines and chucked to the ox; but soon he whoaed the ox again and watched Cean making her way back down the long furrow where her barefoot tracks had made a faint path in coming. The jug was on her left hip again. She was halfway to the cotton before he started the ox again.

He stormed at the patient, plodding beast, "Giddap in there!"

Cean's eyes followed the rows of young corn, all of a size, all of a green. She was thinking how she had dropped the grains of seed corn; and they had lain in the dark through cool nights and hot days; they had burst the soil, new and different, unrecognizable in poison green, disowning the seed that sought sustenance downward with white roots in black earth, sustenance for bright-green blades growing toward the sun, toward far-off tassels high in the air, and heavy ears of corn that would be other new seed grains.

# Chapter 3

BRIER BERRIES covered their thickets, dried, and dropped back into the earth which made them. Now the huckleberries ripened in small purple globes on the sandy slopes. Gooseberries swung, larger but not so sweet, on taller bushes. Cean gathered the bushes of the gall berries for brush brooms and laid them on the top of her wash-shed to dry. The brittle stems, beaten free of leaves, would keep the dooryard clean of trash. Each morning as she swept the yard the twigs of the brush broom left their little wavy marks on the thin sand about her doorstep. The chickens set three-marked tracks across the broom's clean sweep. Lonzo's big feet spread their sign toward the fields. Cean's tracks criss-crossed all the other tracks as she threw scraps to the chickens that flew to a fluttering, greedy cluster over the food, as she carried water to the calf, now nearly grown, and his mother, now regarding him with contented indifference. Lonzo did not need another ox to feed, so the calf would be butchered.

Since she was in the family way, Cean had thought up the foolishest things! She didn't want Lonzo to butcher the little yearling, when she knew good and well that he was goin' to do it. One night as he got into bed she had a mind to ask him to swap off the calf and some corn for a heifer. But they didn't have the corn to swap; they wouldn't be their own man until next year, with plenty of corn in the crib and rations of their own. And she didn't need another milker. If she told the truth about it, she just didn't want the little feller killed. She didn't have to see Lonzo knock him in the forehead with the ax-head, but she would hear him bawl and know when it happened, unless she went to Ma's for the day, and there wasn't no mortal excuse for that. And besides she'd have to help Lonzo with the skinning and the rest, for the blow-flies swarmed in this hot weather.

She never had felt this certain way about any yearling she ever heard tell of. Maybe it was because he was hers, kind of; they had started out on this place. In the mornings Lonzo would go far into the field, and Betsey would wander off by the swamp to graze all day, and Cean and the little feller would keep house, as she called it. She would go to the pen and scratch his back with a stick, and look for ticks in his hair; and he would stick up his tail and lope around the pen, butting at the fence-rails, butting at Cean through the cracks. He was a smart little feller, she always thought; he knowed as good as she did when he was showin' off.

And now Lonzo would butcher him and they'd eat him. Cean would beat the tender pieces and fry them on the fireplace; she would try out the yellow tallow for candles, and boil the tough pieces, and she and Lonzo would carry Ma a half of beef. Lonzo would stretch the hide to the back side of the house, and the sun would dry it. Then Lonzo would tan it, and rub it down till it was soft and giving, and then he'd make shoes for them on the shoe-last that lay under the bed. He had joked about making shoes for the little un, but it would be many a day afore the little un could wear them. It wouldn't even be borned till around killin' frost, or after, but it would please Cean right much for Lonzo to make the little shoes. She would set them away in the chest by the side of her own shoes. Now the calf bawled and kicked up and butted at every thing in sight; soon Lonzo would stretch its hide, bloody on the inside, to the back side of the house, and after that there would be brogans for the little un, to keep the hot sand from burning its feet in summer. It was all like wood beads on a cotton string, coming one after another, as even and close together as beads on a string.

Ma had told her that being like this always made a woman mull over things. Ma said the best thing to do was to keep busy. But Cean couldn't keep from mulling. Her hands worked, but her head was idle inside. It looked like, after all, she might turn out to be like her Ma, sulling over a loom. Strange feelings came and went inside her, shivers, sharp and cold, and waves of heavy warmth hot after them. The little unknown thing was growing within her as suddenly and softly as the first touch of spring on the maples. It was putting out its hidden, watery roots as simply and surely as little cypresses take root in a stretch of swamp water away off yonder. It was coming upon her as quietly as the dark came up from the woods at night and hushed in the little clearing, closing every chink of every shutter tight with nothing. Impulses swelled within her, swelled her body fit to burst; yet they did not come out in words, nor song, nor in any sign. Lonzo said her ankles were swelling. Only her ankles gave a sign as yet.

Magnolias held out big cupped flowers as white as the moon. Cean broke a bloom from a low bough and took it back to her house, and set it in a jug on her eating-table. The heavy white petals curved upward above the hard, white beginnings of seed that grew out of the bottom of the cup. The outer leaves were faintly green and yet showed the tender impress where the calyx, silky and brown like a dog's ear, had pressed close in upon the flower, holding it close until its birth-time. There were magnolias all through the woods. Cean pulled blooms from the lower limbs of the magnolia trees and carried them home to scent her house and to droop, heavy and white, over her eating-table. One day she went within the low-growing branches of a tree and climbed the trunk a little way. Her eyes went through the glossy leaves in search of a bloom near enough for her reach. It was hot there inside the house of branches; the limbs ran out as rafters, the heavy green leaves walled about

[ 21 ]

the space inside. Cean mulled over her thought: this was a magnolia house, green and rustling inside, with great white blooms hung about on all the walls. She would pull no more blossoms; she would leave them high and white on the tree. It was a house, finished and trimmed. She would break no more blooms from it to set on her eating-table.

Cean went to pick huckleberries to stew and sweeten for Lonzo's supper. She pulled her sunbonnet on her head, and put on Lonzo's old boots and walked off to the right, past the new ground where the cotton was growing, into the scrubby thickets of palmettos and dwarf oaks growing on the sandy ridge. Briers caught at her skirt. She carried a piggin in her left hand. Her eyes glimpsed clumps of the low-growing berries here and there, but farther on there would be thousands of them, the leaves and berries powdered in gray as though dipped in dust. Farther on she could stoop in one place and cover the bottom of her piggin with a deep layer of the purple berries, each frosted in gray, with a little puckered mouth at its blossom-end, with a little stem no bigger than a sewing-thread.

She had found a knee-high forest of bushes and had picked her piggin half full. These little slick, hard kernels did not stain her fingers as did the soft, juicy blackberries. It was pleasant to pick them free from the bush, leaving only a few little green fellers to ripen later on. You sweated for corn and cotton; you knocked a pig or a cow in the head to eat meat; but these were free. It didn't take sweat or blood. The ripe ones fell into your hand as though they were eager to leave the bush and find a waiting hand. This was something like dropping corn behind Lonzo; she felt that same satisfaction.

The sun was hot down the slope. No little breeze fanned the scrub oaks. Cean was thinking of the churning left undone; she would hurry back and have the buttermilk ready for Lonzo's dinner. Maybe she ought to have gone on like on other days; Lonzo might not like the fried meat and potatoes and cornbread she would fix up in a hurry for his dinner; he was used to his pot of greens or dried peas.

There was a sudden shaking of the air all about her. It was a harsh, singing rattle of sound, hard as thunder, soft as cornshucks, and it filled her with deadening terror. Somewhere about her there was a rattlesnake, and he was close because she could not tell in which direction he lay. As she stooped, afraid to go, afraid to stay, her mind was benumbed like her body. Suddenly just above her elbow she felt her right arm stuck as though by blunt twigs, and turning, she saw glittering eyes in a small, ugly head hanging there close to her eyes. She reached and caught the pulsing, gray thing in her left hand and flung it away, and it fell among the scattered berries in moving folds and turns.

Cean's hand caught her arm close above the needle-prick wound, and pressed with all her strength where she felt the beat of blood under her thumb. She stood upright and moved a little way back with weak steps, and screams took possession of her body. She heard the screams about her head; they seemed to come through the earth, through her body; they flew about her head, not of her own willing, deafening her ears. Then fear chilled her into silence. Stopping the blood in her arm until the bone ached with the pressure of her thumb, she ran toward her house, down the slope and on under the wind in the pine-tops, the sound of it like the sound of fairy rain starting in steady, delicate drumming, and dying. She ran on across the plowed fields, calling for Lonzo.

He heard her coming across the fields to him and jumped the furrows running to meet her, breaking the stalks of young corn heedlessly. When he reached her her face was ugly with weeping. She was shaking her head, talking loose words:

"Lonzo—Lonzo . . . a rattler struck me. . . . I spilled the huckleberries."

He caught her arm and laid the flesh open with his knife: with his hands he squeezed bright red blood from the wound. Lifting her in his arms, he ran to the house and set her down on the steps. He found a little flask of spirits of turpentine on the shelf in the house, and drenched her arm; the clear spirits, streaked with blood, ran down her arm and stained her dress. He made her drink whisky from a brown jug from the same shelf.

Her breath slowed. Her fear eased away as Lonzo tied up the wound with a clean rag.

Inside the house, she lay down across the bed, leaving the meat and potatoes uncooked, and the milk unchurned. Her breathing came slowly, heavily; her eyelids drooped against her will; thick laziness coiled through her blood and made her sleep while the sun was high; pain stabbed here and there in far places of her consciousness. Lonzo watched a green pallor settle in her face, and saw that her body was bloated in sickly white. He made her drink great swallows of rum, and scolded her when she whined against the mouth of the jug at her lips. She needed her Ma, but he was afraid to leave her, and he believed that she would over it. He had cut plenty deep with his knife, but fear pressed close beside him as he watched her.

As the afternoon lengthened she roused, and her face brightened. Lonzo figured that the poison had worked itself out. She was still foolish in the head, but that was more rum than poison, and the dead feeling of the poison in her blood was gone.

It was an hour by sun when Lonzo said:

"Reckon I'd better go and put 'im out o' the way, if ye'll tell me 'bout where ye was."

Cean was humble before her husband because she had caused all this to-do. Her voice was meek:

"Straight on past the cotton-patch and on up the rise. Right where they begin to grow thick. . . . Ye'll see where I dropped the berries, I reckon."

He spoke gruffly over his shoulder as he turned to go: "After this ye'd better stay at home where ye belong."

When he had gone she lay quietly, pondering his rough words, blaming herself for putting him to so much trouble.

She laid her left hand lightly on the bound wound. Remembering, she trembled anew, feeling again the nasty, slick crawl of the snake in her hand, cold and hideous, jerking in a long pull against her hand. She was scared . . . scared. . . . If he had struck a hand higher, it would have been her face that he found instead of her arm, the horrible head against her head, the beady eyes close by her eyes, the rough mouth stinging her cheek to death with its thick, white spit. And she would have died, tied to the bed, plunging in spasms, and turning cold-blooded and blackish-gray like the snake.

She thought, "This is the first time ever I was scared."

Then she thought on, a little clumsy at reaching her own conclusions:

"But hit won't be the last time, most likely."

And she was proud, knowing that she was now a woman. "Hit all comes with bein' a woman."

Then she stilled herself, her eyes widened, her breath stopped at her parted lips. She laid her hand low on her body where a wing had fluttered deep within her, where a heart had beaten once, soft and weak, trying its little strength, where something of less actuality than a dream had become existent in fact, to be noted surely, unmistakably as reality.

Lonzo came back a little before dark with two silky, limp rattlers hanging from the hoe-handle over his shoulder. They were mates, most likely. And he brought Cean's piggin, with her bonnet lying in its bottom. He slit the long, smooth bellies of the snakes and stripped the scaly gray skins from the flesh that looked like fish-meat. Afterward, he would boil the flesh down and reduce the oil to no more than would fill a little flask. The skins he would spread against the back side of the house and peg them, heads up, to dry. The rattles, fourteen in one string and nine in the other, would hang over the fireplace. Cean could never afterward abide the sound of their shaking, but hung about a baby's neck they make teething easy. The snake oil and the thin, rustly, pied-ed skins Lonzo would trade off at the Coast.

When the dark had come down and they were ready for sleep, Cean tried to make amends for her trouble. She said:

"Hit moved this evenin', Lonzo."

He moved uneasily in the bed, so that the shucks stirred a little, and cleared his throat:

"Y' hadn't oughta be off a-traipsin' after berries. After this, 'lessen I'm with ye, you keep home, little un."

Cean felt comfort in his words.

After this, 'lessen he was with her, she'd keep home.

# Chapter 4

NEIGHBORS brought gifts to Lonzo and Cean through the summer. They spoke slow, hearty wish-you-wells and extended their offerings apologetically: "Mary thought you mought could do with a extry hen or two. The old domineckers wasn't layin' much, so I brung some along." And the speaker would dump a sack of fat hens on the ground.

Cean and Lonzo accepted the things as humbly as they were offered:

"Much obleeged to ye, if ye think ye kin spare 'em."

There were four extra shoats in the pen; a flock of hens scratched far afield or watched the back door for Cean's hand flinging a scrap of food; three old geese and a gander waddled in and out of the cotton rows, hissing foolishly at Lonzo's passing; five guineas, other than Cean's own young flock, alighted daintily from the trees at the crack of day and potracked from atop the rail fences through the mornings. Neighbors had dropped by from as far away as Brushy Creek to set a spell, to eat Cean's hot cornbread and to drink her cool buttermilk; when the sun was low they would set out again for home.

The summer days passed slowly, it seemed to Cean. The little un was making her a little heavy with his weight, was crowding her breath in her bosom, was making her slower in her movements to dress, to water the calf, to hoe the sunflowers. Everything was a little heavy, a little slow, under the summer's bright heat and swift growth. By night the crickets burdened the air with their heavy chirring; by day the locusts sang out their grating monotones. During the cooler hours of the day the air was thick with bird song. Mockingbirds tilted on saplings and briers, chucking fussily, and sang from the top of Cean's chimney in notes that were smooth and heavy and golden—too sweet, like honey. On moonlight nights their singing disturbed Cean's rest, and she was weary when day came, and rose, ill-tempered, to cook Lonzo's breakfast. The ill-temper worked in her body like a slow fever, clouding her eyes, making her weak and easy to cry. Lonzo called her toucheous, and told her if people let their feelings stick out too far, they'd get stepped on. Cean would go off to the cow-pen and cry onto the head of the little yearling that would come for her to scratch his back with a stick. Lonzo would kill the little feller; Cean cried slow tears onto his head. But it wasn't just the calf; she didn't know what was the matter with her.

On these days, by the time the sun was an hour or two high, the air began to still. Long before noon a heavy hush blanketed the bird songs, the chatterings of little creatures in the edge of the woods, the breezes that ran through the lusty, green corn. It was hot and close; heat devils danced far and wide over sandy levels. Lonzo worked through the heat of the day; the sun burned deeper and deeper into his brown skin, his eyes shone blacker when he looked over his crops, green and rustling in the hot sun. Cean was afraid he'd get down with the fever, working in the heat of the day, but he ignored her pettishness. Heat is good for cotton and corn; it won't hurt a man if he will fill up on cool water and sweat it off.

Cean soaked their clothes together in the wash-trough; his garments were stiff with sweat; hers were dirtied down the front with smut from the fireplace, and grease, and dish-water. With the white battling-stick she beat free the sweat and smut and dish-water; she boiled them away in strong suds from brown soap that her mother had made; she rinsed them away in cold water from the spring; she sunned them away as the clothes hung, sweet-smelling in cleanliness, on bushes near the spring. Sometimes while she was washing

[ 28 ]

she would grow weak, and would lean against the trough till her head cleared; sometimes the little un would kick and push at her, and she would stand a moment, smiling, feeling its harsh, small impatience, her hands idling in the suds.

On a hot, heavy day Lonzo butchered the calf. Cean wanted to hide away in the house, but she wouldn't give in to her feelings; and Lonzo might call her toucheous. So she turned only her eyes away when Lonzo called the calf to him, when the little feller came across the lot, butting and bouncing up his back end in silly, put-on independence, when Lonzo laid the ax with all his strength on the little feller's pied-ed forehead. The calf fell to his knees and bawled; Lonzo stopped the bawling with a butcher-knife, slitting the throat. Then the blood came out. Unless you slit the throat, it will bleed on the inside. Cean didn't cry; she wouldn't let the tears come out; she was like the stunned brain of the calf, bleeding on the inside.

She helped Lonzo dress the beef, working at the wash-trough where they could dip water from the spring close by. She cut and sliced with the big butcher-knife, and her hands were soaked red with blood; clots of blood dried on the knife-blade and on her wrists.

And sure enough, a little later, there was the hide stretched on the back side of the house, as she knew it would be, pied-ed in red and white, curing to make the little un some shoes.

Now that it was over, it wasn't so bad. She was glad that she had not let on to Lonzo how she felt; a woman has business to be as strong as a man. No, a woman has to be stronger than a man. A man don't mind laying the ax between a calf's eyes; a woman does mind, and has to stand by and watch it done. A man fathers a little un, but a woman feels it shove up against her heart, and beat on her body, and drag on her with its weight. A woman has to be stronger than a man.

Cean was tired out when the butchering was done. She left the tallow until tomorrow. Her face was red, and the long muscles in her legs ached from much stooping by the fireplace to fry the steak. Lonzo had jerked some of the meat into long, thin strips and hung it in the sunshine to dry out; they would use it when the fresh beef was gone. He dumped the evil-smelling remains of their work into a deep hole in the upper end of the cotton-patch near Cean's sunflowers. He never liked to see the buzzards finishing up a dumb critter.

Long before noon, Lonzo hitched up the ox to the cart and Cean climbed to the seat beside him, and they went off across the clearing and down the slope toward her mother's. A half of the beef lay in the bottom of the cart, staining the old, clean sheet with bright blood. Under and over it Lonzo had piled newly cut palmetto fans that shaded the meat in hot, rustling gloom.

Cean mused soberly as they followed the faint trace of the trail. She had not traveled it many times; only twice had she gone back to her mother's, once for soap and salt, once just to be a-goin'. In between, her mother and father had come to see her, bringing the new churn that her father had made, and a length of narr'd homespun that her mother had woven. Today Cean would bring back her mother's candle-molds, borrowed to form the fat of the little calf's carcass into light. She and Lonzo went to bed with the chickens now, but when the little un came, it might be uneasy in its in'ards in the night, and Cean would need candles. She would mold them, and set them in a piggin of cold water, and loose them from the molds, and set them away in the chest.

More and more she found her thoughts drifting, like a river's current that sets stronger and fuller toward the sea, to that day in the winter when she would lie down for her labor. Once when she was a little tyke her oldest brother,

[ 30 ]

Jasper, had told her that new babies were found in dead logs and stumps, and she had searched through all of a morning for a baby. She remembered the day now, and smiled a little within herself. . . . It was a summer morning of still heat, and Jake was a baby not walking then. She had raised Jake, toting him around on her hip, fixing sugar-tits to hush his crying when Ma was busy with something. She had toted him to the woods that day when she went to find a baby in a hollow stump, a naked, squirming, red-faced baby such as Jake had been when she first saw him; but the baby she would find would stay little, and be cute and lovin' like the little pet coon Jasper had—only better. Cean jolted along in the road cart beside Lonzo, her mind apart in a sober, pleasurable place. She was a thin-legged, serious child carrying Jake on her hip. She could feel the warm sand oozing between her toes; she could hear the sighing wind washing evenly through the tops of the big pines. . . .

The little un suddenly strove against its confinement, striking with quick, soft blows. She would find it beside her one morning in winter, would look for it and find it, little and rose-colored, new and unbelievable. But it would grow and learn to walk.

The slow-footed ox rounded a clump of leaning bay trees and Cean saw her mother's house, weathered and settled on the land that her father had plowed over through the years since he and her mother had come from Carolina to settle here. Cean's mother had never much liked the country here. She was born in the red hills and could not get used to sandy ridges and flat woods, wide and lonely, shaded sparsely by the long-leaf pines that were forever sighing over the land, and moaning in storms, and crashing down in big winds of the fall to lie drying through the seasons. Off there lay the swamp, breathing out fevers and swarms of mosquitoes. She had never admired the pines. They were a black and gloomy kind of tree. The magnolias were black and gloomy, too, and their flowers a little too white, like sickly children. All the land was miserable-looking, to her, low and flat and hard to live in. Back in Carolina there were silver poplars turning their leaves silver-side, dun-side in the wind, and pyeart little cedars were set on each side of doorways, and rows of boxwood grew all the way to the gates. She had brought cuttings of her mother's Cape jessamine and boxwood from Carolina, and some of the cuttings had grown to tall, shapely clumps about her yard here in the piny-woods. She didn't like this country; it would grow good crops, but back in Carolina folks settled closer together, people were gayer, and had frolics at odd times, and meeting-houses with dinner on the grounds, and fairs with people coming from all over the section to laugh and have a big time.

Cean's eyes greeted the shrubs about her mother's clean-swept dooryard. She was glad to come back to the old place; it was secure and finished, somehow, as her own home was not. There were blanks in her new life, about her new house, to be filled in as time should come and go. Here around Pa's place all the rail fences were split and laid years back; all the cribs were built and filled; the house and its surrounding earth were mellowed through many days of living together.

Cean's mother and father came across the thin sand of the dooryard to the side of the cart. Her father spoke welcome:

"Git down and come in."

Her mother murmured in a pleasant silence:

"We're real glad ye brung her over, Lonzo, as well as yereself."

Her eyes rested on Cean's face, loving her shyly.

Lonzo said:

"We thought ye mought like some fresh-killed beef. We butchered Cean's yearling this morning."

He pulled out the piece of red meat from the cart, and they all went into the house and its quiet, hearty welcome.

Cean's father was a slow-spoken, heavy-minded man. He could beat his oldest boy, Jasper, pulling fodder any day, and Jasper was six feet two, and twenty years younger. When Pa was in the field they could hear him bawling at the oxen from as far away as the ten-acre field two mile off, if the day were still. Cean's father ruled his house as he ruled his oxen; he gave commands and they were obeyed. His wife obeyed him as his children did; her only rebellion was mutinous silence as she spun or wove. Her husband knew no command that would open her thin lips closed against him, that would soften the still set of her eyes on the ends of her knitting-needles, pulling the length of the rough yarn between them with little jerks.

His rough manner held all his children at a distance from him; they were ever shy of him and went to him only through their mother. It was so that Jasper and Lias had leave to go to the Coast that first time, years back. From their beds in the loft the children had heard their mother as she begged for them, when she thought they were asleep.

"Vince, you a-aimin' t' take the boys with ye to the Coast?"

There was a short silence; the boys held their breath; then the old man said:

"I hadn't thought nothin' about hit."

"I expect they'd be proud t' git t' go. Not as I've heard 'em say nothin' about hit."

He knew she was lying, that the boys had begged her to get him to take them with him. He turned heavily on his side in the feather bed:

"I'd take 'em along if I thought they wouldn't be a-quarrelin' and a-fightin' like some o' them toughs."

[ 33 ]

They all knew that it was settled. Jasper and Lias lay still in the loft, hugging their stomachs that had risen up with joy. The father settled to sleep, grunting; the mother lay beside him, her arms along her sides, her face eased from its hard lines into something gentler than joy. Cean and little Jake in the other bed in the loft breathed long and deeply, their heads side by side on one pillow, her arms about his body. They understood that Jasper and Lias could go, and that they could not. Women and children wasn't wanted on trips to the Coast.

Lias, Cean's second brother, came in from the lot as they were sitting talking of the crops and the weather. He said: "Howdy, Lonzo! Howdy, Cean!"

He was bright-faced and shrewd-eyed. Vince said that he would drive the closest bargains of any of 'em. Vince had always taken pride in Lias; the mother seemed to think the most of Jasper. Cean and Jake did not mind; it was just Ma's and Pa's way. Vince would give them all a piece of land and some stock when they stepped off, each one alike; but Vince always said that Lias would make the most of his. He was given to making fun of spindly-legged Jake, but Ma always said, "You was little once, yoreself, I reckon."

The family sat about the room, uneasy under the formality of a visit. Lonzo and Vince did most of the talking. After a while, her mother called Cean out to the cooking-shed built apart from the house at the back, and a silence fell upon the men. That was women's talk and they were shy of it.

Her mother showed Cean some little garments, cut and sewed with her fingers. There was one of each thing, to show Cean the size and the cut. Now Cean would make the other things; a woman must make her first child's clothes, all to herself. The older woman gave sage advice to her daughter: she must drink sassafras tea for the blood; she must take care in lifting her arms over her head, and in lifting heavy weights; she should never have gone near the butchering—like as not the child might have a birth mark somewhere about it; she must remember not to grab herself when she was scared by anything, for that will mark an unborn child quicker than anything else.

As she listened, Cean was afraid to tell her mother of her fears that were born out of the words and grew, all in a moment, to horrible, quivering things that would move as her child moved. She could not tell of the rattlesnake, nor of her feeling when the little calf was knocked in the head, a feeling of tears running bitterly down inside from her eyes and her throat, a feeling of bleeding slowly and helplessly inside herself. The thing that stirred within her might not be cute and cunning and pretty to see; it could be blood-colored all over. Godamighty! it could be laid to her breast marked with a flat head and beady, black eyes and fangs for teeth. She could feel it there now . . . coiling . . . pulsating. She reached her hands blindly toward her mother as she felt herself falling.

They were gathered about her; her mother had drenched her face with a dash of water. Cean saw Jake in the door, ready to run away and hide, his face a misery of fear. Cean's mother said:

"Jest rest easy fer a little and ye'll be as spry as a cricket."

She turned to the men, her manner graced with the authority of womanly things:

"The heat give her a turn."

Jake disappeared from the door and ran away to the crib, and burrowed his face into the rough, dry ears of corn. His heart was dancing in his throat because she was not dead.

When they were ready to go, Cean walked around the house, calling Jake. He did not answer, and she went on out to the lot. He came shyly to the open crib door, and stood waiting for her to come up. She stood on the ground; he was in the door of the crib, his bare feet on the sill at her waist level. He was looking toward the house, his lips and eyes uneasy in embarrassment. She looked across the lot to where a flock of guineas pecked among scattered cornshucks. She said:

"Hit weren't nothin', Jake. I'm a-goin t' find a baby afore long, that's all hit were."

She went back to the house, and his eyes followed the back of her head as long as he could see it.

When she was gone from sight he ran back up on the slipping mound of corn, and found the farthest corner of the crib, and lay shivering, his face in the musty, dry ears.

Major, his old, blear-eyed hound, came sniffing under the crib door, and whined. Jake spoke to him from the rough, sliding hill of last year's corn:

"Shet up, Major."

The dog lay down under the crib door, settled his drooping jaws carefully on his paws, and closed his eyes with a sighing breath.

# Chapter 5

Lias thought up a plan of putting logs together on the river two miles from their home, and rafting their goods to the Coast.

He put the plan to his father:

"All ye'd have t' do would be float, Pa."

But Vince couldn't spare time from the crops long enough to fix up a new-fangled way of doing something.

"But, Pa, ye could trade the raft as lumber."

Vince didn't like argument from his children.

"A tree ain't never fed nobody. I've al'ays gone by ox-cart. I reckon ye ain't no better than yore pappy."

Lias's jaw trembled as he set his teeth together. He was bigger than his Pa, but he was a-feared of him.

"I reckon I couldn't put a raft together and take hit down m'self?"

The old man's eyes flared.

"Go feed up, Lias!"

Lias went out the back toward the lot; his face was a little pale, his hands were a little trembly. He'd go down the river when he was his own man, so help him Almighty God! And it wouldn't be forever till he was his own man, neither.

In October the cotton had been stripped of its white puffs and stood in gaunt rows down the field; the fodder was pulled and the corn was gathered, and the cornstalks stirred drearily in the wind. The men about gathered up what they had to trade and packed it in the slow-going ox-carts—cotton, potatoes, brown sugar, wool, cowhides, comb honey. Some had hides to trade—black bear, gray 'possum, shaggy wolf, red fox, and even little soft dun rabbits.

Vince carried cotton and wool and cowhides. Seen sent a keg of lard and three hams that she wouldn't need, a sack of dried peas, and clear honey and beeswax from her hives. This year she sent no goose feathers, because she was saving feather beds for the wives who would belong to Jasper and Lias. The boys would be stepping off any time now. Folks married young down here in the backwoods. She had purposes for all her cloth this year, too, with Cean like she was. She might put in a sack of dried peppers and sage for sausage seasoning, but Vince said that things like that wouldn't bring nothin'.

Lonzo and Cean packed their stuff in their own cart. He bragged a little, and she was overly shy in pride over this first trip to the Coast country with their own things. They had only cotton, piled high and covered over with some of Pa's hides. In the corner was a sack of trinkets that Lonzo had covered over, things such as knitting-needles, hairpins, salt-and-spice sets, that he had carved from cedar and juniper wood at odd times when the corn and cotton were laid by; women took a fancy to such jimcracks; he might trade them for something, maybe, or he could bring them back home and nobody would ever be the wiser. Cean had nothing to send. Next year she would look ahead and have her own things for Lonzo to barter for her. She wanted a gold piece. She would get Lias to trade her things for a gold piece next year. Lias was the best trader for that purpose. Now Pa and Jasper were good talkers when it came to cotton or shoats, but they would not care to fool with women's stuff. Cean wouldn't mind asking Lias to trade her stuff for her. Each year she would send enough to trade for one gold piece. And the gold pieces would grow into a little pile. She would keep them in her chest. She would tie them into a little sack about as big as your hand . . . until it was full.

On the way down, the men walked by the carts for part of the way to ease the loads of their beasts. They could make the trip in four or five days, given fair weather and moonlight nights. Allowing for three or four days there for trading and the Big Court, the trip could be made in about two weeks. Leaves were dropping during the time, and when they got back home it was soon time for cane-grindin' and hog-killin'.

Cean's mother always spent the time while Vince was gone in quilting new cover and making winter clothing for her family. The work lightened with the menfolks gone; there was only the stock to feed and the house to look after. She would be alone this year, for Cean would need Jake to stay with her and help her. Jake was right pleased to stay with Cean, since he was still too young to make the Coast journey.

The men were to gather at Big Creek at daylight on Thursday before the first Monday.

The day before they were to go, Cean and Lonzo came to Vince Carver's, and Cean braved her father's rough impatience to say:

"Pa, I ain't the least bit a-feared to stay by myself. Jake wouldn't be no extry burden to Lonzo. I could keep old Major tied up at our place."

She and her father were standing on the narrow piazza of his house. He looked away across the flat woods to where some of his cows were grazing. The sound of a clanking bell on a bent neck came across the woods. Vince watched the cows in the distance, and Cean could not know what he would answer. He kept his eyes on the cows and said:

"I don't like y' bein' by y'self." Then he spoke roughly, "Tell 'im he kin go."

He walked down the steps and off across the yard.

Cean found Jake hauling manure from the lot to his mother's sugar-pear trees in the far end of the cornfield, jerking on the rawhide lines passed around the head of the ox. He came by from the lot, geeing the ox around a clump of crêpe myrtle. The manure was piled on a flat sled, and Jake walked beside it, shouting at the beast.

Cean went out by the smokehouse to meet Jake. She leaned against the side of the smokehouse. There was always a pain between her shoulder blades now; her mother said that when that pain moved down to the small of her back, her time had come to lay her burden down.

Jake's eyes held to the edge of the sled, smeared with its foul cargo. The air all about was strong and heavy.

She said:

"Pa says y' kin go with Lonzo t' the Coast."

His glance started up and clung to her. Her face was bloated now, and liver-spots were brown on her cheeks. The warm brightness of her eyes was dulled a little. They looked at one other for a moment. She said:

"I'll tie up Major t' keep the boogers off me."

His eyes went back to the sled heaped with manure. When he spoke, he tried to keep his voice hard and manly:

"I wuz a-aimin' t' give Major t' ye t' play with the little un." Then he bawled at the ox, "Giddup, y' lazy old fool."

The ox plodded forward, Jake walking at the side of the sled. Cean called after him:

"I doubt he'd stay 'lessen we kept him tied up."

Jake did not answer; he went on walking across the long-turned furrows of the cornfield where a thin wind sang through dead cornstalks bereft of leaf and tassel and ear.

It was eighty miles to the Coast through pines and palmettos, wire grass and occasional swamplands where the trees leaned upon one another and vines climbed to their tops, casting tendrils every way and knitting the upper air into thin green shadow. The trail forded shallow branches and sandy-bottomed creeks, crossed deeper fords where water ran to the axle even in dry weather, and mayhap crossed a river on a ferry tended by a talkative ferryman full of news.

The men camped at night by oakwood fires. They fried

their rashers of bacon and baked hoecakes over the coals, and roasted potatoes in the white ashes. They drank branch water out of a whisky-keg. The oxen were staked out to graze and the men lay about the fire, swapping yarns about bear-hunts, and rattlers with twenty-five rattles and a button, and balls of fire that roamed through certain swamps at night crying with a woman's voice. The older men laughed over the stories, but those who were young lay spellbound under the words. Jake could not sleep until long after the others were snoring; his skin would creep when the dogs started off to run a rabbit or to tree a 'possum. Old Man Cook from up the country told a story that there was a thumping every evening at dark in the ground under a rose bush in his front yard—thump—thump—thump—like a sledge hammer; and when night came, it hushed. Folks from miles around had come to hear it and would testify that it was so. Old Man Cook believed that there was a grave there, and whoever it was was knocking to get out, but he was a-feared to dig up the rose bush to see.

Jake shivered under his quilt, and turned his eyes warily out into the dark. The stars were hazy far in the heavens, the moon was just rising behind the tree trunks. Jake wondered how Old Man Cook could live at the place with the thumping in the yard; Jake couldn't, even if he was grown and not a-feared of anything. . . .

The nearer they came to the Coast, the plainer the road was to see. Jake's eyes could follow it now until trees at a bend intervened. There were forks every now and then; one way went yonder to houses and clearings and fords, but this way went to the Coast!

In the afternoon of the fourth day, Jake strained his eyes toward the clustering, one-storied houses of the Coast town. Live-oaks grew far as you could see all along the river bluff, and gray moss drooped low from the branches and swayed lazily in the wind. Chickens and pigs and cows wandered around the space between the rows of houses. The road went down between the houses to the river, and the river went down between the bluffs to the sea. Jake's eyes followed the river's course that was heaving a little with a fullin' tide; then his gaze came back, retreating from too much wonder. He would walk out yonder to the edge of the bluff, when he got a chance, and sit and look as long as he liked; he would not hurry about seeing things. . . .

The men unhitched their oxen under the live-oaks and staked the animals to graze. Fires were going before dusk came down, and much loud talk and laughter went back and forth beneath the trees. There was a man there who had rafted down a load of cattle from away up the Alatamaha. He had a jug that circled here and yonder; some men passed it on quickly, others hesitated and tilted it to their lips. Jake listened, wide-eyed, to the rough greetings of the men who remembered one another from other years. Vince Carver was jovial; his lips, hidden in his heavy beard, parted over his big yellow teeth in laughter and loud fun-making.

When the bread and meat were eaten, and the fires were built up, and the night had settled closer about the fluttering clusters of bright flames here and there under the trees, then Jake had but to listen, lying on his back with his fingers joined under his head, and there were greater tales than ever he had heard. The smoke from the fires went up into the live-oaks hanging with moss, and sleepy birds stirred high in the branches, disturbed by the noise. As the fires died, the men's faces were hardly discernible. Jake thought that their stories were better when he could not see their faces. Their strange talk stirred his stomach like that far stretch of sudsy river out past the bluff. There was talk of drought up toward Carolina; that was the place Ma was always hankerin' after. And the Alatamaha had burst out all her banks and flooded all her swamps in the spring.

There was talk of crops and new ways of doing, of people 'way up North that were talking war. The heavy, sunburnt faces of the men were all strangely alike with their growths of beard and their deep-set, somber eyes; their words were slow and stealthy like their mouths hidden in their beards. The old men prophesied bloody war, but the younger men laughed. Not 'way down hyere. Why, it was as far up North as it was Crost the Water! The words surged in Jake's brain; he stretched his mind to its little limit trying to imagine up North and Crost the Water, and War. The men spoke of Africky, where folks was black like razor-back hogs; they brought them in ships and sold them. But Jake would not buy one when he was a man, not if he had a pocketful of gold pieces. One man said a shipload of them stunk like carr'n, and the stink would come down the wind on still days like a herd of cattle butchered and left to rot. What made 'em black? What made 'em stink? The talk rose and fell in the night, reaching tenuous threads of thought past the bounds of experience. Jake slept under the voices that flowed over his slumber as shallow brown branch-water flows over hard ruffles of sandy bottom, disturbing hardly a loose grain of sand.

Lias strolled away from under the trees soon after they had all helped themselves to meat and bread from the spiders over the coals. All this talk was old talk, and half of the men were more than a little drunk. And besides, it was old men's talk; the young fellers had to hold their tongues. Ma said he was gittin' too big fer his britches. Maybe he was. There wasn't no such thing as bein' yore own man, and speakin' yore own mind. Lonzo was his own man. Lias would marry, that's what he'd do. But the silly gals he knew —who'd have one of 'em? They simpered at you; they were tongue-tied when you spoke to 'em, like so many heifers starin' from a cow-lot. Heifers, that's what they was. . . . No more gumption than a heifer.

He kicked the loose dirt of the street as he lounged along in the thin dark. There were fires in the fireplaces of the houses, flooding their light through doors and shutters set ajar to the early night. In a house on the left there were voices and laughter. That would be Kimbrough's. There was whisky there for the askin', for those who had stuff to trade. Lias had never tasted whisky. Pa had it in a jug slung high to a rafter, but it was for rattlesnake bite and fever.

Lias stood a moment in the dark outside the door, studying the few figures in the long bare room. Several men were sitting on a bench along the wall; others were slouched in chairs, their backs to the heat and glare of the fire. There was the smell of tobacco spittle and whisky in the air of the room. Lias stood undecided near the threshold. Pa never came here; Pa would be mad as thunder. . . . Lias stepped into the room.

The men paid him little attention, looking away from their talk for only a moment to size him up. But a girl sitting on a stool in a corner behind a counter spoke gayly to him:

"Howdy!"

She smiled, and there was welcome and appraisal in her eyes. She was full-breasted and strong-shouldered; she was almost as tall as Lias when she stood. Lias looked hard into her eyes under their straight, heavy brows. She had gray-blue eyes like a kitten's and her skin was white, white, white.

He hardly knew how to ask for a drink. His hands were trembling a little, so he joined them behind him.

"Got some whisky?"

She laughed a little, holding to his eyes with hers, taunting him; she knew he was a greenhorn. Lias's face burned, but he would not let his eyes fall from hers. She asked:

"Straight?"

He nodded, red-faced, not sure of the meaning of her words.

She set the drink in a mug on the counter before him, and he picked up the drink and threw it down his throat. He coughed violently; his breath exploded in his throat in panic at the hard, hot taste of the liquor. She pushed water toward him with laughter in her eyes. After a minute his breath came easily again and he cleared his throat, but the laughter was still in her eyes. He felt hidden laughter there in her white throat, down her pink, satiny gullet, mocking him; there came upon him a hard desire to slap her mouth, to choke her throat, to squeeze her pink gullet closed. She had no business to laugh at him just because he was a greenhorn; he'd kill a body for laughing at him. He laid his hands flat on the counter and glared at her. Her eyes and mouth sobered. She glanced at the men engrossed in their talk, and looked back to Lias. Then she reached her hand across the counter and laid it, light and cool, over his fingers. But it burned him like a touch of fire, and the burn ran through his blood, to his head, to his feet, searing his senses. He knew a queer sensation of feeling her inside himself—there inside his skin, breathing his breath, crowding his eyesight and his senses more than he could bear. He saw her hand, white as milk against his hand that was burned mahogany-colored in the sun. He thought: my arm is white, too, where the sleeve hides it from the sun; I take after my mother's folks, blue-eyed, light-complected.

The girl said:

"Want to go for a little walk?"

He was suddenly a man, full-grown and fearless. He nodded quickly, saying nothing. She called to one of the men before the fire:

"Papa, watch the counter!"

The man turned and looked at her; then he looked at Lias, grunted, and turned back to his talk.

They went out into the dark that was thicker and heavier now, so that the light from the moon fell upon it rather than through it; at least it was so under the live-oaks and moss where the dark was heavy and cold in wind blowing strong from the sea, pushing the tide up the river, and across salty, seeping marshes where marsh grass, brown and dead, moved only a little on the swell of a tide at its full.

The next day was the Sabbath. Traders crowded into the meeting-house to hear a preacher in a frock-tailed coat thundering out mighty prayers as he rocked back and forth on his knees, preaching down Godalmighty's wrath from the tall pulpit upon those who drank rum or cursed or labored on the Sabbath day or denied the tithe of their crops to the Lord's service and servants. The Word of God wrastled with the phlegmatic, stubborn backwoodsmen, and when the altar-call was made, a few sought the altar built of pine planks, and prayed and repented with bitter tears, and renounced Old Satan and all his works. Vince Carver and his kind, aliens to town ways and prejudiced against any show of feeling, stiffened their necks and hardened their hearts and remained stolidly in their sins, though some of them were uneasy under the press of conscience.

The next day, Jasper wrastled with a young buck from down near the Fluridy line, and threw him three out of three. The morning was young; the older men were trading about the town, among themselves, and with the store-traders; the younger men strolled down to the waterside where dug-outs and flat-bottomed boats were tied, knocking against big timbers of the docks. There were straining boat-races on the river; there were wrastling-matches, and friendly wagers, from a drink to a shoat, on anything—races, wrastlers, which ox would next switch his tail at a bothersome fly.

[ 46 ]

When Big Court convened, trading and sporting broke off, and the men crowded onto the rough plank benches, and the air of the court-room became a warm, smelly breathing. The cases were dispatched leisurely by the tobacco-spitting, slow-voiced judge, and lawyers who wore hats in court to distinguish themselves. The finest lawyer, a fellow named Hartshorn, wore a high hat and used a knobbed walking-stick. He laid these under the judge's pine rostrum, and argued mightily against a cattle-thief who had lit a shuck into Fluridy and had come back only the week before and was slammed into jail to await trial.

Another case concerned a young man of the county who had been ambushed in the woods by two rowdies who had laid his head open with a turpentine mattock, and had pocketed his gold watch and coins. The argument went back and forth, for in this case Hartshorn was on the side of the rowdies. Solemn jurors spat into the corners that were splattered brown with tobacco spittle of former juries. The men crowded into the court-room shrewdly judged the merits of each side of the case; opinions clashed, and wagers ran high before the jury convened in muttered argument and declared their several verdicts.

There was something stirring in the battle over a man's legal rights; young men in the crowd wished that they could be lawyers, to argue brilliantly on a case—instead of following a plow down corn-rows in the heat of summer to make their bread. If you were a lawyer, other folks sweated for your side meat and meal and syrup, and you wore a jim-swinger coat and swung a walking-stick, careless-like, in your hand.

Arguments over the lawsuits continued long after the verdicts were rendered. Talk went hot and strong around the camp fires. Vince Carver always spoke his mind, and held to his convictions through thick and thin; he could turn the slickest arguments aside like water off a duck's

[ 47 ]

back. Jake thought that his father should have been a lawyer, for he would surely have topped Hartshorn. Jasper smiled a little at the corner of his mouth when his father made a clean thrust of argument and ripped up another's fine-spun web of words; he was secretly proud of his father; and he was proud of himself—he could lay any of these young bucks with their backs in the dust and hold them there with his knee in their middles, making them grunt every time he mashed down on them.

But now Lias hated his father, even when he felt a stir of pride that Vince Carver stood so high among these men. (For Vince could hold his own even with men who were borned and raised here at the Coast.) Lias nearly wished that he hadn't come this fall. This one certain trip to the Coast made him hate his father because he must go back with him to the burning noons of summer and the freezing daybreaks of winter at home, to the long rows in the fields to be broken with the plow, manure to be scattered down the rows, new ground to be grubbed out, stock to be fed and watered. He was glum and sour when spoken to. Jasper said that a fit had come over Lias.

And a fit had possessed Lias, a fit of slow torturing fever, of gentle tremors that ruffled his blood deliciously, of far-seeing day-dreams that brought the girl near to him any time he willed to think of her.

Ma said he was gittin' too big fer his britches. He already was too big. . . . Lias hardly understood his new confidence; he would face his father; he would tell him; he was as tall as his father and as strong; he was a man now.

He went about each day burdened with rage and rebellion; he went away from the camp fires each night, and found the girl's eyes waiting for him across the counter; he met her hand slipping across the counter to meet his hand; and she went with him down under the live-oaks that spread their limbs over the bluff. The gray moss swung in the heavy, steady breath of the tide that came in, pressing closer and fuller onto the land, drowning the tidal creeks and the spongy mud-banks for a time in water that came to its full, then washed back, and back, and back, to the sea until tomorrow.

Her name was Margot—Margot Kimbrough. Her father owned the little tavern where a man could have rum or fried fish or a bed for the askin', if a man had stuff to trade.

Lias called his father apart from the men on the fourth night they spent at the Coast. The two men went apart a little way on the road toward home. Now Lias was not afraid of his father; his hands did not tremble. The two stood still in the road where white sand showed light in the blackness of grass and trees and sky that was threaded faintly with moonlight.

Lias said, "Pa, I wanta marry."

The old man grunted. Lias waited a long minute while the sound of his father's breathing came and went. He'd better get it out before he got scared. He spoke quickly:

"I'm a-aimin' t' marry tomorrer."

Still Vince said nothing, but his slow, heavy breathing made his son afraid. Lias said:

"Her name's Margot Kimbrough."

His father seemed to grow darker and stiller in the night. After a wait, while the clenching of his hands and the swelling of his neck veins were hidden in the darkness, he spoke, in words that were hard and threatening:

"Lias, she's a slut."

The boy's jaws hardened:

"No, she ain't. She's done told me how they told that on her. Hit's a lie."

His father cringed, hidden in the dark. Lias said it was a lie. . . . The old man arranged the words of an answer

[ 49 ]

in his mouth, tasting their rank bitterness, feeling shame go
through him out of them. The words waited unsaid behind
his lips. He couldn't say: I ain't tellin' ye hearsay. . . . No,
he could not tell Lias that it was truth, not hearsay, that it
was truth known to his mind from his own experience. No.
But he could lay his rawhide onto Lias and learn him not
to gad about and be a fool. He was so angry that his voice
cracked in the blackness:

"You cain't marry her, Lias!"

Lias defied his father.

"I'm agonna marry her, Pa. She's already said she'd marry
me. We done been together."

The old man's chin quivered; he was trembling throughout his body. He'd give Lias such a rawhiding as he would
never get again. He'd lay the stripes open on his back. He'd
learn him to trail a hussy around. He made a step to go for
his rawhide whip that lay yonder in the cart, but he stopped,
the thing in his heart heavy upon him, stilling his thoughts,
clogging his feet, fumbling his hands into frustration. How
could he blame Lias? He was stunned; he felt heavy and
solid and immovable as though this dark should always beat
upon his face, this cutting wind always blow past his ears,
this figure always stand tensely before him, damning him
to silence and shame.

He sighed and turned back toward the fire. The men were
rolled up in their quilts, and most of them were asleep.
Vince lay down next to Jake and Jasper, and closed his eyes
against the fitful light of the dying fire. But sleep would
not come to him. Men snored gutturally in the gloom. Vince
lay within sound of the ruffled river under the light of the
moon, but lately full, that rode high beyond the netted
branches of the old oaks. But he did not hear the river, nor
see the moon. His eyes, staring up into the night, ached
from their long, wide-spread vigil. He feigned heavy slumber

[ 50 ]

when at last his boy came stealthily back a little before day, and laid him down on the other side of Jake to sleep.

Jasper and Jake and a Coast man rowed down the river to where its waters poured into the Atlantic. A little island with a sandy beach lay in the tide-water. They came down with the tide and would go back with it. Jake worried over how they should ever get back if the tide happened to fail; never could they row such a distance.

The tide was out.

Jake lay sprawling on his stomach on the hard white sand, his hands pressing his cheeks, his elbows ground into the sea-sand. As far as you could see there was water— blue-green water with white foam furling lazily yonder like suds boiling in a pot. His eyes turned far to the south and moved slowly up the horizon's smooth rim to the north; it curved a little like the rim of an iron spider set on edge. And after a while that same water would be here where he was lying, plunging and rearing like an innumerable herd of strange green cattle on a stampede, pawing lightly across the white sand, climbing the bluffs a little way to fall back into a milling mass of strange snorting voices, slick green backs, and soft shuffling white hooves.

Out across there was Africky, straight across as the crow flies. He sighted an imaginary musket across the green waste. Or would that be the Spanish Country across there, hidden behind the water? or Angland, maybe, where the ships came from, bringing fancy clothes, and all manner of jimcracks formed of glass and tin, and pieces of gold? Jake prayed for a sail to heave up out of the sea and come up the river's mouth where he could see it. But no white ship came. This was a stormy time on the water, the old men said; no ship would come loaded down with gold, or smelling of the Negroes—black folks with their noses ringed like a bull's, and having black wool in place of hair. Gentle tremors coursed through his body as he lay there on the sand with his eyes set across the water toward the east. Names stirred his senses as sounds might do, strange, unbelievable names: Africky and the Negroes; Angland with her ships like sea-birds; other ships that they called galleons, with red Spanish gold clinking in their dark holds as the tall waves washed them across the deep seas; black men, white men, men colored brown like mahogany wood . . . Oh, the Coast was a strange place, a place past believing, whence you could take ship for Spain or anywhere, where you could lie on the sand past which the waves would come, after a while, and wash out your tracks. Jake thought pleasantly that if he lay here until dark, unmoving, the waves would come and drown him, washing and pounding over him in the night, beating him down under the sea that was stormy at this timë of year. The water would be black in the night, not green—black and cold and churning against the bluffs.

Jake straightened his body and rose to his feet, brushing the sand from his hands and elbows and clothes. It was pleasant to walk up from the sand where the sea would come, and thus escape being drowned.

As they rowed back with the tide, sea-sand clung to Jake's hair, sea-sounds hovered in his ears so that he scarce heard Jasper and the Coast man talking of the easiest means of shucking oysters.

The ocean was the pleasantest thing that Jake found, but there were other things, too. There were women in frocks that stood far out around them and wearing curious hats on their heads. You saw them only early of mornings, trading for table-salt or worsted goods or physic across the counters. They were the ladies of the town, and kept to home at other times. And there were the stores to loiter about; he would listen at a polite distance to the heavy-handed trading; his eyes would take in the stores on the shelves—

cloth goods, firearms, jugs, pewter pitchers, all manner of things.

In one of the places there was a box of white rats. They were white as milk, and had cloudy pink eyes and pink feet, and were pink inside the ears. They would climb the wooden bars of their cage to sniff at Jake's finger, their silky whiskers twitching delicately. They were such pretty things to see, so white and not a-feared of people's hands at all! A blowsy, black-haired man owned them, and fed them little hunks of cheese. They reared up on their hind legs and ate from his hand like pet squirrels. Jake would have given anything for one; he would take it to Cean and let it run up her arm from her hand to her shoulder; it could sit there and nibble with its little pearl tusks at her ear. He would trade for one for Cean when he was able to have a cotton-patch of his own at Pa's place.

The white rats were a sight to see. Men crowded around the box, proffering their rough fingers to the delicate noses sniffing in search of cheese. Jasper found truth in his father's words that to keep the rats for pets would be a foolish waste of food. But Lias liked the sleek, gentle creatures; once he took one from the owner's hand and smoothed its fur with his long fingers that were sun-burnt from light to dark. The fur was softer than cotton, softer than a goose's under-wing; it was as soft as Margot's flesh against his work-hardened hand, as white as Margot's flesh in the dark night. If he had his own stuff, he might trade for one of the little squeaking things.

Even Lonzo could not take his eyes off the little dumb-fool critters.

# Chapter 6

High and proud, Margot sat in Vince Carver's cart on the way home. The preacher in the Coast town had said: "I now join you together in holy wedlock, and pronounce you man and wife after God's ordinance." So what did Vince Carver's angry silence matter?—or Jasper's sheep's-eye glances? Lonzo Smith and Lias's little brother Jake came along in the cart behind them. Even the little boy's face seemed hostile as he watched this strange woman who was going home with them; but Margot's head reared high above the hard thoughts which she imagined they were thinking of her; she belonged to Lias now, and she would ride in her Pa-in-law's cart with Lias when Lias told her she could.

Lias's face was set straight toward the northwest where home lay in watery autumn light under long-leaf pines that leaned away from the wind's chill warnings of winter. There were fields there that he had broken and planted and laid by all by himself. He had some rights there, even if Pa was so mad that he might not give Lias the new ground that was due him, and an ox, and help with a house. Lias would build Margot a house; he would have a log-raisin', and tell the men and boys from all around to come; he would butcher beeves and hogs, and cook them over white oak-coals in shallow pits in the ground. Margot would cook chicken-and-rice, and spiderfuls of rising-bread, and potato pies. Whose potatoes, pigs, beeves, chickens? Lias tightened his jaw on his uneasiness; you never knew what Pa might do, and he was all-fired mad over Lias's marrying this woman. He had the wrong notion about Margot, Lias knew. And nobody knew her as well as Lias knew her, so Lias thought. Just as on the night when he had first seen her, so now he could feel her presence within himself, even though she was three foot away from him, there on the seat of the cart. And he weren't a-feared when he thought of her. "A pillar of a cloud by day, a pillar of fire by night." His thoughts swerved suddenly away from sacrilege, for those were words from a sermon that he had heard at the Coast; God led the people through the wilderness with a pillar of a cloud by day to lead them the way, and a pillar of fire by night to give them light. The likeness of those shining things to Margot teased his thoughts, leading them away from sermons back to Margot, where all his thoughts homed like a drove of bees that bear their sweetness ever to the same hive, pushing under the low edge of the gum into the warm murmur and the bitter-sweet climate of honey-making. It seemed a sin to Lias to think of sermons and a woman at the same time; but to him Margot was like a cloud billowing along, going nobody knew where; and to him she was like fire by night, lovely as live blood, and burning with heat that hurts if it come too close. Well he knew that loving a woman overmuch is evil, a thing to guard against, a taint of the flesh to pray away; a man must beget children after him, but he must not worship another body. Lias knew the sin of mixing Margot with higher things; women should be kept in their places, and the rest of a man's time should be taken up with work and clean pleasures. He must put Margot where she belonged in his mind, and plan how he was to build her a house fitten for her to live in. He couldn't build her a house yet, not till Pa softened up. They would have to sleep in the loft, with Jasper in the other bed in Cean's place with Jake. Or maybe Ma would give Margot the spare room.

Margot's garments were under the seat of the cart in a small hide trunk bound with tin bands. She sat above her belongings beside Vince, who was driving. Jasper and Lias sat behind on the floor of the cart that was padded with folded quilts. Each man's thoughts settled about his head in a cloud of abstraction. Lias's thinking was black and turbid, but nonetheless splendid, like an ominous sky shot through with lightning's jagged javelins. Jasper was a-feared for Lias, and for the consequences of Pa's anger over this upstart marriage; and he was a-feared of the proud, white woman, Margot, whose face and body moved in slumberous beauty that disquieted him. Vince Carver could take the hide offen yore soul without raisin' his voice. But most of all, Jasper was a-feared for his mother, who had no expectation of this daughter-in-law thrust upon her—a fine, stiff-necked daughter-in-law from the Coast, dressed in flounces and a black bonnet with blossoms on it. Would this Margot look down on his mother, who had rough, brown hands and weak, near-sighted eyes? Would this woman, who laughed in her eyes while her lips were puckered closed, lie late abed while his mother cooked and churned and hoed?

In Lonzo's cart the thoughts were of other things: one saw a vast green sea with white ships that crossed from Trinidad to the New World, and away again to Singapore, and himself the master of one of those ships, high in its rigging, lashing a shaking sail; he did not know how he would lash it, but he would learn. The other saw a little brown woman with a meek face waiting at the end of his journey, her body bearing his son to meet him a little piece down the road.

The oxen ambled along; white sand spilled from the backs of the wheels in gritty whispers. The skies were clouded over. The woods breathed quickly now in sharp gusts of wind; winter was upon them and they were afraid. The leaves of the trees were flushed with hectic coloring. Small wild trees trembled, turning their leaves this way, that way, any way, to escape the cold wind that breathed death upon them. The old pines sighed and sighed; winter would not kill their long glossy needles; they would retain their green grandeur, growing new needles as the old ones fell, so that no one could know aught of the season from their habit. But the maples would stand, dry and frayed as brush brooms propped against the sky; the oaks would stagger high like dead giant brier berry bushes; for the leaves of all save the pines, winter brought fluttering death and a wide grave on the earth, soaked with rain and hard sunlight, where they would rot insensibly as any human thing. The other living things would go away with the leaves; they would hide out in logs and caves in the dark cold until another year would cause the rattler's pied-ed skin to slip upon his back, would cause the rabbits to nuzzle their soft noses together and join in proclaiming a new spring.

A red maple leaf descended the air, tilted on one point on Vince Carver's rough hat, brushed his humped shoulder, fell to the rut, where a wooden wheel flattened it into the sand. Vince Carver chucked to the ox and roused his body from its heavy quiet. No need to rip and rear. The thing was done. Best give Lias land and a team of oxen and a cow, and get him off. That woman! . . . He could not resolve his oppression into thought; this was feeling that added unto itself in the middle of his body, and left his head light and empty; it grew within him, feeding on his in'ards, his shame, his pride, his love for Lias. Lias was smart as a whip, quick to see a thing, and quicker to do it. He was butt-headed, too, wouldn't listen to nobody. But that woman would learn him; yes, wouldn't she learn him! She'd learn 'em all before she was through. She'd take Lias down to hell, that's what she'd do. But Lias wasn't to blame; he, Vince, was to blame. God was punishing him. He had loved Lias the best, and it was Lias she went after. And she got him. Jezebel! Slut! He had told Lias about her, and Lias wouldn't listen. God had stopped Lias's ears so that Vince could be punished through this son that he loved best; and Satan had stiffened Vince's tongue with pride so that he wouldn't speak out and tell Lias the whole truth. It was Satan against God; and Vince had lined up with Satan and his crowd when first ever he looked at that woman; now he was being punished. Vince dropped his head lower into his shoulders. He must take up his cross; he must shut his mouth and endure. Why had he ever thought that the dark might hide iniquity, that distance might silence evil, that secrecy might pass for virtue? Behold, the God of Israel neither slumbers nor sleeps. Vince bowed his head, acknowledging his fault before a great Judge of infinite wisdom, and an unwinking eye, and astounding cleverness in devising punishments for His sinning children. No need to hate Lias and that woman. She would call him Pa, and he must call her by her first name. No need to hate her. This was his cup, and he must drink it. He comforted his spirit in thinking that she had sinned, too; and God would, without fail, brew her a bitter cup, too.

Margot held her head serene above the sloping white hill of her shoulders that were hidden under black stuff, as was the smooth, deep pit of her bosom, and her arms, full-rounded and soft in the sleeves. Black goods sewed into a tight-waisted, full-skirted frock covered all of her body, down to the soft, heeled shoes. Only the white face and white hands came out with a put-on shame against the black. Her hands lay in her lap, the wrists softened by little frills of fine white cloth sewed into the sleeves. The set of her head and the prideful look in her face bespoke the beauty of her long slender body poised on long slender feet that were tilted on pretty heels of new English-manufactured shoes. Her body told its pride in her eyes that were clear and blue as water that conceals with clarity its true depth. Her eyes were as soft as the flesh in the inner curve of her elbow; they held the delicate sheen of the skin that was stretched taut over ankle-bones where blue veins beat softly and regularly, frangible blue gongs tolling the beat of her heart.

Her glances fell ever and again and hovered before her body as though they said: This is not I that you see; no; you see heavy, black goods, but there are beneath this goods shimmering limbs that give off warmth like comforting white fire; there is skin, as fine-made as the silk of a morning-glory's mouth, stretched across an ivory lattice-work of ribs, where secret flesh swells into pink breast-buds that are like buds of heavy flowers. Beauty possessed her, dwelling in her eyes, weighting them so that they fell from another's scrutiny; beauty slowed her feet as she walked, so that the skin and the carefully fitted sockets of her bones, and the flesh that breathed and beat and nurtured itself, throbbed silently and smoothly as a diminutive creation within a vast creation, as a minute world within a mighty world, pursuing faithfully its little orbit of coarse loveliness, rounding methodically through its several seasons.

She held her head serenely, though fear gnawed at her new-found security. Now she was married to a man whom she could love. All the others were chunky or tall, sweaty or new-washed, but they were all heavy-eyed, heavy-mouthed men. But this Lias, this boy, he was lean and clear-eyed; his mouth was unused to the taste of rum, and smelled clean against her mouth; his young beard was washed clean like the brown silk of corn that is washed in rain and dried in sun and wind; his hands held her firmly—they did not hide and slip and seek furtively about her body, they held her securely and desperately, as one holds a fortune of gold.

She ignored the old man there on the seat beside her, hunched over the cowhide rein in his hand. His glance lay between the ears of an ox, like an ill-wish on the journey. She dismissed Jasper, her husband's brother, as being young and foolish; true, he was older than Lias, but he was different. Jasper was young and would never be old, as some women are never old, but keep always in their eyes the uncertainty of a child. Now some women would settle to a marriage with a neighbor's son, to tending a flock of chickens and a herd of goats and a brood of puny drooling children; some women would take the first man that was proffered them, and be satisfied. But not Margot Kimbrough! She had known what sort of man she wanted, and her heart would not rest with any man but that one man. She had loved Lias's tall insolence when first ever she saw it—when he had asked for whisky and had drunk it straight, not because he liked it straight, but because he knew no better; he had swallowed the strong drink, and his eyes had made her mouth shut up its laughter at him. Oh, she loved this man! She loved this man with her heart; her arms were weary of another kind of love, her lips had been shut many times against other kisses than his, her feet had found their last dark interview; she loved this man with her heart.

She lived by her mother's Irish blood. Mary had danced the lilt on a big table in Kimbrough's place the night before Margot was born. The men laughed about it till yet. And Margot had come catapulting into the world before her mother was scarce decently abed. Mary had laughed before them all because her child was so forward, but later, when nobody saw her, she turned to the wall and wept. She taught Margot the lilt long before the child could write her name; Mary's words and ways impressed the child as the sun impresses, unnoticed, quietly, leaving layer upon layer of brown, light as dust, upon tender skin.

Mary was ever wild and willful and her heart loved no one but herself. Micajah Kimbrough she did not love; he meant bread and meat and drink and carousal, and fine garments, and a place in which to show them, but she did not love him. She flung his food together on the rough table when he was hungry; she poured herself a stiff drink for every one that she poured for him when he had a mind to drink. But when she could do so and not anger him, she kept out of his way. There was a little island that lay in the river's mouth where the ocean washed into the river. With only light rowing, the tide would take her down to the little island and the tide would bring her back when it was ready to come back. Since the time when she first came to the Coast town Mary had loved that little island. Back from sight of the ocean, underbrush was thick, palmettos grew head-high, bamboo vines scratched bloody streaks through her sleeves and across her cheeks. Live-oaks stood thick, crowning the island and trailing curtains of moss. Into this wilderness Mary would go, tramping carelessly, not caring if a rattler sang out suddenly and struck at her leg, for if one should, what did she care? She would lie down and die there; her blood would thicken and stop her heart with purple clots. In lower places where the salt water came inland, she would dawdle in the marsh grass, unafraid of a coral snake's flick of a bite, for if a coral snake should bite her, she would lie down, face upward, and watch the sky change from light to dark and know that tomorrow she would not care if it were light or dark; then she would not go back to Cajy's drunken fondling. No. She would forget him quite. Often as she lay with her body sunken in grass in a solitude of live-oaks stirred with sea wind she would forget Cajy and think of Ireland brooding over her little sea toward the Hebrides; she would think of her mother feeding her pigs, and could imagine her shading her eyes toward the south, toward Dublin and Liverpool. For from Liverpool the little ships sail out; and black, horny-tailed dragons are apt to carry down the ships to their sea-lairs and crunch the bones of little creatures who are foolish enough to be abroad in a domain of dragons. Ah, well she knew, did Mary, that she would never go back to the grunting pigs and the mud cottage with a thatched roof.

Mary loved the outgoing tide, for it was going home. She could fancy it piling its crests yonder on the far coasts of Ireland.

She would watch the receding tide as it surrendered the beach to sandpipers and gulls. Reluctant waves furled in along the beach, each shaking out its lacy ruffle of foam. Old, bedraggled foam moved futilely on muddy waves out yonder. Sometimes she would wade, pulling her heavy skirts to her knees, and would stand in the way of the crusted foam, so that it broke against her legs with feather-sounds that were like minute kisses of innumerable minute mouths. Ever she would go away from the sea comforted by its voices that will linger in the ears as they linger in the ear of a sea-shell, ever to be heard for the listening, though the shell be far from the sea.

Mary died of dropsy when Margot was fourteen years old. She died simply and sweetly, as any proper body should, as she had not lived. She died with her eyes fixed on far space beyond the smoke-stained rafters of her room. At the end, she quieted as though in overwhelming astonishment that stopped her breath; her pale mouth dropped open in wonder; her eyes held their wide and vacant stare till they were closed by a sick-nurse's hand, as though her body had spoken in every dumb cell: This that I see cannot be! But what her eyes had sought, or what they saw, never did she tell.

As the journey wore on, Margot's head and shoulders drooped a little, as a stiff flower wilts against its will. The miles were long, heavy space through which the teams would not be hurried, although the men whistled and cracked the whips over their heads in the dismal cold air. Rain would bring winter any day now, and they must reach home before rain came.

In the broad-bottomed carts the goods which the men had traded for slipped and tinkled and bounced about; gold pieces shuffled together in the leathern pouches in the men's bosoms. The coarsely-woven woolen garments, bunched about their bodies, were warm and comforting. Margot caught her long cloak of sewn squirrel-skins close about her throat. The pink blossoms on her bonnet seemed out of place among the foliage above and beside the road. The leaves of the trees were blotched fever red and jaundice yellow as they died and loosed fragile holds on limbs that had given them sap through a length of days, and then inexplicably denied it.

In the night there was little sleeping for Margot where she lay couched on a bed of piled leaves or moss or pine-needles, wrapped in a padded woolen quilt from her father's loft storeroom. Through the thickness of the wrapped quilt between them she could feel the strong length of Lias beside her; his arm lay heavy upon her, his chest was against her shoulders, his breath warmed her ear that would scarcely note a painter's scream through the heavy haste of his breathing. Hers was a strangely bitter, strangely sweet marrying; her sleepless eyes noted the wind, free and wild in the tree-tops against the late moon; the wind tangled the tree-tops with its black blowing in the night. Now she was Margot Carver, bound to Lias Carver with marriage words, but a secret sense within her taught her reticence; a child will hold its breath against a bubble's thin beauty though it knows that the breath-spun globe of colored crystal will vanish though it be not breathed upon.

Lias's feeling toward Margot was as careful as was her feeling toward him. He was afraid that he could not keep this wonder with him. If his father should drive her away, he would take her in his own two hands and go. But even then there must be moneys to keep her well and happy and content to stay with him. There was sickness to be staved off, and death that loves young flesh as a canker loves a spongy rosebud. And ever Lias was haunted by the fear that this magic creature who said she loved him must surely vanish into thin air, or take back her love from him. For well he knew that it was not right for any mortal to feel toward another mortal as he felt toward her. Some mishap must surely come; he thought that it would be that she would discover that he was not so fine a creature as she thought. Now she vowed that never had she seen another man whom she liked so well, but Lias was a-feared that he could not keep himself up to that opinion. She had told him that she had loved one other man.

She had told him as much as her woman's heart thought it wise for him to know—the man's name, and the account of his fine words.

But she did not tell him all.

The first time ever she saw Audley Peacock she was standing beside a ten-rail fence where gourd vines ran; the green gourds on their pretty curved necks were thick through all the cracks of the rails. Margot was gathering a few small ones to serve as salt-gourds, water-dippers, and such like; the others she would leave to grow large and ripen on the vine for meal or grease.

Audley Peacock came unawares behind her and exclaimed all of a sudden, "By jockey!" loud enough to scare the wits out of her; but when she turned, startled, he was looking the other way and rolling his tongue in his cheek as though he did not know that she was there. Oh, ever would she remember that knave, Peacock, for his fine words. "Hut, lass," he would say, and pinch her cheeks, and buss her straight on the mouth. Oh, his eyes had clapped onto her like a duck's on a June-bug. He could sing "Gloomy Winter's Gone Awa' " till it would make your heart-strings quiver. He had taught her the fine game of egg-pecking on a clear Easter morning when they should have been at the meeting-house a-worshiping Godalmighty; she knew that now, but she did not know it then, for she was but ten-and-five year old, and there was no one to tell her; for Cajy Kimbrough slept till noonday o' Sabbaths, not caring if his little daughter went to meeting or not.

Ever in her heart would she curse him for a knave, that Audley Peacock; but ever would she refrain from speaking her opinion of him to any other—and least of all to Lias.

Audley was a ladies' beau, wise in the ways of the world. She should have known it when he exclaimed that her waist was so small, when he begged to see if he could not span it twice around with his big hands. He had been to tea-parties and balls in Saint Augustine; he had danced the cotillion in Carolina; he gave her golden gewgaws to pin on the bosom of her dress; and he was ever spanning her waist with his hands, marveling that it was so small. He was ever crying, "Zounds! ye're mouth is as red as beat vermilion." He would set his eyes on her lips till she drew them in for maiden modesty. He showed her his moneys that he kept at the bottom of his duffle-bag that he laid under his pillow at night with his dragoon pistols. Later, she had found them there when her hands were fondling his head. He spread his gold moneys for her eyes to see—doubloons, guineas, moidores, johannes pistoles, and dollars enough to blear her eyes. He filled her ears with chit-chat, and her mouth with kisses. He taught her to love him till she could not tend the bar nor bake a hoecake nor boil a fowl nor slice a haunch of venison, nor even mind any other body's words, for thinking of him. She ached for him as an airless void aches for rushing wind, as parched earth must cry for rain.

But he rode away one day on his lean sorrel that he called Sally O'Salt. Down the pike toward Savanna he went, duffle-bag, pistol, hanger, shotgun, powder-horn, shot-pouch, whip, leathern bandbox, and all. And even though she saw him pack his last little belonging, she believed that he would come back within a fortnight, because he told her that he would. He swung his hat in farewell to Margot, and spurred his horse to a gallop with the silver spurs on the boots that Margot had greased for him.

A time later comers and goers brought her word that he died the drunkard's death in Savanna in a public house. The landlord had stobbed a knife clean into his lights because Audley had tampered with his daughter's good name. And out of the wound, they told her, frothy blood spurted as his breaths came, till he died. And Margot heard tell of him no more.

Long she wondered why her father had not stobbed Audley Peacock for tampering with her good name and for his not giving her his own name in place of it; she wondered till the day she found the gold moidores in Cajy Kimbrough's money-box that was set high on a rafter in the loft.

Margot felt fear for other things than life or death that might come betwixt her and Lias. Some man would loose his tongue and tell Lias, and she would lose him. And Lias was the only man whom she had ever wanted to keep. Now she was nighabout sorry that she had not gone back to Ireland to live with her mother's mother in a pigsty. But she would not go. She had liked the rollicking, rough life of her father's place, till she met Lias. Old men with white beards who held themselves as straight as pines, young men with black beards and strong as oaks, would row in from their ships and would hang over her counter with their jackets smelling of sandalwood and tobacco; they would talk of a big blow off the tip of the Horn, or of the lights along the rocks at Rio; and she would listen with her chin cupped in her long white hands, with her neck and shoulders swathed in her long black hair. Her eyes would join with some sailor's eyes in exquisite conjecture; her eyes would fall away from his.

Out yonder lay the wild ocean that rings the earth like a lashing dragon; sometimes he sleeps and sometimes he wakes. And Ireland is far away; hills green as emeralds turn back to misty valleys where little houses cluster, sending their smoky breath into a quiet sky; and a pale road makes its careless way toward the south. But here there was a sailor's bold kiss, hot and threatening like the monsoon in hot waters that he told about. Here were long gold earrings dangling on gold chains below her ears; and the swing of the gold against her cheek beguiled her heart.

She was glad she had not gone to Ireland, after all, for even before Lias had come she had known much pleasure. Margot's mother, when she lay dying, had commanded the child's father to send Margot back to Ireland on a sailing-vessel. Then Margot had liked the thought of going with the wind across the wallowing waves to the Old Country. But her father was a slow sort of person; there was always tomorrow. And before the right ship came up from the Cape, curtsying to every inshore wave, Margot had a silk pouch about her neck on a silver chain from the Brazils. In the pouch she kept the big gold earrings, and a carved piece of jade as big as your thumb, a handful of moon crystals, and an opal finger ring that meant bad luck; many curious things caressed one another, polishing their surfaces with each movement of her slow body that she had scented from a vial of ottar-o'-roses that a young Irish red-beard had given her, saying, "Ye mind me o' someun. . . ."

On the fourth day from the Coast, the oxen quickened their plodding. The air grew familiar to them, somehow; the woods leaned friendlier over the trail. While the sun was yet high in the west the carts lumbered up to Vince Carver's place.

Seen Carver was waiting on the steps for her menfolks. Her eyes had seen the blur on the seat of the cart beside Vince; that must be a stranger to be fed and slept for the night—a stranger in a cloak.

Jake jumped over the side of Lonzo's cart. Lonzo called

out, "Well, y' all be a-comin' over . . ." and chucked his ox toward home where Cean waited for him.

Lias helped Margot down from the cart. Jasper shifted his weight uneasily from one foot to another. Vince cleared his throat.

"Well, Ma, yore boy got him a wife at the Coast. See how ye like 'er."

Vince laughed over-loudly and Jake and Jasper felt better about the marriage. Lias's jaw softened. His mother's porely eyesight found his flushed face and proud dare-devil air; it found his wife, pale, shut-mouthed, looking like you had done her wrong. Seen wet her lips and bestirred herself to make her son's wife feel at home.

"Why, Lias! . . . Y'all come right in. . . . There's supper enough fer all, I reckon . . . 'n' beds, too."

Lias wanted to run to his mother and throw his arms about her skirts and cry into its thick folds as he had done once when he was a little boy, when a chicken hawk had butchered a mourning-dove that he had tamed. Though he was much taller now, a man at last, he knew that she was saying now, as she had said then: "Now . . . now . . . no use to take on. . . ."

They went into the house, Vince talking loudly about the lean ribs of the hounds. Seems like Seen needed another woman about, to help her keep house; a lean dog speaks bad for a woman's table.

And Lias's heart was nigh onto bursting for love of his father.

Margot had to repeat her name twice over for her mother-in-law's ears; no such name as that ever came out of Carolina. . . . But hit were a purty-sounding name.

Vince roared when she said that:

"Shore hit is! Lias had me and Jasper and Jake there to help 'im pick out the one with the right name. Betwixt us all, we oughta brung a good un."

But when Seen showed Margot the spare room, and Margot went in and laid her cloak across the foot of the bed, his heart was nigh to breaking. For that was the glossy cherry-wood bedstead that he had carved and polished years back for Seen's new spare room. But Vince laughed fit to split his throat, and thumped Lias's big shoulders, and bragged on him for getting him a wife.

When the ox-cart had rounded the swamp, old Major ran down the rise, barking welcome to Lonzo.

Cean walked heavily down the slope to meet her husband come home. Her face was full and bright and laden with joy. Oh, the days had been long, and the nights burdened with discomfort and unnamed fears. But now Lonzo was back, first time ever he had left her! Her throat was tight, but she would be a pretty thing to cry with him just home. But when he laid his arms about her burdened shoulders, and smoothed her hair with his hands laid on her head where she stood a little distance from him with his child between them, she wept into her hands. He went on smoothing her hair, saying: "Don't cry, little un. . . ."

He brought his presents from where they lay in the bottom of the cart, along with the gunpowder and the salt. There was the gold piece she had wished for; there were six thin, hand-wrought silver spoons to set on her eating-table; there was a length of store-bought cloth, and spice from Chiny and the Indees; and there was a white rat in a cage of wooden slats, that Lonzo said would climb up her arm and hide against her neck, nibbling in play at her ear.

"Lias has got him a wife . . . pretty as you ever seed."

Cean's mouth dropped open; here were too many things to take in all at once. Lonzo said:

"Skin as white as that rat. . . ."

She said nothing, for the soft nuzzling on her neck distracted her. Her skin seemed browner yet against the white fur; the liver-spots showed black against the mouse's soft pink nose.

Finally she said:

"I wonder if she'd 'a' done hit if she knowed how hit feels t' carry a young un every step y' take. . . ."

But she was not complaining; she was just wondering.

# Chapter 7

LONZO put the winter oats into the ground on a clear, cold day in December. November had been bleak and drizzly; the firewood was soggy, and Cean quarreled quietly to herself, trying to cook the victuals over it. December brightened up. It was very cold for piny-woods weather, but it was dry and healthy. The cold took the feel out of Lonzo's hands when he went out to feed up and milk, a little after daylight; but when the sun came up things warmed up. Cean would have breakfast done a little before day, and they would eat by firelight. Lonzo enjoyed his breakfast the best of any meal—fried bacon that swam in its own grease, grits cooked to a thick, smooth mush, hoe-cake, and syrup. Sometimes lately Cean stole a little flour from her barrel and made leatherbread and baked it on a greased spider.

She liked to cook Lonzo's rations before it was light. He always raked out the coals and built up the fire from the stack of chopped light'ood beside the fireplace. (On the wood-shelf below the closed shutter outside there was plenty more wood within easy reach. Lonzo was a mighty good provider.) She would lie in bed until the room warmed a little; but hit weren't laziness; Lonzo told her to take cyare of herself. By the time the rooster crowed the first time she would have breakfast about done. They would eat as the pigs began to stir in the pen off to the side of the house and Betsey lowed away down in the cold. The fowls flew down with the first light and sidled against the wind across the yard to the sheltered side of the house, where they huddled against the logs; every now and then the rooster stretched his neck like a trumpet to sound his urgent, brassy call:

Ooh - oo - Ooh - oo - Oo - oo - oo

The sky paled in the east while Lonzo milked for Cean; but the dark did not go completely out of the air until the sun slipped into place and began its slow climb; then the skies cleared and thinned; the dark went quite away, even from among the bushes around the wash-trough and under the deep north eaves of the house. There might be wind laying itself against the cheek like a slow-biting lash, but it seemed much less cold now than when it whistled in against the house away in the night. That sound would make Cean push closer to Lonzo and be thankful that she was there in a feather bed under good warm quilts, and not a dumb critter out in the cold with its hind end to the wind.

Now in the cold months sleek snakes had found their holes, and rough-hided toads their burrows of mud. Somewhere deep in the earth the snakes might lie dozing, coiling ever so slowly, now and then, a vicious head laid across the head of its mate. The frogs that had shrilled their brittle, metallic singsongs through the wet summer months were blinking sleepily in the dark somewhere, squatted on their ugly haunches, multiple thousands of them in a thousand burrows. Birds sought through the dead grasses for their meals of dried seeds. In Cean's pea-patch partridges found the dried pods that had split open, leaving dried peas free for the small wild beaks.

All through the flat-woods, pines heaved on their deep moorings in the earth; they rocked to the south when the north wind blew, they rocked to the west when the east wind blew; but when the winds were gone back into the east and north, and there fell a quiet, balmy day, the pines were straight as ever, moored fast to the black, deep-coiled roots of the old earth herself. The myriad swarming insects were gone; they had burdened the air with their cries; the heavy jarring songs of the crickets, the minute peep-peep—peep of other insects that rose from the grass in a swarm of compelling sound, caused the summer heat to seem the more oppressive. In summer nights the katydids cried, clinging to one long, steely-harsh note in the midst of a din of the notes of a thousand other insect creatures. The locust's golden stir-r-r-r-r-r would break out in the night, beating on the hot air. Where were those sounds hushed now? The little creatures were snuggled along a maze of earthy tunnelings; many were dead, leaving their unborn young swinging in warm furry cocoons in the trees where the wind would rock them, or clinging to the underside of a dead leaf, or hugging the low stem of a dried weed; nature was careless, but it did not matter; if a thousand perished, a thousand thousand remained.

In summer the sound of the many little breathing calls and cries paneled the dark as one listened, as thin covering hides a rough wall. But the winter dark was a different thing from summer dark. In winter, the night was a bare, bleak thing without the unobtrusive clickings and peepings of little winged creatures. One could not hear the dark now; there was only silence with the wind howling through it. Sometimes against the black silence there would come the cry of a painter, or the yowling of a wildcat in the edge of the woods near the clearing. Sometimes there would be a racing of the feet of the hounds that went after some timid creature that ventured too near the house.

Cean did not sleep well now, for her breath came hard no matter how she turned. But this was not the fevered worry of the nights when her child was growing; her child was grown now, and her body could rest while it waited. Now she could listen in the night and not be a-feared. Now the light from a log that burned on into the morning might make curious shapes on the walls and in the corners, but she was no longer a-feared.

Now, in this latter state, she was attuned to the same sensitiveness as in former months, but restlessness and foreboding no longer made her sick at heart; now she could wonder, without any great grief, how wild things protected their young from all manner of things, and if they did not grieve when harm befell—the painter burying his claws in a fawn's tender haunches, a hawk filling its maw from a squirrel's nest, an eagle swooping upon a rabbit running back to her young that are not yet dry in the nest, a field mouse that must flee from every shadow that passes on the ground. . . . Oh, the wild mothers must have a hard time, she would think, breeding and bearing and losing their young, breeding and bearing, over and over. They were often heavy in the body like herself, yet in sudden danger they must gather their four feet and flee for their lives. Yet withal they were honest, loving mothers; a partridge is a fear-stricken thing, yet she will stay on her nest and fight your foot if you try to push her off; the 'possum, with a face like a young un, will, when she is caught, play dead, to save her little black-eyed baby that cowers in its pouch on her belly. . . .

And here she was with Lonzo by her side to keep danger offen her and her little un; here she was safe and warm, and not worried up over every shadow and noise as a wild thing must be. There was a stone jug close to the fire, keeping hot water ready for any time that the little un should be ready. There was Ma just six miles off, and coming to stay with her. And yonder in the corner was the deep walnut cradle that Lonzo had built and polished, waiting for her little un to sleep in it. But mostly she would keep her baby with her in her own bed. Lonzo said that women sometimes smothered their babies when they slept with them; sometimes a sow would smother one of her litter. . . . But Cean wouldn't!

. . . A pretty mother she would be, lobberheaded as a sow, to smother her baby.

She ought to thank Godalmighty that things were so easy for her. She was eating her white bread now; both were sent on this earth—fine white bread to enjoy, and bitter black bread to be eaten with hard silence or soft tears. But you had to eat whatever was sent. If you flung it back in Godalmighty's face, you'd live to see the day when you would wish that you hadn't. Cean had often heard her mother tell how Vince and Seen had paid for stiff necks and hard hearts, and exchanged them for sackcloth and ashes, as Ma called it, so that ever after they were sweeter and gentler. Ma had recounted it many a time.

Seen had brought a baby in her arms from Carolina, a girl named Naomi Eliza-beth. Ma said herself that neither she nor Pa had ever loved another child as they loved that little Eliza-beth. They dared not, for "Thou shalt have no other gods before me!" Eliza-beth was born in Carolina nine months before Seen and Vince emigrated down to Georgy away from everybody. Ma said that she sinned a thousand times down here because always when she rocked Eliza-beth to sleep a-singin' "There is a happy land far, far away," she always thought of Carolina where folks lived close together, and had jamborees, and hay-rides on moonlight summer nights; it never crossed her mind that she was sinning in not thinking about heaven when she sang about it. Ma and Pa had a hard pull of it when they first settled here; rain rotted the seeds in the ground; the cow died of black-leg; the pigs bloated and lay down and died; even the fowls sickened, their bills and half their heads rotted off before they, too, died. Seen cooked cornmeal mush as long as the meal lasted, and they ate it without milk or sweetening. Then she stewed rabbits or birds that Vince had snared —because he would not waste his powder. He knocked squirrels from the trees with well-aimed rocks—for they were

[ 75 ]

plentiful and trustin' so that they were not hard to kill; he caught fish with a rigged-up hook; and they ate these things without salt, for there was no salt. Seen rejoiced that she still had milk for Eliza-beth, until that dried up (no matter how much water she drank) and her breasts were soft again and small as a girl's. Oh, it was a bitter time. That was Seen's and Vince's time for eating black bread, and they refused it; or at least they turned away their faces from God's hand and grumbled at His treatment of them. Now Seen blessed God that they had ever come out of it, but then she had not lived so long nor learned so much. Then she had been like Job's wife, nagging Vince on to curse God and die, and Vince was ready to do it. They were bitter and butt-headed and thought they knew more about how things ought to be run than God did. And God had taught them a lesson.

In the sickly late spring of that next year Eliza-beth took fresh cold and lay whimpering in Seen's arms day and night. The cold settled in her head and made a rising in there, too far in for Seen to get to it. She poulticed Eliza-beth's face and neck with wild comfort that Vince dug out of the soggy earth; she gave her snakeroot tea to cool the fever that burned your hand like a hot brick; she mixed catnip tea with squirrel liquor and fed the whimpering mouth that turned away from the pewter spoon in Seen's hand. Finally, Vince roamed the woods for all manner of yerbs that he had seen his own mother treat with—calamus for chills, white sassafras roots that are better than the red, shoemake that is good for skin poison. Vince would come in with his cowhide boots caked in mud, and give-y with wet; and Seen would brew all the roots and leaves in different ways; she used them all on the child. But the fever and the swelling did not abate.

Finally, Vince prayed such a prayer as Cean had heard him make many times since, in her own lifetime. His horny, hairy hands fumbled one upon the other where they were clasped on his breast; his eyes were tight shut, not daring to face his God open-eyed and calm-faced. He shut his eyes and reached for a hold upon God that he might wrastle with Him as Jacob did. But God seemed much nearer the Coast towns and Carolina than He did to this place nigh onto a hundred mile in the wilderness. Did God remember that he and Seen had brought their child away here among the painters and wildcats and moccasins—where just across the Fluridy line the Spanish people spoke another tongue, and wanted another war with the whites—where close to the south and west roamed red devils that itched for the skin from over yore brains? Did He? Hit were mighty doubtful. Vince would have to pray loud and agonize long to make Him hear from so far! So Vince prayed, with his brawny arms reaching into the air for power that could heal this child, this little white god whose body, made of his and Seen's flesh, was an altar at which they had worshiped through all the days of her short lift. Vince prayed: "Almighty God, Thee canst hear though from the wilderness; Thee canst heal though the sickness be sore unto death; Thee canst touch the fevered brow and cool it in the twinkling of an eye." So Vince praised the great God that He might be flattered and heal Eliza-beth: "Thee dost note the sporrer's fall. Heal this leetle sporrer in our nest by Thy loving grace and tender mercy. Not that we be worthy . . . no! We be weak and sinful, no more than pore worms of the dust . . ." He beat his breast; tears of self-abasement rolled down his cheeks and were lost in his beard; he wore himself out praying, bellowing his ponderous words in the silence in which the child's breathing came in gasps in its hurry to take leave of the body.

When the prayer was gone into silence, Vince, still on his knees, opened his eyes, and Seen raised her head from the side of the bed. And they saw their child. Her forehead

[ 77 ]

was still hot, but her feet and hands were cold, and at the edge of her tangled hair, brushed back a thousand thousand times by Seen's yearning hand, there was a dampness which Seen had tried in vain to induce with brews of yerb tea.

When they had boxed their child, they gave her to the earth to keep under the grass to the left of the house. Vince got down his big Bible and finished a line on the page that was the likeness of a scroll. Nearly two years before he had set down:

Borned to Vincent Newsome Carver and Cean Loveda Trent Carver
A daughter Naomi Elizabeth Jun 19 1810

Now he added:

Left us for Glory Apr 9 1812

Seen would tell you now that they had humbled themselves before the Lord there at Eliza-beth's dying bed, but that they was too long a-doin' hit . . . and God had punished them, and kept on punishing them. . . . After that there was one child that died before its heart ever beat, and Seen lost it one day when she was alone. Then it was four long years before God sent them another child; that was Jasper. By that time God was softened by their continued tears and prayers, and he lifted up the light of His countenance upon them and gave them Lias and Cean, and, a little later, Jake. And since they had repented, Vince's crops had prospered; now they were well off and would have something to leave their children when it was their time to pass on.

Cean lay there in bed, praying Godalmighty that He would not let her unborn son die of a rising in the head, nor of fever, nor of anything at all as long as his mother should live. She abased herself before Him, hoping that He would know that she was properly humble where He sat

[78]

yonder on a glittering throne on the other side of gates of pearl that open only inward.

She would name her son for her father and for Lonzo's father—Vincent Rowan Smith. It was a fine, high-sounding name. The next boy she should have she would name Alonzo, for his Pa. And she would name one of her sons for Jake—that would tickle him to death. . . . She smiled to herself as she drifted off into a mingled dream of her little sister Eliza-beth, who would now be a grown woman, but who in Cean's thoughts was always a little child, dead on a bed, just as she was thirty years ago; and dreams of her own sons, who would be grown men in another thirty years, but who somehow could never grow past the size of this little one within her, whom she would see with her eyes and touch with her hands before the moon shrank away to nothing again. Drowsing, her mind moiled about the ponderous spell of time that sixty years inclose.

When the December moon was nigh onto fullin', Cean's mother came to be with her. And Lonzo's father brought Dicie, his wife, to help tend to Cean when she got down. The little un was due on the full of the moon; if it put off its coming on that day, it would wait on for another change; and what's more it would be a girl if it came on the shrinking moon. The child's grandmothers came in time for the full moon, hoping for a boy. Lonzo would need boys to help break ground and pull fodder; girls were good for but little, except to weave and pick cotton.

They waited about the fire, Lonzo and Cean and the two old women, while the moon moved across from east to west in its journey through each day's hours; at night it bulged out of the flat sky, heavy and yellow and full of knowledge. The moon was a powerful thing; she pulled the tides on invisible leashes; she governed the seasons somehow, lengthening or shortening them at her will; she let the rain fall, or she withheld it, just as she pleased; her light made the ground strong or weak, all according to some curious formula which men had learned long before Lonzo's or Cean's time (or Dicie's or Seen's, either). Peas will never grow if they are planted in the time of dark nights; potatoes must go into the ground only on a waning moon, so that the roots may grow downward—and so with all rooty things; bushy things must grow upward as the moon grows. . . . The moon has all power; it even governs women's ways, and who can explain that? It can muddle the wits of a child allowed to sleep in its full light. Now the sun will cut no didos, but the moon is a willful, changeable body, kind or hateful as she pleases, undependable as her face.

Cean spread her extry quilts as a pallet in front of the fire for Dicie and Seen to sleep on where the warmth could bake their gnarled old feet. They would mumble sometimes far into the night, discussing this or that child-bed, or spell of fever, or cut that brought on proud flesh. Each had brought her sack of yerbs, saved each in its season, and tied separately in clean white rags; each had brought her best knowledge to serve the need of her child and the loved one of her child. Dicie lived ten miles off, two miles on yan side o' the river. She knew many people of whom these people had not heard in months, so she brought them news of a big hog, or the killing of a neighbor, a summer hailstorm that cut the corn to ribands, or a child that was born to Timothy Hall's wife, red-mottled, with one eye set high in its forehead. But it died, by God's mercy. Dicie had a bright, sharp wit about her; she talked fast and told many outrageous things, so that Cean laughed a lot at her. Lonzo never laughed much—nor cried, neither; it wasn't his way to show what he was thinking. Seen didn't have much to say, either; she was dreading this thing. Cean didn't know what she was getting into.

Lonzo dreaded it, too, but there wasn't nothin' to do

about it. He had helped many an old sow bring forth her young. And once he had knocked a young heifer in the head because he had figured that she had hurt long enough; and she would have surely died, anyway.

Dicie chattered, wrinkling her thin nose when she cackled over a joke; when she laughed, she threw back her head that was pert and brown and a little like a peaceable hen's. Dicie thought little about this business. Cean was a strong girl; no foolishness about her; she'd get through in a hurry.

On the night of the third day after the old women had come Dicie would make syrup candy and there was much talking and laughing about the fireplace. Syrup blubbered in the iron pot over the coals, and had to be stirred with the long horn spoon to keep it from boiling over. Dicie's and Seen's and Lonzo's faces were well-nigh blistered from the heat. Finally Dicie tried the candy in a gourd of water one last time, and pronounced it nigh about ready to pull.

Lonzo sat in a chair with his hands ready-larded. Cean stood behind him, not allowed to pull. She leaned over the back of Lonzo's chair; his hair brushed against her breast; her hands lay on his shoulders; she moved her hands upward and laid them on his neck where she could feel the blood beat in his veins. Her fingers stroked downward on his beard and rested again on his neck. She could smile now to think that ever she had been afraid of him; for no cow with its first calf was ever any gentler with it than Lonzo was with her. . . .

Suddenly she pressed her hands hard about his neck; a heavy pain had fastened on her child and would not let go.

Lonzo turned and looked into her face. But just then the pain let go, and she smiled sheepishly at him. She was all right; it wasn't time, after all. But the blood beat heavier and faster in Lonzo's neck. He spoke to his mother, who was taking off the pot of boiling candy:

"Ma, ye'd better git things ready . . ."

Dicie whirled about, and the pot of candy turned over on the hearth. Cean heard her mother shout in terror, and saw the syrup bubbling on Seen's bony old feet as she moved them frantically up and down in the spreading pool of liquid that was hot as molten brimstone.

Cean sat in a chair, holding her breath on another pain, while Lonzo raked the blistering, brown mess from Seen's feet. Dicie poulticed them with soft mullein poultices, crooning in a monotonous undertone: "You pore child! . . . You pore child! . . . I'd ruther hit was me. I'd a sight ruther hit was me. . . ."

After the first shock of the fiery pain Seen never whimpered. She bared her teeth against her lips and sat patiently with her swathed feet away from the fire, while waves of fire soaked and washed and soaked them. She said to Cean: "Take yore mind off yoreself, honey. . . . Jest think about somethin' else. . . ."

Till long after midnight Cean walked back and forth across the room, as Dicie told her to do; she walked until she could take not one more step, for Dicie would not let her rest; she must stay on her feet even when the last pains caused her body to tremble as though it were beset by the ague, when these pains that should have been the last pains dragged her down if Lonzo's arms did not hold her up. Back and forth, and forth and back, Dicie made her walk, and her face was green, and sweat and tears were mingled on her cheeks. And with any one of these pains she would have fallen and swounded away if Lonzo's hands had not held her up, if Lonzo had not wiped the wet from her face and talked into her ear, saying "little un," and such-like words. She would not complain, because her mother would not complain of her tormented feet; she would not complain even when she had to take to her bed in the hour before morning and lay tossing between Lonzo's hands on one side of the bed and Dicie's on the other. Seen, with her feet in a fiery hell, watched her child endure another hell, and thought that she would gladly have endured both.

By daylight, Lonzo was sick of it. He went out into the whipping wind to feed up, to milk Betsey and turn her out. But he hurried back into the house. He asked his Ma:

"What makes her git along s' slow?"

Dicie's face was sober now:

"Hit's natural . . . with a fust un. . . ."

Lonzo quarreled:

"This hain't natural. . . . They's somethin' wrong. Ye might ez well tell me. . . ."

"No. They hain't nothin' wrong. They 'most al'ays take longer with a fust un. . . ."

Lonzo turned his face away and growled:

"Well, they won't be no second un. . . ."

A pitiable smile caught at the corners of Dicie's mouth. How many times had she heard that! And always they called her back before another twelve months were out. . . . Her eyes sought Seen's eyes in gentle derision of a man's fool blustering. . . . But Seen's eyes were set on her child's face and would not let loose of it where it lay tossing back and forth; Cean's hair was matted, her eyes were shut and un-noticing; her hands were locked to the bedstead back of her head. It wasn't good for her to reach her hands back of her head like that, but Lonzo could not break her grip without hurting her.

Lonzo turned away and would help no more when Cean began breathing each of her breaths with a low, animal-like grunt. She sounded too much like the little heifer that he had knocked in the head because it had hurt long enough, and would surely die anyway.

He stood before the fire, gazing down into the heat, and great unlikely tears ran from his eyes down into his beard. Lonzo knew that his little un was going to die. He knew from the look in Seen's eyes that never let go of her child's face; he knew from Dicie's hard-folded hands that waited now, having done all that they knew to do; and he knew from the little un that grunted like a little dumb heifer that knows that it is time for it to die. Even as he listened, a-feared, her moaning quieted, her pains ceased, and she lay as though she were already dead.

The dogs made a clamor out in front, and a woman's voice commanded them to keep still. Nobody in the room stirred, for they hardly noted the sound. What did it matter who came or went, now that the little un was dying with nobody to help her?

After a minute there was a framming of a fist on the front door and Dicie opened it. Lias's Margot blew in, beating her hands and stamping her feet that were numb with the cold. She looked quickly around the room and went and stood for a moment beside the bed. She turned to Seen:

"I knew it. . . . I couldn't sleep. Something told me to come. . . . I made Jasper bring me. Lias thought I was the master fool. Jasper's out there in the cold now."

She threw her wraps off, and discussed with Dicie a hasty means of bringing this child to its birth before it killed its mother.

After that, Lonzo heaped up the fire and boiled great pots of water; he lifted Cean when she was a dead weight in his arms; he thought that she was already dead, because her eyelids did not even quiver when he called her little un . . . for she would have given some sign if she had heard. . . .

There was a baby's angry, repeated crying; the sound of it eased the agony in Seen's eyes. Lonzo laid Cean down; still her eyelids didn't flicker when he called her. He held the cord whence bright life had flowed from this woman's body into his child, until that flow stopped; then he cut the cord forever since its use was past. He tied the shred of the child's body back into itself, making it an entity, as one finishes something perfect. Cean had made this thing—a thing harder and prettier to do than weaving cloth or sewing a dress. She was not able to do this little last thing for it, so he did it for her. Then he sat down beside her, waiting for her face to regain its color and its meaning for him.

When she opened her eyes after a while, he could not answer a word to her fearful question. Nor did he know that she was afraid to look on the little thing that she had made so carefully. It was Lias's Margot who laughed away Cean's fears, saying:

"Just as fine as a fiddle. They don't make them any finer. . . ."

Lonzo learned from Margot that Cean's child was a girl, and all the women laughed at his stupidity—all, except Cean. Truth to tell, he had not known—nor cared.

Dicie brought the little thing to the bed for it to lie beside its mother. Margot asked:

"Now what is her name?"

Cean's eyes lifted from the baby to Lonzo.

"Whatever Lonzo says. . . ."

Her eyes went back to the little stranger in her arms, whom she had not expected and for whom she had no name. Her mind went all around and about this new thing in her arms as she lay there, while the other women hovered over the fireplace, a long way off, preparing a belated breakfast. Lonzo sat beside her, a part of her awakening from the dream that had encompassed all her life until now. . . . So it was a Her, like herself, to be a little girl—a big girl— a Woman, at last. . . . Cean's senses were drugged with her past pain; she was unable to believe so much wonder; never would she have believed that the boy-child that had filled her heart until now would go so quickly into thin air, and leave her arms feeling no emptiness or disappointment, but filled with this wondrous woman-child.

Lonzo's voice came from a long way off above her:

"You liked them magnolia flowers. . . ."

Cean's thoughts took up the words—magnolias—high and white—and sweet-smelling—too pretty to be broken and wither in her dark house. . . . But here was a little bloom of some kind, broken for her, given to her to keep, to wear upon her breast as Coast women wear gold breastpins.

She called to the strange white woman by the fire:

"Her name's Magnolia. . . ."

Margot turned and came to the bed, smiling; her long white hands smoothed the cover and the pillow and the child and its mother.

Lonzo said:

"Cean, this is Lias's Margot."

The two women greeted each other with their eyes. Cean said:

"Her name's Mary Magnolia. . . ."

They had forgotten Jasper out in the cold; now they called him in.

All their thoughts and all their desires were toward the little Mary Magnolia.

When Vince Carver had seen her, he went home and set down her name in the big Bible, with the day of her birth. Remembering the little puckered face of his first grandchild, he thought his first kind thought of Margot; for it was because of that woman's knowledge of Coast ways that the child now slept in Cean's arms instead of out there beside Eliza-beth. . . . And Cean, too. . . .

Not till days afterward, when her feet were white and withered under the oft-renewed poultices that Margot made, did Seen remember that it was Christmas morning when the baby was born—a day when back in Carolina they were riding from house to house over the countryside, eating syl-labub and eggnog at neighbors' houses, and shrieking "Christmas gift" to every passer-by. She said to Margot:

"I reckon you don't like the sticks, where they don't even know when it's Christmas."

Margot drooped over the feet of her husband's mother, that were soft and white like boiled bacon. She said:

"I never cared for Coast ways. I wish folks would forget that ever I was there."

# Chapter 8

WHEN Cean was going with her second child, Lonzo moved her to her Ma's because she could hardly stand on her feet, much less wash and scrub and tote slops to the pigs. And the baby, Maggie, was a spoiled little trick, hanging to her mother's skirts and screaming for dear life every time Cean got out of her sight.

When Lonzo carried Cean back to her mother's, cracking the whip over the ox as they rounded the bend in the road, Vince felt that Cean was coming back where she belonged, under her father's roof. He was unaware of his jealousy because Lonzo had Cean off there to himself; she was still a brown, thin-legged child to him, even though a little brown baby dragged at her skirts and another was on the way; he had never been easy in his mind that she was out yonder, six mile off, and had to take anything that Lonzo might put upon her, hard words or a whipping or what not.

Vince wanted to keep his family together. He'd be glad if Lonzo and Cean would move into the house so that they all could live together—he and his sons and his son-in-law plowing and planting together, their womenfolks churning and weaving and raising biddies together. That's the way they did in the old days—Abraham and Isaac and Jacob.

He wished that Lias wasn't so anxious to get off to himself in a house of his own. Why build three houses when one house will do? He had put Lias off last spring with, "I'll give ye a third of all I make; ye kaint better that by yeself. . . ." And again this spring Lias was anxious to cut loose and do for himself; Vince put him off again: "Wait another year; they's plenty of time. . . ."

But Lias was discontented. He found fault with the cooking; he complained that the beds needed sunning; he stormed at Margot to stop primping and learn to put enough salt in the butter. Last fall he had brought a fine new-fangled oven home from the Coast, and it was sitting on its three legs on the hearth in his and Margot's room now, without even the new burnt offen hit; he sulled when his Ma had offered to bake biscuits in it one time, saying, "Hit's fer me own house. . . ."

Lias was restless and ugly-tempered as a young bull; his eyes fairly danced in his head when anybody crossed him.

Once Margot crossed him and got her jaws slapped for her trouble. They were all sitting at the eating-table, eating supper. Jake had brought in a fine mess of bream and jack from the creek, and Margot had fried them brown for supper. At supper, she waited on the menfolks' plates, going behind the chairs, helping each plate from a bakerful of hot fish in her hand. She laid a big jack on Lias's plate, leaning close over his shoulder as she helped his plate. Her cheek lay for half a moment against his cheek; he smelled the warm, sweetish scent that breathed from her bosom. Cean, just to make talk, said:

"Blest if Margot don't al'ays save the biggest fish fer Lias!"

They all laughed.

But Lias pushed back his plate and sulled:

"Don't know as I want any fish!"

Seen spoke up and said:

"Why, Lias, we didn't fix nothin' but the fish 'n' grits 'n' corndodgers . . . !"

He said, "I don't want nothin'," and pushed back his chair.

Margot put her free hand on his shoulder.

"Now, Lias, you eat! You've worked hard all day. You've got to eat. . . ."

She leaned close over him, like a light woman with a mouth full of light words.

[ 89 ]

Lias's face tightened all of a sudden, and he pushed her back from him; he looked hard into her eyes and cast off her hand.

"Didn't ye hear me say I didn't want nothin'?"

Margot stood holding the bakerful of hot fish that were cooling because Lias had a whim against fish all of a sudden; they wouldn't be fit to eat, once they were cold. He could be such a fool when he wanted to be. She had tried herself frying the fish so he'd enjoy them; he liked fresh-caught fish, and everybody knew it; he wanted to shame her, that was all. She had put herself out; her back was fit to break from stooping by the fireplace; she HAD saved back the best fish for Lias, and Cean, like a fool, had to go and make mention of it!

She gave Lias back his hard look, telling him with her eyes:

"I ain't a-feared of ye. Ye're only a tall, uppity country-man. I am from the Coast, if ye will but recollect a little."

With her mouth she told him:

"I reckon ye're no better than the rest of us to eat fish!"

She was NOT a-feared of him. She laughed and went on talking:

"But maybe ye'd like a pot o' stewed swan's tongues for tomorrow night's supper!" She turned to Seen. "Ma, ask around . . ."

And then Lias's hand slapped her a-windin', and the fried fish were scattered all over the floor of the cooking-shed. She lifted her arm, afraid that he would strike her again; but with bunched lips and an angry brow he turned and walked out the back door.

Margot stood with her head high and her mouth crimping with shame and anger. She was mad at herself for having fended off another blow with her arm; she had let him see that she WAS a-feared of him. She sent a cry after him:

"You . . . Lias . . . !"

They finished the food that was on their plates. Margot stooped about the floor, picking up the scattered fish. Jasper pushed back his chair and picked up the big jack that lay beside his foot, its fins and tail burned brown and dry in hot grease. He laid it on top of the other fish when Margot passed his chair. Pa and Jake went on eating, but Jasper found that he was not a-hungry, and pushed his plate away. Seen dropped her eyes to her plate. Cean went on eating, too, but not because she was a-hungry; Maggie had to be fed on hot grits and butter, and, anyhow, Cean's mouth kept twitching with unsaid words. Eating was the best way to keep her mouth out of mischief; this was shorely none of her affair!

When the others went on to bed, Margot hung about the fireplace, scrubbing out a black pot with sand and soap; dried peas had burned to the bottom of it while she was cooking dinner this morning. She was waiting for Lias to come in.

Jasper sat by the fire and whittled out a slingshot for no reason at all; he allowed in his mind that he would measure Lias's length on the floorboards if Lias came in and hit Margot again. His hands were a little trembly with the knife. Whittling, with his mind somewhere else, like a fool he cut his finger, and Margot reached down oint-ment from the mantelpiece and held his hand in her hands and stopped the blood with hen's oil. Jasper was a fool to say anything; in the way of a fool, he said the worst thing that he could have said, for pity is bad for a sore heart. He said:

"Lias hain't got no business a-beatin' ye like you was a dog. . . ."

She pushed the back of her hand against her mouth to make her words come straight:

"He knows I'd get him swans' tongues to eat if I knowed where there might be any."

She rose and set back the pipkin of ointment.

She went on to bed, afraid to wait up for Lias; it might make him madder than ever.

Later, he came and lay down in the black dark, and he must have known that she was not asleep, for he stroked the long length of her arm that lay beside him, and gave her a short penitent kiss on her temple where her blood beat silently as a muted gong. She wanted to fling her arms about him and talk and talk and tell him many things, but she did not know how to put those things into any speech of common A-B-C's.

No, it would please him best if she lay still and gave no sign that she understood that he was sorry that he had hit her as though she was his dog to beat on. She made as though she was asleep, but blue gongs thundered in her head.

Vince felt downright sorry for Margot when Lias was so hateful to her; but all in a minute he would know deep in his heart that she was getting what was coming to her. Secretly he was glad to see her go off down to the branch and stay a long time, after Lias had said some hard word to her. Nobody raised his voice to rebuke Lias for talking that way to Margot; she didn't expect them to; she'd just be all the meeker to Lias and the rest. . . .

Vince understood Lias. . . . Lias thought that he was dissatisfied because he didn't have his own diggin's and because Margot showed no signs of having a child. Here it had been more than a year, and she was still as straight as a peach-tree trunk. She was sinful, that's what she was. And she was sinful in being vain of her looks. Seen had seen her combing her long black hair, combing and combing it to make it shine as it did, like the bolts of silk that were wrapped in homespun and laid high on the shelves of the Coast store-men; Margot's hair was as like living silk as silk was like itself, and Vince knew it. And Margot poulticed her face with meal and buttermilk, and patted the stuff into the skin all over her body. Seen had seen her do it, and Margot had laughed and said that she must be pretty for Lias. She had scented herself for a long time after Lias had brought her home with him. Maybe her scent was used up now. Oh, Vince could read that woman like a book. She tempted Lias, that's what, and Lias hated her for it. Vince knew how Lias felt; never in the world would he have mentioned anything beyond corn or cotton or a brood sow to Lias, but he knew how Lias felt. And he understood that restlessness, that bull-headedness. Hadn't he felt that way when HE was young? Could he rest at home? No! He had to come off down here and bury hisself in the backwoods on the Indian Bank of the Alatamaha where settle-mints are sca'ce as hens' teeth; he had put his littlest child underground long ago, and now he must tough out the rest of his life away from his people. Right now he did not even know if his father was alive or dead. His old mother was gone. He had left her up there, dead from the hips down, from a fall out of the doorstep. On one of his trips to the Coast—it was the year when Lias and Jasper had first gone with him when they were yearling-sized boys, the year 'twenty-eight, if Vince didn't mistake—he had found two letters that had come down from Carolina by post. The letters were soiled and dog-eared. The trader, Villalonga, the Spaniard, had kept them for months, expecting Vince in the fall. One of the letters bore a date in January; the other was penned in June. The first letter was set by his mother's hand, weak and quavery, unlike the fine samples that she had set long ago for him to copy when she was teaching him to write, "An idle brain is the devil's workshop; The wages of sin is death." If he tried, he could nighbout remember that letter now, word for word, without going to reach it out of the chest to see:

Dear Son I take my Pen in hand to let you Know that I am Well Hoping this find you the Same Evaline has a Fine Boy Susanna lost her Oldest in the Fall Hooping Cough Am mighty Poorly hope I will not have many More Months to lie here and complane it would Comfort my Heart if I could See you how is Cean and Elizabeth I never hear a Word no more than you was Dead Why cant you all Come Back to see Us Lovingly Mother.

The second letter was shorter than the first, but was folded like the first and likewise sealed with a wafer:

Vince Carver, Ezquire
————Ga.
Your mother died Monday Nineteenth Day of June of Paralsys of the Back she asked for you

Yrs rsptfly

His                His
x    John Carver    x
mark              mark

Never since then had any word come out of the sunny Carolina country; and ever afterward this land was lonelier for him and Seen, though never did he mention how he felt to Seen; she was dissatisfied enough without that. He had to keep up heart. . . .

But sometime he was going to pack up, lock, stock, and barrel, and go back to his people. Word every ten years wasn't enough. Your folks are your very bone and gristle. Here was Lias wanting to get off to himself. Sometime he'd see why his old Pa had wanted to keep him by him as long as he could. Oh, Vince understood Lias! Wasn't he just like Lias when he was Lias's age? That woman, and all. Lias wouldn't be satisfied if you fed him honey out of a gold dish —not Lias; it wasn't in him. When he got what he wanted, then he would want something else.

Vince was forever worrying: Cean was here in his house, unable to walk and pining for Lonzo, the cause of all her trouble; Lias was rearin' to be off; Seen hobbled around on her old feet that were drawn into knots by the carelessness of that fool, Dicie Smith; Vince was getting so ailing that he could not stand the midday heat and Jasper had to bear the brunt of the farmwork. Oh, it did seem like his old years were harder than his young ones, and a man's old years should be full of peace if his young ones are taken up with strife and worry. Vince wished he could go back to Carolina as Seen wanted to do; he wished he could spend the rest of his days there in peace, and die and be buried in a Christian country with a preacher to lay him away in a buryin'-ground full of folks gone on before. Down here the dead didn't have a sermon preached over them till some journeyman preacher happened to come through. The screech-owls had kept him awake a many a night as they shivered in the trees close to the house, giving warning that Death was hiding about the house in wait for somebody; Vince would lie, unable to shut his eyes, wondering which one Death was waiting for. . . . Screech-owls can see Death; humans can't. . . . How many times this spring had he picked a little green measuring-worm off his clothes, the sly spy sent on ahead by Death for the measurement of a coffin? A score of times he had found the worm and cast it away when it was halfway up his breeches leg or sleeve or shirt. . . . He'd hate to be laid away out here where the water stands when it rains a little, as it stands everywhere in this country. You'd rot s' quick! . . . Eliza-beth's grave had fallen in years back, and Vince had filled in the little sunken space that was the length and width of Eliza-beth; he knew that she was rotted flat, box and all. In the nights of fall he could hear pine-cones dropping down upon her with a soft, thumping sound. Seen kept the pine-needles swept off the sandy mound, but always there would be a few more needles the next day, each lying flat with its three glossy dead prongs spreading wide from the little brown cap at the end that had held it secure on a high bough through many winds. Never did he think, when he was young, that the lob-lolly pine would shed on him and his'n; he would but rush down to Georgy and make a fortune in rich land, and rush back home again; he had thought that different leaves would fall on him. . . . It worried him to see how he thought more about death, and dying, and such like, the older he grew. . . . His Ma's eyes watered and her old face crimped up when he left for Georgy; Pa had wrung his hand until Vince had thought that Pa would take it off. . . . They knew what he was learning, and what Jasper and Lias and Jake would learn when they were old enough; but the bad part of it is that you die about the time you begin to learn a little something. Everybody ought to live as long as Methuselah, then they'd know something. But who would want to? Not Vince Carver. He wanted to go on first before Seen and the chillurn; he didn't want to bury an-other'n o' his'n; giving up Eliza-beth had nighabout killed him.

Cean did what she could with the housework, but that wasn't much because she had to lie down or sit in a chair most of the time. But she pieced two quilt-tops for Margot during the time that she stayed at her Ma's, with Maggie scattering her little squares of cloth and mixing the colors every whichaway. One day Maggie lost Seen's precious little gold thimble that Cean was using in quilting; they looked the house over, up and down and around and about. Every-body looked until they were plum tuckered out. Jake even searched through the cow-lot—anywhere and everywhere that anybody at all could ever have been with that thimble; and still no thimble. . . . Cean cried because her child was to blame and because Seen blamed her carelessness; and Seen cried because her thimble that Vince had bought for her in Dublin thirty year back was gone, and because she had blamed pore little Cean who had enough to worry over without being quarreled at.

Margot tried to talk Cean out of her tears; but Lias stormed out:

"Oh, Margot, behave yoreself. Hain't the world full o' thimbles?"

But then he hushed, for he knew that it is not. Margot cast down her eyes as she cooked supper, and SHE cried, TOO, thinking: "No! No! No!—the world is not full of gold thimbles; once you lose it, there is nary another one." . . . After supper, Jasper helped her clean up the pot-things. He kept silent, for he could see that hot tears were running off her cheeks into the dish-water; best leave alone a woman when she is crying.

Margot gulped back the fullness that pained her throat; but tears pushed past the fullness and wet her face. She was ashamed of herself because she could not keep from weeping any time when Lias raised his voice louder than it commonly sounded; she ought to be used to his ways in this time; she ought to learn, if she had any gumption at all, that his tongue was meaner than his heart. I ought to know— she thought—that Lias loves me or he would cart me back to the Coast before I could say scat. . . . He loves me . . . he loves me . . . but why can't he use patience to fight a thing? . . . Am I to blame because he was born a hothead? . . . He wouldn't do me any suchaway if I hadn't given him strong reason to think less of me before ever I married him. . . . A woman has but herself to blame for the treatment a man puts on her. . . . But I can do for myself any old day. . . . I won't take and take and keep on taking. . . . Any old mangy, starved bitch will bite you if you torment her long enough. . . . I'll not take Lias's meanness from him one more time! . . . He can treat me right or I will manage to get along without him. . . . I lived nineteen years without him. . . . I reckon I can get along without him again . . . if it kills me . . . if it kills me—

Jasper was saying:

". . . and when she heard the horses' hooves and ran out in the dark to the front gate to meet him, there she found him tied to his horse's saddle, with the bloody white skull of his head showing. . . . He was hanging from his saddle, dead as a door nail, and bleeding on her hands. . . . There's trouble fer ye. . . ."

Margot sighed. Jasper went on:

"They say neighbors miles off heard her a-screamin'."

Margot dipped another greasy plate into the pot of hot suds. She thought—What was I a-thinkin' of?—

Jasper said:

"I reckon some people was made to make trouble . . . and some t' stand hit. . . ."

—I could walk off and leave him . . . if I could ever get mad enough. . . . But I can't hate him long enough at the time. . . . I forgive him . . . and he knows it. . . . I forgive him if he as much as looks at me once, or but lays his hand on my shoulder. . . . But I ought to leave him and let him see how it feels. . . . It would wake him up . . . maybe.—

She raked the greasy scum from around the sides of the pot of dishwater.

"Jasper . . ." she said . . . She thought—I'll ask him if he won't carry me back to Papa.—

Jasper carefully passed his soggy dishrag over a wet plate. "Yes'm, lady!"

She knew that he was trying to make her laugh. She reached a soapy plate toward him:

"Jasper, they's not one man in ten thousand like you. I'm just tellin' ye in case ye don't already know it . . . in case nobody else ever told ye. . . ."

Because the plate was slick as grease with soap suds, it slipped to the floor and broke into a dozen pieces.

The crash of the plate annoyed Seen where she spun up

in the big-house across the passage; she was peevish, any-how; she quarreled at Jasper like he was six-year-old!

"Do, Jasper! Don't break every last crock on the place. They don't grow on trees, y' know. . . ."

Jasper fumbled around over the broken pieces on the floor, trying to piece the plate together again. Margot called out:

"It wasn't Jasper, Ma. I dropped it. . . ."

Jasper was a sight squatting there on his big haunches, like a worried honey-bear. Here he was a grown man, still afraid of his mother's tongue. Margot laughed soundlessly at Jasper; the two of them laughed like two younguns over that broken plate.

Lias had lit a candle and was up yonder in the house on the side of Margot's bed, mending the torn lappet of his coat. He was too biggity to ask Margot to sew it for him. He came into the kitchen and found Margot and Jasper laughing fit to kill; then he was madder than ever and told her that she need not patch his coat, he had fixed it already; then he flounced out the door.

Still Jasper and Margot could not stop their laughing. Margot said:

"Let him fix it. Tomorrow I'll steal it off and take out his sorry sewing with stitches long as basting threads, and mend it right. Let him pout tonight, and fix it his own self. . . ."

The next day Cean discovered that Maggie had swallowed the gold thimble that they all had such trouble about. The whole household rejoiced. Even Lias laughed, fit to kill; his blue eyes blazed under his sandy brows, and his big white teeth showed in his silky beard. Margot, seeing him laugh so, flung her arms about his neck and leaned on him and kissed him. Cean thought her a brazen huzzy! But Lias looked down into Margot's eyes and suddenly caught her up till she was as tall as he was, and he kissed her hard on her mouth. Then he set her down and strode out of the room, still laughing; and part of the laughter that she had kissed stayed on Margot's mouth. She comforted herself by knowing that Lias would not be satisfied if you were to pick him up and set him down on the broad turnpike of heaven. . . .

Cean pined for Lonzo. Never had she been able to decide if he were fine-looking or if she only thought he was, because he was her old man. Now Lias left no room for doubt, not with that set of his head, and his roughed hair the color of broom straw in the fall, and his hard blue eyes that looked straight at you when he talked to you. Now she thought Lonzo was fine-looking, though he was not so tall as Lias, nor so straight nor so long in the legs. Lias had legs like the pretty stilted legs of a young buck. Lonzo's shoulders stooped a little, and his face seemed to stoop when he was listening to you, as though he wanted to hear every word you said. His eyes were black as swamp water where a big mud-cat can come to within two-fingers' width of the top, and still be safely hidden. Lonzo's eyes were like that—you never knew what things were hiding behind them except that with her they were always kind things. He had cried when he knew for certain of this second young un; but there wasn't no use for Cean to cry over it. The worst part of it was being away from Lonzo and not seeing him but every two or three weeks, whenever he could spare time from the planting. Last time he was here he told her that he had something nearly done for this baby. It wouldn't be a cradle, nor a fine boughten present. Often Cean's face would set in sweet wonder—what could it be?

She would go back home in time for her second child to be born in its own house, as soon as this trouble inside her stopped. She wished it would be soon, for Pa's house seemed crowded; the work seemed heavy and there was too much talk and argument. She liked her own house, still as death except for Maggie's cooing and crying, and the light sound of the clock's swinging pendulum. Oh, she was proud of that clock Lonzo had brought her from the Coast to tell the time almost as surely as the sun and stars did. It was a pretty clock, with a little brown grapevine carved all around the tall wooden frame of it; at the top there was a cluster of grapes carved in the wood, and there were two brass leaves inside the glass on the round brass pendulum. The brass was as bright as gold. Inside, through the glass that she polished each morning with a rag, the long black hand went round and round on the white face, so slowly that you could never see it move, yet it was nighabout as true as the North Star. It hardly ever lied; you could test it any hour, morning, evening, or night, and the clock would tell about what the shadows or the stars would tell: two hours by sun, an hour before day, whatever time it was. The clock was set in the middle of her mantel, high above her fire that was rarely out when she was home, because of food to be cooked, or smoothing-irons to be heated, or light to see by at night; winter or summer, the fire burned on. And there in the midst of her house was the clock—tick-tock —tick-tock—like a heart in the midst of a body—beat, beat, beat, beat—only faster. She had timed her heart and it was slower than the golden swing of the clock's bright pendulum. When she noted the hurry of the clock it always stirred her to hurry with what she was doing, weaving, or sewing, or peeling potatoes with the butcher knife which she was always careful to keep out of reach of Maggie's eager fingers. . . . What if the baby should stumble and fall upon it, and the blood should gush out from her neck as it spouted from the stuck throat of a suckling pig . . . ? But the clock would swing on then, just as it did now, undismayed. No, not the same! Yes, just the same. . . .

Lonzo was alone back there at home, out in the fields or in the house with the clock. She had laughed to herself when he told her how he had scrubbed the floor. He admitted that he had fed the hounds on the floor by his chair, glad for their company as he ate his victuals. She could imagine him pushing the scrub back and forth over the rough floor after supper—for he worked in the fields all day; the cornshucks, fastened through the round holes of the heavy block of wood with the long handle to it, would brush-brush-brush the soapy water across the soft, shreddy grain of the logs, the water swishing a little at each broad swipe of the scrub. Did Lonzo know to scatter white sand over the floor to loosen the dirt and grease? How could a man get along without a woman to do for him? She smiled, glad that she would do for Lonzo till she died—for Lonzo and his children.

She was tired of lying flat of her back, or sitting carefully in a chair; she was impatient to be up and about, doing around her house, patching clothes, washing, planting seeds. She couldn't drop the corn for Lonzo this year, any more than she could last year. A little youngun can't drag along after its Ma, up and down the rows, with the hot sun bleaking down on its head. Sometimes in summer the sun cooked a man's brains just like they were raw eggs on a hot spider, and he fell down and died. A little child couldn't stand no such as that. . . . No, a woman must bide at home with the little fellers, to keep them out of the fire and the wash-trough and the snake-holes. How long would it be before she could follow Lonzo again, dropping the slick, yellow grains from her hand—like that!—one for the cutworm, one for the crow, one to rot, and one to grow, to make the tall tasseled corn for roas'in'-ears, for meal and grits? And when the corn was done with growing, the long blades would hang, heavy and stiff and drying day by day, waiting for Lonzo to sweep down every other row, like a house afire, stripping the stalks blade by blade from top to bottom, first on the left row, then on the right, pull-

ing the fodder with quick sure movements of his hard sun-
burnt hands. Lonzo's hands were never bothered by the
sharp blades of corn that cut a thousand small bleeding slits
in the hands of greenhorns and young boys. No, his hands
were used to hard work. She loved to feel his rough hands
on her cheeks, pinching them to color. . . . How long since
she had been pink in the face? . . . and light on her feet?
. . . and small in the waist? . . . Aah . . . law. . . .

Even Lias felt sorry for Cean, now—and he never pitied
any mortal thing 'lessen hit were a sheep when some wild
thing got its lamb. Once he had shot a great-antlered buck,
breaking its back, and when he had come up to it it had
dragged itself off a little piece, pulling its weight by its fore-
feet, and lay there panting and watching him, its sad, amber
eyes swimming with fear. Lias did feel sorry for that thing—
a brave, fine he-thing with its back shot through, that
would no more lope across the clear, thin distance cut by
innumerable columns that were dark pine boles over-
lapping one another until the far horizon was a black wall
of living columns shutting in the flat woods.

He did feel sorry for Cean. . . . No use running the
thing into the ground. . . . Before she was through with
one, here was another one coming. He was glad Margot was
still straight and slim; he would hate her if she was like
Cean every year. . . . But Lonzo didn't hate Cean; he was
as gentle with her as her Ma would be; he looked at her
like he could eat her up—no, like he could stay there forever without touching her, and love her till he died. Why
didn't Lias feel that way about Margot? She was fine-
looking; he couldn't find a fault with her 'lessen he made
it up. It was all his fault; he oughta had better sense than
to jump up and marry like a shot out of a gun. Hadn't he
always known that women were no more than heifers?
But Godalmighty could hardly have kept him from marrying Margot. Pa tried to keep him from marrying her, but

Lias wouldn't listen. If she was brown and lean-legged and human like Cean—like anybody else—he could stand it. But she was hardly human; she was too pretty in the face, too goody-goody. And all the time she went around with her meek sheep's-eyes; she waited on Ma and Pa, spoke softly to Cean, chewed Maggie's food for her, like an angel out of heaven to see her at it! Ma loved her; Jake would pretty nigh cut off both his hands for her; even Jasper thought she was "a fine woman"; Lias knew that Cean hated him for the way he treated Margot—her eyes would burn at him, bright and unblinking as a coach-whip's.

They just didn't know, that was all—they just didn't know and he didn't know. He could kill her, he believed, and feel good about it, and she was his lawful wedded wife. Oftentimes he remembered the way he once felt toward her, and tried to bend his heart toward her again, and cursed himself because his heart would not bend, nor go, nor stay, nor feel the way a man's heart should feel. What was this devil in him that kept him from being a right-minded man like Pa and Lonzo and Jasper?

When they were married they had slipped up to the preacher's away in the night, because Vince would start for home at daylight. Lias hammered on the door with his fist, his left arm about Margot, shivering in her cloak. They stood there on the narrow sloping piazza of the little house, and Lias warmed her in his arms because she was cold, while somebody inside the house bumped around and mumbled. And they were married by candle-light, and he kept his arms about her. Margot stood there in the half-light with her eyes black and shiny in her white face, like beetles on a Cape jessamine bloom. Her eyes were blue, but ever when she was worried or excited they would be dark as thunder. They had got away at dawn for the long journey home; and all through the time he couldn't stay away from her any more than a steer can stay away when you pull him to you with a rope. There was some pull in her breast, and in his, that you couldn't keep apart. And when Ma gave them the cherrywood bedstead in the spare room when they got home, where were all his fine plans for rafting lumber down the Alatamaha, and hacking the big pines and gathering the gum for trade at the Coast, as some men were beginning to do? Hoh! they were all buried in this white woman!

But he'd make his mark yet, as soon as he could get away from Pa's apron-strings. He noticed that Pa hadn't settled under his own Pa's nose up in the Carolina country. No. He got as far off as he could. That's what Lias would do as soon as he could, and use some of his own plans. There were a million pines waitin' for him to hack 'em, to let the gum run out.

Cean's staying off her feet helped her, for she was able to walk within a month. Next time Lonzo came, she would go home with him, where the clock ticked stealthily on her mantel, counting the hours.

She went one day, but long would that day linger as a hurting in her mind.

Maggie was in the yard, dressed in her best bib and tucker, running in and out among the Cape jessamine bushes. The menfolks were out in the lot, bragging on twin calves that one of Jasper's milkers dropped last week.

Cean stood by the open shutter while her mother, who was folding clean rags on the bed, talked:

"You must make Lonzo tote the water, and chop the wood, and do the heavy work. Take cyare of yoreself, or the next thing ye know ye'll be sickly and whiney and no-'count, and Lonzo'll be sorry ever he married ye. . . ." She went on in a long meek recital of women's woes.

Cean listened while the breeze came through the shutter, fanning her face. Her thoughts were on her mother's words, her eyes were on Maggie's staggering steps that went in and out among the Cape jessamine bushes away from Margot's outstretched arms. Margot always took up a lot of time with Maggie. Wasps went in and out of the tall hedge of boxwood that grew close along this side of the yard; they must have a nest there. Thick sunshine fell on the white clean-swept sand of the yard where Maggie's little brogans made careless tracks. Yonder was Margot, stooping by the steps, her arms entreating Maggie; there was the child, teasing. Every now and then there came the long baying of old Major, Jake's hound, from back of the house. He had been sickly for a day or two, and Jake was offering him fresh, sweet milk. . . .

Suddenly, from around the corner of the house under the open window where Cean was standing, Major came running, with Jake close behind him. The dog loped to the end of the hedge, circled around by the front steps where Margot and Maggie were standing, and ran back past the window. Cean saw lather dripping from the dog's sagging jaws; she screamed to Jake, "He's mad . . . !" She kept repeating the words as she screamed; for fear beset her soul. She ran in a fury to the front door and snatched Maggie up from where Margot had set her inside the house, for she could not bear for those small arms and legs to be outside her frantic arms. Seen was screaming to Jake to come inside the house. Jake watched the old dog loping, loping, loping. He said:

"Oh, Ma, he ain't mad. He's jest a-hurtin' in his belly. . . . Hyare, Major! . . . Hyare, Major! . . ."

Cean kept on screaming, not knowing what she did. The men came running from the cow-lot, bearing in their hands blocks of firewood or iron spikes or any other thing that they could lay their hands on. Lias ran through the house and brought out the gun from the mantel.

Jake knew what Lias would do. Disaster nerved him to bitter resolution; he ran and grabbed up the weight that propped the front door open, ran straight in front of the dog that was hasseling foam like soap lather, and beat the broad head that he had stroked so many times, until he was sure that it was broken in. Major lifted his bleary, blood-shot eyes to Jake's. Blood ran down his nose, his ears flopped back, his legs sagged under him, and he was dead.

Jake stepped back and defied the men that bore a chunk of wood or an iron spike or a gun in their hands; his features were hard and thin; his lips could hardly form words for crying:

"Ye thought ye'd kill 'm, didn't ye, ye . . ." And he cursed them with every nasty curse that he could call to mind.

Vince laid his hand broadside on Jake's hard-set jaw.

"Shet up that short talk!"

Jake shut up and went around the side of the house, his sobs breaking in his chest because he would not let them out.

Cean ran out the back way to say something to him, but he flung off her hand and stormed at her, with his voice a little lowered so that Vince would not hear and slap him again:

"Leave me alone! You done hit . . . a-hollerin' like a loon . . . 'mad-dog.' . . ." His choked grief mocked her screams; he flung off toward the branch, and she knew from the way that he stumbled that his eyes were so full of tears that he could not see the way.

Vince dragged the dog off to the cornfield. Seen covered the bloody sand before the door with other white sand. Vince and Jasper dug a grave for little Jake's dog that he had played with since he was knee-high to a duck. Vince had brought the puppy home when Jake was running around with his little behind naked, before ever Seen had put him into breeches. . . . Vince dug out the sandy loam, a spadeful at the time; Jasper and Vince lifted old Major

[ 107 ]

and threw him in on his side, where his head crumpled down on his spotless breast and an ear flopped down, covering an eye. They piled the hole full of dirt, trampled it level, and went back to the house.

Vince dreaded to go back and face Jake; he'd give anything if he hadn't slapped his boy. The little feller hadn't known what he was sayin'. Vince was heartsick; he had been a boy once; looks like he'd learn how to manage his boys; but on he went, making one blunder after another.

Cean made Lonzo wait until late, hoping that Jake would come back before they started for home. But Jake didn't come, and finally Cean went off home with Lonzo.

He was off down by the river on the sandbar where the bright-green willows drooped in little lifts of wind that came and went on the river. The sand was coarse and clean-smelling under his nose. Down there, two foot away from his feet, river water lapped softly at the bank. Little ripples ran away to join the full deep current that flowed farther out beyond a black greasy-looking log that had been stuck there as far back as he could remember. Wind stirred the coarse brown hair on the back of his head and the fine gold hairs on the backs of his arms stretched above his head. His hard male sobs slackened and ceased. He had cried himself out. Hit weren't no use to cry.

Coolness came down through the air, and the little willows shivered. Night was coming on, but Jake lay there, not caring, for nobody loved him now—not Ma, nor Pa, nor Cean, nor even Major. He ground his forehead into the sand that was wet from his crying. His jaw still ached where his Pa had slapped him. And Cean had come a-traipsin' out the back door to watch him cry, with Maggie a-taggin' at her heels to gape and stare at him. Now he hated Cean as much as ever he had loved her when they used to sleep together in the loft, and Cean would squeeze her arms around him, and he could feel her breath on the back of his neck. It was a little like the way the wind was stirring now.

He turned on his side so that he could feel the weight of her arm around him, and her breath on the back of his neck. He lay so for a long time, remembering. But not for too long, for this was cool night wind gathering to blow. And he was not a little boy any more, as he had been when Cean had loved him.

Tillitha Kissiah, Cean's second daughter, was born in late October, but never could they persuade Jake to ride over with them and see Cean's new baby.

Ma laughed and told about the little cloak that Lonzo had made for the baby from the soft skins of young rabbits that he had caught in their nest-es. He had cured the skins, and softened them, and sewed them together in a little cloak as something to surprise Cean with.

Jake's lips sneered as soon as his back was turned.

# Chapter 9

KISSIE gave Cean little trouble, even from the day she was born. She lay in her cradle and slept while Cean went about her work. Magnolia played about the yard while Cean washed or cooked, never allowed to stray beyond reach of her mother's voice. Cean always had the child on her inner mind as a loved burden, giving it up never, even when it could be lifted for a time, as when Lonzo would ride to his father's with one of his cows tied to the back of the cart, or to Vince Carver's to swap a pig or a load of corn. Cean would wash Maggie and dress her in a clean apron and the starched bonnet that her Granny had made for her; the tail of the bonnet fell about her little shoulders that set like Lonzo's; her swarthy face, with a knowin' look like Lonzo's, would peer out of the ruffled brim of the bonnet like a little coon's from among bright leaves. Cean would wave good-by to Maggie sitting there so proudly beside Lonzo as the cart disappeared around the slough of the swamp at the bottom of the slope. Her heart would tug after the little body. Would Lonzo take care to keep it from falling under the cart-wheel? Would he remember to keep his eyes on it around strange cow-lots and among other folks-es' hound-dogs that didn't know not to bark at, and bite, this little body? . . . Oh, she wouldn't take a cart-load of gold for that little body with its head hidden in a stiff white bonnet that its Granny had made to keep the hot sun offen its head! "God love it," she would murmur as she turned back to her house, to her work and the other child depending on her. God, love it! when it's out of my sight and out of my reach! . . . All day she would be raising her eyes to look for the loved figure, would be opening her mouth to call the little name.

The child was the nigh like Lonzo!—solemn-mouthed, quiet-like, playing by herself for hours at a stretch, and never caring about another soul. She had stopped her whining after Cean as soon as she got a little growth on her. It always made Cean feel sad when she remembered that the first child had its mother to itself hardly any time at all before its sister scrouged itself into their mother's heart, and the older one had to grow on off by itself and get out of the way. Ma said that it was meant to be like that, but Cean felt that she had never rocked Magnolia enough, had never mothered her enough. Even her mother's milk had been taken out of that first child's mouth, because the jealous presence of the second child was poison.

But the little Kissie—hit were too sweet a child fer anybody, even Maggie—to hold anything ag'in' hit! It had not even cost its mother many hard pains, and it had slept through 'most every day since its birth, in the deep walnut cradle where Maggie slept at night while the littlest one lay close against its mother. . . . For even Maggie's place in bed between her Ma and Pa had been taken by the little new Kissie.

But both children had room enough in Cean's heart. There was no crowding there. Ma said that a mother's heart stretched just as her body did when she was carrying a child. . . . But the heart never rid itself of its burden; it stretched, and stretched again with each new child, being always swollen and tender and hurting. As the babies grew into tall broad-shouldered men and thick-hipped women, there must be more stretching until the heart was fit to burst sometimes with its load. For never did a mother's heart lose one jot nor tittle of its load: if a child died, still its Ma carried it about with her always, a dead weight; if a grown man got into trouble, his mother added that to her load, trying to bear it for him as she had borne his weight within her, safe from cold and sun and grief, long ago. Ma

[ 111 ]

said that was why mothers always fought against dying, even when they were old and tuckered out. She had closed a many a pair of old eyes and weighted the unwilling lids with coppers to keep them shut; she had folded a many a pair of old hands onto still chests. And Ma said that nobody fought death so hard as a mother did, who left children behind her to root-pig-or-die-pore in a hard old world.

There was Old Aint Viney Vickers who died last year, past ninety, with her sons and grandsons doing well on their own hooks here and yonder, and her granddaughters all married off with families of their own. But Old Aint Viney didn't want to go; she begged them to do something for her; she didn't want to die and leave her children to scuffle along best way they could without no Pa nor Ma; she could not die in peace for fear that her boys and grandboys would be drug off to war, as her old man and her brothers were in 'seventy-six, and every other male that was big enough to walk and tote his rations on his back. Old Aint Viney's children soothed her talk of war; they wouldn't be no war. But she grew all the more frantic:

"Ye laugh and go on yore way. . . . Ye're young. . . . Ye'd better listen t' me. . . . They'll be a war wussen ye ever hyeard tell of. . . . Old eyes is keener than young uns. . . ."

Truth to tell, her words had scared all who heard her, for she was credited with second sight; she had foretold her old man's passing to the day and hour. She claimed to see things by faith. Many was the cartload of sparkin' young couples that drove to her house o' Sabbath days to ask her their fortune. She would tell it in tea grounds: a long road winding to the east was maybe a Coast journey; a cross meant trouble in love; tiny mounds of soggy leaves on the other side of a heavy clot of leaves was marriage and . . . The fortune would break into Old Aint Viney's high-voiced cackling, guffawing and back-slapping of the young bucks, and painful proud blushings of two lovers who wished no finer fortune than marriage with one other and a calavan of babies.

Cean wished that she and Lonzo had gone to ask Old Aint Viney Vickers what their fortune would be. Now she must live it out to see; it lay there before her, near as the next day, but she could not see her hand before her face into it. . . . Would there be a war while she lived? Lonzo said it was a fool notion. Who wanted to fight? You couldn't get up a war if nobody wanted to fight.

A war would be a bad thing. Men took sides and tried their best to kill one other, and a many a one was killed and left to the buzzards. Pa's Uncle Jasper was killed in the war with the Redcoats. He had been dead, let's see—law me! moren half a hundred years. The worst thing about war was that men had to go whether they wanted to or not. You couldn't hide out; they had your name, and they'd send a detail for you. She hoped she'd never live long enough to see them come and get Lonzo and carry him off to be killed, along with Jake and the others.

But thoughts of fighting did not often disturb Cean's mind. Older ones spoke of a war over the niggers, but that was fool talk. There weren't a nigger nigher than the Coast, where they raised cotton and rice by the hundred acre. Why folks could wish for slave niggers Cean couldn't guess! She heard tell that some of the niggers that were smuggled in off of the ships couldn't talk a word, and an overseer had to drive them like so many cattle down the rows of cotton or into the wet bottoms to plant rice where a many a one died of moccasin bite. Fine Coast women had nigger wenches in their houses to cook their rations and wash their children's faces. . . . Cean wouldn't abide that! She couldn't stand a black E-thopian hand on Maggie's or Kissie's mouth, or anywhere here in her house with its clean-scrubbed floor and thick rafters bracing the roof overhead.

[ 113 ]

When they needed more room Lonzo would ceil the room and make a loft for another room. Now there was room aplenty; and truth to tell, Cean liked the dim space overhead where the corners were veiled with dusty cobwebs that the little gray spiders had woven, bringing good luck to this house. She loved her house; from the beams of it hung her bronze-red pods of pepper drying for sausage seasoning, her beans strung to dry for winter use, her seeds gathered fresh, season by season, and tied in clean rags to hang safe from the rats' greedy teeth. She hated the wild, slick-tailed brown rats that scuttled across the rafters in the night.

Now the little white rat had been a different matter; he had eaten the choicest bits of everything, waiting behind the slats for Cean to let him out so that he could climb her arm and cling about her throat. Cean had loved that little dumb-fool critter, but it had died—Ma said because God didn't intend for women to fondle anything but a baby. Cean had wropped up the stiff white thing that had died, leaving its pink eyes open, and had buried it by the root of the pink crêpe myrtle that her mother had sent her by Lonzo.

She buried her dead biddies in the row of boxwood; a shoat of Lonzo's that had sickened and died was buried under the Cape jessamine bush by the door. Dead things made the best kind of earth for things to grow in. . . . All these things buried about her house added to it, somehow; the yard was lived in now, like the house; each bush had something added to it, other than enrichment of the soil, for, together with its history of planting and rain and sun and dark, each bush now had, close by its seeking root, flesh that had grunted or peeped or squeaked while it lived. It gave Cean satisfaction to know about it.

She hardly ever went to her Ma's now. She was satisfied to stay home—keeping things going, she called it. When she had come back from Ma's, before Kissie was a baby, she found the clock run down. Lonzo had forgotten to wind it; the house felt as though it was dead, for it seemed to Cean that the ticking of her clock was like quick breathing to her house or the placid beating of a heart. When the clock was going again, she felt that everything was all right.

She would cast her eyes about the big room of her house, and her face would soften in content. Yonder on the wall hung the little looking-glass that Lonzo had brought from the Coast so she could see to comb her hair; on the narrow shelf below the looking-glass lay the fine bone-backed comb and the bristle hair-brush, and the little pipkin of ointment compounded of witch-hazel tea and rose leaves, to soothe her lips and hands from winter chapping. On her floor were yellow shuck rugs of her own plaiting and sewing, and deep bearskin rugs from the backs of the honey-robbing, lamb-stealing beasts that Lias, dare-devil! had killed in the swamp. Far in the corner was her bed, and close beside it was the cradle where her babies would sleep, each in its time. This was what her marriage had brought her—a room, quiet save for the soft voices of babies and the hurried ticking of a clock. And she was content. Why else did she marry Lonzo than to keep his house and raise his children?

Sometimes she wondered how she could tell that Lonzo cared about her at all, for he had never told her that he thought a heap of her, in so many words. He had courted her as other men did their courting, sidling across a room to stand beside her at a pinder-b'iling, or a candy-pull, or a nubbin-grabbin'. She had courted him as other girls courted, with lowered eyes hiding their desire for him and the desire for his presence beside her until one of them should die. Never did he speak fine words into her ear, nor make fine promises. She knew how many acres Rowan Smith owned, and could guess what Lonzo's share would be; he knew what sort of a housekeeper she would be, from the looks of her mother's house. What was the need of words? And truth to tell, words would have destroyed something that lay soft in his eyes when he looked upon her, choosing her to be his own, as he would judge the merits of a fine heifer, or a stretch of timberland, deciding, "I want that for mine!" She had gone meekly to him, quiescent under his choosing, as a pretty, well-tempered heifer follows the gentle pull of a rope in a stranger's hand to whom she now belongs, as the woods take upon themselves new ownership that descends like a season upon them that are at any season's will. Words would have shattered the intimacy into which they entered at any casual gathering of young people when their hands met with exquisite stealth and drew apart again trembling for hunger of that other hand, when their beings ached, one for the other, with a pain they could not understand, a pain which nearness, or any other thing, could never quite appease.

It was at a cane-grinding at Rowan Smith's place when Lonzo spoke out and changed Cean's heart from its fluttering and failing to a steady, happy beat. That was nearly three years ago, before this house and these babies were even thought about. She and Lonzo had been near each other many times, but always there was the hot strangling in her throat when he was near by; and to save her life she could think of no word to say, except, "Hit do look like rain," or, "Hit air mighty hot fer this time o' year." But at the cane-grinding —

The cane juice bubbled and frothed in the syrup-boiler under the outdoor shed in Rowan Smith's yard. Smoke rolled out of the clay chimney overhead in the night, and eddied back under the eaves to sting the young folks' eyes a little and make an excuse for laughter, for, as is well known, smoke follows the prettiest gal in a crowd. Lonzo fed pine knots into the open-necked furnace under the boiler, manifesting a certain mastery in affairs, for this was his Pa's place and this was his own syrup-b'iling to which the young folks from near and far were invited. Dicie and her daughters dipped up the foam in long-handled strainers and poured it back as occasion demanded, to keep the syrup from boiling over. There was cane juice aplenty yonder at the cane-mill that stood at the edge of the circle of light, around which the ox had tramped a rut in his journeyings, pulling the arm of the cane-mill on his heavy wooden yoke. The mill was still now, and the ox set free to rest in the night, but there was juice aplenty in a barrel. Cean liked to rake a cane peeling around the edge of the boiler, and to suck the foamy, sweet skimmings from it. Ever the smoke followed her, and the loud-voiced young males bellowed their laughter and teased her, milling about among the shy, giggling girls like young bulls in a cow-pen. Lonzo's eyes followed that little Cean Carver as she dodged the smoke from one side of the syrup-boiler to the other. He heard the teasing of the other boys, the bold, insinuating laughter. Rank jealousy possessed him, causing him to mope and to take to feeding the fire in earnest, with never a pleasant word, not even when Cean laughed out and said, "If that Lonzo Smith'd stop a-pokin' pine knots in there, they wouldn't be s' much black smoke to worry folks." Lonzo only glowered into the fire and Cean was sorry she had teased him, for she had meant no harm and never had he minded before. Soon the young folks were a-frolicking out in the full light before the furnace, but Lonzo wouldn't dance. Burning pain made him sick at heart to see Cean out yonder going through the figures, with Jabez Hollis holding her hands and measuring his steps to suit hers. Lonzo was as hot and restless inside as the syrup that every now and then foamed over the iron rim onto the hard-baked clay if Dicie and Epsie and Ossie did not watch. When the young folks came back to the fire, hot in spite of the cold, and laughing, and nighabout ready to break up the gathering, Lonzo's pent feeling overflowed upon the face of Cean with

[ 117 ]

its brown eyes warm and bright as fires, and its lips hardly ever shut to because she was so gay. He was back in the dark behind the roaring chimney, and there were tears in his eyes as he watched her. He thought that they were tears of rage, for he wanted to kill her because she was so merry and he was so miserable, because she was yonder in the firelight within reach of inviting laughter and gleaming eyes that followed her. When she came slowly near him there in the dark—for she knew that he was there—rage took hold of him until he hardly knew what he was doing, and he caught her quickly, drawing her out into the dark. His arms crushed her, his lips loved her in quick, hard kisses, as a thirsty man falls beside a branch and gulps water until he is full. When Lonzo's mouth had softened from the clinging press of her mouth, and his arms yielded her back to herself again, he told her: "Ye're agonna marry me. I'm agonna tell 'm so." And he did, bringing her out from behind the chimney to face the ribald fun of the others, who had seen other betrothals such as this. To their questions Lonzo answered that he and Cean would marry in the spring. Jabez Hollis, because he was put out and jealous of Cean's bright eyes, called out: "Why, Lonzo, that's when wild things mate!" And Lonzo bawled, with his hand still holding onto Cean's: "Yeah, hit is, hain't hit!" And he laughed, unashamed. Cean cast down her eyes, shy of the rough joking, but her heart beat proud and high ever afterward—a man had chosen her.

They talked about how high Margot held her head. Cean could hold her own head as high as anybody's alive, higher than Margot's, for Lias treated Margot meaner 'n a dog, and Lonzo was ever good and kind to her. Cean pitied Margot. Sometimes Margot would come over and spend the day at Cean's house, and the two women would talk of their little doings. Margot would humor Maggie's every whim and diddle Kissie on her knees while Cean stirred about, cooking. She would sing the baby to sleep with the lonesome backwoods song she had learned since she came here:

Bay-black sheep! Where's yore lamb?
'Way low down in the valley;
The buzzards and the butterflies are pickin' out hit's eyes—
Pore little lamb cries: Ma-a-a—Ma-aa—

The baby would lie still in Margot's arms, listening to the hard words and soft melody that Margot had picked up from hearing Cean sing it so many times to Maggie as she rocked her to sleep. Cean liked the song, but Margot thought it a mournful thing to sing to a little un warm in its mother's arm. The baby seemed to like it, too; she lay still, her eyes wandering over Margot's long white face, her body at peace since it was held, her mind lulled with a slow song.

In the late summer Lonzo cut the hay on the far side of the cotton-field. Many a day Cean had picked an apronful of peas there, standing knee-deep in the welter of grass and purple-and-white pea blossoms and cool green pea-pods branched on their sappy stems. She loved that pea-field as much as anything on Lonzo's place. It was wild, and yet tamed a little, too. It sloped down to a bog where Lonzo had set beegums in the cool. On past yonder was the swamp. Lonzo would be lucky if the bears didn't steal all the honey that the bees could make. Lonzo said that the little critters liked a place off to theirselves. In the woods around this field gall berries grew thick as hops, and all manner of flowers, too, so that the bees could find a thousand colored cups of sweet, full and waiting for them. Cean liked to think of their land going down into the edge of the swamp, and lived upon, even on this lonely boundary, by something of hers—the bees, children of her hives near the spring, children's children of her mother's hives, six miles to the east. She liked to walk over to this field in the late afternoon and pick peas for tomorrow's dinner, after Lonzo had come in from the field and could watch the children for her. Stooping, her legs girdled about by blossoming pea vines and spidery grasses, she would move slowly forward among the faint odors of growing things and the voices of a thousand insects that made a home of this yellowing wilderness of hay. The sun would move toward its setting as she gathered tomorrow's dinner; the shadows would lengthen toward the east; the air would be a murmurous, hot haze, and the field a wide, clean space engulfing this small, brown woman finding food for her man's brawn and her children's growth. Now and then she would lift her head to look upon the sullen black swamp, or to watch a bumblebee that clung to a swaying pea-vine tendril, its lumbering black body seeming immense and heavy on the delicate curl of vine. Above her bent the white sky, shading to faint blue; clouds reflected the sunlight, dazzling the eye; the dome of earth arched blindly over color and light, holding them under its heat until the summer world was thick with thundery oppression.

When Lonzo cut swathes in the pea-vine hay, swinging the scythe with a long side-swing of his body, a thousand stems gave forth their beads of thin sap; the thousand breaths from that sap mingled with the odor of drying grasses and the death-scent of dropped seeds, with tangy, woodsy air and the earth's own good scent, and made breathing rich and rank for the nostrils.

Lonzo was cutting the hay on the day when Margot came walking up the rise to Cean's house, and Cean knew that something was wrong. She met Margot in silence, and Margot, tired a little from her hot, dusty walk from Vince Carver's place, sat down on Cean's doorstep and said, simply:

"I've parted from Lias. . . ."

There was no need for many words. Cean's heart fell; a parting is sadder than a death, Ma always said, for two people are dead to one another and yet go on living—as though you might cleave a body in twain and set the severed halves apart and leave them to bleed helplessly for one another. A parting breaks the sacredest vow that any woman or man can make, ". . . till death us do part, so help me Godalmighty."

And what would Lonzo say to this?

Cean stood beside the door; Kissie sagged on her hip and lunged toward Margot in happy restlessness that tired her mother's arms and back fit to break. Magnolia sat solemnly beside Margot on the step, setting her feet close together as Margot's were set.

Cean said nothing for a little; she'd let Margot do the talking. Maybe this was just a little spat between Lias and Margot; he'd come around the bend after a little to carry his wife back home. She told Margot this, after she had thought the words over.

Margot set her eyes on the dim trail that went around the bend back toward Lias. She shook her head and her eyes were black as tar.

"No, he won't come for me. I slipped off. He'd see me dead before he'd come and ask me to go home. He'll be glad I'm gone. . . . And besides he wouldn't go and beg nobody for nothing . . . not Godalmighty Hisself. . . ."

Cean wanted to say, "Why, Margot, what in the world could make you leave Lias any such a way?"

She said:

"Oh, I wouldn't pay hit no mind, if I was you. Lias is rotten spoiled 'n' al'ays was. . . ."

Margot spoke angrily:

"I've put up with his notiony ways, but I won't put up with his taking up with another woman. I'm as good as Bliss Corwin, and better, too, if the truth was known. I'll thank her to keep her hands off of Lias. . . ."

Oh, Cean thought, so it's that little Bliss Corwin, no more'n a child and hardly big enough for her foot to reach the treadle of her mother's loom. So Margot is jealous. . . .

Margot went on:

"She's a little nobody without sense enough to get in out o' the rain! Fifteen . . . and running after a grown married man. . . . And him fool enough not to know better! . . . She needs her mammy's hand to blister her good, that's what she needs. . . . I'll do it meownself, ever I get the chance."

Cean held her peace. She could not think what to say. Margot misunderstood the silence.

"I reckon ye'll all side with Lias. . . ." She spat out the words bitterly.

Cean's voice was like her mother's:

"I wouldn't side with Lonzo hisself, if he done wrong." Then she tried to turn off Margot's anger. "Maybe ole Green-eye's jest got ye. . . ."

Margot was following out her own thoughts:

"I saw him with me own eyes. . . . He kissed her . . . like he thought she mought break if he touched her. . . ."

Cean asked:

"What did Ma say?"

"She don't know it. She can think her own thoughts about me. I just told her I was coming over here. Lias don't know that I saw him. . . ." She told Cean of it: last night she and Jasper were sitting on the empty kegs in the corner of the cow-pen, waiting for the cows to come up to be milked. It was nigh onto night. Bliss had driven over a yearling that her father had sold to Jasper. Lias was feeding up at the crib. He must have seen Bliss, for he came down to the cow-pen. He did not see Jasper and Margot in the cow-pen, no doubt because he had no eyes for any soul but Bliss on her way back home. And Lias followed Bliss to the other side of some gall berry bushes, and they hid like two thieves, and he took her face in his two hands, and he kissed her and she didn't say no.

Cean said nothing. Margot went on talking, though her breath thickened with every word and her face changed from anger to grieving:

"Jasper saw it . . . but he wouldn't let me say nor do a thing. . . . I had to sit still and watch. . . . Jasper told me to shut my fool mouth. . . ."

She laid her head on her knees and could say no more for crying.

When she was through with her crying she laid her simple plans before Cean: she wanted to stay at Cean's house for the little time until Lonzo should go to the Coast. She would pick cotton or pull fodder or do anything there was to do. If Lonzo could manage to make his trip alone this year, on some excuse, and would let her go with him, she would pay him with all the fine jewels that she possessed. She brought forth from her bosom the fine leathern bag in which lay the swinging earrings and the little green stone as big as your thumb, and the sparkling rocks of moon-crystals, and a gold finger ring that Cean did not much like, for it looked a little like the clouded eye of a blind man that she had once shuddered to see. But these were Coast jewels, and because Cean did not like an opal was no sign that it was not a fine thing to have. Magnolia watched the pretty things wonderingly. Kissie grabbed her hands after them. Cean's heart gloated over them, feeling a little guilty of its greed.

When Lonzo came in from the field, Margot told him what she had told Cean, as simply as one man tells another of his plans for next year's planting. Lonzo said little, but Cean could see that he did not like this business of a woman's running away from her husband. Margot could feel his disapproval.

"He don't feel about me like you feel about Cean. He never did, I reckon. He used to think a heap o' me, but never like you thought about Cean."

Lonzo felt better about it then. Always, in everything else, he had been behind Lias—Lias was smarter, taller, quicker; but now in this matter, Lonzo was the better man—Cean had not run off and left him! But he did not crow over Lias, even in his own heart; rather, he crowed over himself— Cean would *never* run off!

Lonzo knew that it was worse than useless to go and talk to Lias and have him fling out and want to fight, as he always did when anybody tampered with his business. Lonzo would let this thing drift!

Margot worked like a nigger slave in the field next day. She kept pace with Lonzo down the cotton-rows. Cean kept thinking that Lias would come—for he must know that Margot couldn't be anywhere but here—or that Pa would come to talk Margot into going back home.

Margot bent her back to the beating sun in the cotton-patch. Her heart had never been uplifted so high, nor cast down so low—uplifted because she believed that this was the right thing for her to do, and downcast because she could not make her heart do this thing without nighabout breaking it. For a heart may be lifted up and cast down in the same moment, as sometimes sunshine comes while rain is falling, and builds upward in the sky tall reaches of misty, unlikely beauty.

Rain and sunshine fell together upon Margot in the changeable, equinoctial weather as she worked in Lonzo's cotton-fields. Rain spangled her hair and sprinkled her face when she stood upright and lifted her head to the sky; sun dried the raindrops as she stooped again to a labor which she found satisfying. Here in the midst of black-green cotton leaves, where coveys of bob-whites stormed through like dry leaves in high wind, there was nothing to trouble her heart; here there was only good. True, she pinched a green worm from her arm and it fell on the ground, and red ants tormented it with their vicious, crowding stings; yonder, low on a cotton stalk, a winged bug, created to fly, struggled frantically against a spider's cunning web. That was evil of a sort, and cruelty. But it was all as it was meant to be. There was a difference, though she could not think how. The spider was meant to spin a web for its food. . . . And this . . . well, mayhap this was meant to be so, too—this evil that had come between her and Lias. There was something in this field that came into her and purged her clean, as boneset tea purges disease from fevered flesh. There was no hot distemper in her heart now; there was hurting, but it was healing pain that must come to every wound that does not rot.

Lonzo went off up to the house as evening closed in; Cean might need firewood chopped for supper. Margot finished up the patch in the early dark. She let loose her hair because ever she had liked it loose against her cheeks. Her long black hair loosed in the softly flowing air made intangibly real to her precious secret things which could never be set into words, nor yet thoughts; her self seemed loosed with her hair and was free, unbound from the coil of propriety and the hard pins of busy-day ways.

It was cool now and she was nearly done with the long row. The rough, dried bolls, with their sharp points widespread, gave up to her fingers the cotton that bore its seeds as small, hard cores of life inside it. The sack hanging at her side was heavy; the end of the row was just ahead, waiting there for her in the thin dark. Stars lighted the sky dimly; the moon, come halfway to its full, burned like a curious candle set out in the southeast. Lightning-bugs drifted by in the warm dusk, and one caught in the long black tangle of hair below her cheek. It struggled there, fitfully lighting its distress. She watched the little light, inconstant but brighter than a star. After a little time the bug ceased its struggling in the maze of hair, but the light went on gleaming and vanishing, like a minute candle in an unimagined window, set and snatched away again—a small mute sign not to be understood.

The far clang of the bells of Cean's cows up at the cowpen came to her; the cows were lowing to be milked; she'd better go and help Cean milk. But she did not stir. She heard the cows lowing; she saw the greenish light of the bug's body caught in her hair, and the light was like quicksilver, frantic to be free to spill out onto the night. In her mind she saw Lias with that child's face in his two hands and his lips hovering above her mouth; then he laid her head on his breast, and she closed her eyes, and his face fell upon her face and hid it from Margot's sight, and his bright-brown hair fell down upon her ashy-brown hair and mingled with it; and Margot gasped and would have run to curse Lias, but Jasper pushed her back on the keg so that she fell on her hands to the boggy muck of the cow-pen, and Jasper said, "Shut yore fool mouth." . . .

The furry body of the lightning-bug pulsated with greenish-silver light. Margot lifted it and crushed it carefully between her fingers. The light stained her fingers, and when she wiped them on a cotton leaf the light stained the leaf. Lightning-bugs were thick all about her in the coming night. She put back her hair from her face, and bound it up, and went on to the house.

She found Lias there.

He was talking pleasantly enough with Cean and Lonzo on the front steps. When Margot came through the house, he called out:

"Howdy, old lady. 'Bout through yore visitin' with Cean?"

She did not know how to answer him. When he saw

that she would not answer him, his face sobered, and his words were sober, too:

"If y'are, I've come t' take ye home. . . ."

She went and got her hair-comb and the shimmy in which she had slept, and followed him out to the cart, while Cean and Lonzo made talk to cover Lias's and Margot's silence.

Margot went back into the house and called Cean. Cean went in, and Margot took the opal ring out of the leathern bag which hung about her neck and slipped the ring into Cean's hand.

Margot and Lias were halfway home in the dark before he turned toward her and spoke:

"Don't you never dare walk off from me ag'in!"

She pressed her hands together in her lap and said nothing.

"Do ye hear me?"

Without having thought out her words, she answered him:

"Then don't go kissin' every little fool ye see. . . ."

She heard him take a long, deep breath. He thought—Now how did she know about that?—He said:

"I'll kiss who I please . . . 'n' you kin do the same. . . ."

His words startled her. She thought—Oh, Lias, whom should I kiss but you?

"Jasper told me where you had run off to. . . . Hit must be comfortin' t' have somebody close by t' complain to . . . !"

Margot's hands loosed one another in her lap.—You Lias! Ole Green-eye's got hold o' ye!—

The ox jogged slowly on in the night.

She laid her hand on Lias's shoulder.

"I don't complain to Jasper" . . . she reached her hands to his shoulders and turned him toward her ". . . and you know it. . . ."

The rough cowhide of the lines slipped through his hands, and his hands went about her shoulders as though seeking for her he had found her. She turned about and laid her head upon his hard knees, and wooed his mouth and his head down to hers with the weight of her hands on his cheeks and the weight of her head on his knees.

And the night was the same night that comes down upon the Coast country where the sea washes in up the river, and then runs out again, and mosses swing from the trees like specters swathed in rough cerements.

But now it was late, and Ma would be up and worrying about them out like this away in the night. And for the listening you could hear wildcats and painters meowling and complaining of hunger yonder in the swamp.

Secretly Margot had felt a little guilty when she gave Cean the gold finger ring with the opal setting, for an opal is a curse. Would the finger ring bring Cean bad luck? But no! Cean had a good husband; and no luck can matter to a woman with a good husband; and no luck could change Lonzo!

Cean would never wear the blind-eye ring, because it was too precious and because she could not love the dull, blind shine of it. When Margot and Lias were gone, she laid the ring inside the small chest of cherrywood that was set deep in her big chest; she placed the finger ring with her few gold pieces and her spoons of silver and the first worn brogans that had belonged to Magnolia.

Now in the late fall the sheeps' wool was matted with dried cuckleburs and sandspurs and seeds of beggar-weeds. Broom straw was tall and thick and bright yellow, ready for gathering and tying into house brooms. Goldenrod had bloomed itself out, except for a late clump here and yonder that sprayed up out of its stalk like a peacock's proud fan. Sometime Margot would manage to get a pair of pea-fowls for Cean. The way her eyes had glittered when Margot told of how a flock of them would strut about on some rich Coast planter's place!

Lias liked the goldenrod; it was a pretty sight to see, come to think of it. He spaded up a flower-bed under Margot's sleeping-room window, and set out clumps of the bunched wild goldenrods to grow there near the house; they'd wither and die now, but the roots would live and next fall there would be flower blooms for anybody to see for the opening of the shutter. Lias thought that new gold, untouched in some deep gut of old earth, could be no brighter or prettier to see than those curving rods of living gold.

Lias thought that now he loved Margot more than ever he had loved her before. She was changed, somehow, in what way he could not say or know, since that time when she left him for two days. Somehow or other, Margot knew that he had kissed Bliss. Jasper had seen and told her, no doubt. A fine blood brother Jasper was, working his mouth to make trouble between man and wife! But why had he kissed Bliss that time? Why, she was only a child to him, a little brown child that smiled shyly at him across fence rails, or came across the cow-pen with a fine story of a new calf. Why had he ever fooled up with her? Her child-eyes worshiped him, but Margot's woman-eyes worshiped him, too. Why had he kissed her that time? Furtively he remembered for a guilty moment the touch of her cheek against his cheek, the shy clinging of her mouth, the supple sheath of her hair pressed upon his brow. The feel of her near him was a new thing; he had not known that this new thing could be between a man and a woman; it was something, if he had known how to say it, that was without substance, yet real as the sky's coloring, lightsome as the wanton burst of down from a thistle's bloom which may be shattered by the lightest touch of a pleasuring wind. For hers was the kiss of a child who is almost a woman.

When Lias brought Margot back home, Jasper was glad

[ 129 ]

that the difference was healed; but his in'ards felt as though a hot smoothing-iron was going back and forth over them. And Seen, to comfort Margot, said that such things come about in the life of many a man, and ever it hurts his mother more than it hurts his wife. Margot could not believe that saying, for she could not believe that any other body could hurt as she had hurt when she had slipped away to walk that trail that led to Cean's house, while her feet, heavy as lead weights, rebelled against going since every step was a little way farther from Lias. Jake saw no reason for so much to-do! Men and women were the master-fools; ever he was grown, never would he marry! Vince said less than ever these days; the older he growed, the less he knowed, he said; but one thing sure, a wife has no business a-strammin' around over the country, nor a husband to let her do it. . . .

Cean, back home on a low slope bounded by swaying stretches of broom straw and tilled fields, sheltered by lofty pines and the blazing-bright dome of heaven, prayed God-almighty that she would never have just cause to leave Lonzo; but over and above any other thing, each day raising her heart to an altar, she prayed for patience—patience to listen to a child's fretting; patience to endure a man's hard displeasure over bad weather or the death of a hog; patience to love God as she ought, this being hard to do since never might she see His face until she died.

# Chapter 10

Lias never meant to get into any trouble over that little Bliss Corwin. Margot was more to blame for it than he was, he thought; she set Bliss in his way where he would have to see her and speak to her and remember her afterward.

Lias believed that he would have forgotten Bliss—and glad to do it—if Margot hadn't kept on reminding him of her. Sometimes when he would lay his arms around Margot in the dark of night, she would press her cheek against his neck and whisper, "Am I as sweet as Bliss?" He could not carve out pretty legs for a fire stool without Margot's spoiling his pride in it by saying, though she said it with a laugh, "Is that for me or Bliss?" Lias knew no way to answer her; if he were angered at her childishness, she would fret herself because she thought that he was angry because she had spoken of Bliss; and if he laughed at her, then she would be sure that he took but lightly such a grave matter as Bliss Corwin. If she had quarreled, then he would have known how to answer her; but she would never quarrel. Sometimes when he would be deep in thought over some affair of his own, she would come softly behind him where he sat, sober-faced, and say, "A penny for yere thoughts!" And he would know that she believed that he was studying about Bliss.

Lias believed that he would cheerfully have forgotten Bliss, but Margot made him remember.

This was the third year of his marriage to Margot. There was a cool, wet spring, and a blowsy, slow, over-ripe summer; then before you could turn around, fall came blowing in, and Margot went about the yard budding her winter pinks under the window shutter of her room. Bright leaves went flying down every high lane of wind; pine-needles dropped soundlessly as sand brushed from the fingers; high wind blew black smoke flat on the tops of the chimneys. Soon winter would come in. During all this time Lias had seen Bliss not more than twice, and those times in a crowd; he had kissed her not once more, nor wanted to; he thought of her as a pretty child whom an up-and-coming son of a neighbor roundabout would snatch up and marry one day soon.

Margot gave an all-day quilting in October, during the bright Indian summer weather that followed the first cold snap. Nothing would do Margot but that Bliss should come. She made Lias drive her over to Lige Corwin's; she was careful to invite Susanna, his wife, and Marthy, his fat daughter-in-law—and Bliss, when anybody would know that Bliss wasn't old enough to go to a grown-woman's quilting. But Bliss came as big as you please, diked out in a sky-blue dress not more'n a week out of the loom, with her head in a pink hood trimmed with black worsted blossoms.

The menfolks did not come about such women's doings; they kept out of the way. Though Vince was now so poorly, he rode off to see Lige Corwin; Jake went off fishing; Jasper and Lias puttered around the lot over an axletree, or ground the plowshares, or did any old thing to keep their hands busy away from the house.

In the house Margot stirred about the cook-pots filled with the big dinner; Bliss helped her. The room-wide quilting-frames were set up on chair backs, and the women stood around the sides of them, sewing busily; the air was full of women's talk and laughter with no meaning behind it. The women's hands guided the needles carefully in minute stitches through the top and cotton and lining, following a pattern laid out in their minds. Cean was here, with her babies tugging at her knees and crying so that she could not keep up with her quilting. Lonzo's sisters were here, and women from all roundabout. They could easily put in and take out four quilts before the sun was near down. All hands were busy, and the house was ahum with pleasance.

In the middle of the morning Margot was quilting, too, but all of a sudden she stopped her needle, laid her thimble beside it, licked her lips carefully as though she had something hard to say. She went to the fireplace where Bliss sat quietly as became a younger woman; she stooped and said to Bliss:

"Would ye mind going to look for Lias for me? Tell him I want him."

Bliss's eyes widened a little as she looked up at Margot. "No'm. I'd be glad to."

But she was not glad, for Mister Lias frightened her. She went out the back door in search of him, and Margot turned back to her quilting and her eyes were shining. Margot talked brightly now; she even started Liza Jones off on an account of her grippe of last winter.

Bliss could not find Mister Lias. Jasper was filing a hoe-blade and looked at Bliss as though he had never seen her before. Bliss went up to Jasper, taking upon herself a fine grown-up air.

"Could ye tell me where I'd be likely t' find Mister Lias? His wife wants him. . . ."

Jasper scowled.

"No'm, I couldn't say. . . ."

He turned his back and set out for the cornfield.

She saw Mister Lias a moment later; he was in the crib-loft door, high above her; and he was laughing at her like she had been a fool!

"And what did ye want o' me?"

She dropped her eyes; she did not like to be laughed at. "Ye're wife wants ye. . . ."

"Then why didn't she come fer me?"

He lay on his belly on the hay above her, clasping his cheeks in his hands.

She fingered her wristband that her mother had made a smidgeon too tight.

"She sent me fer ye. . . ."

"*Margot* never sent *you* fer *me*!"

Her face reddened, but she did not know how to answer Mister Lias; his wife *had* sent her!

He took down his hands from his cheeks, and his long, brown fingers drooped over the hay-strewn threshold of the loft door.

"Well, if she sent ye s' big, why don't ye come on up and git me?"

"Ye can come down by ye own self, I guess."

She turned to go back to the house, but she did not much want to go, and when he called her she turned back toward him. Reaching his long arms, he swung himself down from the loft door and dropped to the ground.

Up at the house there was nobody in sight; an old hen with a poor hatch of fall biddies scratched by the back door; around the place there was no sound but the cheerful pot-racking of guineas in the trees around the spring and women's lifted laughter from the house.

He thought, "Ye're smarter than ye look, little sinner with the face of an angel!" Then his face hardened and there were two thin, white lines reaching from his flaring nostrils to his twitching lips.

"Go on back to the house!"

"Miss Margot wants ye. . . ."

"You tell her I cain't come now!" He stood straight with his arms folded hard on his breast: "You go on back to the house . . . and come back some other time. . . ."

She never knew that he never believed that Margot had sent her.

She went up to the house and told Margot what Mister Lias had said. Margot laughed a little.

"Well, I guess I can draw what water we need. . . ."

But Bliss went to draw the water while Margot went on with her quilting and ran the needle under her thumb nail because she was thinking: "I'll make him see that I'm no jealous fool . . . if it kills me. . . ."

In November, Margot persuaded them to give a corn-shucking for Jake's age of young folks. Bliss was there again. Margot paired off Bliss and Jake, and as luck would have it, Jake found a red ear and so had a right to kiss Bliss if he wanted to; but he would not kiss her, though the gathering laughed and tormented him; all he would say was, "Nope, I don't kiss, thank ye!"

Margot had more to say than anybody, until Jake was purple in the face with shame. She kept on saying: "Pore little Bliss! Won't nobody kiss her for Jake?" Lias stepped out finally, but Jasper was but one step behind him, and spoke first:

"I'll kiss her . . . and learn Jake how!"

And Jasper kissed Bliss with a loud smack of his lips; his face and neck were as red as a beet and blood crowded in his head like a fever.

After that you would have thought that Jasper had taken a liking to Bliss. He saw her home that night, and twice in one week he went to her Pa's place on no more excuse than a sick hog, or less. Lige and Susanna Corwin egged it on and were over-nice to Jasper, and sent Seen a keg of lard and more smoked sausage than they all could eat. Jasper was a good catch, not so handsome as Lias, but steadier; not to say that he wasn't handsome at that, with his dark hair falling over his dark brow, and his black eyes bright as black water, and his broad shoulders strong as a young battering-ram. Jasper thought that he would up and ask

Bliss to marry him as soon as he could find out how well he liked her.

But a little thing held him back: if they were talking of banking sweet potatoes, she would say some little thing to stop his thoughts, such as, "Do yere folks like sweet 'taters? Seems like I remember Mister Lias sayin' he wasn't over-fond of 'em"; or maybe they would be talking of hogs, when she would say, "Mister Lias is the proud of his big sow, hain't he?"

So Jasper's hot notion of marrying Bliss cooled in his head, little by little; he found no more excuses to ride over to Lige Corwin's.

In March, Lias carted his big hog to Lige Corwin's.

Any way you looked, the grass under the pines was purplish with wood-violets. Lias got down out of the cart to look at the things; he pulled a few, and some of them had stems as long as his hand; they were a washed-out blue color, pale as a sky or an ocean, with leaves as big as puppy ears, and shaped like hearts; they had the look of blind, blue faces. He cast the handful of them away and went on to Bliss's.

Bliss brought fresh buttermilk for Lias to drink, and sweet-bread still warm from the fire. Lias, with his mouth full of sweet-bread, talked to Lige:

"Y'ought t' see the creek slope betwixt here and home . . . blue as indigo with violets . . . a sight to behold. . . ."

Before Lias was well out of sight, Bliss set out to see those flower blossoms.

And yonder on the creek slope was Lias's ox-cart. He was grabbling out rooted violets to carry home for the bed under his sleeping-room window. Bliss decided she would take some home, too. So Lias dug up some for her, too, till his hands were grimy. Then the two of them went to wash their hands where the creek flowed across the trail. And for fun they took off their shoes and stockings and waded, though the water was still ice cold from winter.

She was not afraid of Mister Lias any more, for he told her to call him just plain Lias, and he seemed no older than herself, for all his beard and deep voice.

The creek was up; the water lapped the under sides of the logs that were set up to carry the trail across; Bliss climbed out of the water to the foot-log; she stood there above Lias with her feet showing red from the cold. She shivered and said that she must put on her shoes and go home. But just then a scorpion ran his pink glossy head over the side of the log not two foot away, and she was afraid to go by that way. So Lias lifted her down and carried her out of the creek, with his breeches rolled to his knees, and Bliss's bright-green skirts and blowsy hair and laughing mouth filling his arms.

He set her down on the ground and put her stockings on her feet; her skin was soft as lambskin to his rough hands; he tied the latchets of her little shoes for her.

They were sitting on violets as though they were common dirt.

He plucked a loose handful of the tender blooms of grimy, wild roots. They had but little sweetness to them, so he crushed them in his hands to make them smell the sweeter. He laid them on Bliss's rumpled hair, and laid his hand, sweet with violet-smell, on her laughing throat. He kissed her, then kissed her again quickly.

Willows swooned, head down, in the yellow water of the creek that was muddied by spring rains. In the brown shallows little frogs spoke with the very sound of many silver bells. High water lapped urgently at the foot-logs on its long way to the sea.

When he went back to get his hog, a week later Lias said nothing of the violets, for they were past their thickest bloom. But on his way home he waited to see if Bliss would come again to see the violets.

And she came.

In September Lige Corwin swallowed down his pride and came to Vince Carver's house, and the two men went off to the ten-acre field and held long converse. When they came back, it was hard to know which face was the darker or which mouth was the grimmer. Vince rode off home with Lige without a word to his womenfolks. Seen and Margot looked after the men, wondering what might be up. . . .

Bliss's face was peak-ed, and her eyes were sunken in dark rings; she was outspoken now, no more a child; she had a woman's courage to tell a child's lie:

"Hit hain't so! . . ."

Vince put his hand over his face and shook his head against this trouble, and said nothing. Lige Corwin said little:

"Tell me his name and I'll kill him!"

But Bliss denied her child even until the night it was born. Her own mother could not shake her denial, though the old woman's face was piteous with shame and grief. Steadfastly Bliss denied her love.

When he saw that he could not shake her, her father said:

"If ye'll not tell me his name, I'll find out fer me own self. . . ."

Vince's eyes were set on the floor, his hands trembled on his knees, and his face was green with fear or some other thing. His tongue would not speak, though words pushed up against his dumb throat. There was no need to speak. Lige knew there was no need, but he could not hold his mouth shut. He knew what they all knew—that the least said is the easiest mended. Finally Vince offered Lige and Susanna Corwin all the comfort that he could give them:

"I'll see to the child . . . once hit's borned. . . ."

When he got home he told Seen of this thing in as few words as he could use. And Seen told Margot. If Margot ever wept over it, they never saw her do it; if she had any hard words for Lias, she never spoke them to him.

Vince went alone to his room, where he stayed much of his time now; he got down on his knees beside his bed, but he could not pray because his back was heaving with soundless, shut-mouthed sobs that bore the likeness of terrible, bitter mirth. He was drinking Margot's cup of gall with her.

No word of Bliss came up at Vince Carver's eating-table. What Lias might have had to say no man can tell, for no man asked his opinion.

Because Margot never quarreled at him, Lias followed her about with his eyes looking like a whipped dog's. He took his father's word as law—and Vince now was hard on Lias who was his favorite. Lias stayed away from Bliss and made no move to see her. It was she who would come, under pretense of driving off the calves, and turn one certain rail so that its bark lay skyward. That was a sign between them, meaning that he must see her tomorrow when the work was done, where the creek with a slow turn of its black current flowed into the river's cunning serpent way that would in time seek out the sea. There he would hold Bliss's pitiful, weeping face close against his breast, comforting her with kisses and bold promises; and sometimes she would comfort him as he lay with his head on her lap, his face turned to the sky, whose hard light she shadowed for his eyes with the bend of her face over him. Though she was not a child any more, always she was a child to him, whom he must comfort, who comforted him with the artless seduction of a child.

Bliss bore her child in a cold night of a hard winter. Her mother, with a bitter face upon her, attended her pains; her father would not come near her. Seen would not go to Bliss, though she had helped every woman of her time to bear her children. This was a shut-mouthed, secret thing. Even Bliss's own father said that if she died he could not grieve; he thought that she would be better off dead. Vince prayed, though he knew that it was a sin, that the child would never draw the breath of life.

When the child was born, taking with it the pink out of Bliss's cheeks and the laugh out of her throat and the lightsomeness out of her feet, Bliss closed her eyes against it and would look at it only when her mother was gone from the room; so she was alone when first she saw her child's thin-skulled woman's head and the clutching woman's fingers. Alone with the woman-child and God, she unwrapped its feet and saw them as they were made, and would ever be, twisted at the ankles and marred in their making so that they would never walk straight in this present world. She hid the feet quickly when her mother came in the door with hot meal gruel.

When the child was three days old, Vince and Seen came to take it home to its father's roof. Seen's heart was touched when Bliss parted from the little crippled thing. Seen said:

"Come over whenever hit pleases ye, Bliss . . . and see hit." . . . When she was going out the door she turned to say, "We'll call hit any name ye say. . . ."

Bliss raised herself on her elbow, for she was still in bed from weakness after three days; her eyes were hollow and dark and deep with tears. She said:

"Call her Fairby . . . if hit's all the same to ye. . . ."

And they called her Fairby.

Bliss had made up the name out of her own head. It minded her of an old song she had sung a many and a many a time when she was little, toting a doll-baby under her arm, ten year back and longer. Till now she liked that song:

Once there was a lady, fair was she,
Loved a fine gentleman—aah, la me!—
To him she gave her heart to keep, sweet fool she!
And o'er and o'er he told to her, "How fair ye be!"

Then saw she him a-wooin' go—aah, la me!—
To court a dame whose lands and gold were fair to see!
She took his hand, she took his name, poor fool she!
For never did he tell to her, "How fair ye be!"

# Chapter 11

FOR two years after Kissie was born, Cean was free to stoop or run or frolic—to pick cotton or to lift the biggest pumpkin that Lonzo could grow, or to scrub down the walls of her house with hot suds—without fear of injury to another being growing within her own.

She liked being lean and light on her feet once more. She dared Lonzo to footraces down the cotton-rows, but he ignored her, too proud to take up with such tomfoolery. She tossed Kissie and Magnolia many times into the air, liking to hear their stopped laughter burst in her face as they rushed down into her arms. She helped Lonzo with the spring planting, because Maggie was a big girl now and could look after herself and little Kissie.

She had felt so hearty that she had wanted to take that little motherless youngun, Fairby Carver, and raise it like it ought to be raised. Margot wouldn't know how to mother a little thing; no woman could know, 'lessen she had borned one. Now Cean would know—she could feel a little thing's hands and legs once and know if it had a fever, and how much; she could hush a baby's crying, no matter what ailed it.

But Lonzo would not hear to her taking Bliss Corwin's child to raise. Let Lias see to it! . . . And Vince stormed out: "No, Cean shain't do hit. Margot can raise hit! . . ."

Margot scarcely ever let the little thing out of her arms. Secretly she greased its little twisted feet with oint-ment, hoping that somehow they might grow straight as the child grew.

Cean kept wanting that child, but when Fairby was three months old she was glad that Pa and Lonzo would not let her have it. For she came down with bed-sickness again.

She mulled long in bitterness and disappointment. Just between her and Margot and Godalmighty she never wanted another child. She sulled for a week or two, before she would tell Lonzo or her mother about it; then she cried for a week or two, just to ease her heart of its worry; after that she was all right again. And now, because of this thing, she was one lesson wiser in living, as Ma used to say; now she knew that hit were a sin fer a woman to crave to be free and easy and unencumbered in this here life. She had sinned in wanting to frolic and joke and find delight in this world. She told Lonzo these things in few words, and made his heart warm and full of satisfaction; to his knowledge he had never sinned after this fashion, and found it easy to forgive Cean for wilfulness and rebellion against nature. But never did she tell him that during those two past years she had planned and managed to have no children for him. That he would never have forgiven her, and well she knew it.

She confessed her lesser sin—that she had not wanted this coming child—to Lonzo so that he might forgive her and make her feel better; but the blackest sin she would not confess to her own mother. Oh, she had sinned in many ways—laughing and frolicking and thinking that this world was a place to be happy in. Now she knew better; this world was a place where a mortal must do his duty and prove whether he was more than a dumb brute. She must do her duty, bearing a life to its birth every so often, washing, minding the little thing till it could walk, then starting on another. But she could not be quiet-minded about it, though she might keep her mouth shut and do her duty as she should.

One day Lonzo watched her studying a blade of broom straw, green before the frost and bearing needle-tufts of down as its seeds. She watched it so long that Lonzo wondered what could be the matter with her. Finally she said, "Hit does hit oncet, and then hit quits!" Never did Lonzo know what Cean meant by that.

Now Cean understood better the words which the old elder had spoken over her and Lonzo when they were married.

Word had gone around that they would be married in the spring; but long before it was needed, Cean's homespun was bleached and folded in her mother's loft; her goose feathers were sunned every week to keep them sweet-smelling; her calfskin shoes, sober new bonnet, black bearskin cloak, and short white shimmies that caused her heart to contract with a delicious withdrawing, waited and waited through the cold, wet days when the grass began to spring green in the black earth, when the bluebirds moved in swift blue clouds close to the earth, when the bob-whites separated, two by two, from the winter coveys and went to build their nests. The elder came late one afternoon when the sky was clear save for tall clouds stacked like piles of pink cotton in the west. Cean felt a new awe of the old man with the snowy beard that reached to his waist, for this man had the power to marry her off to Lonzo tomorrow.

To his wedding Lonzo brought his jean and homespun, his cowhide boots, and his store-bought hat, and the trinkets that his hands had made for his sweet new wife who was thin and brown and sweet-smelling as a dried poplar chip. He told no one, not even his mother, when he was to be married. Lonzo was shy of a big to-do over anything.

The elder said the marriage words without a sign of a book, increasing their respect for him: "Do you take this woman, Tillitha Cean Carver, for your lawful, wedded wife, to live with her in holy wedlock? Will you cherish and keep her for better or for worse, in sickness and in health, in poverty and in wealth, forsaking all others for her so long as ye both shall live? The answer is, 'I will do all these things, till death do us part, so help me Godalmighty.' "

Cean's vow, taken as became her after Lonzo's, ran like her husband's, save that she must cleave unto him through all manner of circumstances, must serve him, and obey him in all things. And Cean took the vow, repeating it fresh from the lips of the silver-bearded prophet of God in this wilderness, and called upon Godalmighty to help her keep her promise.

Now, nearly five years later, Cean was ashamed that for two years she had not truly kept her vow; she had wanted better without the worse, health without sickness. Lonzo had ever cherished and kept her, but she had not cloven to him as she ought.

When she came down with early sickness, Cean complained against Lonzo in her heart. She was grieved with everything; she cuffed the children about, she drove the hounds from the door, she beat a cow unmercifully that would not so for her to milk it. Lonzo had never known her to be like this. He could not make her out until, before ever she told him, he guessed what ailed her one night when she would not rock Kissie to sleep and the little thing went crying to bed and snuffled herself to sleep. He knew that Cean was sorry for that later, for she lay half the night with her arms tight about Kissie and cried softly. She was crying because Kissie was asleep then and could not feel her mother's arms; she cried because another child was pushing this baby out of her arms; and she cried because she could not keep Kissie, nor Maggie, nor any other one, always small enough to lie limp in its mother's arms in its mother's bed as it slept. . . .

Lonzo never scolded Cean. Things will always work out, he said to himself, if you'll keep yore mouth shut and wait. . . . And things did work out to teach Cean a lesson, but

[ 145 ]

not to Lonzo's notion, for the drought fell. . . . Never did it rain after Cean's early sickness, not till the next winter-time. The corn was just in the ground when the last rain fell and the heat came in, hot as dogdays. Never did the crops grow but little after that, so little that in late summer the puny ears of corn would have brought a laugh if they had not brought weeping; they were not much longer than a baby's hand. And the cotton bore but little, and that little looked worse than any storm cotton. Not even hay would grow, nor grass, and the cows were like to die of dry murren. Hot haze lay thick in the lowlands, and the river ran black and heavy to the sea. The spring on Lonzo's place was near to drying up, and he dug a well, and when that failed he hauled river water for his stock to drink, over a hot eight mile, each way. In the late summer the pigs sickened, one by one, and died, leaving two old sows that were too tough for next year's meat even if Lonzo had not needed them to breed more pigs. Last year's corn ran out, and the hogs were turned out to find grass like any pore man's razor-backs. Old Betsey, Cean's first cow, lay down and died without a moan. . . . Oh, there was dead meat aplenty to enrich the ground around Cean's boxwood and crepe myr-tles and English walnuts. Lonzo tied Old Betsey's bloating carcass behind the ox and dragged it off to a peach seedling behind the crib. Cean could hardly stand to look at the wide clean swipe that old Betsey left behind her on the ground as she was dragged off to her buryin'. They must live on deer and bear and other wild meat this winter. But Cean and Lonzo, like other folks that were not wild and savage as Indians, did not greatly care for the curious tang of wild meat, since they were used to the natural taste of sweet fat pork and good beef. Cean could kill her fowls, she reckoned, but what would they do for grits and meal and syrup and bacon? Pa had no more corn than any other body; everybody in this land and country was in the same boat! Every crop failed, and no man could build cribs big enough to hold rations for year after year, as they had done in Egypt once. It was a hard time, as hard as when Ma and Pa had buried Eliza-beth, only now folks lived closer together and knew more about how to get along in hard times.

Through the late summer Lonzo kept on killing coach-whips and hanging them up to dry, to make it rain, though now the rain would do the crops little good. Cean would have prayed, but she figured that this was her punishment and she must not try to pray it off.

Lonzo and his Pa, and the Carvers and the Hollises and Vickerses—all the men hereabouts—must go early to the Coast this year, a month before Big Court. They would miss seeing the fine brainy lawyers argue, and the Holy Ghost preachers pray, but they must have something to eat. And there was little to trade. Everything was lean and hungry. Even the bees could hardly fill their hives, Lonzo said, and bees were the smartest, wisest things living.

There was no way for Lonzo to bring back stuff from the Coast unless he took some of Cean's gold pieces with him. So, when the time came, Cean robbed her chest and bundled up her gold and her finger ring and her silver spoons, and sent them. For once she had something to trade.

But after Lonzo had gone off around the bend, she cried until Maggie and Kissie were crying, too, and she had to hush for their sakes—and for the sake of her other child, nearly ready to be born, that was not yet able to cry. For if a mother weeps over much while she is carrying a child that child will mope its long life through. Cean grieved for many things, but most for this saying; for surely this child must weep through all its life. She had cried a river of tears when she had known that it was on its way, before she cared whether it moped or laughed in its lifetime. Now she would have drunk all those tears, boiled down into one salt cup, if she could have; but it was too late, and she knew it.

Because of her hard weeping in the nights while Lonzo was gone, or because of her worrying by night and day when she would be so distracted that the children would call and call before ever she heard them, or because she must go on with hers and Lonzo's work when never had she felt so porely, never had a child been so heavy and so wild in its plunging against her breath and her heartbeat—because of some of these reasons or all of them, the child was born ahead of its time while Lonzo was gone. Cean labored with no one to help her but Maggie, who wondered at her mother's face distracted with pain, and Kissie, who cried to be held in her mother's arms. Cean tried to stay up for the sake of these children before whose eyes she felt an unaccountable shame that she had never felt before others, not even Lonzo. Mayhap she wished to hide this cruel agony from her girl-children who must soon enough in their time learn it for themselves.

It was a stifling day. Blazing on into the afternoon, the sun made of the earth a still furnace, parching whatever lay under its blazing light. No little bug might hope to creep under a log to escape the heat of this day in September, for the heat lay over and about everything, like burning wool.

Cean's body was clammy as she rubbed down the skin of her arms and legs where goose-bumps stood on every pore as though it were cold weather, where every minute invisible hair reared against the pain that beseiged her body. She paced the floor and hardly heard the whimpering of the children; they were fretful because their mother would pay them no mind and because the heat rash on their bodies stung and itched. Cean made Maggie undress herself and Kissie, and let them run about naked because it was so hot. They raced about the room from one corner to another, content with this novelty for a time, their lithe bodies glistening with sweat, their eyes beady with laughter, oblivious of the passion of their mother's pain. For supper, Cean gave them bowls of clabber with brown sugar sprinkled over it, for she could not cook for them. A little after dark they fretted themselves to sleep and lay on Cean's bed, naked as the day they were born, and left Cean alone, free to weep and pray for Lonzo's coming.

It was after midnight by her clock when she heard her new baby's first cry, and she comforted its wailing with her own hands. There was no hot water, for she had allowed the fire to die, having forgotten everything but the black pain that blinded her and set her teeth to chattering in her head and caused the muscles to coil in her arms and legs like monstrous-strong snakes.

She piled wood in the fireplace and struck fire to it. But before the fire could burn to heat the water, she wrapped the child, unwashed, and crept to bed and pulled quilts over herself and the child. She was cold, cold, though the room was yet hot from yesterday's sun, and sweat beaded her children's bodies.

The doors and shutters stood open to the night. She was not afraid, because the hounds were outside to let her know of any intruder, and never had she been afraid of the kindly, harmless dark save when she was not herself.

She lay, spent and half-asleep, cold under the piled cover, with her first man-child on her arm. He would have no name until Lonzo should come and name him.

Outside in the dark, locusts chirred with long, beating shrillness that deafened the ears; that sound had always made her feel the heat more when she noticed it; now she did not notice it.

Suddenly the hounds growled, and the hair on their backs bristled high down the ridge of each lean spine. So close that she could swear that it was just outside the door, Cean heard a painter scream, and another painter's hoarser scream answered the first. It sounded like women's high, agonized crying. The hounds bayed in dismay, and beat the earth to thundery dust going in pursuit of the painters' crying. Cean's blood seemed to freeze with fear, so that she could not move. The painters were after her new-born child and her. Hadn't she heard her mother tell how the painters could smell childbirth blood for any number of miles? And here were her other two children naked on the bed, and her only man-child still lying as he had lain yesterday and the day before, his chin and folded fists crowded on his breast, his little red legs crossed at the feet and drawn high on his body.

She found the back door and closed it against those jaws out yonder somewhere that slobbered for her children's meat. The dark outside was torn by the baying of the hounds and the screaming of the wild things. She closed the shutters, shoving home their wooden latchets so that no pawing claw from without might loose them. She turned back to the bed, fit to faint from weakness. . . .

Her eyes scarcely knew what they saw. She swayed a step forward, thinking that what she saw was a vision of her weakness or a trick of the firelight that blazed high and yellow in the chimney. A thing like a great house cat lay stretched along the floor between her back door and her high bed. The belly twitched a little on the rough floor, the haunches moved noiselessly, the great tail lashed through the air and back to the floor with never a whisper of sound; the eyes, close above the paws, were set on the bed where the children lay, brown and naked—where the little boy hunched himself in his mother's bed, thinking naught but that it was her body.

Cean could not ever afterward tell what she did when she saw the yellow beast crouched not three strides away from her bed. Godalmighty had helped her to find the musket, ready loaded over the mantel, had driven strength down her arms; for she had gone blindly, not knowing what she did. She could scarcely have believed that she had killed the pesky thing, if there had not been the lank body on the floor, dead beyond any doubt.

Cean fell asleep on the bed, too tired to pull the cover over her body. The child whimpered and she gave him her swollen, hurting breast. In a nightmare she felt again the beast's hot breath in her face and the hot fur of his breast against her hand, the ripping tear of his claws on her shoulder. She rose up in bed, screaming out for Lonzo, and saw the limp body stretched there on the floor, its head shot half away, its great lolling tongue lying on her sheepskin rug; the thick, wild blood had poured out there, ruining her marriage present from Lonzo. She lay back again then, knowing this second fear to be only senseless dreaming; she slept, her breath mingling with the breaths of her children. Two of the steady-coming breaths were light girls' breathing; one of them was short and irregular—a little flutter of breath—and it differed intangibly from the other three, for it was the new, uncertain breathing of a man, safe in his father's house, safer yet on his mother's arm.

Cean waked when Maggie and Kissie waked, shouting over the dead painter, talking to their baby brother, eyeing with awe Cean's marred, bloody shoulder.

She washed the gashes that tapered to scratches down her arm, and caked the open places with tallow melted with clear turpentine. The hot liquid seared with its heat and sting, but she must do this or have blood-poison or proud flesh, and high fevers, and be dead, maybe, before ever Lonzo found her.

Lonzo did not come until three days later. Then Jake drove him home in Vince Carver's cart, for Lonzo's ox had swollen and died on the way home from the Coast, and

Lonzo had left it to the buzzards, for there was no time to bury a dead ox. Cean thought it must be a time for dying. . . . The ox that had hauled her and her'n so many miles by the strength of his back was yonder. The bleary eyes would be staring sightless into the heat, tormented by the blowflies and the buzzards. Dead at the edge of the clearing were two of the hounds that the panthers had ripped to ribbons; their entrails, shining with the shine of the opal in her finger ring, had run out and were soiled in the earth. Outside the door lay the painter, for that was as far as Cean felt like pulling the pesky wild thing that had to come into her very house to die. . . . Oh, it was a time of dying. . . . Before finally Lonzo came, blowflies settled on the dead thing so near her house, and a stink of death went up and made her stomach turn over and throw up its victuals.

Lonzo buried the hounds but he would not bury the painter. He had a nasty time skinning the painter, but he would not have let any stink drive him from it. He would make a floor covering of that skin for Cean's weak feet, or a throw for her torn shoulder, or a fine, outlandish canopy to be over the bed where she slept. Oh, he would do anything at all to please her now. For never had she seemed so fine a wife. He could feel, but could not say, nor yet understand, that she was clean as a sycamore's trunk in spring; brave enough to blow a painter's tough skull wide open; sweet as the breath of a beehive where the bees swarm all the summer through; and quiet in her ways as that hive in midwinter when you strike the gum and hear only the drowsy stir of a thousand wings that are folded close in warm, honey-sweet air, sleeping through all the cold.

It was Jake who named the child.

His eyes had narrowed when he had come with Lonzo into Cean's house and saw the man-child and heard the wild tale of Cean's fight with the painter. Almost he could love Cean again now; but she was changed beyond his recognition. She was hollow-eyed and dark in the face, and said a little of nothing about it all. She was near to crying, though, he could tell that, for he had seen his mother look so, many times, her lips closed, one tight over the other, her brow set in stern wrinkles, her eyes turning away from other eyes. Ma would raise sand when she knew about Cean. He must hurry home with his great news.

Lonzo looked at Cean's shoulder where the tallow held the wound tight till it could heal. He felt a little out of place, for he was forever behind-time with this woman; he would never catch up with her. But he was not put out; he was proud. All her shortcomings were less than naught to him. Had she ever been anything but a little less than perfect? . . . For she had borned him a son, and killed the painter that would have eaten it, all in the same night. His arms went around her and held her as close as he dared with thought of her hurt arm, but never did he tell her how he felt; that would have been like saying "Howdy" to God.

Cean asked him to name his son, when she was no longer so nigh to tears. Lonzo blustered and joked, but in his heart he felt unworthy to name this young creature that he had made in his own image. He didn't have sense enough to name him. What did he have to do with it, anyhow? Nothing —less than nothing.

Cean was shy of this new nature in Lonzo. To cover her shyness she turned to Jake, who was watching her where she sat with the baby on her good arm:

"Kain't nobody think up a man's name for 'im? . . . Kain't you give 'im a name, Jake? Hit's a pity t' be a nobody without ary a name. . . ."

She smiled softly at her joke at the little fellow on her arm.

Jake's eyes went to the fire and back to Cean's face. Pride moved him to think up a fine name for this child. Not everybody was asked to furnish a name. He thought of tales he had heard at the Coast. . . . This year he and Jasper and Lias had gone without Vince, who had been ailing since last year. He spoke suddenly:

"Name 'im Cal-houn! I hyeard tell of a man named that from up where Ma come frum. . . ."

Cean repeated the syllables twice over:

"Cal-houn. . . . Cal-houn. . . ."

She felt Lonzo standing there close, too proud to speak and name his child for himself. She said:

"I reckon Lonzo Calhoun would suit me all right." She smiled a little secret smile, understanding how Lonzo felt.

Lonzo hummed and hawed; that were too much name for a little tyke such as him!

Cean laughed a little, and the sound reminded Jake of her old-time, boisterous laughter:

"Oh, we kin call 'im Cal!"

Lonzo agreed, relieved that the child would not be called by his own name, for that would seem too brazen a pride, unbecoming a plain man from out in the sticks.

So now Jake could carry home news of the baby, and the painter, and a name for the baby that he himself had given it.

And to cap the climax for Cean, Lonzo had traded only the gold pieces for food and stores, and had brought her spoons and ring safe home again to her.

# Chapter 12

CEAN's strength came back so slowly that she thought never would she be well again. Some force of being, some core of courage, had gone out from her on that night when she had born a child, and killed a painter, too. She felt weak as water inside now, and cried for nothing. She was always crying, so that her face, homely enough with puffy eyelids and liver-spots on the thick skin, was homelier still now from crying. Tears slipped down her cheeks from a bank that always stood high in her throat and behind her eyes. She thought that never again would she feel like straddling the ox to ride home from the cotton-field, never again would she sing "Jump t' m', Susie," of mornings because she was too merry-hearted, for no reason at all, to stay still. She thought that if she could not get better she would surely die, and the little baby with her; for she could hardly drag up from the bed to tend to him, and she had no milk for him. The little un cried day and night, except when he was too tired to cry, and lay asleep, a little bag of skin and bones. Cean warmed cow's milk, and goat's milk, and rice water, for the baby, but nothing seemed to suit him. He would scream with the colic so that sometimes Lonzo would walk him in his arms till cock-crow.

A change of the season had always before, since she was a little thing, moved Cean to a sort of season's change within herself. She could tell so easily when a new season blew in on a north or south wind, or crept in, unawares, on the dark of one certain night. Another winter came in when Cean's baby was eight weeks old in November. Cold rain drove down from the northeast and hushed all the staccato chattering and winged singing and shrill peeping of wild things in the woods about Cean's house. Later, squirrels would bark off in the cold, woodpeckers and sap-suckers would call harshly, but such sounds would be but melancholy echoes of summertime. Cean had known the time when she would have loved to traipse off to the woods on the first winter day, to peel away the crusty flakes of bark from the pine trunks, to kick fallen cones ahead of her feet as she walked looking into the far distance, not knowing what it was she would like to see there. But now, that time was obscured by many things, so that she minded not when winter caused her to close her shutters and doors and bundle up her children in warmer clothes.

She had hoped to get to her mother's house once before cold weather, but she had not felt able. Her mother had come to see her, bringing bundles of newly-woven jean and homespun. Seen had stayed a week, doing the housework and sewing up winter clothes for them all. She did this in spite of the fact that Vince was lying sick at home. She felt her heart pull back toward home where Vince was complaining after her, and she felt it pull toward this little house where Cean had to carry a burden too big for her, and she wished that she had a dozen feet, and many hands, and tribble her natural strength, for only so could she go and do and bear for her loved ones as she wished to do.

She went home, comforting herself with the thought that at least Cean and her children would not go cold this winter. She must get back to Vince, for she was a-feared that he would never last the winter through. For he had grieved himself nigh to death over Lias and Bliss Corwin.

Now Margot carried Bliss Corwin's child about on her hip as though it were her own. The Corwins were willing enough to give up the child to the Carvers—all but its mother, Bliss. But Bliss's tears had not moved Vince, nor hardly Seen; for did not Bliss know that she had no right to this child, born out of wedlock, for all the neighbors to make fun of? Vince carried it home, and dared any mortal soul ever to taunt it with its sinful birth. As for Bliss Corwin, let her look to her sin! He'd have no traffic with her; he was only concerned with his son's child, blood of his own blood. He would see to this child, though a thousand times he had prayed that it would die before ever it lived, though every time he laid his eyes on it the sight shamed him. But let Bliss look to her sins! Margot Kimbrough was eating bitter bread now, after too much sweet! It did Vince good to see Margot have to nurse another woman's child; it was meet . . . meet. . . . But, oh! the pain that never left him in peace because his son had done this evil. Mayhap Seen was right when she said that he would never over this sickness 'lessen he stopped his worrying over Lias—and stop he could not. When ye're old and have got sense enough to know that the sands be trickling low, 'tis not so easy to throw a grief from your heart. A-a-ah, law! Toil and trouble, and nobody but God to relieve matters, and He don't seem to mind much. But mayhap that's how-come He built Glory yan side o' Eternity.

Vince would have been all right, he thought, if his nasty sores would only heal. Months ago he had stumped his toe like a youngun, and a sore had come on his foot, and would not heal with any kind of poulticing. Instead, that sore spread until both his feet lay always on pillows, smeared with Seen's salves and oint-ments, and wropped in clean rags. He was all right, he would say—had been all right all this past year and a half, except for those pesky sores and a sort of weakness that made him hardly care if seeds went into the ground and food came out of it or not. He lost all his fat, till Seen could feel the hard ridges of his backbone when she rubbed his back with lard and powdered copperas to ease it of its aching from lying so long. His jaws had shrunken down into his broad cheek-bones, and the skin on his forehead seemed bloodless and thin. All his ruddy color and broad-shouldered brawn were gone, and Seen never let him look into a looking-glass when she could help herself. But one good thing, Vince would eat anything she brought him, and she was glad of that. She fixed good things to please his taste. When the first hogs were killed late in November, she kept the lids jumping on the pots and spiders, stewing and frying and fixing all manner of good sweet pork for Vince. How he did love the taste of it! He ate till his hands and beard were greasy.

And that was the last meal that ever he did eat.

Seen was glad for all the rest of her life that she had taken special pains with those rations.

Late that night she waked and noted a change in the breathing that she had slept beside each night for these many years. He did not answer when she called his name. She lit candles and saw that he was nigh onto dying; from his body there came a dull, unaccountable smell like that of a physic, but not of alum or copperas or any physic she knew. It was Death in the room! He might disguise his scent, but he could not do away with it.

She climbed the ladder to the loft, and did not notice that her bare feet cramped on the hard cold rungs of the ladder. Jasper waked as she came to his bed. Seen spoke in her natural, slow voice, but the sound of it startled Jake in the other bed so that he could not move, and lay with his muscles jerking. Seen said:

"Jasper, yore pa's a-dyin'. . . ."

She went back down the ladder. Jasper got up and dragged on his breeches. He came and took Jake by the shoulder and shook him, but then he saw that Jake was already awake and he said nothing. Jasper went down the ladder, and Jake was left alone for fear to catch him by the throat and shake him till his teeth chattered. He got up and pulled on his breeches, and went down the ladder, his steps lagging, his heart yearning toward yan room where his pa, once strong and tall, was now a ghastly, feeble stranger. Bedclothes covered Vince to the chin; his white beard was streaked with grease from the food he had eaten yesterday; his lips were purple, parted over snoring breath; his eyes were closed in their deep, dark sockets. Lias and Margot and Jasper stood around the bed, and there, too, was Seen, still in her shimmy. Jasper built up the fire and brought his mother's clothes and helped her to put them on. She would not put on her stockings, dressing as though she were in a mighty haste to do something; so Jasper pulled the heavy woolen stockings on her feet that were, and would ever be, rough and drawn and scarred from the old burns.

Seen seemed dazed; she did not at once recognize her duty in this matter. She had handled many another death, but this was her own house, her own grief, and not a neighbor's. Once before to her own house Death had come, but Elizabeth had been too little to be told about it. And that time, she depended on Vince, anyhow.

When she came to herself a little she saw her duty clear before her. For she knew that Death had a habit of slipping inside houses and stealing away souls that might not suspect that he had come for them—unless they be told. Thus it was that so many people died in their sins. Vince was a good man, but he ought to be told that Death was here, come for him. It would be hard to do, for already he was half gone. Death had stolen a march on her. She was comforted by Jasper, who stood there by her with his hand on her shoulder. He had put her stockings on her. As though she cared whether she were shod or not!

She pulled and tugged at Vince until Lias, who was ever short-tempered, scolded her:

"Let 'im be, fer God's sake, Ma. . . ." And then his voice broke.

She waked Vince, though his eyes slid shut whenever she loosed her grip on him. She must be sure that he understood, so that if there were anything that he wanted to set straight, he could set it straight. A body never rests easy in the grave if it leaves something undone here.

She did not tell Vince straight out; she knew that he was nobody's fool.

"Vince, d' ye hear me?"

He grunted with his mouth open, with his eyes set on her eyes, giving assent.

"Is they anything ye want t' say?"

They listened, straining to hear his last words. They must know his last wish and must execute it—for no oath before God, no word of Bible, is so awful, so compelling, as a dying man's words.

Vince grunted, a gruesome, unnatural sound. Lias turned his back quickly and went to the fire, but Jasper stood with his backbone as stiff as his ma's.

The old man's eyes found Margot and set in a stare. Sleep wrapped him like a shroud and made him senseless and careless of death.

Vince had no sin to confess, Seen knew; he was a good man and had ever been.

The old man's eyes were set on the spot in the air where he had met Margot's eyes, until Seen pulled the lids shut and weighted them, as his body cooled.

Seen washed her new dead while dawn was breaking. Margot helped her. The two women were steeled to this emergency. Common words of everyday speech passed between them; they talked to hide the ghastly stillness. They washed his naked, wasted, sore-eaten body. Once the breath was gone, here was an unclean body to be prepared for its burial in the clean earth. Seen could not allow herself to remember now that this piece of flesh had many times yearned to her flesh, creating wonder upon wonder of life— men who stood yonder, shut out from their father's nakedness, grieving for him. She raised the limp body, and Margot helped her clothe it in clean clothing. She set her hand under his chin to see that the jaws were set together properly. She brushed his hair down with a bristle-brush; it was docile under her hand as he had been docile since he was sick, but never before. Margot shook out a clean sheet. . . .

But Seen could not lay it over his face.

Godalmighty, this was Vince she was laying out! This was Vince whose smell she was shutting off under a clean sheet! This was Vince whose hair and beard she had washed, his neck limber in her hands! And he had let her do it; he had been careful not to remind her of what she was doing, until she was through with it—of whom she was laying out to cool. His hands had stayed where she laid them, folded on his breast.

Seen let the sheet fall; it crumpled on his breast and brushed his newly-washed beard. She clumped blindly across the floor of the kitchen-house. Jasper met her and held her in his arms against his breast; she beat her forehead on his hard young breast, crying and crying and telling him, as though she had only just heard it:

"Oh, Jasper—yore Pa's gone. . . . Yore Pa's gone. . . ."

Lias dropped his head into his arms on the kitchen table. Jake rose without a sound, though his mouth was crimping, and went out of the house. Jasper laid his face against his mother's thin gray hair. They wept as strong souls weep, with cries breaking silently out of the roots of their beings; they wept as men weep who know that a bulwark against destiny has gone down, who know that their own tried spirits must henceforth be that bulwark making a stand out in the lonely fore.

Margot heard their grief; she remained in the room where the sheet covered this man that they loved more, now that he was dead, than they had ever loved him while he lived. Now she could almost love him, too, forgetting the loathing she had felt for nim all the while that she had loved Lias. The sheet would never stir now, unless another hand than his lifted it. Seen had closed his mouth and weighted his eyelids; Margot need not hate him now, nor fear him. . . . But It was mighty long and still there on the bed; death had lengthened Its stature strangely. It could bide Its time now; It knew all the secrets of death, secrets of more worth than word or thought. For one ghastly moment she could feel Its eyes staring at her from beneath the concealing sheet; for those eyes had the power of death in them, and could laugh at the futile sheet and the thin, brown coppers on the lids. It was beyond the limitations of the body now, and could see where It liked, regardless of light or dark or any foolish obstruction. She was a pitiful creature beside that Thing that was with her in the room. But she must stand her ground! And she stared the Thing down, her heart hard as iron. Once she could swear that the sheet rose whiter and taller, and moved; but in the next moment she knew that it was only a trick of her eyes that danced with fear. She heard them weeping in the other room—the weeping of the children of these spent loins, the wailing of the beloved of this impotent body. She dropped her face into her hands. She had been afraid of this poor, sick, old man who lay dead. There were no ghosts—and if there were, Vince Carver would be a good, kind ghost. Had he not overlooked her marrying Lias, and never parted his lips against her? She could let him know now that she was a decenter woman than he had thought. But he knew it already, mayhap, for he was out yonder where knowledge of all things floods like a sea of light. She eased her weight down on her knees, and tried to form a prayer to this new spirit in another world—"My thanks to ye . . . my thanks to ye." . . . She dropped her head on the side of the bed; she wished forgiveness from this old man whose heart she had made to ache. Her thoughts reached vainly, trying to tell him that she was not altogether evil, as he had believed. He moved under her hand, and she went cold with horror.

Then she realized that it was only his hands that her own movement had disturbed, since they were not yet stiff. Suddenly, in her relief, she knew why she wanted to say her thanks to him—"My thanks to ye for dying, for getting from between Lias and me. . . ."

Lias rode off to tell the neighbors, and Jasper went to bring Cean. It was two hours by sun then. Seen was surprised to find it morning; to her the air had the feel of late afternoon, it seemed the end of a weary day.

They had gone through the motions of eating the breakfast that Margot had cooked, but not a soul could swallow a mouthful. Vince had eaten his meals in bed for many a day, but never till this day did the head of the table seem forsaken. The empty chair was now a cruel reminder that swallowing and breathing can cease, aye, even in one who is as steadfast a surety as the sun. Now they knew that he would never eat with them again until they sat down at meat with him in the Glory-World. The thing that separated them was Death, broader than the farthest reach of sky from east to west, deeper than the depths of the Middle Passage to the Old Country, blacker than any night, and more to be feared than any demon in hell. They knew all these things. Yet Seen spoke of how happy Vince must be right now, holding little Eliza-beth in his arms. Her eyes filled as she said it, and she yearned to caress that little angel, and to be caressed by the big, stalwart angel that was Vince, striding, broad-shouldered again now, about heaven, with Eliza-beth in his arms, her silver wings folded on her shoulders, and sweet as her mother's dreams of her in a little blue robe that God had given her to wear. Oh, the house ached for Vince and Seen's heart ached for Eliza-beth, too, the while it was aching for Vince. It seemed only yesterday that Seen had watched Vince dig Eliza-beth's grave out yonder at the side of the house. . . . Now Seen went to the shutter and opened it, and looked yonder to the grass under the pines. The day was still and only a little cold, for the weather had warmed up again after the cold snap. Elizabeth's little grave seemed lonesome under the leaning pines, but it would soon have company. The neighbors would dig out another hole this very morning, and Vince would go into it.

Margot stirred about the fireplace, cooking dinner for neighbors who would come. As she went busily about, she carried on her arm the girl-child that had got her pretty puckered lips from Bliss Corwin, and her scornful flaring nostrils from Lias Carver, and her ugly clubfeet from old Satan.

Seen latched the shutter and turned back to the fire. She sat there close beside the fire. Slowly her life showed itself to her to be resolved into two parts, as a sharp knife is passed around a smooth fruit, causing it to fall apart into two perfect halves. The first half lasted until last night, filled with work and care and going hither and yon doing this thing and that thing, making a home, rearing big men and a good woman as her children; the second half began last night when Vince's breath left him. This day—the day when Vince would be buried—was the first day of the second part. (For the weather was not cold enough to keep him out until tomorrow unless they put him in a room without a fire, and even then he might purge a little at the nose and mouth.) The second part of her life would hold neither work nor care, neither going nor doing, for her home was made and her children were grown; this second part would be weary waiting for God to call her home to be with Vince, where she belonged.

Seen said nothing of all these things, but her children noticed that she was different ever afterward from the mother they had known before; they forgot, while she remembered, that before ever she was their mother she was Vince Carver's wife.

Lias wondered over the manner in which Jasper stood his father's death—better than any of them. Jasper was most like his mother, the neighbors said. Cean was like that, too.

Jasper withstood grief as a stone withstands rain. Cean sat in a chair among her little children and never did she break down once; only silent tears slipped down her cheeks. Jake was gone most of the day; he was down by the river, for he was ever a rabbity sort of feller, hiding out when something got the best of him. . . .

Lias did not know how Jasper and Cean and Ma could hold themselves in so. Down in the woods he sat on a log and pulled wire grass, thread by thread, from its roots; then thread by thread he cast the grass away. He stilled his fingers for a time and held them locked on his crossed knees, but before he knew it he was back at the grass-pulling, and his foot was scraping the earth clean between two clumps of grass. A little gray lizard skimmed down the log toward him. He sat motionless, watching it. The lizard lay still for a moment, rearing its head to watch the great unfamiliar hulk on the log, then it moved across a ragged hole where the rotten brown heart of the log lay exposed. Lias watched the lizard's gray color turn to the brown of the rotten wood; then, as the lizard slipped down the smooth, weathered side of the log and climbed across a clump of grass, it turned green as the grass. It crawled across the toe of his dark boot and was dark again. . . . Lias stamped his other boot heel hard on the lizard; it squirmed and lay still, its in'ards smearing his boot—in'ards that were neither brown, nor green, nor gray, but red, like his own, he reckoned. He picked up the crushed lizard by its tail and flung it away, and wiped his boot clean with a handful of grass. "Tarnal thing!" he said.

[ 165 ]

"He kain't be dead," he thought. "He kain't be dead. . . ."

Pa had been his best friend, and he had been a friend to pore little Bliss. He had known that Lias wanted Bliss's little child even if it would limp all its days. Pa had taken Ma to see the child when it was three days old, and they had brought it back to Lias's own house for Margot to tend to. Ma said that Bliss had cried to see the little thing taken away from her, but Susanna Corwin was glad to get the sin-bred child out of her house. Anybody would know it all its life for a sin-child, because of its ugly, stumped feet.

Now Lias could send Margot back to the Coast. . . . No! He couldn't. Pa would turn over in his grave. So Lias must keep on slipping over to Bliss's house, meeting her by the creek when she could get away from her mother's storming tongue and her father's stolid disgust.

Oh, Pa had told Lias that he was making Bliss the laughingstock of all these parts, that he was bringing his own name to be a joke among the neighbors. . . . But Lias would not listen. For he could fall on the grass beside Bliss and feel her cool hands smooth his forehead once, and hear her little voice hush his quarreling, and he would forget that ever he had been worried up about anything. There was something about Bliss that was as good for him as a dose-t of camomile tea. If he was dead and in hell, she could come to him and say, "Oh, shet up yore old quarrelin', Lias," and he'd hush. She always knew how he felt about things, Bliss did; but never did she count them worth worrying over, or quarreling about. She was a sweet thing, a mortal sweet thing, Bliss was. . . .

Through the piny woods came the silver wrangling of cow-bells. Lias heard the iron clanking on iron on the necks of his father's cattle. Without moving his eyes from an ant that climbed along a pine root two foot away from his boot, he could name the cow that bore each bell—Bonnie, or Gypsy, or Bess, or the little pied-ed heifer, Spot. Each bell

[ 166 ]

seemed to sound a tone deeper or higher than an other; all
the varied tones mingled to lull the mind, rather than to
tease it, for wherever the bells clink-clanked in a steady,
patient wrangling, there the cows were feeding at peace, or
resting, stirring their bells only to toss away a biting fly. To
the east, where the ground was higher, the finer clanking of
a sheep-bell might be heard, a thinner sound, as became the
little woolly beasts mincing over the grass on their delicate
feet that seemed too small to bear their fleece-laden bodies.
An old bay-black wether led the flock, the little bell swung
under his neck by a buckskin thong. Lias knew that bell, too.
He knew each bell, and the beast that bore it. These dumb
things were his kin, not in blood, but in circumstance. As
Vince Carver's crops prospered, these bellies would be full
and these backs fat and broad; when the crops failed, these
beasts were denied, as Vince Carver's family was denied, and
not one whit more. Lias listened to the cow-bells swinging
on the necks of the dumb creatures whose bags were drained
each day, night and morning, to feed the Carvers; he heard
the old bell-wether that had led the sheep up for the
shearing these many years, giving up his own reddish-brown
wool first so that his flock would not be afraid of the shearing, holding his tender eyes half closed as Vince Carver's
shears went carefully through his winter fleece. Since Lias
was a little feller that old bay-black sheep had led the flock.
Once when Jake wasn't knee-high to a duck he had cried
his eyes out when Ma sang that old song about the bay-
black sheep; he thought that it was Pa's bay-black sheep
that had lost its lamb away low down in the valley, where
the buzzards and the butterflies were a-pickin' out its eyes.
. . . It made a good joke to tell on Jake now, for the old
wether couldn't have a lamb if he tried.

To Lias the sound of the bells was a forlorn and forsaken tolling, for the man who had been judge and pro-

tector and slayer of these dumb beasts would soon be under this ground that was his, over which the beasts that were his walked grazing, subject yet to his will.

They stood about the hole while the wet earth thudded down upon the yellow pine box. The elder would be along in the spring. Now they would put him away the best way they could. Lige Corwin prayed a half-hearted, choking prayer; the neighbors stood around the grave, sorry enough for Seen Carver to die, but unable to say a word, or to do a thing but cover up the yellow pine box.

Seen had to look away from the soggy soil that was thrown in, a spadeful at a time, on Vince. She must not lose this peace in her heart; it could be but a few short years until she would see him again in the Glory-Land, with Eliza-beth; and they would climb the golden stairs together up to God's white throne, where prayers from sorrowful earth gather about God's ears and are thick and sweet and compelling upon His remembrance.

Cean stayed that night at her mother's house. They lay, each in his bed, with their ears aching with the sound of the hounds' mournful baying. Never was there so lonesome a sound. . . . The dogs slunk through the dark with their tails between their legs, and prowled around the pale mound where Vince Carver lay in the damp earth close alongside Eliza-beth. The freshly turned soil gave up a keen clean odor to the sniffing of the hounds; but among the scent of clay and rain and grass and tree they found, too, a faint, curious odor of their master.

# Chapter 13

THE winter was mild and sweet-tempered. The leaves had scarce a chance to turn for the little frost they had felt, and all through the cold months you could hear the frogs croaking, clinking like bright metals one upon another, for they were out of their burrows, fooled by the warm weather. Men must start their spring plowing early this season, for crops must be up and doing before hot summer; there had not been enough cold to kill the worrisome insects that would swarm alive over the fields in the hot months.

Fairby's first birthday fell in the middle of this warm winter.

Margot baked a sugar-cake and Jasper pared down a candle till it was a little size, and they set the cake and the candle in the middle of the eating-table at dinner-time. Fairby blew her face red, trying to quench the little flame that was so toucheous that it swerved from every least breath of air; but she could not blow it out. She sat in the high chair that Lias had whittled out of a walnut block for her, and frammed against the table with her feet that were crumpled as though a strong hand had broken them.

They were having a merry birthday dinner of it, for who would not love a little woman-child with eyes as blue as Lias's, and a crimped, wet mouth as sweet as that of its mother that it can never have for its own, and little legs that clump like wooden legs across the floor from one's arms to another's? Fairby could never decide in whose arms she would rest; when the family was together, as at mealtime, new arms were always reaching for her and she would pass about amongst them, first high on Lias's shoulder, then low on Seen's knee, or on Jake's or Jasper's. But ever when she was broken-hearted she would run to Margot and be comforted on Margot's bosom that yet was beautiful and high as are new green hills that have not nurtured men.

Seen had baked fancy ginger-bread gentlemen and ladies for Fairby. It was a fine layout and the table was merry, with jokes and a song for Fairby, and a big crock of white winter pinks in the middle of the table, picked from Margot's flower-bed under her sleeping-room window.

All was merry when Bliss and her father drove up in front of the house, and Lige called out, "Anybody at home?" like as though everything was chicken pie betwixt the Corwins and the Carvers, which it was, for it had to be. Bliss was as meek as Seen would ever have her be when she brought in her presents for Fairby.

Now who would ever have thought that Bliss would do a thing like this?

Lias's face was as red as a turkey-gobbler's, and his fingers were all thumbs. Margot felt herself trembling all over as she set extra chairs at the table and ran for more crockery. Seen opened up a churn of cucumber pickles and one of sausage, and what with the chicken-and-dumplings and greens and Fairby's sugar-cake, it was enough for all hands.

Jasper and Seen and Lige kept up loud talk. Bliss said no more than a humble wish to Seen: "I hope I find ye well. . . ." Never did she dare to look Lias in his eyes, and he was as wary of her. Fairby's eyes went from one strange face to another. Finally her little mouth began to primp and she cried for Margot. Margot took her out of her high chair, and Fairby pressed close against Margot's bosom, hiding her face.

In the midst of her eating, Bliss lifted the bundle hidden in her lap and pushed it across the table toward Margot and said:

"We recollected as how it was the baby's birthday. . . . Ma sent hit somethin' fer hit's birthday. . . ."

Then she went on gnawing a hen's breast bone clean, though she was not a-hungry. There was fine sweat on her upper lip, and the palms of her hands were damp, and her eyes had a feverish look.

Margot just went on about the little red worsted hood, and cape, and a string of poplar beads dyed blue and strung for Fairby's neck; and there was a cradle-size comfort in pink and white patches, and stuffed—of all things!—with down from Susanna Corwin's geese. Seen had much to say about the things and pleased Bliss mightily by saying:

"I'll wager ye pieced that comfort ye own self, Bliss!"

And Bliss blushed and said:

"Yes, ma'am, I did. . . . Hit hain't much. . . ."

But Fairby would not even so much as lift her head from Margot's bosom to look at the things, not even the pretty blue beads. When Margot pulled the little red hood over her hair, her chin crumpled and she gave way to heartbreaking screams, and Lias had to take her out to the lot ever to get her quiet. Seen smoothed things over by saying: "Ye'll have to come oftener. She never did like strange faces. . . ."

Bliss and her father didn't stay long. They were in a mighty big hurry, Lige said. Susanna said to hurry right back. They hated to eat and run, but . . .

Bliss was the nigh to weeping all the way home. She'd stay away from the high and mighty Carvers after this!—and, Lias, too, the biggity, big-mouthed thing! They always had thought that they were handed down, a little too good for common folks. She'd never set her foot on their place again for all of Seen Carver's begging her to come back. She'd show Lias. . . . She'd show Margot. . . . She'd show 'em all. . . .

And she'd never spin another strand nor dye another smidgeon nor sew another stitch for that little biggity Fairby. That was Margot's child—like as though Bliss hadn't borned it. It wouldn't look at its mother once, as much as to say: "Yere welcome to yere heartaches and pains on account o' me." . . . Margot Carver had stolen that child. That Margot Carver had smooth, sly ways that nobody suspected; she was slick as the next one to get what she wanted; and she was mean with it, lording it over everybody. . . . "*Do* sit down in *my* place, Bliss. . . . I'm not a-hungry, anyhow. . . ." She gave Bliss her leavin's, that's what, and Bliss didn't thank her for them. . . . That's my child, and she stole it . . . just like any other stealing. . . . But I don't want it. . . . She's welcome to it. . . . Already it's been with her so much till it's out o' sight with Carver bighead. . . .

Never would she trouble them again, and never did she, not until the day she died.

And the fence rail lay unturned. Little gray lizards bred in its bark, and the rail went on rotting like any other weathered rail of Seen Carver's cow-pen where Margot and Jasper milked in the morning and evening of every day. On warm days, Fairby came with them, riding on Jasper's back, and she learned to call the cows by name.

When Bliss and her father had gone off home, Margot felt as though some strength had gone out of her. "As long as I don't have to see her," she thought, "I can stand it. But I can't bear her coming here in my own house, pushing herself in my face, daring me to do something about it. Now that she has come once, she'll keep on coming, trying to wean Fairby back to her with presents. Why didn't she keep her, if she wanted her? No, she gave Fairby up without a word, and now she's made up her mind that she wants her back. And she'll take Fairby back any time she wants her, and I can't say a word because Fairby belongs to her. She'll have everything on her side. Lias will side with her. . . . Even Ma will side with her—and Jasper, too. She'll take Fairby back, now that I've tended to her and learned to love her like as though she was my own."

Margot could not love Fairby more, she thought, if the child were her own. Well she remembered the day when Vince had thrust the little puking, wailing thing into her arms, saying: "Now, Margot, you tend to hit. They's nothin' else t' do. . . ."

Margot had not known for half a day that Fairby's feet were crooked, for no one could bear to mention the vile affliction caused from the sin of its being; and Margot could hardly bear for her hands to touch Bliss Corwin's child, red from its late birth three days gone.

That first night, when she dressed it for sleep, she found its feet; but she felt naught but pity at the sight for they were clammy with cold, and she held them to the fire, and rubbed them with hot tallow, and nested them in her hands to warm them, while the child nursed warm goat's milk from a pipkin with a gut nipple on it. When she had got the child warm and full, it lay on her breast and slept; she could feel its breath on her cheek; she could, for the turning of her head, lay her cheek upon its cheek. . . . She laid her face down against the child's face, and the feel of it startled her, for the child's face was softer than any silk, softer than any imaginable thing. It was new flesh, lately molded in God's palm, yet soft from the touch of His hand, yet warm from the breath of His nostrils, and unspeakably tender since He had so lately set it down in this world. Old Satan never touched finger to the making of such a thing, and Margot knew it, though never did she mouth such heresy; God had molded those little ankles as it pleased Him—with some secret thought, and mayhap a secret purpose, in His mind.

From that time forth Margot loved the little unwanted thing; she thought that God had told a secret in her ear: Take this child; it is from Me, to serve My purpose. Her thoughts ran thus, and farther: His purpose is to give Lias back to me. This was something that God had to cram down her throat—a recompense, disguised in sorrow, that she had railed against. Because of Bliss Corwin's child she came as near as ever she came to kneeling and thanking God for all good and all ill that He had ever sent upon her. She thought: next time I will wait and learn His purpose before I rail against His harshness. God was teaching her a mighty means of battle, she thought—a force stronger than force; He had whispered a secret in her ear—patience.

But now Bliss would be wanting Fairby back. And Margot had no patience. If Bliss took Fairby back, there was nothing Margot could do. But she would not let it matter with her; she would not break her heart over it. If she had a mind to, she could sit down and cry a week, but she would not do it. She had not let Lias break her heart, and if Lias could not do it, Bliss Corwin would have a hard job trying.

The night of the day of Bliss's visit Margot got Fairby to bed, and covered over the cradle with the pink-and-white comfort. I'll not let them see that I care, she thought.

Then she ripped the sole from her shoe so that Lias would have to stay up after the others were abed, and resole it. She sat with him, and sewed by the fire after the house was still with sleep. She held the sewing hard in her hands, to keep them from trembling; it was new pantalets for Fairby.

She dropped her head a little lower over her stitches, and her face was covered with blushes like a silly young fool's, for she found it hard to tell Lias this thing that she had made up her mind to tell him:

"Lias. . . ."

He pushed the bodkin through the leather of her shoe.

"Huh!" he said, to answer her.

"I want a child o' me own. . . ."

His bodkin stopped; she looked at him and could swear

[ 174 ]

that he was blushing harder than she was. And that tickled her. . . .

"I want a man-child with eyes like your'n and hair like your'n . . . a little Lias that I can hold and suckle and raise up for me very own so long as I live. . . ." She was proud of this speech that she had made up to tell Lias.

Lias's face was a sight to see. . . . Margot was the on-gonest woman! Imagine yore wife comin' straight out with a thing like that! The longer Margot watched him, the more his fingers fumbled; he was beet red and plum put out. She wanted to say, "Lias, you fool!" She wanted to hug him fit to burst his lights.

He said:

"I don't see how in creation you ever got yore shoe into any such a fix. . . ."

She gathered up Fairby's pantalets, rose to her feet, and went and hung her head near his ear. She whispered, laughing:

"See if ye can't make out to find me a man-child next time ye go to the Coast."

Just to say something, he said:

"You don't know what you want. . . ."

Then she had him:

"It seems to me it's you that can't make up yore mind. . . ."

He knew that she was thinking of Bliss. She went on to bed, and he went on sewing the shoe. Danged if Margot wasn't worth twenty Blisses. Danged if he'd look toward that fence rail again, let it lie any whichaway.

Seen's altheas and bridal wreath bloomed in March, as is their way. Warm wind stormed through the woods like a thousand horses snorting and tromping up dust. All the dooryard was arrayed in flower-blooms, and bees tumbled, head first, onto verbena blossoms, and butterflies crossing the yard uncertainly halted to drink sweetness from Margot's flower-bed under her sleeping-room shutter. An old hen made a dust bed right in the middle of a bed of pinks, and drowsed there with yellow biddies climbing all over her, but nobody much cared except Fairby, who liked to shoo the chickens with her little apron.

Jasper and Jake and Margot went seining when the swamp water warmed up under the April sun. Margot and Jake scared up the fish toward the seine; Margot waded in Lias's old breeches. Jasper ran his hand inside the old stumps to scare out the big fish in hiding. They waded waist-deep; Margot could feel the big cats shoving between her legs, escaping. When they pulled the seine out on the mud, there were more fish in it than an army could eat.

This was the first time ever she had come fishing. She aimed to come again; it was good for anybody to get away from cooking and sewing for a little spell; and Ma could keep Fairby for her any day. . . .

But she didn't go seining again soon, for Lias was the master-mad because she didn't have any more sense than to wade waist-deep in cold water and to come home, dog-wet, in the cold wind. He did give her a talking-to, but she turned her face away to hide the smile at the side of her mouth. You'd think she was made out of sugar, the way Lias went on! Now she could not lift a keg of lard without Lias jumping up like it was a rattlesnake she had ahold of! You'd think this child of his'n was solid gold, or spun glass, or some such thing, the way Lias cared for Margot because of it. He would not even let her milk the cows now, for fear that one might kick her; he did not want her ever out of his sight. When he came in from the fields, if she were not there for him to see, his first words would be: "Where's Margot?" Sometimes she would stay overlong in the loft, o' purpose, seeing after wool or feathers or seasoning that were stored there, just to hear Lias's quarreling that she ought to be about where she belonged. She would hear his words, and her heart would savor them; they were like the taste of new bay-salt to a body starved on fresh food.

She had a hold on Lias now. He quarreled, and hid his tenderness for her in fault-finding, but she was satisfied; she bore her child gaily, as though a song hummed around her heart night and day, like a clock running down in music. She had never heard anything so sweet as Lias's quarreling at her because she would not rest in bed or eat more. Sometimes she would note him watching her as though she were a stranger to him, engrossed in secret, weighty business which he could not understand.

She passed his interest by, high-headed—So you care more about me than you thought you did, eh, my fine mister?

He never told her of his fear—You are too old to have a child; you will die and I will feel the blame for it; being old and strong, you will grow a child so big that you cannot deliver yourself. . . .

The year enlarged; the earth pushed up against its fully nourished fruiting roots; heavy seed-pods filled and, in time, burst. Never had Lias seen his corn so high nor his cotton so rich in squares. He dreaded the day in September when Margot would bear her child, as a good woman bears her children, upon her husband's knees. Fairby, for all the compassion that he felt for her, was only half his child. This child of Margot's would be his very own, born in wedlock to its rightful place as its father's son. Bliss should never have tempted him. A man is hardly to blame when he follows a woman who beckons to him. Lias thought: Sometime I will tell Margot of that time when Bliss came out to the crib looking for me, and of the time when she came down to the creek looking for me. I will not make mention of the time when I first kissed Bliss. Let Jasper tote tales if he will . . . Let him. . . .

Lias was always possessed of dull anger when he thought of how Jasper told Margot about the time when he had first kissed Bliss; he thought, till the day he died, that Margot would never have known of that if Jasper had not told her.

There was but one day between the births of Margot's first child, a son, and Cean's fourth, a daughter.

Seen would have had her hands full if she had tried to do everything that she wanted to do. But, as was her way, Cean fended for herself and sent word to her mother by Lonzo the next day that they were all well and to come when she could. Lonzo told Seen that they had named this last child for its grandmother and its Aint Eliza-beth—Loveda Elizabeth.

Lonzo reached Seen's house before Margot's child was born, and waited down in the cow-lot with Jasper so that he could take Cean word of Margot when he went home. Jake was shucking corn up in the crib, watching after Fairby so that she would not be in the way up at the house, whistling as though nothing was the matter. They could hear the clean thin air of his whistling; it seemed out of place now that the house was so still.

Jasper was the master-worried over this thing. His knife hacked into a top rail of the weatherbeaten fence around the cow-lot; he cut out a chip, split it into little threads of wood, broke them, one by one, in his fingers and tossed them away. He would give his right arm to be sitting yonder somewhere, so that she could call him if she needed him. He would burn in torment for Margot, if she told him to; he loved her nighabout as good as he loved his mother. He and Margot milked the cows morning and evening. Any time he wanted to, he could call to mind the days of winter, the warm breath of the milk that smoked like fog on winter mornings, the hard trampled ground underfoot, the bleak sky—dark in the early day, dark in the early night—the lazy flank of a cow leaning hard on his forehead; and there, where he could see her by turning his head a little sideways, would be Margot, milking a thin stream from a cow's warm fuzzy bag. It was on such a day that she had told him about this child: "I hope ye'll help me raise it, Jasper. I can never depend overmuch on Lias." ... Up at the house she would be quiet-mouthed with them all, patient under Lias's hard words, putting herself at Ma's beck and call, teasing Jake out of his sullen moods. Down here in the cow-pen she would turn her face toward Jasper and tell him this or that thing that was a great matter to her. He would say little to answer her; there was never much to be said.

This labor had got the best of Seen. She was too old to be steady on her feet or clear in her head, much less to help a woman bear a child. She was too old. . . . She shut her eyes to pray about this thing, for she knew no more she could do for Margot, and Lias's face was as white as a sheet and he was crying like a woman. Margot's lips were blue, and her face seemed unknowin' of anything but pain; her eyes were clenched shut in their sockets. So Seen began to pray. . . .

Margot's eyes opened wide. She gasped:

"Oh, Lias . . . take Ma out. . . . I don't need prayin' now. . . . Go get Jasper. . . . Do ye hear me? Go get Jasper!"

Lias went out the back door and whooped Jasper up from where he stood yonder by the cow-pen.

Jasper's face whitened slowly; his hands began to shake. He threw away his whittling and shut up his knife and went toward the house. Jake, shucking corn, shut up his whistling.

When Margot's child had come safely into the world

without any great harm to itself or its mother, their hearts became light as white feathers. The very air had been heavy with fear that Margot might die. It was hard to say who was prouder of this fine child of Lias's—Lias or Jasper. It was a handsome child, strangely like Lias from the day it was born. Straight across its forehead lay the mark of Lias's high forehead; its nostrils spread at the side as Lias's spread, as though he were always looking for trouble; its little finger nails lay clean on the flesh of its fingers, as Lias's did, not buried in at the corners as most nails are. Oh, well did Margot know each finger nail, each pore of flesh by heart; long before this time she had studied out its features; now she could note each resemblance, strong or faint, which this little Lias bore to her Lias. For her this child would always be named Lias. But Lias reared and pitched and said that they might name the child anything, he did not care what, but his own name.

So Margot named the child Vincent, but to her he was always but a little Lias. In truth, she loved him more than she had ever loved Lias, and that was a small miracle alongside the greater miracle of his lying, alive and with no little bone amiss, in her arms.

After dinner, Lias held his son on his knee, sitting near the fire. Margot was asleep; Seen was resting in another room and had Fairby with her. Jasper and Jake were gone to the field. Lonzo was gone off home with word for Cean.

For no reason, the thought came upon Lias, what will Bliss think of this? . . . He remembered—and tried to stop his remembering, and failed—how Bliss had cried herself half to death when Lias had told her long ago that this son of his was on its way to him and Margot. Since Bliss would not turn the fence rail to ask him to come and see her, he went boldly to her house with word of Fairby, and passed secret words with her, and she met him later by the river. . . .

She kissed him hungrily, slipping her lips across his eye-lids that still would tremble, after all this time that he had known her, at the touch of her. When he told her of Margot —only to make her jealous, only to punish her for being so high and mighty toward him—she stopped her kisses; she slapped his face and scratched his cheeks and bit his wrists for anger. Lias tried in vain to comfort her, but Bliss struck his mouth away from her mouth, and cried into his hair, and scratched red streaks across his face and hands. She cried and quarreled and beat him in the face, but ever his hard hands kept their hold on her waist. She talked many a hard word, but ever, through all her meaningless words, his mouth waited for her to hush her wild talk, waited to meet her mouth and bind her lips shut.

A squirrel chattered . . . chattered . . . chattered. A blue jay sharply questioned his mate; she answered him quietly, as though she said: It is no great matter; they are only little people in whom you and I have no concern. . . .

Lias knew that he should not be remembering Bliss at such a time as this, with his first honest child in his arms and Margot lying there worn out with pain. . . .

But, Lord! how could he put Bliss out of his mind? She was forever there in his thoughts, light as a cork that will not stay under water unless you hold it there.

The baby throve, and why shouldn't it? Margot had no time for anything but that baby. Lias was the put-out be-cause Margot never waited on him any more, never jumped when he spoke, never asked him if there was anything she could do for him. Anyhow, there wasn't anything she could do for him, because she was always doing for the baby. He could not stir her out of her stillness; he would call it still-ness; he knew no better word. She was changed, and she could not change her back to what she had been. She hardly noticed him now that the baby was forever in her arms.

When little Vince was a month old it was high time to lay him down and let him squall if he would. But, no! Margot lugged him with her everywhere, and could not bear for him to wail once. If he but opened his mouth to cry, she would shut it with a kiss of her mouth or milk of her breast. She did not even notice that Lias was glooming and sulling. . . .

When little Vince was little more than a month old, Lias thought that he would show Margot a thing or two. He caught her by herself, and made as though he was going somewhere in a hurry, and said:

"If ye need me, I'll be at Old Man Corwin's. . . ."

He thought she might cry, maybe, or quarrel at him. But her hands only stilled for a minute, then went on patting the baby's back as he lay on her shoulder. She said, slowly:

"You, Lias. . . ."

She spoke to him as though she were a thousand years old and he were only a child, as though she said: There are many things that I would say to you if you were able to understand them.

Her hands went on beating gently on the back of the baby, uneasy over a pain in its little gut.

He had not aimed to see Bliss; he had only aimed to torment Margot. Now he had to go to see Bliss, to make Margot see that he was a man of his word.

Lias went back to his old sulling way. Margot would not let that child rest in its cradle where it belonged. She had to sleep with it in her arms, betwixt her and Lias.

So Lias didn't do a thing but move to the loft, and sleep there with Jasper and Jake. Enough of anything is enough. . . .

Jasper and Jake worked the crops at Pa's place. Lias helped them out when he had to, but Jasper mostly let him be.

Margot's Vince was nigh onto half a year old when it came about that Jasper nigh murdered Lias.

It all so disturbed Margot that Vince vomited back her milk and was sick for a week. It all came about because Jasper for once lost his reason, and told his mother, who was foolish in her mind, a thing that lay deep in his mind.

It happened in the winter-time when cold days come and there is little work to do but the feeding of stock or some such matter. A man's hands are apt to be empty at such a time, and his mind full of this or that heavy matter—last year's loss or next year's gain, or a thing that he has done, or a thing that he desires to do.

With Jasper it was a thing that he desired to do. He had weighed this matter in his mind, and now it would seem a light and easy matter, and then it would seem a heavy, dangerous thing; now he thought it was his bounden duty, next he knew that it was his liking for Margot that ate like a canker inside him.

Ma had second sight; she would know what was the wise thing to do. He would propound this matter to Ma. . . . But he would hide himself, and these others, inside a wild story, and so he would receive Ma's second wisdom without her knowing that she gave it. He and his Ma were, and had ever been, close to one another; he could tell her nigh-about anything. . . . But he would come up on her blind side with this matter. . . .

Nowadays she had a way of sitting lonesomely by the fire in her room, knitting their stockings with never a dropped stitch, turning the heels as smoothly as when she had good eyesight. She had knitted little cream-colored half-mittens for all of Cean's girl-children, and some for Fairby, too. When she pulled the little mittens on Fairby's hands, Fairby laughed and said:

"I spec' ye lef' the fingers out so's ye could al'ays tell if my hands be's washed, didn't ye, Granny?" Seen thought that was a master-smart thing for Fairby to think up!

Jasper sat close to Ma's knees on this side of the closed door. Out yonder Margot was cooking dinner with Vincent in her arms. Lias was sewing boots for himself in the thin sunshine on the back door-step. Jake was gone gallivantin' off to a neighbor's. Fairby was at her Aint Cean's, where she stayed any time she got the chance.

Jasper rubbed his hands together, then let them swing between his knees. He studied the slow-burning fire; he set his glance yonder within a bright cave of coals; the cave was dusted over with fine white ashes, like frost on rosy persimmons.

Jasper could put this thing into few words; he had figured it all out in his mind many times:

"Ma, I hyeard a funny thing the other day. . . ."

The click of her knitting-needles beat softly between her hands, regular as clock-ticks, busy as breathing. Inside the rosy cave yonder, heat, quivering and flame-colored, stirred not at all, but Jasper knew that it was strong enough to melt a metal hard and cold as iron.

"Somebody was a-tellin' me . . . I cain't reckolict jest who . . . that they's a man acrost the river. . . ."

Jasper went on easily: the man was unfaithful to his wife, and was taken up with another woman, and could not love his wife for that other woman; the man had a brother who would, for the saying of the words, marry his brother's wife and leave his brother free to marry the neighbor woman. . . . And a likely arrangement it would be, in Jasper's opinion, if the man would but put his wife away and marry the woman he was running after. . . .

Seen's eyes squinted always; upon her bony brow there was drawn a lasting frown of sorrow. Softly she chucked her tongue between her teeth:

"Tsck-tsck! Devil's doin's. . . ."

She had not waited for him to ask for her second sight upon this matter; a man does not put his lawful wife away for any cause save one that is justified by Holy Writ.

Jasper was taken back; he could not for the life of him know whether she understood the thing in his heart, or not. He was sorry he had made mention of it to her.

All day long the thought oppressed him—I might have kept that matter to myself. . . .

When Ma blabbed it all out, Jasper was not surprised. It was near supper-time when she called Lias into her room. Jasper was beside the fire in the big room, sharpening the blade of his knife on a little whetstone. His heart quaked when he heard his mother call Lias. He spat again on the little whetrock and rubbed his knife-blade around and around in the spittle. The palms of his hands were suddenly moist. He could hear his mother's voice past the closed door, but he could not make out her words.

Then Lias jerked open Ma's door and called Jasper. Jasper laid down his knife and whetrock and went into Ma's room. Margot had not noticed, since her ears were filled with the sound of frying spare-ribs on the hearth. Vince lay on a pallet in reach of her hand; he knocked Fairby's blue beads on a crock and laughed to hear the noise.

Jasper went into his mother's room and closed the door softly. Lias was leaning a little forward on the hearth, with his hands behind him. Between his long, stilted legs, Jasper could see fiery tunnels in the coals, towers of flame, and ashes that were furry-white like frost.

Jasper went up to the fireplace, not daring to look into Lias's face that was green with anger. Lias said:

"So now ye're totin' tales t' Ma!"

Jasper stumbled a little over his words:

"No, I don't know as I am. What are ye a-talkin' about?"

"Ma says that ye be willin' to marry Margot if I will but put her away."

[ 185 ]

Jasper looked at his Ma; she was holding her knitting close against her breast. Her voice trembled:

"No, Lias. I said that hit mought be a likely thing to do. . . . If ye cannot give Bliss up, then set things right and marry her. . . . I said that if ye did put Margot away, she need not lack, since Jasper could make enough for us all to eat. . . ."

Jasper could think of nothing to say; anything he might say would be the wrong thing. Best keep quiet.

Lias's whole body strained toward Jasper through his clenched fists.

"I reckon hit's about time I learned ye how to tend t' ye own business!"

That angered Jasper; he flared back:

"I reckon hit'll take somebody else besides you to learn me anything!"

Lias knocked Jasper down in his tracks, and Seen rose out of her chair, screeching.

Jasper clambered to his feet; his head was singing. Lias swung before his eyes. He struck Lias and reeled him back against the mantelpiece, and Lias's head hit the corner of the mantelpiece. Blood wet the back of Lias's head and matted his hair.

Lias jumped onto Jasper as a painter lights down on a deer; he clung to him in a passion of murderous desire and wrenched his head around as though he would wring it off. Seen cowered in a corner, crying piteously. Margot came, wild-eyed, to the door and stood there shivering and fear-struck, saying not a word.

The two men were equals; neither could best the other, for they were nearly of a size, nearly of a weight. They fell to the floor boards, heavy as a shot steer; they rolled about, wresting their weight each from the other, giving their weight one hard upon the other. Their brother-faces, hideous with hate, clung passionately together. Their mouths

[ 186 ]

grimaced in their beards, their eyes showed murder, their hands fumbled upon the straining mass of their bodies. Lias was speaking such words to Jasper as Seen quaked to hear; he was accusing Jasper of deeds for which men kill other men when they know of them. If Jasper could have got his hands to Lias's throat, he would have choked him to death, but he could not get them there. Lias's length and weight and striving were in the way. But the words danced in Jasper's mind, and in Margot's, and in Seen's—filthy, bestial words whose meanings are veiled in shame so that a woman will hardly admit that she ever heard such words before.

They fought like dogs, each close upon the other's throat, and snarling like brutes. Blood from Lias's head smeared over Jasper's hands, ran in slow streams and was slimy on his face.

Seen came weakly into the middle of the room and fell in a swound on the floor, first time ever in her life she had swounded.

Jasper and Lias got up from the floor, feeling ashamed of themselves, fearing that they had killed their old mother. Margot went for cold water to bring Seen to, making as though she had not seen the fight.

Jasper lifted his Ma over to her bed, and Lias felt for her heartbeat through her dress. Jasper saw his Ma's eyelids shake on her cheek, and knew suddenly that she was 'possuming. . . . But he said nothing. Brothers can find better work to do than drawing blood, one from the other. He had drawn blood from Lias's head; mayhap he had cracked his skull. The brain's a tender thing. . . . He said:

"Go let Margot wash off yore head, Lias. They's blood all over ye. I'll see t' Ma. . . ."

Lias went out the door, slinging his hair back with a thrust of his hand.

Seen opened her eyes, and her face gave up slow tears of old age.

"Oh, Jasper," she said, "I didn't mean no harm, son. . . ."

He rubbed her hand a little, as though it was Fairby's.

"Hit's all right, Ma. No harm done. I was all to blame."

No harm was done. You cannot live in the same house with a man and be brother to him and hate him. Jasper did not hate Lias, and he knew that Lias did not hate him.

Anyhow, when you have done an evil thing, the only thing you can do is bury it and let it rot away like carrion in the earth.

# Chapter 14

CEAN was as good as another man in the field with Lonzo. And it was a good thing, too, for it looked like she would have nothing but gals for him. Her last, born in June, was another little slender-faced gal that they had named Caty Lucretia. Lonzo didn't have much to say, but Cean reckoned he did wish she would have a boy or two, along and along.

Caty, born nearly two years after Lovedy, was now three months old. Cean was skinny as a fence rail, but she could keep up with Lonzo in the field, except for a few times when she would give plum out and have to go to the house and lie down.

Lonzo didn't make her work in the field, like some men made their womenfolks. She liked it. The house was a noisy place that seemed to close in on her. Out in the field the quiet did her good and stopped her mind from straining after what it couldn't have—things too plum fool to name, such as fine clothes and niggers to wait on her. Lord! what wouldn't she give for some niggers now! You could buy them at the Coast, but a strong, young buck would cost more than Lonzo would ever have to trade off, and a wench came nearly as high as a buck. Sometime maybe there'd come an extry good year with the rains right and trading good, and then Lonzo could get a nigger. . . . No! There'd be a house to build for the black to live in and he'd have to be fed, besides. And one nigger wouldn't do a dab of good; it would take enough to fill long rows of whitewashed quarters, like the Coast planters had. They bought wenches and bucks and mated them, and let them breed, and in a few years there were crops of fine, fat blacks to pick cotton and grind cane and shuck corn and plow; or the owners could sell them off around the country for a profit. Oh, Cean knew there was no chance of that for her. She could work her fingers to the bone in the field beside Lonzo and she'd never live like the Coast ladies; they were diked out in silk cloth and breastpins; they could have a black lashed twenty-five times because maybe he didn't bend low enough when they passed by in shining carioles. Those women toted a big iron ring heavy with keys to open the doors of full smokehouses here and yonder on the plantation; or rooms weighted down with big sea-chests full of pyore silver and stacks of boughten bed sheets made of linen from Ireland, or underground stores of rum and sweet wine from Spanish places, dried nuts or spice from Indy, and strange seasonings that come in frigates from 'way yonder crost the Chiny Sea. The big black cooks stir up cakes of sugar and spice for the little Coast children that are dressed in thin, white frocks and shiny shoes that their pas buy offen a ship instead of making them on an old rusty last from under the back side of the bed, as Lonzo must do.

August heat bathed Cean's body as she gathered in the cotton to make warm clothing and thick covering for her children. An old bonnet hung limp on her head, the tail of it drooping about her thin neck. Her lean shoulders were bent, causing her to seem less tall and not nearly so handsome as she had been eight years ago when she married Lonzo Smith. When she was a little thing her mother made her hold her shoulders straight. Now if some one had told her to hold back her shoulders, she might have straightened them for a little moment, but then she would have sighed and straightway her shoulders would have drooped again; for they were so tired; five times they had stooped, long and patiently, to carry a child; and many thousand times they had curved inward to rock one of those children to

[ 190 ]

sleep. A million bolls of cotton her fingers had plucked, and a million rattling blades of corn her hands had sheaved. Great mounds of potatoes she had grabbled out of the earth, a little field of watermelons she had lugged home in her apron to give her children pleasure. No, she was tired, her body was no longer unyielding and valiant, eager for what lay before it. Once she had held her head as high as Lias's, and her shoulders as straight—but not now.

But however high Lias held his head, he was oftener drunk than sober now, and Bliss cried for him now as much as Margot ever had, for it was a woman at the Coast now. Three trips Lias made in one year just to see that woman. Never had any of them ever heard tell of the like! It must be like Ma said—a man that will not cleave to one woman will not cleave to any other one.

Cean liked to work out in the field, for here she could think, while at the house the air was a babbling of children's voices. Lias's child, Fairby, came often to her Aunt Cean's house to stay, and she was welcome, too. Fairby was never ready to go home, and Cean could not much blame her, for Ma's house must be a dismal place with Ma half crazy, Lonzo said, and babbling out to Pa everything that went wrong. Like as though Pa could do anything about it now! Oh, Ma was so pitiful now that Cean could hardly bear to see her, nor to hear Lonzo bring word of how she had said, "Tell Cean her Pa says everything will be all right." Things were not as they used to be. Ma sat in a chair now and knitted. Margot ran things, and it was a God's mercy they had Margot to depend on. Even Margot was changed so that nobody would ever know that this was Lias's fine wife that he had brought home with him from the Coast; her hair was streaked all through with white, and she didn't seem to mind. Once last year she had minded; Lias had found her combing sage-tea through her hair to bring the color back, and he had picked up the little pipkin that held the tea and threw it aside, and it hit her in the face and knocked out one of her fine white front teeth and left a thin red scar across her chin till now. Margot was plain as any backwoods woman now with her snaggled tooth and her streaked hair and sunburnt, pied-ed cheeks, liver-spotted like any other woman's.

She was little older than Cean—born in 'seventeen she said, 44 take away 17 eq'als 27. Margot was seven-and-twenty, then. Cean was six-and-twenty.

Jasper and Jake worked the crops over at Pa's place. Jasper was away past being a full-grown man now, but there was no sign of him a-courtin' or a-wantin' a wife. True, last year he had told Ma to get the elder to let Lias put Margot away, and he would marry her—or some such words as that. But Ma had blabbed the whole thing out, without a thought of being secret about it so that Jasper could work things out underhand-like, for the good of everybody. Margot told Cean that Jasper and Lias fought like dogs. You'd 'a' thought that Lias had loved Margot all along, the way he was insulted when Jasper went about to fix the mess up, aiming to take Margot for his and let Lias take Bliss and live with her as a decent man should.

Yonder at the house Maggie would keep the fire going under the pot and would bake the hoecake and fry the meat when it was dinner-time. Sometimes Cean was glad that four of her five were girls, for girls can cook and sweep and rest their mas' backs from aching. Men always want boy-babies, but sometimes Cean was glad that she had aplenty of girls. But girls could not help make rations as boys could. Maggie and Kissie could look after Cal and Lovedy and Caty, and have dinner done when Lonzo and Cean went up to the house at noon, but Lonzo still had to do all the plowing unless Cean holped him. And that was a pity, for he had plowed since he could reach the cross-bar of the plow. Time he was a-restin' a little. He'd be ready for a little help by the time Cal was big enough to learn to lay off a row straight as a crow flight across a field.

At the thought of Cal's learning to plow, Cean's heart weakened a little. He was so little, just three this year. Before she could catch her breath, he'd be out yonder in the bleaking sun a-geeing and a-hawing, a half-grown boy. Hadn't she seen Maggie shoot up like a dog-fennel in wet weather? Before Cean could turn around, her baby was keeping house for her, and minding the other babies out of the fire. Oh, time goes in a hurry. She must learn Maggie and Kissie their letters before they were so big that they'd be ashamed to learn from their Ma. Pa had learned her. . . . A is for apple. . . . Still, Cean could hear Pa tell what an apple looked like, round, red, shiny, sweet. You could grow apples up in the Carolina hills. Never had Cean tasted an apple. Fruit trees wouldn't grow down here. She had a clear-seed peach tree, a seedling from her Ma's tree, but nearabout ever peach would be as wormy as the wild plums in the woods. A is for apple. . . . Cean always liked the lessons Pa made up better than the ones he got out of the books, such as

> In Adam's fall
> We sinned all.
>      or
> The cat dothe play
> And after slay.
>      or
> Xerxes did die
> And so must I.

"A is for apple" was better—a ripe apple that will fall. Once Pa had told her how he had shaken down ripe apples into Ma's lap one time. They were not near grown-up then; one apple, falling, had struck Ma on her forehead and raised a knot nearly as big as her fist. Pa always laughed there and said, truth to tell, her fist weren't very big then. That was the first time ever Pa kissed Ma, when the apple hit her on her head and raised a whelp for him to kiss. A is for apple. B is for ball. . . . The world is a ball. . . . But never would Cean believe that fool thing as long as these flat woods stretched yonder straight and flat as leather-bread, through the pine boles. . . . C is for cat. . . .

The children had their mother's chairs turned down, making them serve as wagons on their journey to the Coast in Cean's house that was filled now with persuading magic. Lines were passed around the knobs and came back to the hands of the children, who sat on the back rungs of the chairs, riding in majesty to the Coast. It was two more months before their father would go to the Coast; and five of them were girl-children and so would never smell a Coast journey. But now they journeyed to the Coast, shrieking at the passage of fords where their ragdolls were prone to fall into perilous deep water; the hounds, lying stretched on the floor in Cean's absence, waked and howled as the children's shrieks and cries mounted. Painters! Tigers! Rattlesnakes! . . . and worse, perhaps, a Raw-head-and-bloody-bones to ha'nt the trail and scare their livers out of them!

Kissie and Lovedy rode in one cart, for Lovedy was not quite big enough to sit safely on the rungs of a chair alone. Maggie carried the baby, Caty, in her arms. She was ever having to say, "Wait! I ain't a-playin' now. . . ." She would dismount, and go across what was a raging river out of its banks, or a swamp trail infested with all manner of terrors, and poke up the fire under the dinner, or stir the pots with a ladle half as long as herself. Cal had a cart to himself, being fully a man. Fairby rode to herself, too, for nothing ailed her at all save her poor stumped feet; she banged them against the hide bottom of the chair that was a horse's hard, smooth belly. Never had they seen a horse, but they had heard tell that there were horses at the Coast for fine, rich bullies to ride on, and Fairby chose to ride ahorseback, since one could ride any way at all for the wishing.

Fairby made more noise than all the others. Cal tried to hush her big mouth, for her horse's prancing in its gold fixings was like to scare his oxen.

So they went the long way to the Coast. They left this wild Indian bank of the Alatamaha, crossed over at Stafford's Ferry, and took a safe trail down the White Man's Bank across hot sand, alongside the Alatamaha, down far slopes of the curious, bewitching Coast country of MacIntosh County; out past MacIntosh County the water of the strange thing called the ocean rips and fulges like suds a-b'ilin', all the way out to, and beyond, the Middle Passage that is beautiful with terror. Uncle Jake had told them so.

They would bring back many wondrous things.

Maggie would fetch back a monkey like Aint Margot told about, for little Caty, to hush her crying so much. She kissed her little sister on the top of her fuzzy brown head where hair the color of Uncle Lias's was beginning to grow.

Fairby would bring a cartload of breastpins and finger-rings to dress in.

Here Kissie spoke up sharply, as matter-of-fact as her grandmother Seen Carver:

"I thought ye was a-ridin' a horse, s' fine."

Contempt was strong in her words.

Fairby's fine manner was dashed by those chill words of truth, but not for long. In a trice, like the sight of a shoot-ing-star, like the passage of the wind, her horse was changed to a cart behind an ox, but larger by far than the small puny carts of the other children—large aplenty for all the gold of the Coast.

Cal studied when it came his time to declare his lading of fantasy.

Then out of a sturdiness that came from the heavy set of Lonzo's shoulders and the still strength of Cean's face that hated weeping, he said:

"I'll fotch back a hundred niggers fer Ma to beat on."

And all the others were cast down; his man's wit had outdone them all.

August sunshine beat iron-hot on Cean's bent shoulders. She would need more quilts; the feel of the cotton in her fingers reminded her of it. This fall she must learn Maggie and Kissie to spin; they were not a mite too young. With seven mouths to keep filled, everybody must help. Five little mouths—and how many more? She sighed because there could never be any fine, lazy ways for any of her girl-children. They would have to work. She must learn Maggie and Kissie their letters. Cal and Lovedy could wait yet awhile. Caty, bless its bones, was not yet big enough to know nothin'—nothin' but how to suck its mammy's milk. Hit were an angel-child, and hit's mammy loved hit nigh onto death.

She'd quit at the end of this row and go up to the house to see after the children. She couldn't be easy in her mind to stay long away from them. And the baby mought be a-hungry.

Lonzo was ever shy of his children.

He answered their questions short and quick, abashed at his strong feeling for them. Once Kissie, sharp-witted as she was, stood shyly at his knee and asked him:

"Pa, Ma told us they was peacocks and parrot-birds at the Coast. They hain't, air they?"

He answered that in short order:

"They air, if yore Ma says they air. But I hain't never seen none."

Cean turned her face away when she heard his answer. No! . . . Lonzo wouldn't see peacocks if they were to strut in gold and silver feathers before him, nor yet parrot-birds if they had ruby claws and beaks! He couldn't see nothing but corn on a stalk, or cotton in a row, or a hog fitten for nothin' but butchering. Then she felt ashamed of herself. Pore old Lonzo! working till his tongue hung out to feed her and her'n.

Lonzo sometimes wondered meekly why Cean should not be like Margot; Margot seemed to be barren save for a son. His own mother had only three children; Seen Carver had only four living. No use to count the dead. They do not eat, nor disturb sleep. How many times, when he was tired enough to die, had Cean waked him in the night by stirring up the fire to warm a little youngun's feet, or to change its wet clothes, or to rock it on her shoulder to get the colicky pains out of its stomach!

But Cean was a good wife. His mother, Dicie Smith, had only kind words for his wife, and a mother-in-law's praise says more in a woman's favor than anything else in the world.

Dicie and Rowan were left alone now, for Epsie and Ossie had married off and had households of their own. The old Smith place was not what it used to be; the fields had shrunk back toward the house since Lonzo was not there to plant them. Rowan had let the hired boy go back across the river where he belonged, for the old couple did not need much. Lonzo did his father's trading for him now; for none but strong men can sleep out nights on the way to the Coast and back, and Rowan no longer claimed to be strong. Milk and butter, a little syrup and a garden patch will suffice two old folks who are never very hungry any more. And Lonzo traded his Pa's honey and hides when Rowan had them to trade.

Lonzo worried over his pa and ma; they ought not to be

away off yonder ever so far from nowhere. Pa had lain a week sick of hard ague last year before Lonzo happened over there; and there was nobody but Ma to tend him and tote slops to the pigs and do all the work all that time. He wished that he and Cean lived nearer by, but a man can't build a new house as a bird builds a nest. Ma and Pa wouldn't live always; mought as well show some favors while the two old folks were alive. Pa was sixty; that was plenty old for a man to move in close to somebody that could listen out for a call in a cold night. Old folks drop off, dead as a wedge, sometimes. Pretty sight that would be, for Ma to wake up some morning and find Pa cold under the cover by her, staring up into the ceiling with the dead whites of his eyes shining like new money.

Oh, many times Lonzo was worried up with such thoughts. Like as though he didn't have enough to worry over with Cean here, a baby in her arms, a little un in the cradle by the bed in reach of her hand, and three more older uns in a bed together in the loft! This was a purty pore arrangement where a man had to worry over two families.

Yet Lonzo could laugh sometimes like a bull a-bellerin'. Cean did love to hear him laugh. Sometimes men would drop by from here or yonder and stand till the sun was low, one brogan wedged in a fence crack, squirting tobacco juice to drench one certain weed's stalk, swapping accounts, telling news of this or the other settlement. One joke she heard—a joke that Lonzo laughed over for a long time afterward—it took Cean the longest time to figure out. It was a tale about katydids. One night Bub Allnoch was listening to some neighbor gals that were a-singing inside his house; his brother, Zeb Allnoch, on the porch with him, was a-listening to katydids a-singing out past the house. Bub said, "Weren't that purty?" Zeb, thinking that Bub meant the katydids, answered, "Yeah. They make that noise by rubbin' their hind legs together." The men roared at that joke, and slapped their thighs, and hawked and spat, and roared again, each taking on new merriment at the sight of other laughing faces. Cean finally pondered that joke out, and she thought it a vulgar, brazen thing to joke about women's legs. Lonzo would raise Cain if she were to tell a joke like that.

Lonzo was of the opinion that the way to take whatever came was like the cat et the grubbin'-hoe. There weren't no other way. If Cean had forty-'leven younguns, and they turned out to be all gals, there weren't nothing to do about it. If the crops failed, or ran the cribs over, there was nothing to do about it but do his hard-down best through it all, and leave things be. Some gaumed up their whole lives by a-hasteing in this or that thing, taking out their impatience on this or the other body. No, Lonzo would never blame Cean if she had a hundred for him to feed. He'd make her something for her house this winter, when the long, cold days would hang heavy on his hands—a new-made bed, maybe, with a fine criss-cross bottom of new rope for the mattress to rest on. He would carve out the headboard and footboard like those of a bed that a journeyman wood-worker had made for Ma. Cean should have as fine a bed as any woman hereabouts, for God knew she was as fine a wife as they was. . . . And the years would bobble along, bobble along . . . and they would be old and well-off, with their sons and daughters married off through these pinywoods. Dang his lights, but Cean would people these backwoods in no time at all! He laughed a little to himself, but there was pity in his laughter. Cean had been a sweet little thing when he married her; reckon she didn't expect all this hard work and all this great passel of younguns when she came here with him. Never would he forget the words she had spoken to him when he had told her, long ago, that Lias had brought a fine Coast wife home with him. Cean had said, "Wonder if she'd adone hit if she'd a-knowed how hit feels t' tote a youngun every step y' take. . . ." It was pitiful, sort o', to Lonzo to remember that, for that had been when she was going with her first one, and there had been four since then, as heavy and as cumbersome. No, Cean would hardly have stepped off with him if she had known then all that she knew now. Through long, pleasant ways of thought his mind traversed old years. For no reason at all, his thoughts clung to a day when he was eight or ten years old; somehow now that day was related to his thought of Cean. Ossie and Epsie were older than himself by several years. The three children were sitting on the floor close by the back door. A heavy summer rain was falling on the earth outside, and splattered inside the door from the doorstep. Cool spray sprinkled their faces. They were chanting an old, silly child's verse:

> Rain, rain, go away:
> Come again another day;
> Lit-tul Lonzo wants to play!

He was the baby, so the last line always held his name to please him.

The rain plunged from off the eaves and splattered high on the hard ground; the million drops crashed to the earth and were shattered into white mist low on the ground. Wind swept the yard in gusts; the high, thin chant of the children's voices went out upon the wind and was lost. Behind them in the room their mother turned a hoecake on the fireplace; far through the blowing rain they could see their father in the crib door, waiting for the rain to slack up so that he could run across the steaming, puddled yard to eat dinner.

The little verse stuck in Lonzo's mind now. The children up at the house sang it every now and then. Lovedy's name, or Caty's or Cal's would come in the last line to please the baby to a shy smile, if they sang it now as they used to do when he was a boy. . . . A-ah, law! That was a time gone.

He raised his head from the cotton stalks and wiped away the sweat from his face. Yonder was Cean, plugging away, her sack as heavy as his own. She was one wife that earned her keep! He would put her a lane of pink crêpe myrtle down the slope in front of the house. She would like that. He could nighabout see her driving home from her ma's some day, years from now, with the pink blossoms a-fluttering down on her and her cartload of younguns. First thing anybody knew, she'd be a-having twin boys for him! Then everybody would sit up and take notice. Boys choose a strong-minded woman for their mother, and Cean was having all girls. Truth to tell, he would not like her to be strong-minded like some women that had to rule the roost. He'd wear the breeches at his house! He eased his hand down across his back where a pain kept gnawing into his kidney. Then he stooped again and went on picking cotton.

# Chapter 15

WITHIN little more time than a year Cean was in bed, and flat on her back, too, with another child that they named Wealthy Tennessee, not because anybody cared what its name was, but because Margot thought that would be a likely name. Lonzo had to go for Margot before this child was born, for Cean gave plum out, the only time he ever knew her to do that except with her first one. Margot left Seen Carver babbling that Pa said that Cean was going to be all right, and came to Cean and helped her to give up her child.

Cean was the master-weak now. Lonzo knew it wasn't put on, for Cean would go as long as she could put one foot 'fore another. Margot stayed on for a few days, toting her son about on her hip half the time, for, being the only child of his mother, he was mighty spoiled. He was a big, fat-cheeked boy with shiny blue eyes like Lias's, with a primped-up mouth like Lias's, with a biggity, bossy way like Lias's. Margot was always saying, where Lias couldn't hear her, that Vince was even spoiled to death like Lias!

Cean's children were sprangling out now; the biggest of them could pick cotton and dig potatoes; they roamed through the fields like so many happy pigs rooting chufas, while Cean lay in bed with her youngest. To save her life, she could not get her strength back. When the baby was three days old she had tried to walk from the bed to the fireplace, and fell flat on the floor in a swound; never did ⟨...⟩ ⟨...⟩ ⟨...⟩ 'till Lonzo dashed a piggin of water in her ⟨...⟩ng her. Never had she been this sorry and ⟨...⟩ brewed her a crock of physic that never ⟨...⟩kness—three gills of bamboo-brier root, one gill of dogwood bark, two gills of cherry-tree bark, thirty-six roots of star grass, sixteen roots of buttonsnake, two gills of red-oak bark, the same of sassafras root, two jugs of water boiled down to one, two gills of rum, the same of syrup; let the mixture stand one day and night. Cean took a doset morning, noon, and night; if it did her one grain of good, she could not tell it.

She lay huddled in the pillows, wishing for her ma, who was too feeble to come, and too witless to remember any treatment if she did come.

Margot made the children go and play in the shade around the wash-trough by the spring so that their noise and rambunctious play would not be a worriation to Cean. She had brought Fairby along with her, and with Vincent and Cean's five that were big enough to run and scream bloody murder and bounce across the floor, they could make a heap of noise. The children were as well satisfied away from the house, anyhow. They were playing under the swamp maples that leaned over the wash-trough; the leaves were touched a little, for it was the middle of October. But the weather was warm as summer-time. The children were playing school, and it was a school like they had in the Coast country, too, as fine as any that a Yankee school-mistress might set up in any white house on the Ridge at Dari-an. Maggie, being the eldest, was the swallow-tailed tutor from up North who lived in the Big House, paid guest of the rich planter, deigning to teach the little planters their letters.

Maggie was tall and skinny, and wiser than her nighonto nine years would warrant, had they not been overly full of responsibility and knowledge of grown folks' ways. Hadn't she stayed with her mother all the time while her father was gone for Aint Margot, while this last youngun was a-comin'? Hadn't her mother told her all about it, and what to do if she should get too sick to be in her right mind?

The other children sat on the ground before Maggie, each in a rough square drawn on the earth about his bottom that did not know but that the hard, warm earth was a boughten school-seat from Angland. Margot's Vincent, three years old, wore fine, sewn linsey breeches, but the other two younger children, Lovedy and Caty, wore nothing between the smooth, unblemished skin of their soft little bottoms and the tolerant earth. For Mammy was sick, and Maggie was plum tired of changing their didies. Hit weren't no use, time she got one dry, t'other un was wet. Anyway, it saved washing. And Aint Margot wouldn't tell Ma, and Ma would not notice, lying yonder in bed with a new baby.

Maggie minded the children out of fire and water and such dangers the best way she could. Her face was still the nighlike Lonzo's, with beady black eyes and straight black hair that was parted in the middle and hung down her back in a plait to her waist. The plait was blowsy now, for nobody had combed it in three days, and she could not manage it in the back, because the plait started at the back of her head wrong-side to her fingers. She combed the hair of the other children when they got up in the mornings, but her own would have to go till Ma was well. She had a big, quiet mouth like Lonzo's; she didn't screech and make up loud songs as little Fairby did, but she would slap one of the little ones down for taking another's play-pretty or saying a bad word. She was like Lonzo in that, too; they never ran over Maggie; she would pretty quick put them in their place.

Kissie quarreled with Maggie more than any of the others. She had yellow hair that curled and blowsed over her head; her mother let it fall loose about her neck because she liked it so. She would toss her head when Cal called her

Miss Blowsey-head. Didn't Coast ladies crimp and tangle their locks?

Cal was four and a worriation to them all if they would not let him lead every marching of the Redcoats, every war on the Indians, every storming of a Spanish fort in Fluridy. He was nighabout as old as Kissie, he thought, and forty-'leven years older than Lovedy, who was only three—and he was his pa's only boy. Oh, he could look down on them all when Pa took him up on his knees and told him how to catch a rattlesnake with a fork-ed stick and sling it by the tail and pop its head off. Ma said that Pa loved him the best of all of them, but Pa always denied it. Cal looked more like Cean now; his eyes were mild and brown, not beady-black like Lonzo's; his forehead had Cean's own little inquiring frown stamped upon it.

Lovedy was a fat-legged, mischievous little trick, staggering and chattering and pointing. Now she sat on the ground with her pudgy legs outspread, with her frank, undisciplined little bottom flat on the warm old earth.

Fairby, five years old, was not yet old enough to care whether her feet were straight or crooked, and played as happily as any perfect-limbed child.

Maggie was telling the story about A for apple. Apples were bright, shiny, red things sweeter than persimmons after frost; apples were fruit that you could gather in your apron if somebody would climb up and shake the tree. Cal interrupted, butting in to be first in everything, as he always was:

"I'm agonna be the one to shake the tree! I said it first!"

Up at the house, Margot tried to soothe Cean's baby with a little tit of sugar tied into a clean rag. She gave it warm catnip tea till its stomach stuck out, but still it cried, expending its little anguish on each short-drawn breath.

Cean was crying, too, with her face turned away to the wall. Margot would have taken the baby out so that its crying would not worry its mother, but it was just eight days old. Truth, it was fine October weather, warm as June, but she didn't want the little thing to catch cold and die on her hands.

Cean asked for the baby so that she could feed it and hush its crying for a little while. Feeding the child would cause her pangs nigh onto as bad as the pain of bearing it. Always her breasts had given her trouble, grease and poultice them howsomever she might. Now they were hard as rocks, and fevered; sharp pains darted down the blue, distended milk veins that spread from the white pit of her breast-bone like a curious blue vein growing inside her body.

She set her teeth and gripped her hands and suckled the child. Get it full and maybe it would sleep. Sweat gathered on her temples, and Margot wiped it off with a wet rag wrung out of witch-hazel water.

Lonzo was gone to the Coast with as fine a cyart-load of cyored t'baccer and cyarded cotton, pressed bees-wax, tallow candles, bearhides, and hen eggs as ever you seed in yore life. . . .

Jasper kept house for his ma while Jake and Lias were gone to the Coast, and Margot was yonder, taking care of Cean. He liked being here with just Ma. She was a pitiful, puny thing now. Every night he had to rub her with witch-hazel ointment to keep the bed sores from eating her up alive. Margot did the rubbing when she was here; but Jasper didn't mind doing it for his ma. Hadn't she done enough for him?

He slept in the room with Ma now, for somebody had to. She would get up if she weren't noticed, and bumble around and hurt herself. In the night he would have to keep saying:

"Lie still, Ma. They hain't nothin' the matter. Go to sleep."

But she wouldn't sleep. She'd lie and talk half the night, till sometimes in the dark the hair would rise on Jasper's head—and he was a grown man not a-feared of most things. It was the way she would talk:

"Set there in that chair by Jasper's bed, Vince. My back's a-painin' me so's I caint think. . . . No, don't bother Jasper. He's got to work tomorrow. Anything ye want him to know, tell me, and I'll tell him." She would talk on until Jasper could swear that his father sat there, silent, within reach of his hand, wishing to speak with him.

It was a horrible fancy, for Jasper could not see his father now save with the stamp of death set hard on his face, with sickly glaze filling the eyes that had once looked on him familiarly. In the chair—if it were there, and Ma had second sight now that she was old and sickly—that figure stank of grave-horror, frightened him with mystery too deep and solemn to think on. He wished his mother could get her sense back; many times in the night he would get up with his legs quaking under him, and light candles all about the room and sit up with her till day came straggling in through thin chinks in the wall. Ma was a trial now to him and Margot; her joints drew with rheumatism; her knees and ankles were swollen into big knots for Jasper and Margot to rub and poultice, turn by turn. Jasper had to bear her about in his arms wherever she would go, like she had been a baby. But hadn't she born him amany and amany a time? He reckoned so.

Always Seen would have family prayer night and morning, if there was a hayfield nigh onto being soaked by a rain coming up, if a cow was dying of the colic. She would sing one psalm, and read one chapter from Pa's bible, and pray one prayer for each of them. Many times Ma sang the psalm that she liked best now—"How firm a foundation"—

lining it out for them. Nobody but Margot ever sang with her; they knew the words of the old psalm as they knew the name of Godalmighty, but, being men, they were too proud to join in women's weak devotions.

Ma was the pitifulest thing when she sang; her voice was so weak and cracked that you could hardly follow the tune, but she would clear her throat at the end of each line and go on:

> "How firm a foundation, ye saints of the Lord,
> Is laid for your faith in His excellent Word.
> What more can He say than to you He hath said?—
> You who unto Jesus for refuge have fled."

Ma always pitched the hymns too high, so that her old voice could scarcely reach the upper notes but by a thin little screech. Hardly could her children a-bear to hear her sing the last verses of the old psalm that she loved:

> "E'en down to old age all my people shall prove,
> My sovereign, eternal, unchangeable love;
> And when hoary hairs shall their temples adorn
> Like lambs in My bosom they still shall be born.

> "The soul that on Jesus hath leaned for repose,
> I will not, I will not desert to his foes;
> That soul though all hell should endeavor to shake,
> I'll never, no, never, no, never forsake!"

Seen would throw that promise back into God's eternal face in the weak song of her lips. He had promised, and repromised to bear her like a lamb in His bosom, never, no, never, no, never to forsake her.

She was just so pitiful, old and witless and with one foot in the grave, talking to God or Vince Carver like they were Margot or Jake. They knew that their ma was a saint as good as Abraham ever hoped to be off yonder in the Old Country. Hoary hairs had come on her temples from work and worry and grief; now she looked to Godalmighty to bear her in His arms as Jasper carried her from her bed to her chair, where Margot set pillows to protect her poor old backbone, on which sores clustered like it was a sick cat's. Ma's head with its hoary hairs was pitiful, bald as your hand in patches, lean and bony, with her hair screwed into a little wad in the back hardly big enough to pin up. The old knobbed cedar pin that was stuck through her hair-ball was used for the first time on the day that she married Vince Carver. Then the cedar pin had been clean as a reed whistle and bright colored as honey; now it was black and greasy-looking, though Margot washed it every whip-stitch.

Seen couldn't do enough to make one of her children turn against her. They would as soon talk back to God as they would answer short to any of Ma's whims. They would keep on humoring her, no matter what she did. Pa would turn over in his grave if one of them were to talk short to her; for she was their mother now the same as she was before ever they were breeched, when she was strong and young-bodied and could cuff them about as a bear does her troublesome cubs. She would be their mother till she died, and afterward, they reckoned, if earthly kin know each other in the Glory-World. Like Ma said, heaven wouldn't be heaven 'lessen she could kiss Eliza-beth and sit down and talk with Vince in the flesh; never could she figure out how twice-married widows would come out with two husbands to please. But why should she trouble herself over that, since there would be only Vince to claim her?

Jasper missed Margot from the place. He felt closer to Margot than to anyone else. She came inside his thoughts, a familiar of his intimacies. There was no concern of his life that she did not know about, and understand as he understood it. No sister could do that. Compared with Margot, Cean was a stranger to him. His mother had never come so close to him, nor his father, nor his brothers. So it must be that he loved Margot with the love that Ma some-times spoke of: it comes not to every sorry soul of earth, and when it comes it goes not away again, but to attend life out of the body. Ever a man is like to join lust with love in his mind, but Jasper did not so. He did not lust after his brother's wife; truth to tell, he had foolishly let Ma know that he would marry Margot if Lias would put her away by the elder's lief. Until yet, Jasper's face would burn, fire-red, when he thought of that blunder he had made. He had meant only to straighten out a big mess. . . . Ever when he came to this little dark lane of thought, a timorous question scuttled by his reason—did he really want his brother's wife for his own, and cloaked his desire in other, high-sounding motives? But always he went on past such argument, pushing down the blunder into the past.

Jasper had not licked Lias nor had Lias licked Jasper, they had only wearied each other, bruising, pounding, draw-ing blood. They fell to the floor and rolled about with their teeth set in brother's flesh, with their arms and thighs strained hard as iron. Neither licked the other; remember-ing this, it would keep them from fighting again. It had bred a mighty respect in each of them for the other one. Always since, Jasper had felt differently toward Lias con-cerning his evil ways. Lias was as good a man as himself. What right had he to judge? And Margot was still Lias's wife.

She minded Jasper of a woman he had seen once when he was a little boy. A cart had come through, going to the Coast, in the middle of winter. That was an unheard-of thing, for there was no call for journeying in winter. The people had stayed overnight at Vince Carver's house; they were going back to the Coast out of this infernal country, the man, his wife, and their children, no matter if it were winter, no matter that they had left a clearing and a house yonder to the west. They brought a wild story along with them—a story bound up in Jasper's memory with the woman's sunken eyes and slick, scarred forehead, and the healing gashes on her face and neck; she showed Seen Carver that the gashes were so all over her body. The man had told the story, but the woman interrupted shrilly, making the horror seem real as though the Carvers had seen it with their own eyes. . . .

The woman was off in a field to the west of her house, setting traps for bob-whites. She had a notion to tame the little wild chickens and have them breed and nest and run about her door, for the batch of hen-eggs that she had brought with her across the mountains from Tinnysee were broken on the journey; and the hen that she had brought with her all the way down to Georgy would lay, but the eggs would not hatch down here, because there was not a fine, red-combed, loud-crowing rooster to be with her. By the time that the man told the story to the Carvers the hen was wild in the woods, or eaten by some wild thing, for they were six days from home. The woman had wanted chickens about her door. The place where she had set her traps was a fur piece from her house. And she went alone. And wild Indians swarmed out from a pine thicket and came upon her; they caught her and tied her wrists and ankles with buckskin thongs; they whooped up their lean, hungry hounds and set them on the woman. The dogs fell upon her and had a big time of it, while the red savages laughed, shut-mouthed, till their sides shook, standing in a still row, watching the dogs hound a white woman as though she were a hare. When the savages had taken their fill of silent laughter, they went back to the west, calling their hounds after them. At dark, the man came to look for the woman; he found her still grubbing her way back toward her home, blind with blood and dazed like a loon. The buckskin thongs had eaten through the flesh of her wrists and ankles, but they still held tight where the gristles lay close to the bone. And the bites of the dogs' teeth festered and ran and were a long time healing. When they were healed, the man and woman set their faces toward the east, sick of that place.

Always Margot reminded Jasper of that woman, but he could not say why. Mayhap it was the look in her eyes, or the way, when they were milking, that she would turn suddenly about on the little three-legged stool to tell him of some new thing that had hurt her. She would draw back her lips so that the little gap in her teeth showed, and she would say, as though she shouted it with only a meager breath:

"I'd ruther be dead. . . ."

He did not know why Margot reminded him of that woman that he had seen when he was just a little feller nighabout too little to remember it atall.

Lias, at the Coast, kissed the woman hard on the mouth. Then he pushed her away so that she fell back on the bed again. She was more than a little drunk, and Lias's tongue was loose enough to speak his frank thought:

"Ye ain't no more than a dirty trull. . . ."

The woman bristled, pushing back her heavy red hair from her forehead. She said:

"Ye're someun t' be a-callin' me names. . . ."

Lias rose unsteadily to his feet:

"Nothin' but a dirty trull. . . ."

He went out of the house.

He had drunken too much; his in'ards were turning over; he was going to throw up.

The sea wind from the bluff came cold in his face and freshened him. He went out toward the way the wind had come. He blew out his breath in sick gusts, lurching along in search of a place where he could be alone and lie down away from people who might say in an undertone as they passed:

"There's Vince Carver's Lias . . . drunk again. . . ."

He went out to the bluffs, high and stable above the washing water. Live-oaks were massed thick and green. Their low branches swept the dry, white sand of the bluff. Moss draped the limbs, high and low, in a gray, noiseless curtain that hid the sea water from the houses and the houses from the sea water.

Lias lay down, full length, on the earth. The wind sucked in and out of the trees. A twig broke under his thigh as he turned. He felt the feathery, fine sand clinging to his cheek where he had turned it to the earth. His stomach rolled and retched.

Waves swept against the foot of the bluffs and went back in swirls of blackness. Lias heard the sound of the waves—Wash . . . sh . . . sh . . . Wash . . . sh . . . shh—the waves that were washing the land clean shore by shore. The sound reminded him of something, but he could not remember what it was. He wished the sound would go away; it troubled him—Wash . . . sh . . . sh . . . sh . . .

He fell asleep. The wind blew the fine, feathery sand across him in gentle, airy rifts.

# Chapter 16

IT WAS dry as a powder-house in the summer of '49. A cow could stomp her hoof in the earth and dust would rise like smoke. The swamp went báck into its sloughs and bogs, and wild things retreated with the water to the deep morasses far from Cean's house. (Half a hundred miles to the south there lies a deeper swamp, mother to these little swamps. There the bogs are but a layer of slimy mud over a vast sunken sea; there you can set down your foot and cause the earth to tremble with your little heaviness, though you be but a light-weight creature; wild Indians call it Okefinokee, their unknowin', heathen way of saying "Trembling earth.")

Along the edges of the swamp near Cean's house the receding waters left wide stretches of muck that cracked into rough furrows as it dried out; a carpet of dead fish lay rotting there and blowflies swarmed in the stink. In other places, where the water was not quite gone, Lonzo and Cal caught fish in their bare hands and Cean had fish for supper every night until Kissie complained of it. Cean made the children tote water to her rose bushes to keep them from dying, until the water went too low in the well. And till it rained she must leave the floors unscoured.

Cean had caught cold in her eyes, and they were red and weak-sighted. She tried May rain water. Always she had set cedar piggins under the eaves for the first rain water of May; it was a cure for sore eyes that the children caught in summer-time. Now Cean washed her own eyes in the water saved from warm May rains, but it did them no good. Some things just wouldn't cyore up, she reckoned; you jest had to grow out of them. Such a thing was the loss of her twin sons, born a year and a half after Wealthy, born before their time, and dead before ever they breathed.

It was a pitiful thing to wrop the little things in a new length of her homespun and lay them in a box in the ground as you would do with two pink still-born pigs. Lonzo could hardly abear hit. And how Cean did grieve over them! as though she did not have six other children besides. Long afterward, she would sit on the doorstep late of an afternoon and stare off toward the swamp while hushed tears rolled down her cheeks for the little lost boys. Her other children would be romping across the yard, maybe, making the warm air beat in her ears with their noise; but Cean seemed not to hear them. She were a-grievin' for the little boys.

She tried not to cry any more than she could help, for crying made her eyes worse. First thing she knew she'd be weak-sighted like Ma used to be; and now Ma was nigh-about blind as a post. Sure enough, like Jasper said, Ma must have second sight now. They had tried her out; she could feel them come into her room even though they might steal in ever so quietly.

Cean took care of her eyes, washing them many times a day in salty water, in May rain water, keeping out of the sun as much as she could. She didn't want to go blind in this world; there was too much to look at. They said second sight was a finer thing to have, for by second sight a body can see visions and all manner of things that the ordinary eye cannot see—streets of the Glory World, the Pit of Torment, folks who are dead to this world but walk alive again, seen only by second sight. But Cean didn't want to lose this first sight of hers. Sometimes while she nursed her eyes under a poultice of big white blooms of wild comfort, she would name over in her mind the many pretty sights she would never see again if she were blind.

A pity Godalmighty had to threaten to take your eyes away before ever you would look and see what a pretty place He had given you to live in! With her mind dark behind the cold poultice, she could see clearly a thousand sights; she could lie quiet—till somebody came and called her—if it were a whole enduring hour, going from one thing to another, examining each of many remembrances, in no hurry to pass it for another that was no lovelier, only different, in a small or great degree. Once, long ago, before that rattler had struck her when she was new in this house and scared her nearly to death, she had thought a snake a powerful pretty thing. And it was a pretty thing yet! so she decided. Just because a rattler had struck her was no sign that God hadn't made him pretty in another way from a coon or a frisky-tailed squirrel or a flower bush. When she was a little girl she would drive Ma's calves away from the cow-pen to the river bottom, where they would forget their mother's full bags in cropping the wet, sweet grass. The sun would be an hour high, for the cows were long since milked and turned out. So, on such a trip one morning, she had seen a moccasin, with her five rosy, shiny-skinned babies twisting about on the ground around their Ma before an old stump that would be their den. Cean would never forget that, for it was a rare sight. Hardly ever could you catch an old snake with her young; she would scatter them, daring you to find them. Cean never told her pa that there was a moccasin den in such and such a place. Let the old snake have her home that she had made in a rotten stump! She would have wild enemies aplenty to fight, without taking on a grown man who would fire the stump and drive her out in the open and beat her head flat with a stick.

Law! the sights Cean could see inside her head when she tried! There was fog lying flat and thick yonder when you looked away through the pines early on some fall morning. Fog was a mystery to Cean; it was as like smoke as two peas, and yet different—no smell, no nothing. Let the sun come up and fog skedaddled off into nowhere, leaving the leaves of the low bushes slick and wet and spangled with a thousand spider webs that were built into the air of last night. And maybe down the throat of a flag-lily you would find a drop of dew formed into a flat shining bead, or a little bright-green spring frog sleeping high up into the morning hours. Oh, there were a thousand sights for folk-es' eyes to see!

But sometimes hard sights slipped in behind her eyes, too, as she lay holding her eyelids closed. She would move her head to the side, dodging them; that was no way to do, mulling over something you couldn't help, looking at something you couldn't change. But the sight of those two little boys, alike in every way, would not leave her mind in peace. It was a new marvel to Cean; always before she had looked and found two crumpled hands, two little folded feet, two eyes to look blindly into her face through the cloudy gray-blue that saves new-born eyes from the first cruel light of this world. And here were four little hands in a row, twenty little fingers with a finger nail on each one, and here were twenty little toe nails. Cean marveled most that forty little nails could have come perfect out of her body! No, not perfect! for they were white as fish meat, not pink as babies' nails should be. Oh, the ways Lonzo did try to make them little boys live! . . . and never would they breathe once.

Cean would sit on the doorstep in the early evenings and cry. It was a pitiful thing to her for the little fellers to breathe never once, to cry and be hushed in her arms never once, to taste their mammy's milk never once.

Never could she figure out why the little fellers had not lived unless it was Godalmighty's way of showing Cean her place. You didn't get off with just praying and crying over a sinful thing. God would hold your feet to the fire; He'd cause you to remember again and again, as long as you lived, and just so often must you repent all over again. Weren't hit exactly two years that Cean had made out, between Kissie and Cal, to have no more children? Well, then! These two little boys, given cold and white to her arms, were children that she had murdered in her heart ten years ago. She had murdered them because she denied life to her seed for two years before God outwitted her and sent her Cal. And she had thought to get off with crying a little in repentance, and bearing her children that had come since with patience and a quiet mouth and heart! Godalmighty had His own way of showing her the children she had laid out dead, slain by her own selfishness, by her own hand that had followed Margot's evil talk of Coast ways. It did undo her to see Lonzo drive off that day, carrying the little boys in a box in the back of the jolting ox-cart. Cean wanted them buried by their grandpa, by their Aint Eliza-beth. It would be too lonesome for them to be buried away off here by her house, six miles from nowhere; the dead like company, too.

Oh, Cean was heavy-hearted, fit to die, but nobody ever heard about it. Lonzo thought she was weak and sickly; the children thought nothing about it, for the way of his own mother is the natural way to a child's thinking; all else seems foreign and remarkable.

There was always work to do to distract Cean from black thoughts; there were always fresh accidents to hurt where others had healed in her thoughts. A snapping-turtle bit off Cal's trigger finger on his left hand, and Cean always afterward felt that she had too many fingers, since Cal lacked one of his. It was a pitiful thing to do—to wrop the bleeding stub, to hear Cal tell, between his snubbin' breaths, that he hadn't meant no harm to the old turtle. The other children crowded around, hush-mouthed in amazement at this new happening, a little envious of Cal. Fairby comforted Cal, telling him that it was a sight better for the old turtle to bite off his finger than to hang on till it thundered, as everybody said turtles did. When the hurting had stopped and the bite was healing, Cal had to unwrop the stub many times a day for the children's eyes to see, for in the puckered flesh their credulous eyes could see the mark of a turtle's hard teeth. And Pa said that a turtle hain't got no teeth!

Cean was always a-treatin' something. In the cold rainy spells of the year, Wealthy and Caty, and sometimes even Lovedy, would take turns having croup of nights. Cean would keep her tallow and turpentine and camphor ready-mixed and warm on the fireplace; she would dose and rub the little chests, tight with cold, and sometimes she would crawl into bed beside Lonzo's heavy snoring only when the roosters were crowing for day, to catch a cat-nap before the children would be up, quarreling over their wool stockings and hide shoes that lay fresh-greased before the fire from last night. One time Kissie ran a big sliver deep into her foot, and Lonzo had to split the flesh as you would a squirming fish, and dig out the frazzled wood, piece by piece. Cean had to fight Kissie like she was a wildcat, to hold her still, and since Kissie was now nighabout as big and strong as her mother, Cean and Lonzo swapped places, and Lonzo held Kissie down, who was fit to go into a spasm, and Cean dug out the leavings of the splinter from the bloody hole in Kissie's foot where the leaders were drawn like cured rawhide. Cean drenched the wound with clear turpentine, knowing that it burned her child's meat like living fire. Oh, some bad thing was always happening. . . . Even Maggie, careful and slow as she always was, slit her hand through one morning when she was slicing potatoes to fry, and Cean sewed the meat of Maggie's hand together like it was a seam of homespun! The needle would hardly push through; the skin was tough like leather.

But there were good things, too. Lonzo brought her a little case of Promethean matches from the Coast. It was a big surprise, and when he struck one between his teeth, she screamed out at the unlikely sight of fire in his mouth; it scared her till she trembled all over. Now the children would be powerful good and powerful smart for a whole day just to see their pa strike a match in his mouth. Cean was glad of the matches; they were better to hold in Cal's contrariness than a dozen larrupin's.

And there was the gold and silver money in Cean's chest. Each year Lonzo would trade some of his goods for silver dollars to take home to Cean; he cared little about the things just to hoard them, but Cean got a mighty lot of satisfaction out of it. Last year, because he could not forget her face as she looked when the little boys would not breathe her breath that she blew into their nostrils, he traded all the cargo of his cart for two gold eagles to carry back to Cean. And when she saw the two gold pieces, she did not complain that he had not fotched home to her the little things she had expected—pepper and cinnamon and cloves (from the Brazils or Chiny or even Moscovy, who could tell?), and a three-legged oven like the one Margot had, and a candle-mold of her own, for she was tired of borrowing Ma's.

How Cean did gloat over those gold and silver coins! Somehow to Lonzo it was worth his doing without all the things that he had wanted to buy for himself when he saw Cean sit before the fire of nights and run her brown fingers through the pieces of money that clanked softly together as they fell through her fingers, catching gleams from the firelight; Cean would recount to her children how gold lay deep in the black guts of the earth, yellow and heavy until some adventuring man found it and brought it to the light of day and to the hands of greedy men. The children would listen, and even Cal would be hush-mouthed while his mother talked; in the procession of Cean's words they could see men, sick of the gold fever, hasting westward by foot or ox-cart, wandering westward across trailless deserts where there is never a tree—only sun and sand; they could see ships straining westward with the wind strong in all their sails. Once gold was struck in the up-country of Georgy at Dahlonega and Lonzo—if he had been old enough—might have upped and gone to dig the bright riches out of the ground if he had so willed; surely it would be a quicker, easier labor than sweating and straining, year after year, where rain was uncertain and crops came hard even with the best of seasons. But Lonzo would never up and dash to a fortune; it was not his way.

But he had brought her two gold eagles from the Coast, and maybe that was a wiser way to do. Lonzo would have liked to buy himself a new wool hat at the Coast, and a pair of boughten shoes with the wooden measure left in them, a handful of iron door nails, and plowshares that shine new and cut clean. But remembering Cean's face, white and scared at the sight of the two sweet, death-blighted babies that had come out of her living body, he called out the Spanish trader, Villalonga, from his counting-room, and offered him all that was on the cart—hides and honey, a load of white cotton and a measure of fine seed corn, syrup, brown sugar, and sweet cyored hams, all for two gold eagles that would bring a smile to Cean's mouth when she saw them. Lonzo chose two gold eagles, rather than one double eagle. Cean liked to drop the coins through her fingers in the firelight of a night, and two are better than one for such a purpose.

Sometimes in the night Cean would mull over this matter of gold until she could not sleep. There were four-teen pieces in her chest. You must stack ten pieces like them into the hand of a slave-trader before you could buy one little nigger slave. . . . But in California gold grows in the ground like pinders or 'taters. And at the Coast there are women who have nothing to do but work a little silk-cloth sampler with red and yellow worsted; yet these women eat rich food and wear soft, silk shifts next their hides, and live all their lives without sweating or digging or hoarding to have such. . . . Cean could not make sense out of it. . . . Why should some ground grow gold secretly in its in'ards, while other ground, like this of her'n and Lonzo's, will grow only weeds unless it be tended like a sick baby? She did not know. . . .

How Jake did want to go West; but, no, he must stay home and help Jasper manure the garden patch and tote splinters to Ma's fire, and help Fairby and Vince on and off an ox's rump any time it pleased them to ride. In the first place, he was hardly old enough to go; he begrudged Jasper and Lias their ages and beards and deep voices. He wanted a hairy chest and a bellowing voice and haunches strong as Jasper's; instead, his chest was white and blue-veined as a girl's; he was tall, but his legs could not take Lias's big stride, nor his arms Lias's heft; his voice was but little deeper than Margot's. Jake was jealous of his older brothers.

He liked to lie out in the woods; he was a rabbity little feller, Ma always said. Now since he was grown he would lie out for days and nights by the river with a quilt and blazing fire to keep him warm at night. For his hunger he would have a few potatoes to roast in the ashes, and besides he could kill any wild meat and clean it and prop it on a spit to roast; he could cook a big venison haunch through so in half a day. Jake sometimes thought that he would like to have been born fresh to the woods like any little beast, forced to find food and shelter here and yonder like a fearsome thing. He thought that with his tinder-box and dog-knife he could get along forever but for the hard, wet cold of winter, and he could stand that, if he had to, in a hollow log out of the wind like a 'possum, or in a dark cave like a bear. Not a bear, not even a rattler, would harm him, for they would be sleeping off the cold, too, and he could scare off any hungry painter by pitching a chunk of fire at him. Wild things hate fire; it will sweep through the woods in rolling smoke and waves of flame that burn out their dens and singe their young and mayhap hem them in between two walls of fire and roast them to greasy cinders.

With his turkey-yelper that his pa had made for him while the old man lay sick, Jake could lie behind a fallen log, and if he were patient and yelped carefully on the resined strings of the little box he could make a strutting, bronze-green hen come to the other side of the log and peer over at him; he would freeze his muscles and lie so still that she saw nothing amiss in the long, scarce-breathing figure that lay still as the log itself. She would strut away again, searching for that impatient mating call of the yelper. Gobblers were harder to fool and took fear when they came near, noting some unused quality in the scraping of the yelper on the string; but they would call through the still woods, distressed by the yelping they could not understand. At the close of day, when the great birds would beat through the darkening air on their wide wings and would settle on their accustomed roosts in the trees, Jake would creep near and disturb them as they settled to sleep; they would stir and call and ruffle their feathers and drowse, impatient of that fellow yonder who would not come to roost when dark fell, as he should.

Sometimes Jake would lie against the wind and watch deer feeding yonder like a herd of beautiful, strangely-made kine; many-horned, dainty-footed, they would lope by him if he stirred, hardly afraid of him; he would feel toward them a hopeless yearning. "I would not harm ye if ye would let me lope with ye to yere strange homes and wild bogs;

I would crop grass with ye and drink from the same springs; why should not grass and water satisfy my gut if it fills yours? For ye are but blood and flesh and bone like myself—only ye are fleeter and sweeter flesh, brighter blood, whiter bone made from wet grass and clear water and clean wind." But never could he go with them; they would take fright, if he tried, and outrun him, leaving their tracks thick in the earth, like prints of violet leaves; they seemed to fly low over the earth, all their feet together, lighting on the earth but to brace themselves for skimming flight. Jake tried to run as the deers ran, springing in swift leaps that are like the beat of music. . . . But his feet were too heavy, his weight was too much. He felt angry disappointment that he was made to walk heavily on broad soles, and not on light pointed feet that are able to fly with only brief and lightsome reaches back to earth.

It happened one day when Jake was going down the river to look at his fishing-lines that were set on tupelo-gum sticks along the bank, that he heard voices. He crept closer like a wild Indian that looks where he is to set his stealthy foot, and sets it flat so that it may sound like the scurrying of a squirrel or the falling of a dead pine-cone. Jake did not care so much whom he might find; but he would like to steal upon them and steal away again, as wild Indians do. . . .

And he saw Lias and Bliss.

And he stole away again.

Never would he go so far past the river's bend again. From that day forth Jake could hardly abide Lias in his sight.

Jake felt sorry for himself. Even Pa, as he lay dying, had forgotten Jake. Ma could never talk with him now; her voice went off in feeble mutterings, her eyes strayed away to places beyond the reach of Jake's eyes. Jasper was taken up with work and worry over a yeaning ewe, or the well gone nearly dry, or some such thing; Jasper paid Jake no mind; though Jake was more than full-grown and as tall as Jasper, yet the older man with gray in his hair treated Jake like he had been a youngun, and Jake resented it. He hated everybody but Margot, and she could hardly ever tease him out of a smile now.

Little Fairby loved Jake; if she had been older Jake would have taken up more time with her; but she was a girl-child, not nine years old, and full of questions. She thought Jake was the finest man in the world; Jake liked for her to look upon him as a full-grown man, able to do a man's work, able to hold a little girl's worship of a man. Uncle Jake could rob a bee-hive and receive never a sting; he had a way with him; the bees knew him; he would go softly about removing the honey, holding his breath long and hard in his body, troubling the bees as little as might be; and with never a sting he would garner the honey in crocks for the sweetening of a honey-cake, or to fill a finger hole in a cold biscuit when Fairby or Vincent was a-hungry. Jake took down dirt-daubers' nests from the ceiling to show Fairby how the wise, winged creatures had laid their eggs in dried-dirt cells that were stored full of bugs and worms that were still alive but overcome in some curious paralysis; they were for the little grubs to eat while they grew, as a biddy eats the meat of an egg yolk before it cracks the shell, as baby bees eat bee-bread in the mother-queen's hive. It was a master-wise arrangement to think up. Wild creatures have more sense than tame ones, Jake always said. He told to Fairby many a tale of queer happenings; he showed her many a nest of twigs lined with down, many a spider waiting craftily under a leaf with his leg set on a spoke of his web until it shook with the struggle of another creature, winged, living, unwary, trying to shake itself free of the sticky web.

If anyone came close to Jake, it was Fairby.

After a windy day in hog-killing time, there was not even Fairby. . . .

Over at Cean's house Lonzo killed three shoats, laying an ax-head between their too-small, greedy eyes fringed with sparse, stubby lashes. Cean had a hogshead tilted sideways in the earth, ready for hot water for the scalding; the children kept up the fires under the two wash-pots which they had filled with water from the well.

When the first shoat had ceased his brief death struggle on the earth of the boggy, shuck-strewn pen, Lonzo dragged him to the hogshead and scalded him there where Cean had poured in boiling water till it sloshed over the tilted, iron-bound rim. The children could help to scrape the tough white hide free of bristles; all hands found work to do. Wind whipped the children's hair into their eyes, and blew Cean's skirts flat on her lean body. Soon the pink, naked carcasses were hamstrung to a rafter, their scalded hides clean in the cold wind, their ribs hanging lank on the emptiness of their bellies that were rid of the in'ards from a long gash that reached from their throats down the length of their bodies. Purplish-pink bruises discolored each dead forehead, where the ax had been laid with an exact lick of metal on skull so that the brains might not be crushed and ruined with blood. Blood stained each down-hanging mouth open on its discolored teeth.

Lonzo was proud of his first kill of corn-fed winter meat. The shoats were fat and the moon was fullin', so the meat would not shrink in its curing. There would be meat aplenty for all the little mouths that looked to him for food, chitterlings, haslet, souse, good green pork to eat these next few days; and for next year there would be cyored hams, sweet and dry to make red gravy, and kags of white lard, links of cyored sausages, and big kags of side meat salted down for next summer's peas and okra.

The yard was swept clean by fall wind; fire swirled under the sooty iron sides of the wash-pots.

Now the scalding water was cold in the hogshead. Lonzo and Cean were cutting up the carcasses in the wash-trough, dividing the ribs from the fat-lined skin, chopping out the backbones down to the pig tails that would go to Wealthy, the baby, when they were bogged down in rice.

It was a busy day for Cean: there would be the fat to try out for lard, the sausage meat to grind and season and stuff, the heads to clean and boil for souse. When the meat had taken salt, Lonzo would light up his hickory fires in the middle of the dirt floor of the smokehouse where the hams and shoulders and sausages were hung to the dark rafters, and would cure the meat to keep. Lonzo loved to cyore meat, making the smoke just so thick for just so long. Lonzo could cure as fine meat as anybody in the country. Cean thought it was because meat-curing was a slow and patient work, suited to Lonzo. Lias, now, could never cure meat; skippers, and, worse, maggots, would be in his meat before the hickory ashes were dead, because he would go at it like fighting fire and ruin everything.

Tomorrow Cean would make soap-grease out of the scraps, when her lard was cold in the kegs, and her sausages were all strung up in greasy links in the smokehouse. Not every woman knows how to make good strong soap that will not shrink away to nothing when you lay it out in hunks on the smokehouse shelf. But Cean knew how, for her mother had taught her when Cean was not knee-high to a duck. Like meat-curing, there is no quick way to make good soap. Wait till the dark of the moon to cook up your soap-grease and pot-ashes, and while the mixture is boiling stir it from left to right with a sassafras paddle; when it is thick and ready, let the fire die under the pot. Next morning you will find the soap shrunk a little from the sides of the pot, and a little wet like dew will be gathered upon it; then you can slice it in hunks and lay it away, sure of fine, strong soap for another year.

Cean and Lonzo were yonder, cutting up pork on the wash-block, washing it free of clotted blood in the wash-trough. The children brought fresh firewood and heaped it to make tall blazes under the pots. Shouting and laughter flew across the windy yard, for hog-killing time is a merry time. The children—seven of them, with Lias's Fairby—played at their work of toting water and mending fires.

And one little hissing flame licked out its tongue and thrust its way into Fairby's skirt, catching and thrusting and eating its way with its bright, forked tongue. Wind whipped about, blowing the children's hair, beating the flames on the wood to fine, fair mischief.

Caty, next to the baby and five years old this month, was standing close beside Fairby. She saw the sly flame in Fairby's skirt; the flame seemed strange and lovely there on Fairby's long frock; she had never in all her life seen a flame in a body's frock. The older children did not see the flame till it shot upward, feeding on Fairby's hair, till it leapt like a lively snake to Caty's sleeve, dartling across her body, flying before the wind. Maggie and Kissie and Cal were yonder, toting meat to the smokehouse. The wind blew cold out of the north, changing to hot breaths on the bodies of those two children who were amazed and frightened, and so young that they knew no better than to run in the wind, with fire eating on their bodies.

Cean was scraping a dead hog's skin where the children's careless knives had left bristles in the hide.

Screams of the burning children made Cean and Lonzo drop their knives and run. But then the little bodies were flaming like dead pine stumps in a woods fire.

By the time that water was thrown upon them, Fairby's fair brows and long, fair hair, yellow as broom sage in the fall, like her father's, were burned away; her little face, grimaced in death agony, was parched and dry as a fried meat-skin.

Cean carried Caty in her arms to the house, and where she touched the child's skin it slipped and came away.

By nightfall, Cean's and Lonzo's hands were risen in solid, clear blisters where they had fought the flames on the children's bodies, but now they did not notice that they were burned.

They laid Fairby out on the bed and covered her over with a clean sheet. Cean made poultices and larded Caty's burned body, and laid cooling cloths on the roasted flesh. Caty screamed and screamed, so that Cean was hardly ever afterward able to remember her child's voice without remembering the sound of it as it fought its way out of her blistered mouth.

Lonzo went for Margot, his hands and arms swathed in white rags, and all the way he could think of no way to tell her that Fairby was burned to death at his house while playing with his children, while he was at the wash-trough butchering a hog.

Caty must have swallowed some of the fire. And that is ever death. On the next day she died. They had believed that she would over it if they watched her faithfully and renewed the healing poultices and brewed cooling bodywashes. But she must have drunk some of the flame. And once a flame is inside a body, that body cannot live, though it may linger a right-smart while.

Oh, it was a dreary way to go down the slope between the bare crêpe myrtles, around the swamp, across the cold six miles to Ma's house to lay away Fairby and Caty.

The road had never seemed so rough as now. With every jolt Cean cringed for her child's body lying hard and stiff on the pine planks of the box. Oh, she wanted to bear Caty in her arms, to save her from jolting, to warm her who must be so cold in the pine box, for she was laid out in a little white frock without a coat or a quilt. Cean would have felt better, though it might be foolish to feel so, if Caty were wropped warm against the cold.

Somewhere behind Lonzo and Cean's cart, Bliss Corwin rode above her child who was taken from her now in a second, crueler parting. Margot, for very pity, had said, "Let Bliss ride with Fairby." Bliss was crying like her heart would break. Cean had cried but little; she seemed dull and blind, and her heart was a load of iron. She thought: That Bliss Corwin did not love her child as I loved Caty. No. For there were six of mine, and I loved Caty best of all. So it seemed to her now. She thought that she could have found a reason in her mind why any other one of her children should have been taken, but not Caty, not Caty. . . . So, she thought as she jolted along the road back toward Ma's.

There ahead was Margot who had tended Fairby since she was a week old or less. Margot did not weep, but grief made her droop like a frostbitten weed. Margot did not love Fairby as Cean had loved Caty. Oh no. . . . So Cean thought. Caty was so sweet . . . she was her mother's heart-strings. . . . Cean counted over a hundred ways of Caty's, a hundred little happenings in the house or about the yard, when Caty had come running to her, or had told her this or that thing in a child's impetuous words. Caty was the center of Cean's thoughts. Here was Wealthy with her head on Cean's lap, asleep; yonder, in other carts, neighbors brought along her other children. . . . Cean and Lonzo were bearing their youngest two back to Ma's, the baby with its head warm in Cean's lap, the next to the baby in a box in the bottom of the cart, with its head as cold as clay. Now Cean understood that verse: "And the Lord God formed man of the dust of the ground and breathed into his nostrils the breath of life; and man became a living soul." You know that it is so, once you feel dead flesh with

Godalmighty's breath gone out of it. For you can verily feel the wet earth of any dead brow. Dust of the ground wet with God's spittle, that is all we be.

Cean's heart was well-nigh breaking; she would have given completely away if Lonzo's heavy, swathed hand had not come down hard on her thigh, if it had not lain there, pressing hard on her flesh, giving her strength, forcing her to courage. She shut her cries in her throat, and watched the trail ahead where trees and bushes on each side came up and passed slowly behind them, giving way to other trees and bushes.

But when they rounded the bend and saw the old house sunning itself on the slope—when Cean saw the familiar porch that opened now to her, taking her back home,—not even Lonzo's hard hand on her knee could hush her crying. For Lonzo was crying, too, with no sound but a hard shaking of his breath in his chest. To Cean, tears, birth-pains, weariness of body, or any varied pain that she had ever known, seemed sunken away into this void where her child had gone, a void that will not echo any cry of sorrow or fright or longing.

Above the grave they sang a plaintive psalm. Cean could hear her mother's cracked old voice carrying the high tribble that wound above the air of the song—a weird and beautiful harmony that brought the tune ever back to a sweet, flatted minor:

"When I can read my title clear to mansions in the skies,
  I'll bid farewell to every care, and wipe my weeping
    eyes.
Should earth against my soul engage, and hellish darts
    be hurled,
Then I can smile at Satan's rage and face a frowning
    world.
                .   .   .   .   .   .   .
"Let cares like a wild deluge come, and storms of sorrow
    fall;

May I but safely reach my home, my God, my heaven,
        my all.
    There I shall bathe my weary soul in seas of heavenly
        rest,
    And not a wave of trouble roll across my peaceful
        breast."

Cean had never seen a sea or a wave, and never would
she see one, but she could understand the welling flood of
such a sea as the old psalm talked about. Surely there is a
better life after this one, she thought, in a place built upon
the white roof of the sky where there are mansions for all.
Yonder is a city not made with hands where saints throng
the streets singing praises, where even little children are
crowned with diadems—of stars or flowers or a plain little
halo of earthshine—of whatever thing shall be their deserts.
But there would be one there nighabout too small to wear
even a little diadem unless it were set carefully on her head,
too little to sing any but simple praises, for she was but five
years old. . . . But Pa would be there beyond a doubt; he
met little Caty at the gate and led her in. And Fairby was
there, familiar to Caty; she would hold the littlest child's
hand and hush its homesick whimpering as she had done
many times here on earth. And there, too, would be Eliza-
beth, familiar with the beautiful ways. Sister Eliza-beth
would welcome Cean's shy little stranger yonder.

Cean felt better about her child; she was not here in a
cold box; she was yonder, learning to sing to harp music,
feeling the big angels brush her with their wings. Caty would
never cry again, nor hurt again; ever now she would wear
a white robe; ever now her feet would fall lightly on the
bright gold of heaven's floor where there is neither moth
nor dust nor corruption. Cean was comforted: this is such
a mean, nasty, sorrowful world; she was glad Caty was out
of it. . . .

But ever afterward she did as she had heard her mother

say that women do—though her child was dead, still she carried it about in her heart, a dead weight.

Cean was a little angered at Lias, if a body can feel anger in the midst of grief. He was not here to weep with Margot and Bliss over dead Fairby. . . . No, Lias was not here for God to strike him with grief over little Fairby's broken feet and bright hair, and eyes soft as blue water, and gay lips that never spoke a curse nor told an evil lie nor breathed wrong against any soul. Fairby is in the ground —and God have mercy on Lias's soul, wherever he may be . . .

In the fall of that year there was talk at the Coast of deep fields of gold to the west, free for the digging. It was away yonder on the other side of rivers and mountains and dry, deserty places. When the year's trading was over, Jake and Lonzo went home without Lias; he was gone to the gold-fields of California. That was the word that Lonzo was to carry home from him to Margot.

So Lias could not know that Fairby was dead; they felt pity for him because he did not know. Sometime he would come home again bringing cartloads of gold; then they would all eat out of gold mush-bowls and sleep under quilts of gold cloth. Fairby, when she lived, had excelled in ac-counts of these imaginings, and stood high in the opinion of the other children. Was it not her Pa who had gone to bring back gold? And when he came back, Mammy would hush her crying and would wear gold rings on her fingers thick as feathers on a bird's back.

Now of a rainy night when the daylight had gone out quickly under lowering clouds, when wind howled over the roof and rain beat hard against the sturdy logs of Cean's house, she would wonder where Lias was, and how he fared, and the children would speak softly among themselves of Uncle Lias. A rain drop might sizzle into the fire from down the chimney . . . what roof did Lias have to keep his head dry on this night of wet winter? . . . As Cean went to see if the children were covered against the cold, she would wonder, Does Lias sleep warm and have cover aplenty where he is? . . . Mayhap he is dead in that wild land of buccaneers and trollops. . . . If it had not been for Fairby, then Caty would be alive today. . . . If Fairby had never been borned. . . . Oh, Fairby was innocent. . . . It is Lias who should bear all the blame for this sorrow. . . . Lias brewed the grief for us all, and left us alone to drink it for him. . . . But vengeance is mine, saith the Lord. Had God-almighty aimed at Lias and struck Fairby? . . . Lias, may-hap, was out o' His reach! . . . But, no, that could not be. . . . "Though I take the wings of the morning and fly . . ."

"May the Lord have mercy on ye, Lias, wherever ye may be," Cean prayed.

# Chapter 17

War talk flamed around the camp fires under the live-oaks at the Coast. As far back as Lonzo could remember, men had talked of war with the North; but now there were stronger arguments for and against War. Now there were hotter heads. Always slow-tongued, Lonzo had little to say; he listened, and kept his own counsel. He would lean over a trading-counter and listen while some young blood of a planter's family harangued over states' rights. There were fire-eaters among these planters, Lonzo thought; they would fight at the drop of a hat. Their eyes flashed and their skins darkened when they recounted some new tale from up North—some runaway slave, mayhap, that was petted and pampered when what he needed was fifty lashes on his greasy back. Rich planters would tighten their fists, wishing for a war so that they could go and lick the Northern upstarts who hadn't learned to tend to their own business. The planters argued that the Negro was well cared for under slavery. Didn't the overseer dole out corn and bacon every Saturday noon, so much to a man and so much extra for every black that was in his shanty? Didn't every house in the quarters have its garden patch to go with it? Weren't the wenches busy in the weaving-sheds from dawn till dark, making cloth for the slaves, and didn't the mistress herself oversee them, holding them to so many lengths a day before they could leave the looms at night? The sempstresses sewed the cloth into garments; black cobblers cured cowhides, tanned them, dressed them, and made winter boots for young and old to wear to the meeting-houses o' Sunday. No nigger in slavery went hungry; it paid to feed the blacks well. They would fall sick if they were not fed well, and planters who denied their slaves meat and lard found them to be lean and scrawny and weak, not fitten to bring a top price when they were placed on the block. Besides, no number of lashes on his back can keep a black from stealing when he is hungry—a pig in the dead of night, or a side of meat from the smokehouse—if the overseer does not hand him out his rations Saturday by Saturday. For a nigger does love hog meat. As for the matter of the rawhide lash that the cantankerous Yankee preachers had so much to say about, was ever a black whipped unless he had stolen from his master, or played sick to keep from working, or sassed a white man? One overseer at the Coast had a stiff right hand on which the thumb and fingers stuck out like a dead man's; he had broken it on a Negro's blackbone skull when the black man sassed him. That man's hand was a sight for Lonzo to see.

The talk went on about Lonzo; he listened to planters, overseers, backwoodsmen, merchants, gleaning knowledge of the strange life that went on here at the Coast. The planters made out an easy life for the Negro; never did one lie sick without a physic, for the mistress would visit the quarters herself, carrying physics and ways of treatment. Some plantations even had hos-pi-tals where the blacks were treated like you would put a fine hog in a pen by itself and tend it till it was well, for niggers cost more than any hog. Unless you raise him in the quarters, a healthy buck will cost you five hundred dollars.

That was a mystery to Lonzo—how a man could be worth so much. He would nighabout sell himself for that much, if it were not for that lashing business. He'd never let another soul whip his hide like he was a yaller dog, not 'lessen he was dead.

Talk of states' rights was too deep for Lonzo; the sovereign right of a commonwealth to secede was an argument that he could not follow. Talk of Tar-heel fire-eaters in Carolina, and Copperheads in the North who would fight on the side of the South if it came to that, was interesting, but outside the bounds of his own life. He owned not one black; never would he own one; he would be a master-fool to run off up North and fight over a nigger! And as for the sovereign right of a commonwealth to secede, he did not know.

He would squirt his tobacco-stained spittle accurately to a wet corner where other spittle lay, spat from other mouths that were noisy with argumentative words, or still with heavy reflection, like his own.

If Lias had been here, he would have interposed questions where he did not understand, and later he would have argued as Vince Carver used to do. But Lias was away yonder in California. Lonzo was ashamed to show his ignorance; he would rather listen and let come out what would come out; later, back home, he would argue the matter in his own mind as he ground an ax on the whetrock, or mended a wheel on the ox-cart, or carved a wooden doll of a winter night for Wealthy or Lovedy. But to save his life he could not understand, for all his thinking, why the Coast planters wanted a war. He would scratch his head, plum bumfoozled over that.

The moon waxed and waned, month by month, riding away yonder above Cean's house set low on its blocks and sleepers. Her cabin hugged the slope of sandy earth, withdrawing a little way from the swamp that teemed with wild things and black muck and mosquitoes.

Cean's house was weatherbeaten now, a little shaggy at the eaves where so many raindrops had rolled to the earth in sheer wide waterfalls. The bright gold of the new logs was vanished away under the beat of rain and wind and sun. The house was dove-colored now, and weathered; fourteen years will put a little age on a house or upon anything.

Cean's yard was a pretty place as long as some old hen with a brood of new chicks did not scratch up her sprouting seeds, as long as there was rain enough to make her flower bushes grow and bloom.

Her boxwood put out a few new leaves each spring; her privet bushes grew taller and broader, year by year. In summer the crêpe myrtle made a flowering lane down the slope to Ma's. Through the varying seasons the crepe myrtle shed its bark, its fluttering foam of bloom, its leaves, like a pretty woman changing her garments of differing colors and texture, as befits the season. Cean sometimes wondered how a senseless thing like a tree or a flower can feel heat and cold, can count days and months like a body, can change her garb to suit the weather. Two years gone, Lonzo had brought her a century plant from the Coast, and Cean set it in a far corner of her yard and watered it. She wondered how anybody would ever know if it counted a hundred years right till it was time for it to bloom. She would not be here, nor Lonzo, nor the last youngest child that she might bear. She would never know; the only way would be to write this flower bush's true age out in Pa's bible, and let her grandchildren wait and see about it. But she did not like to ponder over such matters. In a hundred years the almanac would say Anna Dominy Nineteen-Fifty, and she would be dead and rotten long ago. There would be nothing alive that she had known—not a child, nor a cow, nor a bird. Yes, the 'gators were long-lived creatures; they would go on bellowing in the spring; and the turtles would go on sticking out their ugly heads on leathery necks. The pines would go on living, and Cean's boxwood and evergreens. But she and hers would be gone, like prince's-feathers and old-maid flowers and bachelor-buttons that die with killing frost, leaving only dried seeds for a careful hand to garner if it will; blazing-star and mulberry geraniums will leave roots to sleep in the earth like a wild thing; Cean would leave no roots to wake again to the sun of another year. Her children, she judged, were her seeds and roots and new life. Godalmighty must have meant it to be that way.

It was a thing to mull over; but Cean would reprove herself for thinking too long on such matters. It was not her business that her century plant might break into flower when she was dust without even a stink to it, that these same tough-hided 'gators might bellow in the warm dark of some far-off year, that her boxwood might hoard a nest of hornets in its green fastnesses when she was not here to see it put out its few precious leaves, spring by spring. Cean would remind herelf that by much worrying and thinking Ma had driven herself to where she was mighty nigh as crazy as a bat.

The clock on Cean's mantelpiece, marked the hours carefully, alloting so much space here, and here, and here; the hands moved around the clock's inscrutable face, careful not to haste in their ways for any great matter that might lie ahead, nor to pause for any brief, perishable happiness.

The moon came and went high in the sky over Cean's house. She liked the way the wild Indians called the months; she always called them by Indian names in her mind. Of course, to set down a birth or death, or in trading matters, a body would give the months their rightful, reasonable names. But Cean liked the wild flavor in the sound of the names of the Indian moons: January is the Cold Moon; February is the Hunger Moon (and were not the victuals like to give out along then before the garden patches were sown?) ; March is the Crow Moon (and did not the crows caw after every grain of dropped seed corn, flocking black in the wet March winds?) ; April is the Grass Moon, when dusty-colored wood violets wither out on the slopes among the new grass; May is the Planting Moon (but there was something amiss here, for Lonzo would be a pretty sight to leave his fields bare until May); June is the Rose Moon, and the seven-sister bush and the moss rose and the climber by the chimney are laden with blossoms, thick as stars in a wintry sky; July is the Thunder Moon, when heat devils dance across fields and thunder cracks like iron in the hot sky; August is the Green-corn Moon (if he could catch the seasons right, Lonzo's corn would be tall as his head with tossels as yellow as butter and ears as thick on the stalk as scales on a fish's back, or nighabout that thick); September is the Harvest Moon; October is the Hunting Moon; November is the Frosty Moon; December is the Long-night Moon. . . . Cean thought that the wild redmen were not so savage as people said, for they had the gumption to name the months of the year better than ever she could if she were put to it. Cean had never seen a redman, but Lonzo had; they were the color of old copper money, naked except for a rag about their hips and groin, and shiny with bear grease; they wore eagle feathers in their hair, and silver handwork, set with moonstones and chalcedony and bloodstones, about their necks and arms. She would love to see a redman who was tame and good-natured as some were reported to be, friends to the whites.

And the full, frosty-white moon of another November—the Frosty Moon of the redman—came to its full and stood high over Cean's house along about the middle of the month. It shone like a polished silver thing, white as the frost that lay thick in the still woods on every bent weed and fallen pine-cone, along every shining brown pine-needle that lay on the floor of the forest, part of a springing, soft carpet for timorous, furry feet.

And the Frosty Moon brought with its fulling Cean's second son that would cry for her, and take warmth from her warmth, and grow, if she were careful of him, into a man.

But Cean, weak and fearful and prone to mull over any little thing, could hardly be proud that it was a son. For Lonzo said that it wouldn't surprise him much if some of them hot-heads at the Coast were to bring down a war upon everybody's heads with their wild talk. Girl children could never go to war; nighabout Cean could wish that this were another whimpering, hatchet-faced gal in her arms.

They had food aplenty ahead. If the red Indians would stop their roaming and set their hands to work rather than to mischief, they could make food aplenty, too, and there would be no Hunger Moon for them. Cean had heard tell that squaws sometimes came to houses in the settlements and held up their hands, begging for something to eat; they did not know white man's talk, so their mouths were dumb, and their empty hands spoke for them. Cean wished that a friendly squaw might come to her door, some day in late winter; she would be glad to give the red woman enough to fill her belly, and her children's windy bellies that growled with hunger. For Cean and Lonzo had aplenty and to spare. Out in the smokehouse there were kegs of lard and sides of meat, sweet brown hams and shoulders, and sausages fried and buried in lard; piled back in the corner were pumpkins, pale-colored in the half-light; behind the corn-crib were mounds of dirt and pine straw covering banks of potatoes—all Cean had to do was go and grabble out as many as she needed; in the loft were dried peas aplenty; in stone crocks Cean had preserved all manner of things in thick sweetness—mayhaw jelly, blackberries, huckleberries, water-melon rind, wild plums. Like her mother, Cean set a good table. With corn aplenty for meal and hominy, with potatoes to fry, with syrup to be sopped up with a hot biscuit, and preserves to be had for the asking, it was no wonder that Cean had only a coming war to worry her. When her table was set, neat and tidy with its crockery plates and bone-handled knives and forks and pewter spoons, it was a pretty sight to see. Maggie and Kissie would rake the coals from the top of the oven, would push the coals from under the pots and skillets, would lift the pot lids and let the food cool a little. Rich simmerings would mingle with the floury, fresh odor of buttermilk biscuits and varied scents of boiled beans, stewed pork, and such like—all fitten to stir the hunger of a stone man. The roasted potatoes would come out of the hot ashes to be peeled and buttered. "Fine rations," Lonzo would say as he sat down to eat; at his words a satisfied smile would settle on Cean's lips. And for the next meal she might stir up a sugar-cake to please him and make him eat the heartier.

Vincent Jacob, Cean's youngest, throve under his mother's and sisters' care. He was a fine, big-chested, big-bellied child, heavy on Cean's arm, and Lonzo was the master-proud of him. After all those girls, he was glad to hold a son on his knee again—a son, broad in the shoulder and lean in the hip joints, to fight with his fists and earn his bread by the sweat of his brow, bread for him and his'n when it was his time, after Lonzo.

When little Vince was old enough, Cean had Lonzo carry her to see her mother; for Margot sent word that Seen Carver was failing fast. They rode through the woods on a December day when the birds were all out, rustling through the bushes and twittering in the warm sunshine. Their mating songs had been forgotten in the cold peril of winter, but their tremulous chirpings made the morning seem gay and springlike.

Cean brought her broad-browed, big-jointed man-child up to the bed for her mother to see; but Seen paid him no mind. Her mind was nighabout plum gone now, and only once in a long while would she call for one of them, or talk with any sense at all.

Cean sat beside her mother's bed. Her children, gawky and abashed at the sight of this sick old woman under the cover, stood about for a while, watching Seen's sunken eyes and drawn mouth curiously, as they would note a dead snake or a new calf; then they straggled out to the yard to play with Margot's Vincent, to hunt hen nests in the hay of the crib loft, or to beg Uncle Jake to tell them about the Coast country. Maggie carried Cean's baby out with her, and left Cean alone with her mother.

Lonzo was out on the porch, talking with Jasper about some day soon when Jasper and Jake were to help him with the deadening of a strip of woods to the north of his place that he was taking in as new ground for corn.

Cean watched her mother's shrunken, unknowing face; her heart was too heavy for weeping. A blue vein beat on the temple of Seen's dried, bald skull; her lids twitched now and then over her blind, white-skimmed eyeballs where cataracts grew thick and white like gristle.

Seen's horny, restless hands moved restlessly on the quilt; her breath came softly and quickly out of her shrunken chest, and went again, sighing.

Cean bent over her mother's face and took her hand and called her softly:

"Ma. . . ."

She called her again, hoping that they might talk once again, as they used to do. But Seen would pay her no mind; she mumbled words that Cean could not understand; Cean knew the words were not for her ears. . . .

(For Seen, with all her mind a-dream, was talking with her mother.

She was a child in a long, full-skirted dress of blue-barred homespun. It had little flecks of red and green in the center of each check; her mother had woven tips of bright flannel into the length to make it please a little girl.

Seen was proud of her dress; she herself had stirred the indigo liquor for the blue of it; she herself had held the

[ 243 ]

swift for the cloth of this dress, had sorted out the reed quills from the quill-gourd, handing them one by one to her mother to be set in place on the loom.

Seen liked this dress. Her hands smoothed the pretty length of it that went down to her shoe toes, new and heavy and stiff; this dress was so new that it had never been washed.)

Her mother's restless hands on the cover worried Cean. They kept reaching and reaching over the cover, caressing and smoothing, and would not stay still even when Cean tried to hold them in her hands.

(The pretty blue-barred frock fitted close about Seen's neck, the narrow belt was tight about her waist, little bone buttons went down the back of it where her mother's hands had buttoned it closed. Her oldest sister, Mirandy, was helping Ma with the candles; when they were all molded and cold and set aside, Seen would be allowed to count them out and lay them away in the candle-box—four hundred and eighty of them, a year's supply. It was tedious labor; sixty times must the mold be filled and cooled, and the eight candles loosened from it and laid out. Seen would like to help, but her mother would not let her because she was too little, and besides didn't she have her new dress on her back? Ma minded Seen away from the hot tallow; the candle grease bubbled . . . bubbled . . . bubbled . . . yellow and heavy and hot. Ma and Mirandy lifted the pot from the coals. And the pot turned on its side and the yellow candle grease streamed over Seen's feet. . . . Then strange to say, there was Dicie Smith wiping the candle grease from her feet; and it was not candle grease at all, but syrup-candy bubbling between her toes. And there was little Cean having birth pains with a little youngun on its way into the world. . . .)

Cean bent over her mother and tried to hush her thin,

piteous screaming, to quiet her weak plunging under the cover. Seen shrieked and went on shrieking:

"Oh, hit's a-burnin' m' feet. . . ."

They did not know that her mind had gone back, gathering up a horror of another time, and living it again. Their mother must have viewed the flaming brimstone pit; and the flames had lapped over and licked at her feet that were so near the brink of another world.

If the fires scorched her feet where now they lingered, slow in leaving life, what chance did any of the rest of them have to taste eternal joys? If Satan pulled Ma down to hell for the sins of her soul in this world, then must they all burn in the deepest, darkest torment where shrieks ride the blistering winds of hell forever and forever. And, oh, the thirst for one drop of water. Have mercy on me . . . and cool my tongue . . . for I am tormented in this flame . . . !

But yonder saints sing praises in God's face and droop their bright crowns low before His throne. Day by day new souls lumber up through infinite space to the shining gate of heaven and beg admittance, and they are wearied from their flight, for they are heavy on their wings like birth-wet butterflies. But their weariness vanishes away when they see the face of Mary as she leans her cheek against each new face and whispers, "Hush, child! Thy little grief is past. . . ." And there they see John, his hand clasping the hand of God's Son, and Peter is healed of his lying tongue, and Stephen bears no more the wounds of stones. And eternal light blossoms suddenly into bright halos about their foreheads, and the sight is more beautiful than the rising or the setting of earth's sun, or even the greenish-silver of a glow-worm's light in earth's dark. And the wonder of that place is that a new soul is so changed that never does he note the lack of mortal breath (the breathing of a mortal is foul so that he must be forever washing his mouth with table salt and fire coals) ; he does not miss his earthly flesh that weighted him down and caused him to sin (and was so loathsome a substance that it must be washed day by day with strong soap) and was so jealous an evil that it persuaded the soul to fear and rail against dissolution. Ah, when all is said and done, the body of even a new-born babe is but decadent flesh that will grow for a few little years, deceived by the beauty of its growth, then age in subtle corruption.

The hearts of Seen's children quaked. Well they knew that when she died Ma would go as straight to heaven as a bee-martin to his gourd. If God were faithful to His promises, she would!

But even Ma had seen the fiery pit, had felt the touch of the flames upon her helpless feet before she died. Seen's children fell silent about her bed. Voices of the children came in from around the lot where they were playing hide-and-seek and roly-poly.

Cean sat beside her mother, not comforted by Margot's telling her that Seen had many nightmares and fancies to worry her.

When the others went out, Lonzo stayed with Cean in the room, propping his chair against the wall. Deep in thought, his tongue went over and over a hollow in one of his jaw teeth; he'd have that tooth pulled, first chancet he got. . . .

Jasper went into a shed-room where he slept when he was not looking after Ma at night. He sat in a chair, and his hands drooped limply between his knees; his head fell on his breast. . . . Oh, his ma was a dead woman, a dead woman! . . . He could see it for himself; her vision of fire was a sign; she would not be here many more days. . . . It is a hard thing for a man to watch his mother's last breath leave her, a hard thing. . . . A father is a father, but a man has lived by his mother's milk, has gone a thousand miles in her arms before ever his own legs will carry him a step.

Margot came softly to the door; he was not ashamed for her to see tears for his mother wet on his face. She went close to him; she put her arms about his shoulders and laid her face against his face. His arms reached and held her as though he had been waiting for her to come and fill them.

For a moment he forgot his grief, and she forgot it, too. There was nothing to remind them of it. In the shed-room there was only silence filled with the diverse smitings of their hearts. Tenderness stirred in Margot like a slow quickening, as spring sap stirs low in a tree that is dead since last year, as a river's current stirs to gather all its little currents into one long flow when it sights the sea beyond the headlands. Jasper would not let her hands go from his shoulders; the touch of her fed a hunger that possessed him; now he knew that she was a sweet-water spring, and he was athirst.

Margot pulled herself away from him. She was the first to remember that Seen Carver lay dying yonder in the next room. She was ashamed later to remember how she had fondled Jasper's head when Seen Carver's breath was like a brittle thread running down her throat, a thread that might break if one but blew upon it. They went back to the room, where Seen lay, now asleep. They saw Cean holding her mother's hand as a mother holds a child's hand so that it may go to sleep without fear of the dark or an uncertain tomorrow.

Cean held her mother's hand so until Maggie brought Vincent in to her for her to suckle him to sleep.

Four nights later, in the blackest hour that comes just before day, Seen Carver's soul went lightly away from her body on the last of her sighing breaths,—breaths thinner than a spider's weaving. When the quivering cord of her breath broke, her face changed subtly and settled into the secretive serenity of the dead; no least stir of restless breath broke her consummate peace; heart-worn, her flesh had accomplished its repose. She had left them behind. But they felt no fear for her on her long journey; they believed that her soul would find its way home, as a bird homes over half a world to an old nest, with never a chart nor a mile-post to show it the way to go.

Margot and Cean laid out the wretched, sore-eaten body. Had they not loved it in life, it might have brought a sickness to their in'ards to wash the withered, bald-skulled flesh.

When the body was laid out, washed clean, shrouded and still under a clean sheet, when Margot and Cean had gone out to the kitchen, Jasper went in and kissed his mother's body on the temple, on the cheek, and wet her shriveled hands with his strong tears. For ever he had been his Ma's boy, as Lias was Pa's. She was dead, as he had always known she would be on some unbelievable morning. She was dead, and all her mulling and wishing had come to this—a clean sheet to cover a sight that might cause a body to turn away with a sick stomach, if he had not loved her as Jasper had.

Jasper took down the family bible and, when he had looked in the almanac, inscribed his mother's death date beside the date of her birth:

Cean Loveda Trent Carver  9 Aug. 1790  15 Decembre 1850

By ciphering in his head, Jasper judged Ma to be sixty year old when she died. Often had he heard her tell how she and Vince had settled in a home on a slope from which Cean Trent could see her mother's house on a clear day. She set poplars and boxwood, and a row of peach trees to be a screen for the cow-lot. When the roses were grown and the day was fair she could sit on her piazza with needle work on her lap and look across the roses and the clay

[248]

hills and see her mother's house set yonder on the ridge. She carried her first child, and topped her rose bushes, and looked across the hazy hills to her mother's house, hardly homesick at all because home was so near—and because it is fitting that a woman leave her father's rooftree and make a home for a man. Her child was born when the brier roses in her front yard put out their first blooms.

But then the State of Georgy had to buy up the Creek Indian land, and have it surveyed like it was something fine, and better earth than Carolina's stiff clay where they lived. And settlers went south like it was something fine to do. . . .

Vince Carver would sell out his land and move to Georgy in spite of Cean Trent's tears. But worse, he would not stop in the up-country; he must go on south where grazing was good the year round, where swamp muck was rich as manure. Mealy-mouthed, oily-tongued land agents told Vince that you could plant one crop after another the year round, because the weather was so fine, the earth so rich. Frosts did not kill in South Georgy, they said, and children could go barefoot the winter through. So the palaver went. And most of it was true, and Vince believed it all.

But the crops grew no faster than in Carolina. As dark fell, mosquitoes swarmed through all the land, so that you could listen and hear the air beat in your ears with their high, thin singing. In a long, wet spell, all but two of Cean Trent's rose bushes died, and never did her cedars and boxwood seem so thrifty and bright-leaved as Ma's back in Carolina.

And Eliza-beth died and was buried in the wet ground.

The piny woods were as flat as your hand, and were forever wet with the last rain, for there was no place for the rain water to go. Oh, Seen could never glimpse the Carolina hills from here, no matter how fair the day might be! Ever

Carolina was a little like heaven in her mind—distant, set on tall hills, never to be glimpsed with mortal eyes.

But when she was old and afflicted and lonely—old enough to learn some sense—she set her heart in a right relation to God and He revealed to her why her life was lived out here in a land she could not love: four years after Cean and Vince had come off down here, yellow fever broke out in Charlestown and half the people died; those who were able to leave, fled from the pestilence and spread the scourge far and wide, even back into the hills of Carolina, even to Cean's mother's house, where they welcomed in a stranger and fed and slept him. He sickened and died in Zilfey Trent's spare room; they tended him, not knowing till too late that it was the pestilence that gripped him. Anyhow, would you turn a sick man from the door, or leave him alone to die? Zilfey Trent would not, nor John Trent, her husband. So, leaping from one body to another, the fever carried away the Trents, all but Cean, who was safe away down in Georgy.

A neighbor of the Trents wrote a pistareen letter to Cean in Georgy; it told of the people that were carried off by the pestilence. It told of the word from Charleston: hardly a house but had buried its dead; all night long dead-carts had rumbled over the cobblestones, bearing the dead to their burial in one long grave. Those who were sick, and those who were left to watch, could hear the muffled wheels of the carts whose iron tires were bound in cotton bagging so that the sound of the piled bodies traveling over the stones might be stifled a little for those who listened in the dark houses. Cean Trent grieved most that she had not held her mother's hand, nor washed her fevered face, nor comforted her as she died. . . .

Jasper closed the bible and set away the quill and ink-horn.

He had set the last day of her life down, in the early

morning of this new day, as she would wish it done. Her record was there, midway of God's word, on a thin page that was banked on each side by the solid weight of eternal, immutable Truth.

He went out and closed the door softly, shutting away the still figure that lay under the clean sheet.

# Chapter 18

LONZO was a Democrat, though never
did he declare his views. No one ever asked him to state
his opinion, for he was not easily drawn into talk. But well
he knew which side of the fence he was on; he belonged
with the wool hats and copperas breeches and cowhide boots
and oxcarts. The Whigs had nothing to do with such. No.
They cavorted and pranced on fine, long-tailed mares, nam-
ing them such names as Daphne or Ariel, and fondling them
as though they were women. There was one mare, Ariadne—
Lonzo would have given the shirt offen his back if he could
have straddled her once, if he could have felt her sleek
body answer a gentle pull of the rein, if he could have seen
her toss her head and shake her bridle when he called her
name. Aryadny! That was the purtiest name ever he had
heard, even though it might be a horse's name; ever he had
another woman-child, he'd name her Aryadny, Cean willing,
for Aryadny was a woman's name, Lonzo never doubted.
These Coast bloods gave women's names to their horses, and
said such love words into their ears as Lonzo had never
said to Cean; the mares would roll their eyes at the sweet
names, would twittle their ears and snort and paw the earth
lightly with one fine-shod hoof. Lonzo would give his 'tarnal
soul for a mare to ride!

But a pretty thing he'd be a-prancin' around a cotton-
patch on a mare! Nobody but Coast planters—Old Line
Whigs—could own horses. Not all the gold he could ever
manage to trade for would be enough to buy one mare. No,
he was definitely a Democrat. Not even a fine saddle-horse
garbed in an Anglish-make saddle with a silver horn to it
could make a Whig out of him; he would still be a gawky

hayseed from out in the sticks, in jeans and a homespun shirt, the smile or the grief of his mouth hidden in beard that had never felt a barber's shears.

Lonzo hated the Whigs, though never did he part his lips against them. They were the hot-heads that itched for a war; they were in correspondence with Copperheads in the North. At the Coast, the mail-coach dashed in twice a week with letters from the North, the driver sounding the horn for all to hear. Letters came for the planters,—but never a one for Lonzo. He would watch the Coast men open their letters that were folded up like thumb papers for a little feller's horn speller, one end slipped under the other end and sealed with a wafer. He would like to have a letter come to him from somebody somewhere; he would answer it importantly; the fellow at the other end of the line would have to pay the postage, anyhow. Lonzo was nighabout a mind to sharpen up a quill and pen a letter. . . . But he knew no name that he could set on the front to receive that letter. Oh, since he was wishing, he would like to up and pay his fare and ride off in a mail-coach in a cloud of dust as Lias had done! Tenpence a mile it would cost him; and where would he land up at? But pish-tush! a grown man hain't no business a-traipsin' off like a strange dog that will take up here and yonder, and be gone, and first thing ye know, be back again! Lias had no business gone yonder like a jack-rabbit when a shotgun discharges.

Now the Coast bloods came and went as it pleased them; some of them had been across The Water, and could tell of The King a-ridin' to Parlymint; some had been schooled in Princeton or Philadelphy—or even away in Angland—and could reel off by rote long rhymes of this or that. The rhyme that Lonzo liked best to hear was one that a tall, carousing young squirt would say whenever he was half full of rum:

"My name is Norval;
On the Grampian hills my father feeds his flocks . . ."

Lonzo would hear it through, wishing the others would hush their noise. The sound of the thunderous words of the young planter satisfied some need of Lonzo's soul, but he would have been hard put to it to say why he liked the rhyme.

He hated the Whigs, but more than ever he hated them after the young Whig, Aspinwall, killed Aryadny.

Aspinwall dashed down the street on her back and turned in a close quarter where carts of the traders were thick before doors of storekeepers; the slim, sleek beast whirled on her hind legs, showing the whites of her eyes, and came down against a cart; her left foreleg snapped as though it were a dried reed, and she fell and lay on the earth with her sides blowing. Aspinwall knelt beside her and hugged her shining neck and whispered into her ear as though she were a loved woman in childbed. When he saw that her leg was past saving, he drew a pistol from its hanger, and laid his cheek on Ariadne's head and told her good-by. Then he shot her in the head. She floundered once, trying to rise, and he laid his hands on her head, caressing her; her eyes, terrified like a human's, found his face as they glazed.

Young Pope Aspinwall drank heavily that night, and cursed and puked over the table in Kimbrough's tavern. Lonzo thought that he felt nighabout as bad over the thing as Aspinwall did; but Lonzo did not drink; he had not the liking for the taste of whisky, nor the money to throw away. Never did he forget Ariadne's eyes as she died. Late in the night, friends carried Pope Aspinwall home, dog drunk; the next day he took passage on a schooner that lay out in the river under sail for Savanna, and Charlestown, and finally New York; he was a-grievin' for Ariadne as though she was a woman that he had loved, and killed with carelessness. And Lonzo could nighabout understand; Lonzo had heard more than one young sport brag that no woman could please him as his horse could, for a horse is dumb-mouthed but understanding, full of spirit, but ever submissive; she will force her gait till she drops dead, if it be her master's will, and she will not complain at any saddle-gall that he is careless enough to inflict upon her; a horse is a sweet thing, a pretty thing, a long-lovin' thing—thus thought Lonzo, though he had never bestridden a horse.

He would wish for a horse if he were a rich planter, but that could not be. He would wish for blacks such as Coast planters have, if he were a Coast planter; he would have a head cook and a cook's helper, a chambermaid—though that seemed a brazen term to him—a sempstress for Cean, a nurse-girl for every girl-child and a play-nigger for every boy-child, a stableman and a carriage-driver, a gardener, and a dairy-woman; and he would have plenty of young niggers besides to drive up the cows and sweep leaves and scour the pot-things, and come running every time you clap your hands. He would have slaves such as a Coast planter has, if he were a Coast planter. But that could not be.

He finished his trading, jewing with the wool-stapler over the long-staple wool he had brought. Ever Cean sent her best wool to the Coast, parting off the long from the short, the coarse from the fine, in the washing; she would rather sell off her best wool for a high price, and gower along the best way she could with the sorriest grades for stockings and undershirts.

Lonzo haggled with the bootmaker over the worth of the tanned hides he had brought. And he bought for Cean a pair of fringed doeskin moccasins such as redwomen wear.

Cean was at home, suckling her two babies, Lonzo reckoned. She was the master-proud of her twin sons, James and John, born in the last hot summer-time. No danger of the Smith name running out. First thing you knew they'd have a pyore Smith Settlemint hyere, danged if they wouldn't!

The carts lumbered along on their way home from the Coast. Jake and Jasper had brought two carts this year, for Jasper was a master-prosperous farmer; he was even talking of buying mules at the Coast to plow his fields. They were strong as oxen and ten times as fast, but the cheapest of them would cost nigh onto a hundred dollars apiece. Lonzo thought such doings would be a foolish waste of money inasmuch as oxen would serve as well. He would not care to trade all his hoard for an ugly-faced mule. Now a horse would be a different matter. But not to save his right arm from being cut off would Lonzo have told any soul of his fancy to buy a horse; they would think he was fitten for Bedlam!

They came back across the creeks and sand-ridges, betwixt p'lmeters and scrub oaks; and their hearts were as light as their carts, for a Coast journey is a pleasuring time.

As they neared the river that ran close to the old Carver place they could hear one of Jake's hounds giving tongue deep in the river swamp: that would be some fox or wild-cat or rabbit. Six mile t' other side of the Carver place would be Lonzo's place, with Cean waiting by the fire with a man-child of Lonzo's on each arm for him; he knew that she would be glad to see him, since he had been gone all these long days at the Coast.

When they came in sight of the Carver place, when the hounds ran, baying, down the trail to meet the carts, Lonzo and Jasper and Jake saw figures, many of them, standing yonder in front of the house. Lonzo strained his eyes to see, and his heart failed him. For he made out Cean's figure, and all her children were about her. She was carrying one baby, and Maggie was carrying one. . . .

There was sickness or death or heavy trouble ahead of him. He gave his long whip a mighty crack in the still air above his tired ox.

The days seemed dull and lonesome when Lonzo was gone to the Coast.

Cean did not know why this should be. There was as much work as ever to fill her hands—more, if anything; there was but one mouth less to sit at her table and eat. The days were like all the other days when Lonzo was at home—the sun rose, noon came, dark fell, night lasted till the sun came again; but to Cean there was a strong difference. She was glad that Lonzo went to the Coast only once a year, for the two weeks seemed longer than any month when he was home.

To pass the long hours, she spun after supper when the little children were in bed, or sewed or quilted with Maggie and Kissie by candle-light. Maggie had three quilt-tops of her own put away, and Kissie was working on her second one. Cean could sigh, if she had a will to, over her daughters' long legs and swelling breasts and eyes that were learning more than their mother ever wished them to know of this world's ways. Each of her girls had a homespun sack in the loft, filling it with saved goose feathers. Law! Cean would never have another feather bed of her own; she had too many daughters to save feathers for. Maggie, little as Cean liked the notion of it, was nighabout ready to marry right now, for she would be fifteen in December, the twenty-and-fifth day. And Kissie was but a year behind her. But what young stripling had Cean seen to whom she would be willing to give Maggie or Kissie as a wife? There was no man living good enough for her little girls, wide-eyed and inno-cent-hearted. But all the time she went on saving goose feathers, one plucking to Maggie, the next to Kissie; all the time she went on piecing quilts o' winter evenings, and weaving lengths of homespun to bleach for the white sheets of their marriage beds; all the time she went on weaving fancy dress lengths, with short lengths of plain color to frill the neck and wristbands, and to flounce the foot of the full skirt. Lonzo said there was a linnen-mercer at the Coast; Cean coveted a length of linnen cloth to make her girls their wedding shifts when they should marry; and their top clothes should be of fine boughten stuff, if there were time and money for Lonzo to buy it. What made her dread their stepping off with a man, and yet plan ahead for it like she looked forward to it? She did not know. She went on saving the sorriest wool, too short for spinning, and planned bright-colored, tufted, woolen comforts for her daughters; she wove yellow homespun till Maggie and Kissie complained of helping her, asking her what she could ever find to do with so much yaller homespun to lie in the loft and rot. Cean answered such questions sharply:

"Ask me no questions and I'll tell ye no lies!"

Sometimes she would watch Maggie out of the corner of her eye as the child went to the looking-glass when she thought no one saw her, when she smoothed her hair or fastened her neckband with her eyes set on those admiring eyes in the glass. Maggie was a gentle, brown-eyed thing, meek-hearted and pretty to look at, but when one of the children aggravated her beyond reason, she would slap him a-windin' before ye could say scat. . . .

Always before she lay down to sleep, Cean climbed to the loft to see how her children slept; and she would find Maggie sleeping, her full young bosom rising and falling in slow breaths, the buxom length of her body as untroubled as her face. Cean would not go close to look into Maggie's face, nor would she stand but for a moment watching her as she slept, for she could remember waking in years long gone to see her own mother standing above her bed, looking hard into her face. There had been something frightening in the look of her mother's face, something that Cean had never understood until now. She would not for the world wake Maggie and let her see her mother staring at her. . . .

Cean had never loved her mother as she did now when she saw her own girls nighabout old enough to leave their mother's roof for a strange man's, now that she knew how her mother had loved her. She was walking the way her mother had walked before her, and never did she recognize that road until her mother was dead and her girls were grown about her. A pity it is that nighonto twenty year must come between a woman and her daughter that is the first fruit of her flesh and the very blood of her heart; a pity that Cean must feel as much a stranger to her own girls as her mother had felt toward her. . . .

How was she to tell her daughters all the things that she had learned, all the secrets that take root in the heart of a woman and grow into evergreen things and put out new leaves as the boxwood does, slowly and faithfully, year by year? She could not tell such things; she could only lean upon the foot of their bed with a candle in her hand; she could only pull the cover close about their throats where soon a hard hand would stray roughly; she could only rest her eyes a moment on their soft, child's lips that had suckled at her breasts but a little while since, and soon would have a man's kiss set hard upon them. No, she could tell them nothing more than her mother had told her—that a girl-child's bosom grows when she begins to be a woman, that living with a man whom a woman loves will cause her body to swell and bring forth children that favor him. She could tell them little; she could let them see not one fear in her heart, nor one tear at the back of her eyes.

But she could smooth the cover on their beds, bearing a candle for light in her hand; she could pray that the days and nights might go slowly, slowly . . . until these children were scattered here and yonder away from her.

For some unknown reason, Cean was jumpy as a cat the day that Lonzo left for the Coast. She made Maggie sleep with her that night.

She could not think what might ail her; she jumped at every noise and her heart was heavy as lead. Surely one of her children was sickening unawares, or some accident was lying in wait for Lonzo, or some sickness was in her own blood, not yet having brought her down. All signs pointed to calamity. Straight out in front of her foot on the first morning that Lonzo was gone she saw one of her pins lying on the floor, and the point was sticking yonder the other way. Further than that, didn't her right ear hum all day long so that by no shaking or turning of her head could she dislodge the sound? On the next morning, when she went to milk, she was halfway to the cow-pen before she noticed that she did not have the milk-piggin in her hand; never before in all her life had she done such a fool thing as that! She made a cross in the dirt with her left foot, and spat on it, and turned back to the house for the piggin. Now she knew that some ill-luck was close by. But worst of all, as she went to milk a little before dark, she found a snake-track across her path; she stooped on her hands and knees and rubbed it out with her face, to beat the luck, but the track had been there all the same, a warning in the sand!

Through the next day, she stayed close to the house and took good pains to watch after the children. But when she went to milk that night, didn't a rabbit run straight across her path in the failing light!

That night she dreamed that she saw a green flame in the leftmost corner of the ceiling over her head; it stayed the same size, and it was too high for her frantic hands to reach it and put it out. Next morning, mulling over the dream, she could not figure it out. But it was a mortal bad sign.

Three nights later, she remembered the dream when she waked and saw the leftmost corner of the ceiling over her head strangely lit by flames.

The loft was afire! And in the loft were all her children, except the little twins in the cradle by the side of the bed!

Outside in the yard, the hounds set up a baying. Cean climbed the ladder and shouted Maggie and Kissie awake. Smoke muffled everything; it burned her nose as acid poison would, and made her lungs seem hard-pumping bellows. The children were coughing and stirring in their sleep.

Cean handed down the drowsy, lumpish children to Maggie at the foot of the ladder. Kissie carried them out to the front yard, where they lay on the cold sand of the boxwood walk. Cal stumbled about, half-asleep; his muscles jerked as though he were cold.

Save for the howling of the hounds in the yard, everything was strangely quiet. Cean could hear the sparks popping in the timbers, and the soft roaring of fire gathering air in a draught to hasten its burning. She screamed to Maggie to get from under the loft hole. When the space below was clear, she dragged the chest across the floor and pushed it over the edge of the loft hole, and it fell, breaking loose its leathern hinges pegged with hickory pins. Cean piled her belongings into the dark hole of the loft opening and trusted to Maggie to throw them free of the house—quilts, bags of feathers, wool, the hair-bound trunk, feather beds, children's mixed pairs of calfskin shoes. She felt her way through the boiling smoke; her eyes and nose burned as though fire was in them; she breathed bitter draughts of black air; tears flooded her face, though she was not weeping. When she knew that she could stay no longer, she went down the loft ladder and helped Maggie drag the things out the door to safety in the yard.

The little twins cried where they lay yonder in the cradle in the yard. Lovedy and Wealthy took them up in their arms and hushed them. Little Vincent was wide awake, but he was too frightened to cry.

Cean commanded her children as though they were little tugging oxen. When Cal cried, she boxed his ears till his head rang, and told him to tote out the cook-pots before the roof fell in on them all. They worked like ants in an ant-bed.

When the roof fell in, showering red sparks far into the sky, and the flames rolled up into higher billows, Cean was yonder on the smokehouse pouring water on its roof. Maggie was drawing water, one hand over the other on the well-sweep as fast as they could go, till her hands blistered and the blisters broke. Cal and Kissie toted water to their mother, running so that the cold water from the full piggins sloshed on their legs and feet and made their teeth chatter with cold, though they did not notice it. Chickens cackled and guineas potracked, disturbed by this weird waking in the middle of the night.

Out in the front yard, Cean's children huddled among her piled possessions, lit by flames of her burning home. Lovedy held one little squalling twin, and Wealthy, who was only six herself, held the other. They were singing at the tops of their voices, trying to hush the yelling babies who wanted their mammy's milk to hush their crying.

But their mammy was yonder top o' the smokehouse, try-ing to save Lonzo's meat. She could not hear the brave, thin singing of the little girls' voices, trying to hush the babies:

"Bay-black sheep,
  Where's yore lamb?
  Way low down in the valley;
  Buzzards and the butterflies a-pickin' out hit's eyes;
  Pore little sheep cries Maa-maaa. . . ."

Little Vincent, two years old this very morning, if Cean had stopped to think, sat close to his big sister, Lovedy, and watched the house burn; he was afraid to cry, afraid to move; he could not hold himself still; his leaders jerked, his teeth chattered, but he did not once cry out for Mammy. But because he was so afraid, he wet through one of Maggie's quilts and ruined it, for now it must be washed, and marriage quilts should be laid fresh on the bed so that dreams that are dreamed on that first night under new cover will come true if they are not told before breakfast of the next morning.

The house was long in burning itself down to ashes, for the logs of it were bigger around than yore waist and the timbers were a hand's-span thick. But after the first tall flames, there was no great danger to the smokehouse and the corn-crib.

Cean and Maggie and Kissie and Cal came and huddled with the little children among the piled quilts, case-knives, washed wool, grease, gourds, bedding. The little company sat and watched the house burn down to flaming embers of logs,—door-sills whence their feet had gone in and out, rough-hewn clapboards of the roof that had sheltered them. The heat burned their faces. Far around the house, the fields were lit with lurid light. Cean could see her cows huddled in fright yonder in the far corner of the cow-pen. Out behind her and her children, the hounds sat on their haunches, or loped about, baying; they were distraught with fear, too, but they bayed defiance at that flaming thing that menaced the woman and the little women and Cal, who fed them, and the little things that cried.

The night spread, wild and black, above, for the light of the fire dimmed the stars. Cean took her twin sons on her lap and suckled them to sleep. Vincent laid his head on her knee, and after a while he went to sleep, too. Sweat dried on her body and made her feel the cold. She made Maggie hand quilts around; so they sat wrapped against the cold of the late night. Cean looked up at the sky, wondering what o'clock it could be; her clock lay face down, its pendulum still, under a pile of babies' didies; never, after that night of lying out in the cold, would it keep true sun time again.

The lips of the babies loosened on her breasts; she laid their limp bodies on a feather bed and covered them over, and fastened her bosom against the black night vapors. The children were quiet. Maggie spread out the beds, and Cean made the other children lie down and go to sleep.

"Shet up and go to sleep," she said.

But their lips were tight shut, anyway.

She walked a little way down the slope between the bare crêpe-myrtle trees; she cupped her hands to her mouth; she filled her body with breath fit to burst her lights; she called for help, turning her face yonder toward her Ma's and Pa's place. Her cry went flying into the night, the weird distress call of these piny woods, high and clear and long-drawn, sent on two long, distinct notes like the beginning of a terrible song going through the death-still woods in the night-time:

Whee-e-e-e-e-e        Poo-o-o-o-o-o-o-o-o

She called again and again into the dark. Mayhap some soul had seen the glare in the sky and would know that Lonzo Smith's place was burning down over yonder; for fear that they had not seen it, she would try and wake them. And they would come if they heard her; they would lash their oxen to a run, for they would know that somebody was in dire trouble—fire, or cruel danger of death, with no time for sending word.

The hideous, piteous distress cry of the piny woods went ringing out across the swamplands. And the lonesome echo of the cry returned into Cean's face, breaking in mocking cries softly in her ears, "OO-OO-oo-oo!" lessening like her courage.

O-oh, Lonzo! her heart shrieked. Oh, Lonzo! Come home to me—for yore house has burned down to the ground and yore little younguns are here in the cold. . . .

She hushed her calling; her hands fell away from her mouth. It was no use to call; Pa's place was six mile off, and that was the nearest house. She had called with all the strength of her body, but that was not enough.

She listened; if the night would hold very still for the space of a clock's tick, mayhap, oh, mayhap! she would hear a cry coming from Margot's in answer to her crying, or the sound of three gun-shots to tell her that help was on the way. The answering wind might blow strong in her face from home, telling her to keep up heart. Tight-lipped, she faced the dark. . . .

An arm's-length before her face, a night bird—an owl, or some such thing—lumbered by with dark wings fanning the cold air. Across Cean's face, there passed the brief, wild scent of its flesh garbed in unwashed feathers. The sudden bird startled her so that all her body trembled.

And no answer came, save a lonesome echo that mocked her cry. No sound could she hear but the soft roaring of the fire behind her in the ruined timbers of her home that Lonzo had built for her when she was young and pretty as a pine sapling, and merry-mouthed as a guinea-hen.

No, there was no help. For the men were all at the Coast, trading and tippling and kissing the mouths of strange women. Lonzo, too! What did he care, and him merry-making yonder, leaving her alone to fight fire or to do any other hard thing that came along to be done? Had not she killed a painter oncet when Lonzo was gone yonder a-traipsing to the Coast, and her with a little youngun not yet cooled off from her body's heat? And had Lonzo ever parted his lips to say a word about it? No. He went on, cold as a stone, deaf as a cypress log, blind as a bat, dumb as a bump on a log, saying nothing, doing nothing, but plant and crap, plant and crap, leaving her to herself like she was somebody not good enough for him since he was a man! . . . And now his house was burned down from over her head . . . and him yonder doing God knows what—smoothing a Coast woman's legs, maybe. Hadn't Margot told her how the best of men act up at the Coast, once they are out of sight of their wives and childurn? And God help the wives and childurn left alone with hound dogs and a charged shotgun to protect theirselves with! Cean leaned on the trunk of a crepe myrtle; the tree was cold and soothing on her cheek that was nigh blistered from the fire. Tears rolled down her face in the dark; her breaths came in a tempest of despair.

When she had cried some, she felt better. She wiped her face on the tail of her shimmy. Here she stood in the cold, nighabout as naked as the day she was born. Enough to give her pneumony! A pretty thing she was to cry like a baby! Wasn't there trouble enough without her a-bellerin' over it? With daylight she could load the things that she had saved onto the cart with the children; she could hitch the old ox to it—the old feller that was too old for Coast journeys—and call the hounds and go to Margot's till Lonzo came back. If the cows came up at night to be milked and there was nobody to milk them, she didn't know what to do about it; if the calves got lost off, she couldn't help it; she didn't have but two hands and two feet and one head; she couldn't be Godalmighty out here in this on-gone place to stave off trouble; she had done the best she could do, so there wasn't no use to cry. . . .

And Lonzo had done the best he could, so there! Let him

hug a Coast woman if he got the chance! Hadn't he yearned a little fun here in these God-forsaken backwoods? What she didn't know wouldn't hurt her!

She went back and lay down alongside the children till day. They were all asleep; but sleep would not come to her, for there was yet a glare spreading all about, there was the sickness that went through her now that there was nothing to do. When the first light came, she raised her head to see her shrubs. The leaves on the side next the house were blackened and limp; ever afterward the shrubs grew one-sided, for the limbs on that side were killed, and for years afterward long scars stretched down the trunks of the cedars where the meat had bulged white and healed over the old burns.

Morning light hard in their faces waked the children.

Cean fried bacon and cooked mush on a little fire near the smoking ruins of her house. When they had eaten, she set about loading her provisions and furnishings.

No one had heard her call for help, for no one came.

At the Coast Lonzo stirred under his quilts where he lay under the cart. He yawned in a loud, long relaxation, and stretched his body in every sleepy muscle. He must be up and about, for today he would start for home.

From under the moss that made his bed he raked out his money-pouch and twist of tobacco and the soft doeskin moccasins that he had bought for Cean. He gnawed off a chew of tobacco and laid away the pouch and moccasins in a deep pocket of his cloaths.

# Chapter 19

LONZO'S new house was nighonto
finished in the next spring; it had taken many days of hard
work, from away before day till away after dark, to do it.
For spring planting had to be seen to, howsomever other
things might go. Neighbor men came from here and yonder
to lend a hand in the setting up of Lonzo Smith's house;
Jasper worked like as though it was his own house; Jake
strained his back fit to break over logs and beams and j'ists.

Oxen had dragged in the logs, one at a time, from the
woods. Lonzo did most of the felling and stripping and hauling alone. There was not time for the trees to cyore; they
must be set up green. For this was no bridal house on which
girl-and-boy love was waiting; a roofless family waited on
this house. Lonzo knew well that his folks were right welcome at Jasper's place, but he wanted them under their
roof again with him.

Through the winter, when the weather was not too raw,
he slept on the old site, rousing up the old ox long before
cock-crow. He cooked his victuals there to himself over a
little fire, and hauled logs a second time for a second house
—alone as he was alone that first time as a single man when
he made ready Cean's bridal house. It was bitter-hard work,
but no fool would blame a spark for falling just so on a dry
pine-needle in one certain place on the roof, nor the pine-
needle for catching fire and burning on and on until the
house was ashes.

March came in like a lion and went out like a lamb.
Lonzo named the day for his log-raising in the last week of
the month. He killed two beeves and three shoats. Jake
brought in two bucks from the woods, and went back for

wild turkeys and a sackful of partridges and a backload of squirrels, and finally a big mess of fish. Margot and Cean and the children came from Jasper's with three carts loaded with wash-pots, cleaned chickens, flour and meal, sausages and wild rice and lard and seasonings. They set up the pots over fires of oak wood; they dug out a shallow pit, laid a rack across it, and burned down oak limbs for hot, slow-cooking coals. The men came from all around and brought their womenfolks and children for a great day.

It was a Thursday, dry and mild. The wind lay, and sunshine fell in bright reaches across Lonzo's fields. The leafless swamp lay off to itself, still and harmless now that summer heat did not draw out the malarial miasma from the mud. Lonzo was ever careful not to plow the bogs, even though they would grow corn green as p'ison and high as a house, nearbout. Let that muck be, if it would; turn it over, if you dared, and summer sun would draw out evil vapors, and the wind would blow them all over this land and country.

The pines stood still on this calm day when Lonzo's house went up a second time. The air was quiet save for the shouts of the men, heaving and setting in lifting the logs into walls that grew taller with each new log. Axes made the chips fly from notches where each log was made to fit into the side of another log, heart to heart, bracing one another in steadfast fealty, making a wall to turn aside the wind in its blowing, to beat the rain back against itself as it lashed in on hissing tides from the north.

Yonder the women stirred about the wash-pots that were bubbling, full to the brim of good, rich food over the fires. Yearling-sized boys shoveled hot coals carefully into the roasting-pit to keep the heat slow and even under the quarters of pork and beef and wine-colored venison. For the noontime meal there were stewed turkeys with tender flour dumplings in the rich gravy; there were partridges fried crisp and brown in hot grease; there were squirrels boiled tender in a big wash-pot full of rice. Oh, there were rations aplenty—fried fish and hot hoecakes, stewed chicken and rice, fried sausages, preserves, jars of cucumber pickles—and other things more than you could name. Through the afternoon the coals would go on smoking under the roasting meat; that meat was for supper.

After the men had gorged themselves, they lay about for a while on the dry ground in the sunshine, letting their dinner settle. Then they went back to work while all the mothers filled their children's hands with food, leaving themselves last to scrape the pots and to eat what was left. Hounds gnawed greasy bones in the grass. The children, thirsty from bellyfuls of rich, salty meat, went often to the spring and drank from cupped bay leaves, disdaining the ordinary gourd dippers which the women had brought for the purpose. The women babbled pleasantly together, exchanging all manner of women's news. All the younger women bore children in their arms, and older children tugged at their skirts. When a baby cried, his mother brought out her breast for him, in a quick, rounding movement of her hand, and he sucked and drowsed with his head against the soft, white flesh of her breast—drowsed and waked and drowsed again under the gentle sound of her palavering mouth.

When they sat down at sunset to eat the roasted pig and beef and venison, they could look on the house with satisfaction. It was done, all but what Lonzo could finish up any old time. It was a finer house than the one that had stood there before; this was a double-pen house with a passage down the middle. Lonzo could put on the piazza any old time; he could add shed-rooms to please himself; here was his house ready to live in.

All the company stayed there and warmed the house that

first night. It was too late in the day for journeying; tonight they could rest themselves and swap yarns to their hearts' content. The boys had gathered wood for the clay chimneys that were still wet where the men had daubed them together. They piled firewood on the fireplace in the big left-hand room, and Lonzo stooped with his tinder-box and struck fire to the dead pine-needles and rotten punk and fat-pine splinters. It was a sign: if fire were easy to strike, it meant good luck. The sparks flew, a spark caught the punk, a flame climbed, and the fire was made. Voices rose in excitement; it was a good-luck sign.

As the night deepened, women unrolled quilts and laid pallets on the earth floor where knots of grass-roots were growing—for Lonzo would set the floor in as he had time. Children, whimpering and sleepy, were laid on the pallets and covered over to sleep in the warmth from the great fire that was heating the room and drying the clay of the chimney hard as flint, er nighabout that hard.

Then it was that the men began to shift their quids; and out of the mouth of a speaker would come a labored narrative of some happening on Harrican' Creek ten or twenty or fifty year gone. As the man told the story, all other mouths held silence, save for tobacco spittle that fell, hissing, into the fire, and an anticipatory rumble of mirth before the climax of the story was thrown solemnly into their midst with scarce a twitch of the lips of the narrator. It would be rank self-praise for him to laugh at his own joke. One story brought another, of the War of Independence in 'seventy-six, or a water-journey down the Alatamaha to Dari-an. The women laughed discreetly as the stories broke; they were but shut-mouthed listeners to the talk of their menfolks. The children snored softly on the pallets.

Two women there in the chimney jamb whispered together of Tildia Comstock, who could not come with her husband because her first was expected any day; but she had sent a big pot of chicken and dumplings and a deep huckleberry pie for the log-rolling, and a ham for Cean to start housekeeping on. When that word was told, it was a great joke on Lonzo and Cean, and they both turned as red as a good hen's comb, and laughed, ashamed. Start house-keepin', like a young man and his new wife—the la, me!

True, they were starting housekeeping again, but it was not the same by a long shot as it had been that other time when Lonzo and Cean had come alone to this place in the far woods, burdened with shame because they were alone for the first time and married.

Cean's eyes watered a little, where she was listening, back in the dark. . . . That was a sweet time here alone with Lonzo those first few months. A mortal sweet time it was! . . . Now eight children slept here on her pallets, and three slept yonder alongside Pa. Now, the space which monotony of time, and sorrow of death, and pain of labor lays between two people, lay between her and Lonzo where they sat to-night, with the width of the room between them in their new house. Their bodies were filled with weariness of labor and heaviness of worry, and slackening years that they had not borne on that other first night in their new house. Soon they would be married seventeen year. "Mayhap", thought Cean, "my time of bearing children is over. My hair is gray streak-ed-y; my body is heavy. Mayhap I have done my do. . . ."

But on the eleventh day of April two years later, she bore another daughter whom Lonzo named Epsy Ariadne.

And on the ninth day of the next February after that she bore yet another daughter whom Margot named Eliza Bethany.

And in that same year of Bethany's birth, on a dark night of December, the twenty-and-fifth night, she bore another soul with the hardest travail that she had ever known with any of her children. Lonzo despaired of her life and blew his own breath into her nostrils when her face was purpling with cooling blood, when Margot dropped her head into her hands and wept hard tears for this woman whom she loved more than any sister. The new-born child wailed unnoticed on the bed while Margot grieved for Cean's dying. Lonzo did not take time to grieve; he ceased not to drive his breath up her nostrils. And finally she took hold of his breath, and took it inside her body, and breathed it—Lonzo's breath—till the day she died. They knew that this was so, for Cean was certainly dead and her breath was gone from her when he forced his own breath inside her body.

Hot blood came back to her cheek bones and drove out the ash-gray color of death. When she opened her eyes, there was another body beside her for her to weep over, for her to bury some hard day, or to leave behind her on some harder day, whichever should come to pass. She named it Zilfey Trent for her mother's dead mother in Carolina; she gave it her breasts to drink from as she had done with all the others; she bore the gripping after-pains in silence as becomes a strong woman who knows that no child can be born without pain to its mother.

The child throve, and Cean regained some of her strength, though well she knew that each time that she lay down in childbed, a portion of her strength and life-blood and time of living went quickly away as another being wrenched loose its hold upon her.

So it happened that her first child for Lonzo Smith, and her last for him, had the self-same birthday. For Zilfey Trent, born on a Christmas day, was the last child that ever she bore for Lonzo.

In deadening a strip of land over on the north side of the place he laid the instep of his left foot clean open with the ax.

With a growing family, a man must ever be taking in new ground for corn or cotton or peas or potatoes. Lonzo could not say just how it was that he cut his foot; it was a fool thing to do—a grown man letting an ax slip in his hand as a tampering youngun might.

He was laying the ax into the heart of a great-girthed pine, dead from last fall. The chips flew from the growing notch; breaths went driving from Lonzo's lungs in soft, regular grunts. The notch ate into the wood until the tree quivered through all its formidable, many-seasoned height, leaned its branches a little way toward the earth, swung in a slow arc through the air, and so thundered down in a mighty cracking of limbs, a cruel tearing of the body from its wounded stump, a frantic lunge upward and back to the ground like a beast in its death-throe. Then, the old still-ness fell upon the woods; birds, hushed and flown away at the hacking of the ax and the falling of the tree, flickered back through the quiet. High above in the air was clean, windy space where the crown of the tree had lived, roaring its needles when the wind was high, soughing like a phantom sea when the wind was in the south.

Lonzo's hands had nighabout lost their knack with a knife and a piece of creamy poplar wood or sweet-smelling cedar; now he had to lay his weight on the drive of an ax into a tree trunk for rails to fence in new ground. And he had only Cal to help him; out of fourteen that he had fathered, eight were female, and two of the males were too weak to breathe once. Now Cal was sixteen, and gangling up as tall as Lonzo; he could lay as straight a furrow across new ground as Lonzo could, he could keep his pace with Lonzo pulling fodder or cutting hay. Lonzo was forty, come summer. It was hard to believe, for only a little spell back he was a yearling-sized boy, whistling while he shucked corn in the crib of a rainy day, or grumbling at the grist-mill as he swung the stone around in the cypress gum, fill-ing a peck measure that Pa had set there for him to fill. Aah, la! Pa was dead since the cold, wet winter of last year.

Lonzo and Cean had brought Dicie Smith home with them for the rest of her days, another mouth to sit at their table and eat of their victuals. Pore old Ma, so puny and fault-finding that Cean was hard put to it to please her. . . .

Such thoughts were thick in Lonzo's head as he laid the trees low in this ground that was to be a new field for him to plow and sow and harvest. . . . Suddenly, he stood amazed. Deadness spread from his foot through all his body. He looked down and saw the ax buried in his left instep where it had cloven the rawhide boot through—uppers, tongue, and sole, and held his foot to the earth as a man pegs a leathern hinge to a post.

He pulled the ax out, and in the silence he heard the leather squeak and saw blood well into the breach in the bony flesh of his foot. He called Cal, who was at work yonder on another tree. Cal leaned his ax against a tree and came at his father's call. He was in no great hurry, for he thought his pa had found a rattler or a curious locust sleeping in the bark of a tree. He came through the clear, sunny air, wiping sweat from his bulging brow that was like Lonzo's.

He cut off his father's boot with swipes of his Barlow knife, and bound up the halves of the severed foot with the shirt jerked off his back. Lonzo hobbled up to the house, leaning on Cal's shoulder, resting his weight a little on the heel of the cut foot as he walked.

Cean saw them coming; she came flying out to them like the wind, her face drawn and brown as a cured hide. Cal had never seen his mother's face as it looked now, for mortal fear darkened and drew down her features.

Lonzo made light of his hurt, though he was white around the gills, though the shirt from off Cal's back was soaked through and dripped blood like a dead gobbler's neck chopped with an ax.

Dicie was standing in the door. Her hands fluttered

around. She went to moving chairs, and to quarreling that never could she make Cean keep hot water ready.

Cal helped his pa to sit down before the fireplace, and Dicie threw pine-fat splinters onto the slow fire and set a pot of fresh water to heat.

The children crowded around. Cean stormed at them: "Git out! Don't stand there starin' like lobberheads!"

She boxed the ears of James and John, who were slow to move away from this spectacle of pain, and Maggie and Kissie herded the children out the door, where they waited in the passage and peeped through the door crack, wide-eyed with curiosity and fear.

With all her body trembling, Cean went to the loft and climbed and stooped, gathering her hands full of soft, dusty webs that friendly gray spiders build, bringing good luck to a house.

Blood kept on running from Lonzo's foot. Cean set a knot on the inside vein of his ankle, and swathed the gash with clinging spider webs. They will ever stop bleeding when nothing else will.

When the bleeding had stopped, they set a pot of old cotton rags on the fireplace and lit them from the fire, and held Lonzo's foot in the thick smoke so that it might kill any poison that might be in the wound. Coppers tied on a wound will take out poison, too, but how many coppers would be needed to hide this gash!

Lonzo held his foot in the smoke till noonday, when Cean washed it with hot water and drenched it with clear turpentine; but that started the bleeding again and she had to use more spider web to stop it. She poulticed the foot in tallow and turpentine, and wropped it in a clean rag.

Lonzo lay down, first time ever he could recollect staying in bed in broad-open daylight. He had to bear the healing pains the best way he could. Dicie and Cean did all they could for him, but they knew no cure for healing pain.

Anyhow, it is well known that if one can but bear them, healing pains will purify a body better than physic salt.

It was not for lack of care that Lonzo's foot did not heal. For four days Cean slept but little, and that little in a chair by the fire where she could keep meal and water and poultices hot for treatments. She did all she knew to do, and all that Dicie could tell her.

If Ma were here, she would know what to do. . . . But Ma was not here. She was six year dead; her hands that had a way with sick folks were gone back to the clay and water and dusty bone that made them. There was only Dicie here, complaining that Cean must not have used the remedies right, making them too hot or too cold or too suchaway; else Lonzo's foot would surely get better. . . .

But his foot did not get better; it swelled to twice the size of his head, and stunk. Proud flesh came along the edges of the gash, puffy and white and puckered; Cean burnt it away with burnt alum, but it came back. The meat of his foot turned purple and then green; red streaks went reaching up his leg to his groin. His fever ran so high now that he had no sense, and when he had sense he was wild with pain. Cean gave him fever tea and broke him out in sweat, but before she could change his shirt he was burning iron-hot again. Once when she was burning out his foot with turpentine, he groaned like a bull and looked hard into her eyes, and begged her:

"Cut hit off . . . er let hit be . . . fer God's sake . . . !"

Cean could not chop it off, though in her own mind she thought that would cure him. That foot was mortified already; it was carrion fitten for the buzzards; if it stayed like that and reached upwards he would die.

The poison reached upward, bloating his knee and thigh, turning the meat into purple, stinking putrefaction.

In a black dawn of February Lonzo died, plunging in spasms, when Zilfey Trent was less than two months old.

So it was that Cean bore him no more children.

Never did one of her children see Cean weep for Lonzo's passing. Ever she had felt contempt for loud grief from a woman. She had wept quietly when her father died, and she had wept when her mother died; now her grief was bound in her heart by some restraint that was hard and strong as the iron rim that a cooper sets about the head of a cask to make it hold its shape and serve its purpose. She could not cry now, not with all these children gathered about her, a-feared of something which they could not understand. Solemn-mouthed, still-tongued, they stood about their mother, waiting to see how they must act in this emergency.

Dicie began to wail and to wring her hands and to beat her breast. Her voice shivered, high and thin, and descending in mournful monotony like a screech-owl's.

Cean's eyes hunted about the room; she could not think what to do, now that she had loosed Lonzo out of her arms to death. The baby, Zilfey, waked in the cradle and squacked in short, sharp, hungry cries. Cean took her up and suckled her quiet. No, Cean must not cry, for tears poison a mother's milk for her child. The baby's clothes were wet all the way up its back. Cean motioned for Kissie to hand her a dry hippen from a chest in the corner of the room.

Maggie, slim and straight and proud-faced, stood behind her mother's chair. She was twenty and pink-cheeked as a mayhaw, bright-eyed as a young 'possum. She was crying softly, and the sound of her breath catching distractedly in her throat disturbed her mother. Cean thought: "She can cry, but I must not. Hit's only her pa, and she hain't but twenty year old last Christmas mornin'. Now I am going on full thirty-and-nine. That's old enough fer a woman to be able to hold her tears. . . ."

Maggie was to have stepped off last October with Will

Sandifer, the oldest boy of Dorcas and Zeph Sandifer's. But Cean was then heavy with this last child, puny and hardly able to go, so Lonzo had persuaded Will and Maggie to wait until spring. It was a pity, for Maggie was already nigh onto an old maid. Now that Cean was well again, and Lonzo's last illness was past, Maggie would marry and move off yonder to Dicie Smith's place, for Dicie had willed her place to the first of Lonzo's children who should marry. . . .

Cean clutched suddenly at Maggie's hand that lay on her shoulder. She stared grimly into the fire; she thought, "If Lonzo's ma would hush her screeching, I could think what to do. . . ."

But Dicie would not hush, and all that Cean could think of was Maggie's hand there on her shoulder: "Oh, you little girl-child hand that will soon be patting a hoecake on a hot spider for William Sandifer's belly, don't go off now . . . not now! . . . with Lonzo gone. . . . I named ye fer a magnolia blossom. . . . Lonzo thought hit mought be a likely name. . . ."

The word that was her oldest child's name reeled crazily through her head, repeating itself like the sound of a loom's treadle: Mag . . . nol . . . ia. . . . Mag . . . nol . . . ia. . . . It was a maddening sound. . . .

Cean found herself standing there in the middle of the room with a desperate cry gone out of her mouth across the still form of Lonzo. The baby, Zilfey, was there in her arms, waking and pulling again on her breast for milk. Cean walked to Cal, bearing the baby in her arms, and shook his lean shoulder with a free hand:

"What 'r' ye a-standin' there a-starin' at me fer? Why haint ye done gone frum hyere fer yore uncle Jasper and yore aint Margot?"

Cal hurried out, glad to be told something to do.

Cean turned harshly on Maggie and Kissie:

"You gals! Don't ye know dinner's got to be got fer the folks that'll come? Looks like yere old enough not t' look t' me fer every blessed move ye make! . . ."

Cean drove the children out into the passage and across to the other big room. She threw more wood on the fire, and went up to the back of Dicie Smith's chair.

"Now, Ma, you know and I know that hit hain't a grain o' use to cry. . . ."

Cean spoke to Dicie as she might have spoken to Zilfey. Dicie stiffened her back and hushed her weeping.

"Oh, let me be! . . . Ye younguns don't know what hit is t' be left here withouten nobody . . . nobody . . . nobody. . . ."

Cean led the old woman out across the passage to the other room, where another bright fire burned in the chimney at the other side of the house. The children would comfort Dicie. It is a hard thing to grieve when children are about.

Cean went back to Lonzo's room to lay him out. Her fearful children heard the wooden bar slipped home on the other side of the door on the other side of the passage, and knew that their mother was alone with their dead father. No, she was not alone with him; little Zilfey, his last child, was in there, too.

Here in this room whispered talk rose among the children. Dicie, as is the way of some women, talked to ease her grief. She began to relate this or that account of Lonzo when he was this or that many years old. Ever he had been a mild-tempered child, she said; never had he caused his mother worriation, as some sons do. . . .

Maggie carried Bethany on her arm as she measured and sifted meal for the hoecakes for dinner. Bethany was just old enough to toddle and whine at Maggie's heels. Maggie had no notion of hearing her whine now, for she could hardly keep from crying, herself, so she carried Bethany on her arm.

The little twins, Jamie and Johnnie, grabbed the tongue of a little wooden wagon out of Aryadne's hands and caused her to fall and crack her head on a chair post; it was Aryadne's wagon, in the first place, for her pa had made it for her. Kissie slapped the twins so hard that the palm of her hand stung; then she shook them till they hushed, and sent them for firewood, to get them out of the house. They were a troublesome age—four-and-a-half—good for nothing but to make a fuss and tote in firewood. Vince was going on seven now; he could feed the pigs as good as any man. Wealthy was eleven, and Lovedy was fourteen—buxom, fat-cheeked, sweet-tempered girls.

Cal must be a man now, whether he was full-grown or not. Maggie must put off her marrying for a while longer, and if Will Sandifer would not put it off, then he must find him a wife of another name than Smith. Kissie must stop her traipsing around to cane-grindings and pinder-b'ilings and candy-pullings; she must stay at home and help her ma make a living. Lovedy and Wealthy must take more of the work on their shoulders, and not play yonder most of the day with the younger children under the trees by the wash-place. These children's pa was gone, and they would all have to move in closer together, trying to fill the gap where he had been. . . .

For Ma was in yonder, grievin' alone over Pa. . . .

Kissie set her teeth as she washed the brown rice for dinner; she'd get her a handful of switches and she would tan the meanness out of Jamie and Johnnie, if it took her till Christmas. They must learn to quit their impishness; they must learn to watch after Aryadne and Bethany and little Zilfey while the others worked.

Maggie diddled Bethany on her knee beside the fire,

stooping every now and then to rake coals in or out beneath the pot of greens or the hoecake-spider or the oven set on the trivet.

Aryadne leaned on Dicie Smith's knee, sucking her thumb; her eyes were set on the fire that licked the fluttering tags of soot on the back side of the chimney. She laid her head on her grandmother's lap and her eyelids drooped in the warmth of the room. Dicie lifted her and rocked her, talking all the while of some doing of Lonzo when he was her age. She hushed her talking to weep, and hushed her weeping to talk of him who was the only son she had ever borned, the only soul that bore her name, save these little ones that he had begotten of Carver blood.

Cean opened the door and came to the fire. She gave Zilfey to Kissie, saying:

"Her dress tail's wet ag'in. Change hit 'fore she ketches cold. . . ."

Cean stood with her face turned down toward the fire.

Maggie grieved to see her mother's face so hard and full of sorrow.

Cean did not turn her face to any of them, but they all knew that her words were for Lonzo's mother when she said:

"Well . . . I've fixed him up the best way I could . . . with his leg like hit is. . . ."

She laid her arms on the mantelpiece to hide her face. They saw her shoulders shake a little, but she stared steadfastly into the fire that was busy making coals to cook his children's dinner.

They held silence, save for Aryadne's sucking lips that caught a fresh hold on her thumb every now and then.

Now Grandma was quiet, too, for there hain't a grain o' use to cry when a dead body is washed and laid out in another room and a-gittin' cold. . . . Lonzo was not now absent at the Coast, nor at Jasper's, nor at a neighbor's. He was gone forever through a dark door. Never till the last dawn broke would she see his face, or hear his voice, again. Cean's teeth chattered if she did not hold them carefully shut to; the leaders in her neck strained as though they held up a heavy weight. Her flesh trembled in its struggle to hold itself serene in the face of this grievous soul's hurt. Her mind seemed sluggish and ponderous; it was laboring to encompass a thing too vast to be encompassed in mortal thought. She dared not even imagine the depths of this grief. He was gone through the door that opens into darkness. Hardly any soul is so brave that it does not shudder when it hears the door opening softly and knows that it must go out into the frightening dark; for the door will close as softly as it opened, will close upon the light of a sky set with hot sun or tremulous stars, upon the unlovely human face of a soul's beloved. Lonzo was gone, and to see him again, after an unknown length of years, Cean must follow him through the dark door. Shaking heart and uncertain feet! Where is Lonzo and which way did he take? No Solomon could tell her.

Margot and Jasper came to help Cean make plans for the buryin'.

But they could hardly grieve with Cean, for they were but a month since married; and no single sorrow outside themselves can come betwixt two lovers who have been but lately joined one to the other.

Never a line had come from Lias's hand in going on eight year since he had deserted his wife. When the elder came through in January before Lonzo died, Jasper put the matter before him, and the elder was willing to pronounce Lias Carver dead and to join Margot to Jasper as his lawful wedded wife. A congregation assembled in Jasper's house and agreed to Lias's death. They heard the whole matter, and any man was free to speak his thought. In the end, the elder raised his voice and said, as though to notify Lias:

"I now declare Lias Carver dead!"

So Margot was a widow.

Her breaths quickened, and Jasper leaned his weight on his other foot where he stood beside Margot, facing the elder. As Jasper changed his weight, his sleeve lay close against Margot's sleeve. They were comforted at the touch. Though they hid the fear from one another, each was afraid that somehow Lias would come betwixt them yet; Lias was mean as a very devil, when he wanted to be. If he knew that Jasper was marrying Margot, he would come back and take her away from Jasper.

With hardly a pause after he declared Lias dead, the elder married Margot to Jasper. Jasper did not like the elder's hurrying into the marriage. Somehow, in Jasper's mind, Lias's name was mingled with the marriage words; somehow Lias thrust himself between Margot and Jasper, cheating them of proper intimacy. To spoil this sweet marriage, there rose in Jasper's mind an ugly memory—I once cut blood out of his head, and he bled into my face; likewise to Margot there came a memory—He put his arms about me all the time I was being married to him, how long ago at the Coast.

Now, at Cean's house, making ready for Lonzo's buryin', Jasper could hardly let Margot out of his sight; he was forever straightening her shawl on her shoulders, or stroking her sleeve as though it were rumpled. And Margot, for her part, could not sit beside Jasper without resting her hand lightly upon his long thigh, as though she laid new claim upon him whenever she came near him.

Cean did not note these little things, but curious neighbors at the buryin' wondered that Margot and Jasper could not hide their feelings, for God knew that they were plenty

[ 284 ]

old and stable to know better than to flaunt their ardor at such a time as this.

To Cean, the bitterest thing in Lonzo's dying was the letter that came to him after he was eight months underground and could never read it with mortal eyes.

In the fall, Cal went to the Coast to do Cean's trading, and found a letter for Lonzo waiting in Villalonga's counting-room. Cal brought it home for his mother to read, fearful of its consequences, once he had seen its mark of the post. Cean took the letter from Cal's hand; it was sealed with a little wafer that she found hard to pull away, for her fingers were rough with trembling. It was a letter demanding much postage. Villalonga had handed back only sevenpence out of a silver dollar. Oh, the way it had come by ship and by stage, across stormy water and high hills and mayhap desery places. For the letter was from Californy, and it told them that Lias was alive and well, that he wished Lonzo to make peace for him with his family.

Tell Ma [he wrote in a tall, mannish scrawl] that I have got her a vermilion-dyed merino dress picked out and linnen cloaths aplenty to dike herself out in Tell Fairby that her Pa has got boughten for her a silk dress and a book of needles for her to sew it with for he would like to see her sew it up her own self being as she must be a big girl in this time Tell her that she shall have a red head shawl to boot if she be a good sempstress by the day I come For my son Vincent the rascal I will try and rickollect a polished rams horn and a jews harp and a bord shotgun to kill molly cottontails by but if he is hard to make mind and is give to sassing of his mother I am apt to disremember Tell little Cean to get her a hole ready for a Californy plumb tree I will bring her For yoreself Lonzo you lousy old buckkiller I will try and manage a jug of wisky to warm yore innards Look out for me when you see me coming But I swear that you will hardly know me when you see me coming home.

At the bottom of the sheet there was a line for Margot:

> Tell my wife if she be willing I should wish to take up where I left off and give her such a bridal party as she will not be ashamed of.

Cean's face had a cruel look from the tears which she would not allow herself.

> I submit myself respctfully yr brother Lias Carver.

That letter! It brought Lias before Cean's face as though he were standing there. Never would Lias follow a letter-form, nor pen his letters precisely, saying, "This leaves me well truly hoping it finds you the same." No, it took Lias to make a sheet of fool'scap talk.

Cean did not know but that she would do better to burn the letter.

But she shut up the children's questions over Uncle Lias's letter, made Cal hitch up the ox-team, and rode to Jasper's to tell him. She did not know what else to do. She might 'a' knowed Lias would do a fool thing like this, thinking to ride up some fine day, feeling proud as Lucifer, and rubbing his fine fortune in on them all. So Lias thought to bring whisky to warm Lonzo's in'ards when they were rotted away! And a merino dress for Ma's pore old body under the ground! And a needle-book to please Fairby, now that a dozen needle-books would not make her smile; her finger bones could not curve to the learning of stitches now; now she could not run out to greet her father if he rolled up in a gold coach pulled by white horses.

Cean did not thank Lias to come here bringing a plumb tree for a peace offering, making more trouble than they all could ever patch up.

For in this time Margot was eight month gone with Jasper's child.

When he read the letter, Jasper turned white and said

nothing. But Margot went into a hard spasm of weeping, and neither Jasper nor Cean could say anything to quiet her. When she got hold of herself, Margot turned it off, saying:

"Ye'll have to overlook my taking on so. I'm toucheous and heavyhearted. . . ."

So Lias was not dead; and Margot had lived in adultery with Jasper and was bearing a child outside of marriage. . . . Till death us do part . . . ! No opinion of any man, no word of any elder, can set aside those words between a man and a woman.

Margot went off to the spring-house to set away the butter and to be alone . . . —I am Lias's wife—she thought— and when the elder married me to Jasper the words were air . . . and no more. . . . From this hour on I must live apart from Jasper. In another month I must birth his child, but he must not help me do it. For I am but his sister. Jasper helped me when Lias's child was born; if he is here in that time, Lias will help me when Jasper's child is born. Or will Lias kill Jasper? God-almighty! why can we not see a little time ahead and so step aside from a mess that lies ahead of us! or do we walk straight into a mess, shut-eyed, and biggity-hearted!—

She stood watching the spring water boil up out of its dark hole; it circled up as water in a pot circles before it boils, but it was icy cold. Men told that once an Indian woman had fallen into this spring and quick as thought she was sucked out of sight. You could not find the bottom of this spring, even with a long stick.

—If I stepped in, I wonder if that would be the last of me. . . . But it would be a horror to be swallowed down into this loose gullet of the earth, to be churned around for no telling how long, to be spewed out yonder God knows where on a bleaking mountain hot with volcano flame—

She knelt beside the spring, and leaned her weight on

the palms of her hands, and studied the dark depth of the spring. The welling of the water troubled the likeness of her face as she stooped and looked into it; the spring was black and gluttonous, an insatiate mouth. Oh, the earth has mouths; the swamps are full of them, slobbering and sucking and trembling for greediness!

She thought—Lias is alive and well. . . . I should wish to take up where I left off. . . . Take up and leave off and take up again . . . like an old shoe. Hard new boots are a trial to the feet. . . . Lias, I have shed enough tears for you to fill this spring. If you have ever shed one for me, I do not know of it—

She pulled up to her feet again, and nigh pitched into the spring, for the weight of Jasper's heavy child. She would ask Jasper if this spring would truly swallow a body if one were offered it.

Cean bore the letter back to her house and laid it away in her chest of precious things. This letter was nighabout as precious a thing as a gold piece, for all his life Lonzo had coveted a letter in his own name.

On the children's birthdays, Cean took the letter from the chest and read it to them; but never to them did she read the line of the message to Margot. It had been set at the bottom of the sheet, and Margot had torn it away to keep for herself, and the written likeness of Lias's name set down by his hand.

The twins dug out a big hole on the slope and hauled manure and dumped it in the hole, ready for the Californy plum tree. Each of Cean's little girls coveted for herself little dead Fairby's silk dress and needle-book that her pa was bringing home to her. All the children worked hard and were extry good in hopes that Lias would bring them jew's-harps or Barlow knives or any old thing, so long as it was from Californy.

When Cean was gone back home, Jasper took down his

old rifle from the buck-antlers over the fireplace; he wiped it out carefully, rubbed the pan with a woolen cloth, drew a piece of tow through the touchhole, poured in powder, sprung open the grease-box in the breech, put a little grease on a little piece of patching, laid it on the muzzle with the greasy side down, set the bullet on the patching, pressed the bullet down with his forefinger, carefully cut away the extry patching, primed carefully, and laid the charged rifle back on its buck-horn rack over the mantel-shelf.

Lias was slow in coming, for some reason. He should be here in this time. But he did not come.

A month later Margot bore a son; and Jasper, brash and reckless in the face of Lias's arrogance, gave his son his own name and the maiden name of Margot's mother—Jasper O'Sullivan. Though Margot was not his wife, and before God had never been, Jasper could hardly do his work for hurrying back to the house to see if Margot needed anything. He could sit by the hour, holding his child. A frown on the child's brow tormented Jasper; he did not want his child to be sad-hearted and heavy-mouthed like its father; he wanted this son to be like its mother.

Jasper bore the trouble in which he found himself as lightly as might be, for he took full blame upon himself for it. Always he had known that he had no right to marry Margot.

Now she quarreled at him for any little thing; she sharpened her tongue upon him as any wife might do; she said no strong, hard thing, but was apt to find fault with anything he did, and taunted him with being slow and shut-mouthed. To answer her, Jasper only sighed and heaved his shoulders a little. He was willing for Margot to quarrel at him; she had enough on her mind to drive her crazy as a nit. If he and Lias had left her be, she might have been happy. As for himself, he was being punished and he would see to it that Lias was punished, ever he came home.

Each day they thought: This day Lias will come; but day after day went by and he did not come. They tired of looking forever down the trail toward the east; they tired of keeping themselves cocked and primed to meet Lias. They did not know that Lias could not come now, howsomever he might wish to. And for Margot's quarreling at Jasper, and for his humble care of her and the child, they were as well as married.

# Chapter 20

LONZO's death was no great matter to the crops that were planted in his ground; pea-fields blossomed and bore as heavy a hay-crop as ever; as in any past happy year in Cean's life, corn stretched its brazen-green stalks upward to golden flower-heads.

Cean seeded her land and brought it to bearing and stripped it of its harvest nighonto as well as Lonzo had done these things. Her mouth lost some of its gentleness and became hard and tight; the children would whine back at her if she were not firm with them as she set them to hoeing out the weeds in the fence corners or to setting cabbage plants or potato draws; they would lag along behind her now that Lonzo was not here to threaten them, until Cean learned to threaten, too—and to carry out her threats when they were not heeded. She trounced the children sometimes until she would be ashamed of herself; when she scolded one that would not hush his whining, and raised her hand to strike, and saw him dodge as a hound dodges a stick, she would be heavy-hearted because she must use hard measures with her children. Oh, how they needed Lonzo over them to draw obedience by the simple, gruff calling of a name! Cean sometimes exhausted herself in switching the twins, and when it was over, went up in the loft and cried about it. She did not know what she was to do as her children grew older; what if they should turn on her and jaw back at her? She did not know what she would do when she was too old to whip one till he gave in to her.

She was too worried up over many things to grieve overmuch after Lonzo. She had cried for the little twins that she lost, she had cried for Caty who swallowed fire, but she had cried no great deal for Lonzo. She had too much work to do to sit and cry after him; there were too many noisy mouths to call after her and quarrel among themselves. But, oh, sometimes in the night when the house was still but for the clock's ticking and the soft snoring of her children, she stretched her hand to the left of her where he had always slept, and her whole time of life seemed as empty as that little stretch of feather bed that he would never warm again. Never had he been much for kissing and fondling, but well Cean knew that he had loved her as a good man loves his wife—without any great change or much talk of it till one of them is put underground. For a time after Lonzo died Cean wished that she had been the one to go; but now she could see the wisdom of His ways. What in creation would Lonzo have done, left alone with this passel of younguns? He would have got him a new wife before a new year. Cean would not like a young and foolish stepmother over her children; no, she could see that things were better as they stood.

The country about was opening up and filling in. To the west, families had settled, and Cean felt safer. It was a fur piece yonder to the Mississippi where the county line used to run; for in the old days, Georgy stretched from Savanna to the Alatamaha and westward to the South Seas; and there was nothing between here and there but walls of black pine forest sifting down dead needles in the wind, and wide rivers, and fever swamps, and wild Injuns roaming about like pigs in a chufa-patch. The Georgy Indians were kind Indians, folks would tell you, but Cean wouldn't put no trust in a man that lived wild in the woods like a black bear.

On a bright morning in the early fall of 'fifty-eight Cean and all her children drove to Margot's, where Maggie was to be married to Will Sandifer when Margot and Cean had all the preparations made. The new preacher, Dermid O'Connor, was staying at Jasper's house. And, anyhow, somehow Cean wanted Maggie and Will to stand where Seen Carver had set Cean's and Lonzo's feet when they stood up to be married.

Maggie's was a finer wedding than Cean's had been. Margot and Cean cooked up pies and sugar-cakes for days ahead, and scrubbed the walls and floors of Seen Carver's old house until everything smelled of pot-ashes. In the middle of the front-room floor, clean now as an eating-table, Cean marked with a dead fire-coal the place where Lonzo's feet had stood, and another mark to the left of it where she had stood. She stayed on her knees a minute, recollecting; yonder was Ma's place behind Pa's shoulder; and beside them had stood Lias and Jasper and little Jake—who had cried when Cean married—who was now thirty-and-three year old and was breaking land to the north across the river from Pa's place and a-courtin' little Kish Acree. After the last longest, it looked as though Jake might grow up, after all, and be a man. Kish was a little thing, not half as old as Jake—fifteen come June. She had slapped Jake's jaws one night before a crowd of them all when he had teased her past endurance about having such big feet; then they all knew that he would marry her, for her feet were not much bigger than a child's, and Jake could see it for himself. Kish had cried when Jake teased her so, and slapped his jaws for him. When Jake saw her tears he went and sat quietly behind her through all the loud talk and merrymaking, trying to make her laugh by put-on crying over his jaw that he claimed she had broke with her fist! They two would not frolic nor join in the singing nor pull candy; they sat in the corner away from the others. Cean watched them with sheep's-eye glances. Until yet she loved her little brother fit to kill. Kish sat with her childish, puckered chin tucked down into her shoulder, with her blue eyes cast down to her stiffly-starched bosom, with her fingers working at the little hand kerchief that lay in her lap. Jake's eyes were cast down, too, for he was ashamed that he had teased her until she cried; he could not think what to say to her to make amends. But when the new preacher, Dermid O'Connor, brought out his banjo from the shed-room that used to be Ma's, and plunked the heavy wires a time or two, and raised his voice in that sweetest song that Cean had ever heard in all her born life—"Ever of thee I'm fondly dreaming"—Kish's little brown hand went to hide under the full, wine-colored skirt of her dress that was spread out on the wall bench, and Jake's hand went and found it. Jake and Kish sat so through all the sweet length of that song. Cean had to turn her face away to keep from crying. It was all the same as it had been more than twenty years gone, only it was Jake and Kish now, and not Lonzo and Cean. Before she could turn around there would be another wedding. . . . She thought: Time does not pass in a clock's ticking; oh no! It goes like gusts of wind past the north corner of a house. Stay in the sun on the south side and you never know a wind is blowing, but breast around the north corner, and it will jerk your breath from out of your ribs. It is blowing, but you don't notice it; always time is passing, but you don't notice it, until that baby-chile, Mary Magnolia, is ready to stand up and take a husband and go yonder to Dicie Smith's house to live.

Cean went about helping Margot with preparations for the bridal feast. Margot was planning such a time as people have at Coast weddings; she had enough victuals to feed an army—meats, preserves, pickles, pies, cakes. And in the loft stood crock after crock of brier berry wine. Cean doubted that Pa would like liquor in his house, but folks must change when times change, and mayhap brier berry wine is no crime. Anyhow, Cean would make no objections to any of Margot's plans; for Margot had worried so long over Lias's coming that Cean was glad for her to have some big thing to take her mind off herself.

When the Irishman stood Maggie and Will up to marry them, Cean's eyes went to Maggie's face and stayed there. Maggie stood shyly beside Will Sandifer's straight, lean figure; her eyes were bright and soft and trustin' as a young squirrel's. "Do me no hurt," a little squirrel says to ye, as plain as eyes can speak, "for God knows I mean no harm to ye!" Cean could not bear to see the look in Maggie's eyes; she moved in behind Jasper's shoulders, so that if a foolish wet came to her eyes Maggie would not see it.

There was merrymaking all night long in the old house when Maggie was married. Even Dermid O'Connor, the New Light preacher, drank goblets full of sweet brier berry wine, one after another, in the course of the celebration. When the fun was loud and plain-spoken—and truth to tell, Cean was growing a little squeamish—the preacher came over to where she was sitting and asked her how the Widow Smith was feeling; and she answered, "With my fingers, the same as always!" And the two of them laughed at the joke, sorry as it was. He said, "And how does it seem to have a grown gal married?" She could think of no smart answer to that and answered, simply, "I reckon I feel no different from before." Still he would not hush his talking. He went on, "A body would never think but that ye was sister to Miss Maggie, t' look at ye!" Cean blushed at that; her heart thudded like a girl's, though well she knew that Margot's brier berry liquor was making him lie like a sinner, and making her have no more sense than to listen to him. Not in years had a body paid her so much mind.

When no one was looking, she went into Margot's room and looked at herself carefully in the looking-glass set in a brass frame on the wall. (Jasper had brought Margot that present from the Coast like as though she was his wife.)

Sure enough, Cean saw that her eyes were bright as shoe-buttons from the Coast, though she knew that was because she was excited over Maggie's wedding—and full of brier berry liquor. Alone with herself in Margot's room, she wet her lips with her tongue and smoothed her cheeks with her hands. No, she was not ugly; wrinkles lay deep across her forehead and around her eyes; her face was fagged and worn; but she could still be a handsome woman if she would poultice her hide in meal and buttermilk, as some women do, and wash her eyes in brine night and morning, and grease her hair with goose grease to make it sleek and shiny.

When she went out to the big room again where Margot was ladling out sweet brier berry liquor, Cean took another goblet that was pushed upon her, and drank the goblet empty. She sat in a chair along the wall, and laughed to see the young folks having such a fine time. The back of her neck tingled as though a poultice were laid there; she felt warm and content; she thought it was a happy thing when midnight came and Maggie and Will went off to the bridal chamber that Jasper had given up for tonight so that Cean and Margot could dike it out to be Maggie's room. For very brash deviltry, Cean drank a new goblet of wine every time one was offered to her, until her head was nigh onto falling about on her shoulders. She thought—and could not get away from the thought—That was Ma's best room, and Pa carved her a cherrywood bedstead for it. Nighabout two years ago it was Jasper's and Margot's. And, la me! twenty-and-two year gone Lias led Margot in there to sleep . . . and that was when I was new-wed to Lonzo . . . afore Mary Magnolia was a baby.

Cean was like to cry for sadness; she thought—Still, I am not sad; it's but them brier berries that Margot made into wine.

She sat along the wall, watching the frolicking and fun-making on this side of that shut door yonder, and she was dreamily content. Nothing disturbed her, not even the thought of the least baby, Zilfey; if it waked and cried, Wealthy would turn it over and hush it.

Earlier in the night she had looked toward the loft hole, and had seen Wealthy with heavy-eyed Zilfey in her arms, and Lonzo's Vincent holding Margot's baby, Sully; Jamie and Johnnie and Aryadne and Bethany were ranged on the floor at the edge of the loft hole, peering down into the room like shy little animals watching how foolishly men may disport themselves. Here in the room were Margot's son by Lias, the gangling-legged Vincent—more like his father now at sixteen years than he was the day he was born, and he was much like him then; Lias's frown was stamped between his brows, Lias's quick step and high-tossing head haunted the body of this youth as though it were possessed of a spirit. Down here capering with other young ones were Cean's other children. Kissie laughed too much and turned her head if Seeb Ingle but spoke a word to anybody at all; Cal was nearly a man with the best of them, seventeen, and beginning to try out the young girls with a joke in his mouth; Lovedy was the age of Margot's Vincent, lacking one day, and the prettiest child Cean had at all.

Cean leaned her head against the log that she had washed down with strong soap suds the day before yesterday. She was satisfied; it was worth any pain to see Maggie happy; it was worth all the labor of her and Lonzo's hands to see their children step off in turn, well provided for. A pity Lonzo was not here to see Maggie's wedding. . . .

Words of the new preacher fell dully on her ears. He had come to sit beside her. She could scarce hear him for the warm, singing sounds that were all about her, obscuring the meaning of his words; her blood worked in her body like sweet brier berry juice that turns to wine. Margot had showed her how to give away a daughter—not with tears and fears and solemn good-bys, but with jokes and laughter and wine to kill the uneasiness that must rise at the marriage of a woman's child. She would give away the others in a proper manner; she would set wider reaches of cotton; she would raise more goods to trade off for linnen shifts for her girls to be brides in.

And for Kissie's wedding she would poultice her face in meal and buttermilk so that she would not look like Kissie's granny; that O'Connor had said that she looked like Maggie's sister. She turned her head and sought through the pleasant, heaving haze that enwrapped her, and found the preacher's face and laughed into it. He answered her laugh:

"Ye're that handsome and sensible-hearted, Cean Smith, that I could nighabout forget me mission in these backwoods. . . ." She laughed again: "And ye're close onto bein' a black sinner fer sayin' any such a thing. . . ."

She turned her head to rest it on the wall behind her, and closed her eyes, curling her lips at his lying.

The next she knew, Margot was shaking her shoulder and laughing at her for falling asleep at a bridal party. Soon the sky in the east would be gray with day. The merriment was dying down; everybody was tired and sleepy.

Cean went out to the well to draw water for breakfast.

She found Dermid O'Connor there in the half-light, dousing his face in freezing well water. For the first time she saw him clearly, though there was only half light to see him by. He was tall as Lias; he favored Lias with his sandy hair and eyes that were blue as plumbago blossoms. A new thing in his face held her eyes, and she knew that she had never seen him as a man before: his brown beard was cut away from his cheeks and mouth and only fringed his jaws; his face was clean-shaven all about his mouth; his lips were free to come and go over his teeth that were big and clean and bone-yellow; gaiety came shameless to his lips and stayed there, unforbidden.

He smiled at her now with bright drops of well water clinging like trembling dew to his hair, to the clean flesh of his mouth. She closed her mouth that had fallen open as she stared at him, since she had never seen him before. She said:

"Good mornin', Brother O'Connor. I hope ye rested well. . . ."

He laughed at that foolish slip; and she had to laugh, too. He bade her good morning, calling her Cean Smith, and surprised her by asking her what her maiden name had been. She said:

"Since ye ask, it was 'Tillitha Cean Carver.'"

He nodded his head and said m-h-mm. She saw his teeth catch his lower lip and gnaw it, as though he were thinking of something. She was a little disturbed over her meeting with this stranger. She had taken him to be an ordinary preacher, and he had turned out to be a man, forty or fifty year old (old enough to know his mind), who paid her compliments of words.

She went back to the house with her mind full of the sound of her maiden name and the sight of his nagging teeth on his naked lip.

But she forgot all about it when she climbed to the loft to wake the children and to change little Zilfey's hippin.

Cean and her children and Dicie stayed on for a day or two at Margot's house, after Maggie and Will had ridden away to their home at Dicie and Rowan Smith's place. Dicie had stood on the steps, calling advice after them: such-and-such a field would never grow potatoes—"all vine and no 'taters; Rowan, nor Lonzo after him, could never make it bear."

After the younger children were asleep at night, Margot

and Jasper and Jake, Cean and Dicie and the older children, sat before the fire while Dermid talked and told of this or that great thing. Cean longed for Cal to be here and hear all these things, but he was staying at home to look after the stock and fowls. O'Connor could tell of Ireland's Big Wind of 'thirty-nine, till you could nighabout feel the houses rock on their sleepers with the force of the blowing. All Limerick and Galway and Athlone suffered in the Big Wind; houses fell in and hearth fires were scattered; the wind blew destruction everywhere like a raging beast loosed upon helpless little people whose little houses were frail as fool's-cap in the grip of the wind.

Cean's thoughts followed the sound of the soft, clean-spoken words that came from Dermid O'Connor's naked lips, and midnight would find her with her chin in her hands, her eyes set on the lean, clean face of that preacher who had eyes like a child's, though he must be older than herself.

Jasper might tell a tale for their ears, but Cean had heard all those tales before, from her father's lips. There was a hurricane in Carolina in the year 'four that lifted cattle off the earth and set them down a field's wedth distant; chimneys cracked away from the houses, and scattered fire had to be put out then, or not at all. Where there was not water enough ready-drawn to hand, by grace of Godalmighty, houses flamed sky-high in less time than it takes to tell it. Pa had told that the night was made light as day with whistling, beating flames of homes afire yonder in Carolina. And many houses were laid low like so many stacks of split pine-fat kindling.

Down here in the pinywoods, there was a harri-can, in 'twenty-four. Cean was but just six year old then, and could just remember her ma running out of the house with Cean in her arms; Jake was born in the night of that day, and Ma said that was why Jake was puny and gal-like when he was little—the life was nearabout scared out of him before he was ever born. They had heard Pa tell about it a many a time; a steady blow came hard against the house, and went away, and came again harder than ever. There was scarce half a piggin of water on the table by the fireplace; if the chimney had gone down, there would have been nothing to do but let the house burn. Only God's mercy had saved this house in which they all sat now, recounting exciting tales of another time.

Dermid O'Connor had helped to drive out the Cherokees from the up-country of Georgy in 'thirty-eight; they started with up'ards of fourteen thousand reds—male, female, and their young—but four thousand died before they got to Tuscumbia. They wouldn't eat, and died like flies along the way, grieving for the red-gullied hills where they were born. Little copper-skinned papooses sickened at the breasts of the squaws, and died, and were borne on, on the backs of their mammies, till they stunk; for the redwomen would not lay them down on this foreign ground, nor bury them away from their fathers. Dermid O'Connor had learned to shoot an arrow like any Indian, and in those days he could hamstring a deer as easy as he could hawk and spit on a weed. And in Ross Landing, Tennessee, there had been a prisoner by name of John Payne that could make a fiddle wail like a child a-cryin', his music-makin' was that sad.

Now O'Connor was ashamed of all his wild and woolly younger days. That was all when he was foolish and adventuresome, he would say; now he was old and settled. His eyes went across the fireplace and met the eyes of the little widow-woman, Cean Smith. He reached down his banjo from the mantelpiece, stooped and threw on another light'ood knot, and beat the taut wires of the banjo in thrumming tunes that he had danced to when he was young and foolish. He kept time with his foot on the floor, and before they knew it all their feet were beating the floor and all their faces were set in smiles as they heard of the frog that went a-courtin', um-hum. . . . O'Connor could throw the banjo into the air, and catch it again, and go on, with never a beat in the music gone awry.

Cean's face would be as sour as vinegar when he sang "Ever of thee I'm fondly dreaming." He would nearlybout pull the breath from amongst her heartstrings, with that song, but she would give no sign. What woman could he be such a fool about, as to dream about her like that forever? Some Tinnysee lady in Ross Landing, doubtless. Nothing so fine in a Tinnysee lady! Cean might have been born in Carolina her own self, if her mother had so decided. . . .

Or maybe he bore in mind a rich coffee-planter's daughter in South Ameriky—or a half-black signorita . . .!

O'Connor had traveled all through the Brazils where there are noddy-birds and boobies that have no more sense than to lay their eggs on the bare rocks; where butterflies grow big as a man's hand; where people sleep on straw mats for mattresses, and eat breadfruit and baked cassada, and call beans feijao; where common swamp ferns grow tall as trees and vampire bats suck horses' blood; where ants build nests twelve foot high and roads are marked with wooden crosses where murder has been done; where winter is summer, and summer is winter, and cloves and peppers grow on trees like mayhaws or acorns, and cinnamon may be found in the bark of a tree. Oh, Dermid O'Connor would tell of South Ameriky until Cean could nigh see the thorny acacia trees grown to ugly, wry-armed shapes that bend away from the sound of the sea and the steady blowing of the trade-winds.

Why, Dermid O'Connor had even fit in the Mexican War, ten or twelve year gone, when Cean and her people had only heard that war was going on to the west of them!

He could tell about Sam Houston, barricaded in the Alamo, till Cean's blood ran cold for pity.

Was there anything that Dermid O'Connor had not done? she would think. He had fought, caroused, chased Indians, gone from one land to another like it was from one settlement to another; and now he was preaching. He called himself a missionary to the pinywoods, as the Wesleys had come to the wild Indians away back yonder a century gone, and more. O'Connor knew all manner of matters. And he could sing "Blow ye the trumpet, blow!" till you could nighabout hear Old Gabriel cut loose on the Last Day. . . .

Here it was that he would set up a brush-arbor church; here he would set up a school presently for all the children round about who would come. Margot would have her big long-legged Vince taught free, for the use of her big front room as a school-room, and O'Connor would work in the fields with Jasper for his victuals. On every Sabbath Day that was fair, O'Connor would preach in the arbor, and the women would spread dinner on the grounds. Cean thought it not nearly so lonesome a land as it used to be.

She was proud of the schooling that her children would get from this O'Connor. It was to be a first-class school, with everything from a fescue to point out the letters to the beginners, to a dunce-stool for the laggards. Cean told the preacher that he must surely set up two dunce-stools for her twin sons, but he said that he much doubted it if they anyways took after their mother; there would be ciphering and penmanship and spelling. Cean used to be a good speller herself, with Pa hearing her the words; she could reel off her abiselfas and anpersants as fast as Pa could give out the words. She had no doubt that Dermid O'Connor would learn her children well; he could read the hardest words and the longest periods of a late gazette from Charlestown—or even Boston.

After Cean and Dicie had gone back home, Cean would catch herself humming "Ever of thee I'm fondly dreaming" over her quilting or sewing, till she felt like slapping her own mouth to make it behave. Never had she been a light-mouthed woman; she was too old to begin now. Once Dicie looked sideways at her daughter-in-law from the other side of the quilting-frame; her face was sour as though she had stuck teeth into a green persimmon when she said as how the preacher would be a fine catch for some woman without a husband. Cean stormed an answer at the old woman as though Dicie had insulted her. That was the first time that Cean could remember talking so to one of her betters; she could not think what had possessed her. Dicie seemed not to mind; she dropped her face lower over the quilt, and said nothing, drawing her lips inward upon her thoughts.

Early in the next spring O'Connor's school opened up. On that first morning, Cean and all her children were up long before day, frying meat and baking hoecakes and potatoes for dinner for the children. Cean sent all of them this first day—all that were old enough to take anything in; the crops must wait on schooling for her children's heads; she must spare the ox from the planting and plowing. The older children all rode away in the cart—Kissie, Cal, Lovedy, Wealthy, Vince, and the twins. She would pay for their schooling with cotton or lard or hams, or even a gold piece out of her chest.

She minded the littlest children in the house—Aryadne and Bethany and Zilfey. All day long, the house seemed strangely still; there was only the sound of the voices of the little girls who played on the floor, and the steady ticking of the clock on the mantelpiece. Now and then Cean could hear the grit of Dicie's needle on her thimble through the cotton of the quilt. This quiet minded her of long since when she watched after her first babies in the house while Lonzo was yonder in the fields making his crops; here were the same sounds, the same work to do, the same peace in her heart and head; nighabout she believed that she could go to the back door and whoop Lonzo up from the far cotton-patch. The long time that had passed seemed not to have left any mark, but the mark was there; she felt it when her back ached with her old weakness, and when Dicie complained overmuch, and when Lonzo never came in from the far cotton-patch.

This country was not as lonesome a place as it used to be, and that made a big difference; cartloads of children went by her home morning and evening, going to and from the school. Some children, whose parents were hardest up, came walking, or caught rides on other folks' carts. The trail came through the lane of crepe myrtles and went away yonder to other houses. Hardly a day passed that there were not comers and goers. It was a pleasanter place to live in now.

There was more to see, more to do.

In June, Jake had corn tall as his head on his own land, and cotton green as p'ison in rows back of his house that was ready for Kish Acree, not half his age, and hardly big enough, Cean thought, to do her own washing by herself. If ever Cean saw a man that thought a woman was made out of pyore gold, that man was Jake, and that woman was Kish, hardly a woman yet. They two were married on a hot day in June. They were married by Dermid O'Connor over at the old Acree place. The old elder was dead, and the new elder had washed his hands of this settlement that ran after a New Light preacher.

Kish was a sweet bride in a dress as blue as her eyes; and it was a good sight to see Jake standing there, lean as a bean pole, beside her. He was proud as Lucifer over Kish. He had to look a far ways down his shoulder to find her eyes, for she was little more than half as big as he was. She was fifteen and he was thirty-and-four; it was a matter of merriment among the young folks to think how Jake was nineteen year old before ever Kish was born.

At this bridal frolic, Cean drank more brier berry wine, and heard Dermid O'Connor say at her shoulder:

"Would ye ever care to be a bride again, if the right one should come along, Cean Smith?"

Cean lied like a sinner; her heart thudded:

"Don't know as how I'd care to make the same mistake twicet. . . ."

She turned her back upon him, but not before she saw how angry she had made him by laughing away his offer. Well she knew what his few words had meant. She saw him bite his lip to hold back words that he might have said to her because she was fool enough to make a jest of a tender compliment.

Her unthinking words spoiled the party for her, and she got no more pleasure out of it all.

After that, O'Connor came near her no more, and she went early to the loft and lay down to sleep; but she lay awake till dawn.

They drank the last of Margot's brier berry wine at Cean's house in the summer of that year when Kissie stood up to marry Seeb Ingle, Lissie and Martin Ingle's oldest from yan side o' the river. Dermid O'Connor was there among many others, but he said the marriage words and little else, most especially to Cean. Cean laughed more than anybody there, and joined in the frolicking until Maggie, sitting in the corner at her sister's wedding and six months with child, was ashamed of her mother showing her petticoats in a dance. Late in the night when O'Connor went out to the well, Cean saw him leave the room, and taking her foot in her hand, as they say, she went after him and found him as she had seen him that first time, his face dripping water like a dog-fennel dripping dew, his eyes still as blue as the blue flame at the heart of a coal, though he must be a half a hundred year old.

She said what she had to say in a hurry:

"Mouths talk without authority sometimes . . . and tell lies when they shouldn't, Dermid O'Connor!"

She meant to tell him:

"Ye asked me oncet and I lied to ye, for that I was so ill-at-ease."

He shook the beads of well water from his hair, and wiped his face in a white linnen hand kerchief. Then he set his eyes on her face and watched her close as a hawk:

"Ye're drunk, Cean Smith."

He hoped she would answer:

"No, I ain't drunk. I'm sober."

But she did not know what he wished her to say.

She caught her breath in her throat; she clutched her hands together and turned and walked to the house as fast as her feet would take her; and shame dyed her face red as a rose. Never had she been so outdone; never had she been so sad over a little matter that was less than nothing to her. For she had offered herself to him, and he had as good as slapped her in the face in return.

Now she would see him in burning torment before she would marry him, though he should beg her till his tongue dropped out. . . . But she kept wondering if ever he would ask her again. Oh, this mulling over a man would surely end her vanity over her eyes that yet were bright though she was forty-and-one year old. An end was put to it.

For a month following Kissie's wedding, she would not let her children set foot in Dermid O'Connor's school, claiming that the weather was too bad. But that was no reason; before this she had sent them when they had to spread cowhides over the cart to keep rain off their heads.

And well O'Connor knew it.

# Chapter 21

MAGGIE died in childbed the year that Kissie was a bride.

When Maggie began to sicken with fever when her child was three days old, Cean took the baby away from Maggie's breast and fed it on goat's milk weakened with rice water. Between the baby's crying for its mother's milk, and Maggie's fever that would not slack, Cean got no sleep for a week.

When Maggie went, and was laid out, Cean fell in a heap on the bed in the cold, damp shed-room of Dicie Smith's house, and felt that she was going to die, and hoped that she would. She was but a lone sojourner in this world now; heaven was a happier, warmer place by far.

Cean did not hang over Maggie's dead body, grieving as some women make grief over their dead, kissing faces that have the feel of drying, newly-dug clay against their weeping lips. Some women will scream out when men let down a coffin into a grave, as one man stands in the hole to let one end of the pine box down, then climbs out so that the other end may thud into place; any woman knows that such treatment will jar every bone, every inch of flesh, though it be dead. Cean would not scream out. Is a dead corpse more knowin' than a planking of wood or a stone, than cold dirt or dead leaves or any poplar chair? Cean would not stand over Maggie, grieving because her eyes were shut, because her mouth was speechless and could never learn words again, because blood was clotted cold in her veins by the hard ague-fit of death.

"I did not love my child's soul enough," Cean grieved. Oh, she had loved Maggie's body that was part of her own even now, as surely as her own hand or her lifting breath was part of her body. "I loved the body overmuch, I know." Now when she must give the body to the ground, and never see it more as she had seen it in this world, it was like to kill her. She grieved for Maggie more than she had grieved for Lonzo, or her mother, or little Caty. "Ma was an old woman, and it was time for her to go. . . . Caty was a little child and missed all the hardships that this life brings a woman. . . . But Maggie was a woman old enough to know her mother's heart without sayin' many words about it. . . . I loved Lonzo more than all my children put together, but never did I bear him about with me for nigh onto a year till he was grown enough to breathe for himself. . . . I carried Maggie . . . and quarreled to myself because of the burden she was to me. . . . I did not give Lonzo his breath and his heartbeat and the very blood in his veins. . . . I never suckled Lonzo in my arms a thousand times over, as I did this baby, this woman-child. . . ."

Oh, Cean could not have hurt more if her heart had been ripped out of her body and set yonder on a hot spider to fry and be eaten. "Can it be," she thought, "that griefs cut deeper when we are past bein' young?"

She was like to lose her mind, for she kept thinking that breaths were like threads on a mighty loom, drawn tight, woven among one another, broken singly as each life reaches its frayed or short-cut ending. She could hear the treadle of the loom knocking in her ears—but that was her heartbeat. . . . No, it was surely a loom, working secretly at its business; and every knock of it brought her nearer to the end of her own thread of breath that was drawn yonder closer and closer with every rise and fall of her breast; and finally it would be cut, as she cut free the threads of a web of homespun, and wove the loose fringe of warp threads that were left on the loom beam into a thrum towel with tassels tied along its lower edge. She had lost her breath, Lonzo had told her, when Zilfey was born, and he gave her his own breath; mayhap that cut his breath short so that now he was in his grave, two year since, before ever he was old enough to die. Still, there would be found her lost breath in all her living children, for they had drawn it from her as they were born; each child cut her own breath short by that much. The more children a woman bears, the sooner she dies. Now her first little twins had never been able to catch their breath from her, since she had murdered them in her heart long ago; for the seed of a woman's waiting children lie in her body from the day she is born, and she must watch that her head nor her hand nor her heart do them no hurt till they come to their birth, each in turn; that is why a woman-child must be purer in heart than a male child may be, careful of her body, holy in her mind, for she bears within her the seeds of souls, like a green seed-pod that will ripen in time and scatter itself before it dries and dies and is empty.

The knocking of the loom in her ears, the weariness of her body, the labor of much long-thinking, were like to drive Cean out of her right mind.

Margot tried to cheer her; her children hung over her bed; but she would not rise nor eat nor do anything that they asked her to do. She let them take Maggie and bury her yonder in Pa's buryin'-ground, and would not even rise from her bed to go and hear the last words said over her child. She stormed hard words at little Will Sandifer who had brought this on Maggie and had stood about like a dolt while Maggie was dying. Lonzo would have done differently, thought Cean; Pa would have done differently; Jasper or Jake or Lias would have done differently. This was no man, but a spindle-shanked child, that Maggie had married, for he laid his empty hands against his face and cried like a woman.

Dermid O'Connor came and prayed over Cean because Margot asked him to. He set all the others out of the room, and spoke to Cean as though he were a warning angel from God. But he talked to the back of her head, for she had turned her face to the wall and shut her ears to his words. Well she knew that Margot had sent Cal for him.

His words fell slowly; she listened because he spoke so low:

"Cean Smith . . . 'tis yours and Godalmighty's business, the settlin' o' this matter. Another human has no business a-comin' atwixt the two o' ye. But a sarvint o' His'n that takes a powerful interest in the peace o' yere sowl can bid ye to take on yere showlders inny burthen that He chooses to lay there. They're plinty sthrong, Cean Smith, yere showlders. 'Tis a woman that ye are, such as God but rarely chooses to make up. 'Tis top place I'd be a-givin' ye. Yere plinty sthrong to bear this, yere plinty able. 'Tis only yere heart that's a-wearied and a-tired, but mind ye, He told ye a long while sincet, 'Come unto me, all ye that labor and are heavy-laden—and I will give ye rest. . . .' "

Silence fell; Cean went on listening through the silence.

"Yere eyes were not meant to laugh all the while, Cean Smith. 'Tis grievin' that makes the eyes o' a woman deep with understandin' and sweet with the love o' God. Me mother was o' Catholic faith. She prayed to Mary, Mother o' God, and found comfort for her sowl when she lost a son at sea, and another in the war with Bonaparte. Meditatin' on Mary comforted her grievin'. I buried her one day. I doubt not this very mornin' she and Mary be a-sittin' Yonder Some'eres a-talkin' over the little boys that the two o' them washed and kissed and buried in this world. 'Tis Mary maybe ye'd better think on. Ye're child was not crucified in shame. Kneel at the foot o' yere cross, ye that are only another little Mary, and God will give ye comfort,

[311]

too. . . . Cannot ye turn yere eyes thisaway whilst I say a little prayer fer ye?"

His voice dropped nighonto a whisper as he entreated her as he might entreat a hurt child.

She said:

"God's forgot that ever I lived . . . He's forgot . . . and He never cared, nohow. . . ."

He smoothed her brown, rough-palmed hand; he held her hands to keep her from jerking herself away from his admonishing:

"Oh, 'tis not true, the words yere a-sayin', Cean Smith; and well ye know it. Never does He forget a child o' His'n. 'Tis His children that forget that He is rememberin'. Get on yere knees and climb on them up to the shelter o' His arms. Knock on His ears with yere prayers. Creep into His arms, Cean Smith, and lay yere head on His bosom, and He'll hold ye closer than inny man ye ever love can ever hold ye. He'll lay His hand on yere head and ye'll stop yere restless fightin' against His will. He'll shut yere pitiful little mouth from complainin' against Him. Ye'll hush and be comforted. . . ."

She dared him to prove his saying:

"Then pray fer Him to do them things fer me!"

He prayed; and when he had finished, Cean's will was as water to God's will, and Cean's tears were softening and healing to her heart.

O'Connor parted from her with the words:

"Rest yereself, Cean Smith, and pull yereself t'gether. 'Tis others ye must think on, and not all yereself. There be others that be thinking on ye when ye don't know it. Whin all this grief has lessened, I mind me o' a question I'd like to put to ye for ye to think on. . . ."

Cean began to mull over what that question might be before little Levie Pleasant, dead Maggie's girl-child, was three months old. But other griefs intervened between that question and Cean. Bloody flux carried off Levie Pleasant and Cean's own last baby, Zilfey, in the spring of 'sixty.

Early in May, Dicie went off in the night, from heart failure; Cean found her stone-dead early one morning, with her eyes staring at the ceiling, and her hands hard in rigor mortis on her chest.

Cean stood these griefs far better than she had stood Maggie's death, for through them she leaned hard upon Godalmighty and Dermid O'Connor.

The brush arbor was hardly big enough to hold all the folks who came from round about to hear O'Connor preach on Sundays.

Cean sat on a narrow plank with her children ranged on the right and left of her. Willow baskets were in her cart, full of good things for the dinner on the grounds.

Dermid O'Connor would eat no pickles or preserves but her own, and would so make her feel faint from blushing. As he preached, she would lean forward, and all his sermons seemed messages for her alone—words which the others could never understand. His words fell into her heart and lay there for later remembering; she turned them about and gloated over them as one gloats in secret over precious letters from a loved one far yonder.

Wagons and road carts, oxen and mules, and sometimes a bushy-tailed horse hitched to a swinging limb were halted all about the brush-arbor church. The animals stamped their hooves and switched their tails at flies that settled on their flanks in the drowsy heat. Away from the brush arbor leaves of the trees murmured a little in a breath of air; and a louder murmur of a man's voice preached heaven and the remission of sin, hell and sin's sure punishment. He was preaching the glory of the "New Light" that falls into the minds and hearts of men when they seek God carefully with tears and prayers. "And as he journeyed, he came near Damascus; and suddenly there shined round about him a light from heaven. . . ."

Last year's oak leaves and pine-needles lay thick on the sandy ground that was marked by hooves of animals and feet of men and women. The brush arbor sat in the midst of the wilderness on a sandy slope above a sweet-water spring not far from the crossways of three trails of the settlement. Its sloping roof of thatched palmetto fans was reared high on cypress poles; planks were ranged on wooden blocks, forming rows of seats for all who would come; the rostrum was a tall cypress gum with a puncheon seat behind it for the preacher of God. At the left of the rostrum there was a water-shelf holding a water-piggin filled with water from the spring, and a drinking-gourd. Through the preaching little children would come for water, and go back down the wide aisle, and rustle softly across their mothers' knees to their places.

Dermid O'Connor's church was formed from this beginning.

In time a weather-boarded house was set up; the boards were riven from logs and dressed down with a builder's adze. Elders were elected from the assembled congregation by common acclaim, and rules of church order were formulated and penned by Dermid O'Connor into a church record.

By common usage, the church came to be called Sweetwater Church. O'Connor left the name at that, and preached a sermon on how one might come to this house of God and drink of sweet living water to quench the bitter-salt thirst that sin leaves in the soul.

The rules which the elders formulated were read for the first time on a first Sunday of July. O'Connor stood before a pine table which had a drawer in which to keep the record and the quill and the ink-horn; he read the rules slowly and solemnly, letting each rule sink into the minds of the people, so that each man and woman might hear and judge if he wished to become a member of this congregation:

1. There shall be no whispering nor show of disrespect within this church, nor fighting nor use of profane language on the grounds thereof.

2. There shall be no taking by stealth of any article that is another's, by any member of this church, whether it be a house, a wife, a water-piggin, or a shoat, or any other thing.

3. There shall be no swapping of horses on Sabbath Days, nor wagoning save to and from the house of God.

4. There shall be no getting out of temper nor acting un-Christian-like.

5. There shall be no shows, nor vain display of things of this world.

6. There shall be no corrupting of the soul by sins of the flesh.

7. One member may accuse another member and bring a grievance before the congregation that shall try him openly for his sin; but such accusation shall be made only to the glory of God and the redemption of an immortal soul; in such case, the congregation may appoint a committee to wait upon a malefactor.

8. When a member has conscious guilt of sin within his soul, he shall by his own compulsion rise before the congregation, accuse himself, express contrition, and be forgiven by God and man.

9. No member shall be admitted to communion with this congregation save by earnest confession of faith in God, and the witness of the spirit.

When the rules were read, O'Connor preached a powerful sermon on "Repent ye!" The very air stilled at the recital of the visitation of the wrath of God upon brazen sinners. O'Connor told of that day when the moon shall turn to blood and the sun shall become black as sackcloth of hair, and the earth and sea shall heave up their dead, and sons of men shall flee and pray for the rocks to fall upon them and hide them from the wrath of Godalmighty, who shall have borne with sins of men till He wearies and takes His revenge.

Little children hid their faces in their mothers' laps, and strong men trembled, as O'Connor read the dreadful words, awful by reason of their truth, from the Word of God, and expounded them for the salvation of lost souls.

O'Connor opened the doors of his new church and commanded the people to fall on their knees, elders and all alike, and pray for a sign that God had forgiven their sins, that He would take them within this church whose members would be caught up in that great day of wrath, safe from the belching flames of hell, safe from walking pestilences and plagues that shall besiege the earth when the vials in the angels' hands are emptied and the beast riseth out of the sea to make war upon the saints.

"On yere knees, for 'tis black with sin ye are!" the preacher shouted.

And they fell on their knees.

There rose from the plank benches murmurs of the voices of terror-stricken souls, and the whimpering of babies whose mothers ignored their children's hunger in their own greater hunger after righteousness, in their fear of eternal damnation.

They labored in prayer, as the preacher had told them to do, for a sign that their prayers were heard and their sins forgiven. On that Sunday, dinner was not spread till the sun was low in the west, for souls were seeking entrance to this new church; their names on its roll would admit them to Glory when this world goes up in fire.

Many mothers went home without the blessing, for their thoughtless children at their knees kept them from seeking with all their hearts as a soul must do. But there were many who fought their way through and found glory in their grasp; one by one they laid their hands in the preacher's hand, confessed their sins, and asked entrance to this church, and cleansing baptism under water.

Margot was among those who confessed their sins this first day.

She stood before the congregation with the horror of hell set on her face, and confessed her sins of twenty-year-and-more gone, and later sins of not so long ago—her love for Jasper while she grieved after Lias, and the sin of Jasper's child. All the country round about knew of this last sin, but none blamed Margot nor Jasper; no man knew but that Lias was dead when she married Jasper. But no soul that heard Margot confess knew of her sins of twenty-year gone. An awful hush fell upon them; so this good woman had a heart dyed black in sin; all the while she was carrying about a load of sin in her breast! No wonder God had visited sorrow upon her. Their faces hardened, judging her sorrow just and her heart mean and hard. But Jasper dropped his head in his hands and groaned like a death-struck bull. Little Sully tugged at his mother's skirts as she stood in defiant shame, easing her soul of its load; the child was troubled and wept because his mother was troubled and wept. But Vincent, son of Lias, and now nigh eighteen year old, did not weep, but hung his head and could have died for pity that he felt for his sweet mother.

But for all the belated peace in her heart, Margot never again held her head proud and tall as was her old way; never again would she meet a body's eyes when she spoke, but dropped her own glance nigh onto the low hem of her dress; rarely did she speak save when she was spoken to.

Neither did she fear Lias's coming now. Lias was a thing that she had lived past, with pain and length of time and patience, as Seen Carver used to say that a woman must do with some things.

Bliss Corwin, now a thin-bodied, ashy-faced little woman, accused herself before the congregation, and was forgiven of her heinous crimes of many years gone. Bliss was an old, dried-up woman, nigh onto forty year old. People said that she was light in her head, and her own mother would not deny it; for Bliss was forever holding converse with the guineas or teaching an adder to know her. Under her mother's front step there lived an old frog that Bliss fed night and morning as though it were a beast. When any comer appeared, Bliss made it to the crib or the woods, and no persuasion could make her come out to talk with a body. Long ago she had begun to drop her eyes before other eyes, and to murmur meekly when she spoke.

She made her confession with her eyes set on Dermid O'Connor's feet. Her face had the look of a child in it, though age-wrinkles were thick across it. Mayhap her confession made changes in her; it is not given to curious, eagle-sharp eyes to see into the placid or turbulent hide-outs of the heart.

When she was through speaking she stood for a little minute with all her body trembling with the beating of her heart. Dermid O'Connor said, "God bless you, sister!" and all the elders breathed "A-men." Then Bliss hurried down the aisle and ran to her father's cart, for she was sick. She lay for a while on a quilt in the back of the cart, but soon she lifted her head and spilled her breakfast over the cart-wheel.

Dermid O'Connor began to feel a fearsome doubt: Mayhap I do wrong to ask these people to turn their hearts wrong side out for all the people to see. It is not meet for a minister to come between any soul and its God. . . .

But he could not think how to mend matters now. Truth

is, he had not deemed these simple people to be so deep-dyed in sin.

Cean confessed her sins with her eyes set steadfastly on a trembling scrub-oak tree that showed through an open shutter: she had acted un-Christian-like a thousand times; she had fought against Godalmighty's will in her life; she had ever loved her loved ones' bodies more than their souls; she had lived selfishly, thinking more of her own woes than of the griefs of another; and she was ever hoping for peace and rest and happiness in this present world before she reached heaven—which cannot be. Her own mother had confessed this last sin many times, Cean said; Cean was thribbly guilty of it.

As Cean confessed, Aryadne and Bethany sniffled into her skirts. They could not understand what their mother's words meant, but it seemed a sad thing to weep over.

Cean told the congregation that yet, for all her praying, she had no witness of the spirit to relate, but she would pray on; and she asked for their prayers.

She sat down with blood storming in her ears, and breaths short in her chest. Never before in all her life had she said so much without halting.

Two days later the witness of the spirit came to Cean after she had fasted two days and nights till she puked from emptiness. She had sworn to take no food into her body until Godalmighty should give her a sign. Through her fast she kept her thoughts on heaven, she prayed unceasingly, she repented of her many sins with tears.

On the second night she got the blessing, the seal of God's approval. Never did she doubt that it was a vision that came to her in her sleep. . . .

She was walking across a swampy place where her feet sank into warm muck that oozed pleasantly between her toes. A red bird sat on her shoulder and sharpened his beak on her ear that was become white, new bone like that which sprouts from a heifer's skull. Undergrowth and swing-ing tendrils of vines grew so thick before her that she could not see the place to which she was hastening; it lay yonder beyond, pulling her feet toward it. The red bird, ever whetting his bill on her ears that were of horn like a heifer's, flew about her head and settled in her hair, and blinded her eyes with red from his wings. Then slowly, out of the muck, her toes that had been bare flesh showed bone gray like a heifer's hooves. Inside herself she felt bones bulging and crowding and falling loosely together, so that she was that weak that she was like to fall from faintness. And ever the red bird dartled about her head, and alighted upon her toes, and struck his soft, feathery blows about her body. Then the red bird troubled her no more. . . . She was walking up a green slope, and her body was feather-light, so that walking was no labor. She knew herself to be beautiful and strange-appearing, for where her limbs had been there were left only bones shaped in the shape of her former body, molded of cloudlike, shining substance, soft to the touch, and more pleasant to behold than words can tell. Her flesh had fallen away in the red bird's beak. But this was she in pearly raiment that was not flesh, but bone, that was not bone, but some other substance. Never at any time in all her life was Cean able to describe that substance. She walked, swift and light as wind's passing, over the green grass to a place where children were playing under an apple tree that was laden with blossoms and fruit, so that every heavy bough was smothered in bloom, so that apple-fruit fell in a bright, soft storm all about her head and crowded under her feet until she could not walk, but must float above the ground cluttered with fair fruitage. The oldest child that was playing there was Mary Magnolia, white of body like Cean and formed of smooth and lovely flesh such as magnolia blossoms wear. She bore in her arms a small, white child whom she called Levie Pleasant. There were with her other children, white as the moon and as softly bright: there was Caty, with a smile on her mouth; there were naked twin boy-children who caught Cean's feet in their bright hands and pulled her out of the air that gleamed like an opal, down to the green grass. The twin boy-children whispered to Cean their names—Timothy and Titus—and Titus was the more beautiful, if they could be said to differ. . . .

The vision broke, and Cean rose in the night and broke her fast with cold cornbread and fried meat. Her prayers were answered, and in no ordinary fashion; she had seen heaven before she died, a vision commonly granted only to saints.

Now that her soul's salvation was attended to, Cean took a smart set and caught up with her work in the fields.

And O'Connor started in to court her in earnest.

He did not ask her outright to wed him. He sent her an album by the children—a thing that he had bought at the Coast last fall and had penned full of tender verses for Cean Smith. The verses had come out of his head, telling her of his love. Cean's heart fluttered over each verse, like she was sixteen:

> Whose fair face lights my deepest dream
> With light celestial, Pure.
> But day shall have no sunlight Beam
> Until that I am Your
> > Dermid.

Cean had never seen a swan, and well she knew that her neck was noways like a swan's; but one verse read:

> A swan's Neck Graceful is as well.
> And sweet the Turtle-Dove.
> But brings no word that Any Tell
> Of One like You to Love
> > With all my Heart.

She had learned all the verses by rote long before he came up the slope between the showering pink of the crêpe myrtles to ask if it may have happed that she had come into possession of a little book that was sent her by an unknown party. She sent the children away to chop and tote firewood. She smiled to herself, and feigned ignorance of any such book, until he thought a prank had been played upon him and felt himself a monstrous-big fool. Gloom settled upon his clean, naked face with its short fringe of brown beard. Then she laughed at him:

"Ye be a mighty foolish man, Dermid O'Connor, if ye believe anything a woman tells ye!"

He laid his hands on her shoulders and, retreating from his nearness, her head pressed into a branch of crepe myrtle and shook free a little shower of blossoms that fell upon her head and his head as he kissed her mouth that had the sorrow-wrinkles set about it and the weight of years pulling it down. They stood in the midst of the low tree that was full of plumes of puckered blooms that fall if a breeze but shake them a little—much less the leaning of two strong bodies—that smell a little like four-o'clock flowers, that are thinner than butterflies' wings, softer to the touch than a bumblebee's worsted garb, sweeter as they fall than any other flower even as it buds.

He laid her head upon his breast and did not note that the hair upon it was nearly white. Cean did not remember, either, under the drifting tide of blossoms and green leaves as she leaned against the clean trunk of her crêpe myrtle tree with her head on the breast of the minister of God-almighty. The touch of his naked lips on her mouth was a sweeter, more comforting thing than any sermon he had ever preached. Here was a new sacrament—a new way of tasting bread and wine for the remission of pain and death.

Then she turned her face fearfully up to Dermid O'Connor's.

[ 322 ]

"Dermid O'Connor! Hit mought be a sin fer me to find such pleasure in yore kissin' me! Hit mought be carnality, moughtn't hit?"

He laughed, with his eyes shooting blue fire upon her:

" 'Twould be a mighty shame if that were thrue. But we must gower through this world as best we may. Mayhap Godalmighty forgives carnality if we be ashamed for it. . . . 'Tis foriver kissin' and repentin' I'll be. . . ."

Cean felt the nigh like a fool on her second marriage-day, in August. For Margot would have her garbed in frilled pantalets under her wide-skirted, full-gathered white frock. Cean could not get used to the feel of the pantalets all up and down betwixt her legs.

To be fancy, Margot set a dish of pick-tooths in the center of the table at the bridal party, and there was much laughing and cleaning of teeth when dinner was done.

And the press of Dermid's mouth upon Cean's lips, against her neck, within the blue-veined inner curve of her elbow, made her forget that ever her mouth had wept, that ever her shoulders had bent under sorrow like a tree under a storm, that ever her arms had ached with being full of love for a dead body—for now her arms were filled again.

# Chapter 22

WITH her new name Cean had taken upon herself a new life that was different from the other two lives that she had lived under her other two names.

Cean Carver was a pyeart, shy-mouthed, swift-fingered helper to her mother, and a nurse to Jake, and a pupil of her father's tutoring; Cean Carver was a girl-child of unexpressed fancies and long imaginings.

Cean Smith was a woman that Lonzo Smith made from a brown child that had no more sense than to let a rattlesnake bite her when she was growing the dark bud that was to be Mary Magnolia, sweet as a white tree-flower and dead now as the magnolia blooms of year before last; Cean Smith was shut-mouthed instead of shy-mouthed, and browner and swifter of finger than was Cean Carver. She would slap the jaws of a child that did not mind her; she could make up her mind in the flick of an eyelash, and stick to it for the rest of her life. Cean Smith made her children keep their teeth clean with fire coals and salt swabbed on a chewed sweet-gum twig; their bodies must be clean and sweet-smelling before they got into their beds at night; before they fell asleep, they must say their grateful prayers, thanking God that they were still alive, though heaven was a wondrous happy place. Cean Smith was sensible and careful in all her ways.

Cean Carver learned of her mother how to keep a house and how to tend a child and gave her knowledge to Lonzo Smith's wife. Cean Smith learned of Godalmighty how to bear a grief without complaining, and passed that knowledge, like a secret gift, to the woman that married Dermid O'Connor.

Cean O'Connor was the object of gentle envy among other women of the Sweetwater Settle-mint. The New Light religion had come upon them like a bright light, and those who had not yet the witness of the sperrit were wrastling like Jacob of old for it. Now, Cean Smith had been chosen to step into that holy of holies that was the preacher's life. None doubted that he was a true minister of God, that his way of preaching was The Way, The Truth, and The Life. None doubted that he would see Glory, though they might fall short of it; for he was a good and wise man, gentle in all his ways, kind in his judgments, patient in all his ministering. Now, Cean Smith was to live with him as wife, feeding his hunger, knitting his stockings, greasing his boots, quilting his bed-covering.

From the day when he married, the preacher fell a little way from grace in the eyes of his church; he was not now the Christlike saint with his eyes set on heaven, for he had taken to himself a woman to comfort him, and she was his first wife, though he was fifty-one come October, by his own admission. Never again did he seem so holy-minded, so set apart in God's service, after the day when he said his own marriage words over himself and Cean Smith. Never again did the laying-on of his hands upon the heads of the women so move them as a witness of the Indwelling of the Holy Spirit. For now he was Cean Smith's husband.

Cean was a good wife to him. She rubbed the silver communion chalice and the pewter plate until they shone. Each Sabbath morning she had Dermid's articles of service ready for him when he was shaven and ready to ride to the church —tuning-fork, psalm-book, Holy Word. She learned history from Dermid's lips and could tell you all about the great revival of eighteen hundred, and greater farther-back revivals than that one. She knew to keep her lips close shut-to

[ 325 ]

when some woman came to the house in a pet, telling of the scandalous life which this or that church member was leading. Always Cean let the matter come to Dermid's ears from another tongue than her own. But he never was swayed by idle gossip; never would he accuse a member, nor allow an elder to do it. By the power of God in his sermons Dermid forced a sinner to accuse himself. He pulled quietly on a sinner's heart, preaching around and about and over and under the sinner's misdoing, and never flinging a hard word straight into his face; then he would swing a tune into a swelling call to prayer—for he could pitch a tune as well by ear as with a tuning-fork—and the sinner would come stumbling down the aisle and, grasping Dermid's hand, he would pour out his confession before the whole congregation. Such a confession is good for the healing of a man's soul; a carbuncle will never heal till it be opened.

O'Connor set apart the first Sabbath of each month to be a Love Feast Day. On that day the converts gave their experiences—new light on some passage of Scripture, the strengthening of some weak sister's faith, homely instances of God's mercy and understanding and answers to prayer: Old Mis' Autrey lost her gold thimble on a Wednesday, and prayed to God to help her find it, and, lo! when she raised her face from between her hands on the bed, there lay the thimble where her face had been; Sallie M'Namara was sifting flour for biscuit when it came to her what The Word meant when it said "pressed down and running over." Each testimony was offered in humility to God's eternal glory; Dermid O'Connor approved each witness of God with a gentle nod and a fervent "God bless you."

Cean could never testify, and it was a shame to her. God-almighty had gone away from her when Dermid O'Connor came close. She could not think hard on Dermid's sermons on the Isle of Patmos, or Calvary, for as the words came out from his clean face, she remembered the touch of his naked mouth. And that was a heinous sin, for she was forty-and-two and a grandmother three times over. (For Kissie now had twin girls named Evaline and Angeline.) Many a time as she sat under Dermid's preaching, her conscience would nudge her, saying, "Rise up! Confess before them all that you are yet full of carnality, though you be now an old woman. That the preacher is your husband is all the more reason why you should empty your heart of sin."

But she would sit unmoved, asking God for mercy, knowing full well that mercy comes after repentance, never before. This was another thing to mull over in the night, long after Dermid was snoring close by her shoulder.

When she knew that she would bear a child on the same moon with Kissie's next, she was so ashamed that she cried, and would not tell Dermid for a week. When he knew, he would not let her grieve, but chided her, laughing, and kissed her face and called her his darlin', but she could pay him no mind for thinking: This Dermid needs to have his mind on God's Word, and not on a woman. I betrayed him away from The Truth. Anyhow, what will I do in Glory, if ever I manage to git there, with two men a-standin' a-waitin' fer me?

But the very next Sabbath Day, Dermid preached such a sermon on "The Witness of the Spirit" as Cean had never heard fall from his lips. She looked for God to strike him dead in the pulpit, but God did not, and from that time on she looked to die in childbed where this child of Dermid's would bring her in no time.

The strangest fancies beset her, so that Dermid grew ever more gentle with her, and ever more anxious in the face. Through the days she had heartburn and sour stomach; through the nights she had visions. One vision came to her which she would much have liked to tell; but the congregation might think that she was taking airs upon herself now that she was the preacher's wife. But she could think on that vision, and so forget any earthly worry, for she had seen Heaven. . . . Alabaster walls encompassed Heaven about, walls that were as tall as the skies of the earth that she had left below. Morning-glories clambered in green fountains on all the alabaster walls. And their trumpet-mouths of blood-red and thundery-blue and moon-white and wine-color and cinnabar—oh, all the mouths of all the colored trumpet-flowers—blew music through the vast breadth of Heaven. But that music did not blare and break upon the ears as does earthly sound; no, that music was soundless and airy; more, it was the air of Heaven, as wind is the air of earth. The very angels breathed music and it was life to them. But Cean could hear the music that had no sound,— as could God and all the saints. She had new hearing; her former hearing had passed away. Past fleshy comprehension was that music compounded of brassy, gay notes of red flower-mouths, muted melody of dusky blue blooms, thin tribble of flaunting white blossoms, and heavy bass of wine-colored ones, and those of cinnabar. Cean could hear that music yet; though the mouths made no sound, yet they filled all the white vaults of the Glory-World with praise: Holy-Holy-Holy!

After that vision, Cean confessed her sense of sin to Dermid. He laughed at her sense of sin. She said:

"What sort of a place might heaven be, Dermid?"

She meant to draw him on. If his answer suited her, she would tell him of her vision. But his mouth filled with argument, and he harangued that heaven was not such a place as mortal man would make it out to be. Only spirits dwelt in heaven, he said. Cean would have none of that, for well she knew that never would she care to strive for heaven if, once there, she could not stroke Dermid's very cheek (and

Lonzo's beard, but she said nothing of that to Dermid), if there she would not see the white scar in Maggie's hand where Maggie had sliced it through once, long ago, as she helped her Ma cook breakfast. How was Cean to know little Caty in heaven if she could not look into her child's cloudy blue eyes nor fondle her soft, fat hands?

Dermid convinced her in long arguments that there is no heaven save a spiritual heaven. Former things shall have passed away, he said. He showed her that she could not have a heaven for the bodies of her loved ones by wishing for it. So she lost her heaven, and she grieved more for it than for any other loss that she had known, for Cean's heaven would have made all things right. Her sense of loss brought fresh upon her grief for those of hers who were dead, and other grief for those of hers who were yet living; for if she would not again see these children, as they now were, once they were dead, then it behooved her to grieve for them now, since they would so soon be spirits, unrecognizable and alien to their mother's heart. And it was so with Dermid and herself; when one of them should leave the other in this world, it would be without hope of a good-morrow on another day. So she went about grieving as Dermid's child grew heavy; and every day that it grew, it reminded her— the thing that is born, it shall die!

Dermid tried many a trick to make her laugh and come out of her long fit of sadness. He sang "A froggie went a-courtin'" till all the children smiled; but Cean would only break into weeping, thinking on how her children would be sour-faced as herself when they were as old. Dermid sang "Ever of thee I'm fondly dreaming," and only made her the sadder because he could not carry such a feeling toward her into a far heaven. He cracked jokes and related many a tale of this or that wild adventure; he told tales of history; but Cean could not bear them once she knew that all the people of that time were long since dead.

Finally he argued at Cean: "Then since the life of a man is but a little time at most, we'd best laugh a little before it be too late. . . ." But that was the simplest of all his foolish arguments, for how can one laugh into a face when one sees it to be a grinning skull beneath the skin? How is one to frolic when he may for the listening hear the beat of time in his ears like a tolling, and no heaven beyond!

Margot laughed at Dermid's worry over Cean, and told him that a woman was like to be a fool at such a time, that all this would pass in the spring of next year. But Dermid could not believe but that Margot was laughing only to cheer him; he could not forget that Cean prophesied that never would she rise from her next childbed.

Late in an afternoon, Aryadne and Bethany strung long necklaces of four-o'clock flowers and brought them to Cean for her to wear about her neck. Because the necklaces minded her of heaven's morning-glories that she had seen in her vision, Cean went into a fit of weeping and groaned in her sleep all night, and spoke out of her head like a woman in a trance.

But when war broke with the Yankees, Cean quieted off and came to her senses; for a captain's detail came from the Confederacy and mustered the men of the settlement.

Cal volunteered and passed muster; Maggie's Will and Margot's tall Vincent did likewise, being of the proper age. Being young and unencumbered, they marched away to shoulder arms, and thought it was a fine thing to have a war to go to.

Cean stormed and raged. A fool thing it was for Cal to go yonder and fight a war over a black nigger. If the nigger wanted to be free, let him fight, his own self! Oh, she could not abear the thought! She lost all her religion in her hate of the men that had made this war. She had begged Cal to slip away from the Confederacy and come back and let her hide him in the swamp. She kept thinking that he might desert and come home, but days passed end on end, and Cal did not come. He did not mind the going, she knew; he was too young to have learned any sense; he was but twenty in October.

Cean bore a girl-child in the early summer, and Dermid gave it her name; to make a difference in his wife and child, he called it Ceany.

She walked to the well before the child was a week old, and looked abroad on her land that was unplowed, unseeded, and it was well into summer. Dermid could preach and teach, but he was no good for farming. And she was sick and had not cared whether seeds went into the ground or stayed out of it. Anyhow, she had planned to die this year, and she was grieving for Cal gone yonder to fight a fool war. Them Coast planters was too hot in the sprocket; if they wanted a war, let them fight hit! But she must get a hump on herself, for some sort of a crop had to be made, some way or t'other.

Dermid tried to keep his school open, but with war talk abroad in the land, and wild rumors on every hand, and many men conscripted and gone yonder God-knows-where, women kept their children at home; anyhow, all hands were needed with the crops now that men's hands were yonder toting muskets with spikes on them to split Yankee bellies.

They made potatoes and meat and a little corn. Dermid did not go to the Coast that fall; there was nothing for him to trade.

Details came oftener as the need for men grew sharper. Bugles sounded in front of the houses, and track-dogs strained on leashes, for the chasing and treeing of deserters. When Jake counted his age and knew that soon he would be called, since he was in the ripe thirties, he brought Kish and her two little boys to Cean's house, and bore his shot-gun and powder-horn and shot-pouch and tinder-box off into the black swamp—and stayed there.

Afterward, sometimes deep in a night, Kish would hear him knocking on the outside of the wall where her bed was set. She would rise and let him in, and gather up meal and powder and shot for him to carry back with him. Once she left her children with Cean, and stayed a week with Jake, deep in the swamp, and they slept on the braced branches of a tree like two wild things. Jake was glad of the war then, for he had Kish with him, and the 'possums ate leather-bread out of his hand.

When it was Jasper's time to go, Dermid went with him. He had wanted to go the whole enduring time, but would not say so; he went with Jasper because he would not stay safely at home with women and children while a war was going on. Margot, left alone with little Sully, brought her oxen and cows and pigs and fowls to Cean's house and set up her bed by Cean's fire. Kissie and her children were already there, for young Seeb was gone to war long ago.

Cean's flour had given out long ago, so they had only hoecakes for bread. The salt gave out and they boiled the dirt from the smokehouse floor and distilled salt from it. Now what would she do for her winter meat? Do without, that's what. She learned to do any work that a man can do. She sawed wood and fixed leaks. She killed hogs and calves as good as Lonzo ever did—and smiled sourly when she remembered how she had grieved when Lonzo killed her first calf at this place.

The bees made sweetening for their hoecakes; the cows let down their milk morning and evening; if the cotton made and the sheep found good pasture, the children would keep warm. If only they could have a good salty piece of meat one more time. . . .

One day broke like another over the backwoods, and

[332]

water must be drawn from the well for every day of cold
or heat, war or peace; cloth must be woven and sewed, and
'taters must be raised and fried, though niggers may be free
to roam the land and take a white man's house away from
him. If only they could get word now and then, maybe the
days would not pass as slowly as a death-watch. At such a
time all a body can do is wait. And it is a good thing to
keep the hands and feet busy at such a time, for work
keeps a mind from wandering; no good can come of a
wandering mind.

To the east, details sallied out, looking for more men;
to the north, the war lay, to the south, the Spanish peril
had settled; from the west, Indians might come down any
dark night, as they used to do in the old times, and scalp
even the smallest screaming child and leave its skull bleeding red, with the soft spot throbbing plain on the top of
its head.

When Cal marched off with a grin on his proud face, he
slung his hand up in farewell to Cean, and she would not
wave her hand to answer his fare-you-well, for she thought
him a fool to go before he had to. Now the remembrance of
how she would not tell him good-by made her thoughts of
him a misery. "If only I had waved good-by to him!" She
had a feeling that she would never see Cal again. "He is
my dependence, now that Lonzo is gone, so he will be the
one to go." For all that he was so good to her, Cean never
put much dependence in Dermid. Dermid was a good man,
but he could not manage a crop or a woman as Lonzo was
able to do.

Cean dreamed a dream of Cal one night, and she knew
when she waked that he was dead. The dream, or more a
vision, came to her in the night of the thirtieth day of
August. Dark closed in on a wide field, and she was seeking
across it, calling for Cal. It grew ever darker as she walked,
calling his name. On the ground all about her feet lay The

Enemy gnashing its teeth; it had no eyes, but ravened wildly over the ground, slobbering red so that the earth was slimy. As long as she kept out of its way, going quietly, it might not harm her, but, oh, what have you done to Cal? O-o-o-o-oh, Cal! Son, hit's yore ma a-callin' ye! . . . She found Cal fallen in a shape that no one but herself would have known, for his face was buried in the hot black earth. But well she knew the way his hair grew on his neck, and the set of his thin shoulders that had holp her plant and crap ever since his pa died—all but these last war crops when he was fighting. She fell on the ground beside Cal. She had no time to lift his head out of the earth so that she might see his face and tell if there were not some breath yet left in him, for buzzards swarmed out of the hot night and settled on his legs and feet and tried to jerk them off in their beaks. Then she knew that Cal was dead. The buzzards told her. But still she fought over Cal. She clenched her arms around his head and would not let go; the buzzards set their claws in his legs and ankles and gnawed as far up as his knee joints, and would not leave him be for all her fighting. But they could not reach his head nor his scrawny little shoulders, for Cean had these hidden inside her arms on her breast, and the nasty things must eat off her finger bones and pluck away her lips and eyes before they could reach Cal's head in her arms. She fought with all her might, but before she knew it there was a black beak hacking at the breast bone over her heart. . . .

Near the battle-ground there stood a large brick building that could serve, if put to it, as a hospital; and through a glade of willows there ran a little stream, and water is useful to a surgeon. The night was bright with moonlight, running water was near, and litter-bearers brought in the dying who cried for water; all night long the surgeon probed for Minié balls or reached for a scalpel or a saw. . . .

Here is a boy with his legs shattered; his mouth cries, his wounds weep blood. The surgeon reached for his saw, but even as he reached, the boy flung back his head, turned aside his face as though he hid it, and died.

Cean's vision was a heavier grief than the word, coming to her long afterward, that Cal fell at Second Manassas—and that was the thirtieth day of August. . . .

—I birthed him by myself while Lonzo was gone to the Coast. . . . I killed a painter that wanted to eat him. . . . He was my first man-child. . . . Seems as how God might have let him die at home and not off there for the buzzards to eat him. But mayhap somebody dug a hole for him to rest in, away from their greedy beaks.—Never did she know, and it was a sorrow to her; death is bad enough at its best, when ye can bury a body and lovingly tend the earth that lies above it. . . .

The war was long over when Margot saw Jasper again.

It was a queer thing to do, but one night she dreamed that Jasper was at Ma's place. Next morning she said to Cean:

"I've got to go home this mornin'. . . ."

Cean argued with her, but Margot would not listen.

"Ye'd be a fool to go traipsin' away over there. They hain't a thing ye kin do but stand and look at the house. And hit hain't hardly burned down without no fire in hit. . . ."

But Margot would go.

And she found Jasper there, jaundiced and out of his head with fever. It was a full week before he knew her or noticed her; he had outdone his strength in trying to get home to Margot before he got down with this sickness.

One night as she held Jasper's head so that she could get him to drink a fever-brew without spilling it, Margot nigh dropped the cup when she chanced upon a thing that came into her mind without her having thought of it. She turned the thought over and over, and the longer it lay in her mind the more beautiful it grew. This was her thought: I have you back, Jasper; your head lies here on my arm; but if you had never come home again, yet I should never have lost you. It is precious little difference that a little time or a little distance can make, once a woman loves a man through and through, the way I loved you, Jasper; and it is the same with Lias; I loved you and I loved him, and though I never set eyes upon his face again, yet neither is he lost to me. I have the both of you fast in my heart.

In the same week as Jasper's return, Margot's Vincent came home, helping along Kissie's young husband, Seeb, whom he had run across in a haywagon in Carolina. Seeb had lost a leg at Petersburg and was a sight to make the eyes weep.

Cean stayed on the lookout for Dermid, thinking every day to see him. Somehow she did not feel like Dermid was dead; and seems like he could have got home in this time, if he wanted to. . . . But la me! Dermid was nigh onto sixty; maybe he was down sick some'eres without nobody to look after him. . . .

She could not help with the planting this spring. She could tell Jamie and Johnnie and Lonzo's Vince how to do it, but she could not help with it herself, for she could not stand the heat. Twice she had swounded away in the furrow and nigh scared them all to death.

She saw to little chores around the house.

On a June day she was grinding the ax on the whetrock at the other side of the crib. She turned the rock slowly, and spat on the edge of the ax every now and then. Hot afternoon sunshine fell on her bent head; the heat of it gave her a smothering feeling in her chest. She lifted her head to blow a little and chanced to glance down the lane of blossoming crepe myrtle.

She saw Dermid walking slowly up the lane toward her. He was footsore—or else a cripple—and he looked like a beggar in gray rags. His cheeks were as thickly-bearded as Lonzo's. He did not look like himself, but somehow she knew him.

When she caught sight of him, he waved his hand to her and hastened his steps.

He had walked from Virginny, catching cart-rides as he might, sleeping in haystacks or on the open ground or in a friendly bed, as chance allowed. He had begged meal, and a little grease to sop it in, wherever he could find it. He had not had a horse under him when Lee signed out. Those who had horses were lucky, for such a man could sell the horse, or ride it home and make a crop with it. If Dermid had a horse, he could have got home in no time; it is a right smart piece from Virginny to Georgy if a man must foot it.

Dermid came slowly toward Cean and bared his head, taking his old slouch-hat in his hand. She saw that he was an old man, bent and lean; his eyes no longer shot blue fires, for they were clouded over. He held out his hand toward her, saying nothing, for he thought—If I tried I could not tell ye how glad it is I be to see ye; so I'll not try; ye'll have to guess at it or leave it be. . . .

His face swam before her face. She was bent and lean, too; her face was furrowed and her hair was thin and white and tightly drawn over her skull.

Neither did she say any word more than he did; she did not even take his hand, for she was thinking—I have hurt so much and so long in my heart that I reckon I don't feel things much any more, not even yore comin' home. . . .

Slowly he spoke:

"Don't ye know me, Cean?"

Her mouth crimped up:

"I reckon hit must be Dermid O'Connor. . . ."

She leaned on the whetrock stand, trying to find words to say to him; he leaned upon the very sight of her face before his eyes.

She called out shrilly:

"You chillurn! Hyere's Dermid O'Connor! . . ."

The children came running, but Dermid could but guess at which one was his child. And that child was afraid of him.

They talked far into the night, for there were a thousand questions to be asked and answered; and between the questions there were silences to be honored, when words were helpless as they are helpless in any silence of a lover or a mourner.

Out of a silence Dermid asked after Lias. Cean shook her head slowly:

"Hit would be comfortin' t' know, no matter what may have befallen him. . . . He was but a year older than me. . . . Aah, la! In this time he is an old man with a white head and a troubled heart. . . . Somehow I kain't think of Lias bein' old and worried out. . . ."

He reached for her hand and held it, turning it in his hand and gloating over it as though it were a new-found treasure he had chanced upon. Presently they lay down in the dark and slept. As the hours wore on, the slow fire in the fireplace died among persimmon-colored coals and warm ashes white as frost.

"So I am bound for Californy," Lias thought, soberly, as the stage rattled down the post road toward Savanna.

As the stage passed, dust settled behind it all down the road on the leaves of the wild myrtle bushes that were still wet and shiny from night vapors. Morning sun peeped through pines yonder in the east; Lias could see it every now and then betwixt pine boles that grew in a clear space.

The air of the early day was cold, and mist hovered low over every softly-flowing branch of dark water; but Lias was warm in a new olive-colored great-coat. The coat's broad lappets were pierced with big worked buttonholes—a meaningless vanity, for there were no buttons to go into those holes; now there were buttons to fasten up his stuck-out chest, but the lappets were but vain show.

Lias settled his head low within the turned-up collar. He might have slept but that his in'ards were yet weak from being corned last night. And then besides his unsettled stomach, there was the rattling of the coach to disturb him, and the thudding of the horses' hooves, and the lifting before his eyes of an horizon diurnally new.

At the end of this road was Savanna, and straight around The Horn was Californy.

But he could find no ship in Savanna to suit his needs. There was a small Spanish schooner there, swaying on her hull in the tidewater, and a few little catboats. There was a brig in the West Indian trade. And there was a dingy old Canton trader deadened by her cargo of copper basins, reels, duffle, stroud, powder, lead, guns, cassia, and a hundred-weight vermilion. But the old boat would beat up the Coast and back before she saw Californy. As for a straight-out Californy ship, there was none.

In a gropshop, Lias stood a glass all 'round, old sailors first, claiming an ill-humor of his in'ards to excuse himself from drinking.

Soon the sailors were bellowing "Poor Tom Bowline" and "Captain Gone Ashore," with all heads close over the glasses. Lias, not knowing the words, joined in the bass, trying to pick up the words as he went along. A brawny tar in a red shirt and a Scotch cap leaned into Lias's face:

"So it's Californy fer ye. Then it's Ann Street, Boston ye want. I'll pen ye word to the right place, and my Rory can give ye victuals whilst yere there. Ye kin tell her that Jack sent ye, but mind out ye don't kiss her fer me. . . ."

Before Lias saw Boston, he learned to sleep in spite of horses' hooves and rattling coaches; and ever there was new land for him to see, like as though he was sailing a discovery-ship to unknown parts.

All the way as he went thick dust settled behind him, or mud closed in on the furrowing wheels, so that before an hour was gone, sign of his passing was effaced in late dust, or mud over a swift furrow.

Jack's Rory filled Lias well, and before he was through with eating with her he tried to kiss her because Jack had told him not to do it; she slapped him back'ards nearbout acrost the room for the trouble he took.

"Looky hyere," she says, with a Northern twang as hard as ice, "see't ye mind yere own business!"

Lias roared at that; he had not wanted to kiss her any old how. Never yet had he failed to kiss any woman that he wanted to kiss. This Rory was beef-colored and coarse as the sole of yere foot, and no more than a callet at long last.

Eighty days from Boston to Callao was a short shuffle— better than Lias could hope for. It would take him forever to get to Californy, but the overland route would be nigh-about as bad, and anyhow Lias purposed to sail in a ship.

In Ann Street he found a shipping-office and a shipping-master and shipping-articles that were open; he signed the articles with his new name, Vincent Trent, received his advance, and was so bound to the northwest coast—ship *Maidenhead,* Joseph Tyler, master, for Callao and California, by Gorton, Dancie & Co., for a two or three years' voyage. What mattered it how long! He was but thirty and two over.

Rory outfitted him with go-ashore trousers and jackets, pumps, stockings, neckerchiefs, a blue jacket, and a straw hat; he stowed them away in his sea chest along with Bowditch's *Navigator* and Bulwer's *Paul Clifford* and a jest-book. Rory gave him the books and a big silk hand kerchief for a bad cold or a greasy mouth or any such thing.

He learned a thing from Jack's Rory. As he left her, she said:

"Now that yere leaving and no harm done, I'll kiss ye good-by to say good-speed to ye. But don't go along kissing lightly. A kiss oughta be a tedious thing to come by." Lias never forgot her saying.

They made sail late in the afternoon when the sky was the color of a dove and the sea was as gray as cold iron. They dropped slowly down with the tide and a light wind. The ship stood still and the land went away from it, sinking into the water. Gray sky, gray water, gray sails curved down into night; yonder were a few lights that the eyes must strain to see, and then there were no lights.

Wind sang past Lias's ears; the ship settled into a gallant pitch. A sense of desolation came upon Lias's heart—If I could go back now, I would do it.—

She had a good breeze on her quarter, and every stitch of canvas spread. I left Margot with a man-child to raise and she will be hard put to it, for he is much like me. And now Fairby has neither mother nor father. We will put in at Saint Mary's for water, and that will be close home, but I will not go home, now that I have set my head.

—She's steppin' down to Cape Horn. Watch her toss her head and strain her flanks! But never shall I set eyes on my old mother again. She's steppin' down to Cape Horn. Hear her snort and paw the foam!—

When the empty kids were sent back to the galley, Lias looked up the scuttle and saw certain stars swing out of his sight and back again. A qualm seized him like a hand that wrenched his stomach. The first night out is apt to be the lonesomest, so the men set up their voices and sang, and the sound of their singing was worse on Lias than his sick stomach:

"Perhaps like me he struggles with each feeling of
  regret;
But if he loved as I have loved, he never can forget. . . ."

Lias fell into his hammock and covered his face, although
no one could have seen him for the dark. The men roared
their songs, but the green hand did not join in:

"Oh no, we never mention him. . . ."

Hove to, with bare poles shrouded in sleet, she took The
Horn.

With ears laid back, she plunged and kicked and reared
and leaped. The steep, icy waves all but killed her, the gales
punished her, so that she was like to lay herself down dead
in the water that was as black and wild as torment. The
ocean froze in Lias's hair and eyelashes, and the flesh of his
face and hands cracked and bled.

Then she shook from her wet flanks the water that was
thick with ice and cantered up to Callao. Soon she scented
Californy on the warm wind and went galloping chock up
to windward.

But now Lias was so sick of lung fever, or some other
thing, that he did not know when the shipmaster anchored
off Santa Barbara and set him inshore in a dinghy.

There was a low sandy tongue of land and little boats
were a-fishing beyond the point.

An old woman nursed him; the shipmaster knew her
from other voyages. Lias had spat blood until the shipmaster thought it scarce needful for him to put in for this
man, Vincent Trent, on the return voyage; Trent would be
dead in a week.

But Lias Carver lived nighonto seven years.

Sometimes in a bad spell he bled until his hiccups shook
the bed, so near was he to death. But after these mouth-
bleeds he would feel stronger and his fever would assuage.

Sometimes for weeks he was able to be up and to walk slowly about in the hard sunshine and to watch the bright sea that bore ships dipping upon it like gulls.

He had clothes and money aplenty. Anyhow, these Californy people were thriftless and extravagant and kind; he would have eaten if he had not possessed a real to his name.

The old woman grew a liking for le Inglis mariner. His sunken eyes were like those of a child who is too frightened to complain; the long white bones of his hands all but showed through the pale skin. He learned the old woman's heathen speech from her and came to feel dependence upon her. When half his blood had gushed away as she held his head that went limp in her hands, he would lie at peace, shuddering, and was thankful for her as he had never been for any other woman.

He came to like the taste of the baked meats, and the frijoles stewed with peppers and onions, and Californy flour baked into macaroni; but much he would have liked to taste a cornpone again, and a pot of Ma's greens seasoned with green pork middlin'.

An old monk made friends with Lias. His head was shaven and a long silver chain swung from his neck. When Lias was abed for weakness, not a day passed that the old friar did not come softly in on his sandals and talk with Lias of this or that matter. When Lias was able, he visited the friar in his plain room that was furnished with a chair and a table and a hard bed and pictures of the saints.

When Lias's enfeeble ' body could not much longer support the weight of his soul, the old friar made the soul ready for its passing.

Then it was that Lias wrote his letter home.

He thought deeply into the matter.

"I want 'em always expectin' me," he said. "Till they die, they will be sayin', 'Lias may come tomorrow.' . . ."

The monk counseled him against dying with a lie between himself and other souls, but Lias would have his way:

"I want Ma and Margot and my children to know that I would come if I could. If they knew that I was dead, they would not look for me to come any more. . . ." Suddenly his eyes brightened: "It may chance that I can go, after all. . . . My fevers have run as high as this a many a time. . . ."

The gray friar shook his head and shuffled his sandals on the earthen floor. Beyond the stone threshold the old woman drowsed, her hands folded in her lap. In the hot sunshine at her feet, an old brindled cat gave suck to three new-born kittens.

As he wrote the letter, Lias had to lay his quill aside time after time, for weakness made his blood as water. He would back his letter to Lonzo, since never had Lonzo been hard against him for his misdoings.

> Tell Ma that I have got her a vermilion-dyed merino dress picked out and linnen cloaths aplenty to dike herself out in. . . .

That was all he could write now. The quill fell from his fingers and his head sank into the pillow. Cold sweat wet all his body, and weeping wet his face. His fine teeth showed in his bright beard; they were bared in anguish; his mouth seemed as though it might be laughing at some strange and cruel jest. After a time, he took the quill again:

> Tell Fairby that her pa has got boughten for her a silk dress. . . .
> Tell my wife if she be willing I should wish to take up where I left off and give her such a bridal party as she will not be ashamed of.

—Godalmighty knows that I meant well by ye, Margot, when I got ye to marry me! . . .—

Scarce a week after he had written the letter, Lias fought through a day and night for his lessening breath. With each

short, expiring breath he adjured his Maker: "Have mercy!
Have mercy! Have mercy!"

He could not put full faith in the prayers of the old friar,
howsomever kind he might be. He turned back to his
mother's God: "Have mercy! . . . Have mercy! . . . Have
mercy! . . ."

Sundown was not far off; in the smooth, bulging distance
the sun eased himself into the ocean to quench the boiling
flame that studs his breast. Shaking water crumpled the
gold pavement of the sunset. Lias ceased his praying, for
suddenly the compelling hunger in his breast no longer
tortured him. Above his head he heard the sound of a
woman's soft weeping, and the sound was like the sound of
an outgoing tide's little waves that caress the sand monot-
onously, sibilant, and as precious as tears.

Little boats were a-fishing beyond the point.

Cean had said:
"Aah, la! In this time he is an old man with a white head
and a troubled heart. . . ."

It might have comforted Cean to know that Lias's heart
was untroubled as he slept whilst she was here with Dermid.
And upon his head where it lay encased in peace there had
been not one thread of white; all his hair was the color
of topazes and autumn-flowering saffron and gold leaf made
of beaten gold—the like pleasing color of Fairby's hair.

**THE END**

# Afterword

As the first novel by a Georgian to win the Pulitzer Prize, *Lamb in His Bosom* enjoyed enthusiastic national and regional attention during the mid-1930s. Indeed, its success has been credited with prompting Harold Latham of Macmillan to make the trip in search of "southern" material that ultimately resulted in publication of the next Pulitzer Prize-winning novel by a Georgian, Margaret Mitchell's *Gone With the Wind*. Although Margaret Mitchell's novel rapidly overshadowed Caroline Miller's in the popular imagination, *Lamb in His Bosom* retained the devotion of readers and the admiration of critics. In 1934, the year when *Lamb in His Bosom* won the Pulitzer and the French prize, Prix Femina, it ranked first on the best seller list, and during the first fifty-three years after its publication in 1933, there were at least thirty-seven editions. The first edition alone went through more than thirty printings, followed by numerous reprintings as well as translations into French and Dutch. Yet, in the interim, by the time Caroline Miller died at age eighty-eight, in the Haywood County Hospital in Waynesville, North Carolina, copies of *Lamb in His Bosom* had become virtually unobtainable.

When *Lamb in His Bosom* appeared, Caroline Miller was, to her chagrin, a few days beyond her thirtieth birthday. She would have preferred to have made a mark while she was still twenty-nine. This concern to accomplish something noteworthy before the age of thirty contrasts sharply with the apparent circumstances of her life at the time: wife of a school superintendent in the south Georgia town of Baxley and mother of three sons under seven. She had been born in Waycross, Georgia, seventh and youngest child of a school teacher, Elias Pafford, and his wife, Levy Zan Pafford. Both sides of the family were well rooted in Waycross and featured a long line of preachers and teachers. Her maternal great-grandfather, a New Light minister, had settled there during the frontier period, and her paternal grandfather had built the country church at which all of the family was buried.

Throughout childhood, Caroline Pafford had demonstrated a variety of artistic and literary talents and, while in high school, had written a play, "Red Callico," which won first prize in a contest held by the Little Theater in Savannah as well as a prize in another competition in New York.[1] Two months after graduation from high school, when she was just seventeen, Caroline Pafford married William D. Miller, her English teacher, and settled down to raise a family. In 1936, after the publication and success of her novel, Caroline Miller divorced her husband and, in 1937, after a year in Biloxi, Mississippi, met and married Clyde H. Ray, Jr., a florist and antique dealer from Waynesville, North Carolina. They had two children, a boy and a girl. In 1944, she published a second novel, *Lebanon*, also set in south Georgia, which proved much less successful than *Lamb in His Bosom*. Thereafter, she published some short stories, but never another novel. She nonetheless continued to write throughout her life, although she seems to have written at a slower pace as domestic affairs consumed more and more of her time. At her death, she left a number of unpublished manuscripts.

According to one story, Caroline Miller had begun to write when her children were young and she wanted to supplement the family income. As a young mother, she spent what time she could collecting stories of frontier life from her family and people in the countryside around Baxley. She would go on excursions with her children, keeping her eyes peeled for old people in old houses who might have stories to tell. Frequently, she would introduce herself to them under the pretext of wanting to buy butter and eggs.

The evidence suggests that, from an early age, she was ambitious and viewed writing as a serious craft. Various accounts of her success in the Georgia newspapers of the 1930s emphasize her devotion as a wife and mother, insisting that, for her, womanly responsibilities always came first. She herself once noted that housekeeping and homemaking were not exactly the same thing and that although she cared deeply about making a home, she did not worry compulsively about the finer points of domestic neatness and order. Like many nineteenth-century women novelists, she seems to have written comfortably amidst her children's comings

[ 348 ]

and goings, stopping in the middle of a sentence to answer a question and then returning to her work. Even if one discounts for some retrospective sentimentality, those stories conform to her portrait of Cean Smith as a young mother in *Lamb in His Bosom*. But it would be rash to take them as evidence that she did not take her own craft seriously.

Caroline Miller's correspondence with Frank Daniel, a reporter for the *Atlanta Journal* who had reviewed *Lamb in His Bosom* enthusiastically (10 September 1933), reveals a lively, sophisticated intelligence and considerable cultural breadth. She may not have had a college education, but she seems to have read widely and paid close attention to the ways in which other writers accomplished their purposes. She acknowledged, apparently in response to a query from Daniel, that she had read some of "Chapman's and the other woman's (Roberts) stuff, but I always confuse the two writers; perhaps they did influence me, I don't know, but certainly not consciously." She liked Sigrid Undset "better than a dozen others all rolled together." She claimed to know none of Erskine Caldwell's work and to remember almost nothing of Frances Newman's. She read and liked Pearl Buck's *The Good Earth*, but only after the publication of *Lamb in His Bosom*, so it cannot have influenced her.[2] In subsequent letters, she referred to Victor Hugo and D. H. Lawrence, as well as to some of the better-known southern writers of her day—Stark Young, William Faulkner, Ellen Glasgow, and Thomas Wolfe, whom she judged by far the best of the group.[3]

Early reviewers, almost without exception, praised *Lamb in His Bosom*, normally emphasizing Miller's uncanny ability to make the plain folk of south Georgia come alive. And since then, the novel has been recognized as one of the best existing examples of Georgia dialect during the period before the Civil War.[4] Frank Daniel associated the novel with those of Gladys Hasty Carroll, Marjorie Kinnan Rawlings, Elizabeth Maddox Roberts, and Maristan Chapman. He praised Miller's insight in finding "the poetry and dignity and beauty which were obscured by the apparent drab monotony and bleak hardship of pioneer life in south Georgia," and for giving it "glowing reality and a rich, lasting appeal in a superb novel."[5] Louis Kronenberger, reviewing the novel for the *New York Times*, offered more qualified approval than most other reviewers, but, like Daniel, began by comparing it to the work of Elizabeth Maddox Roberts. In his judgment, *Lamb in His Bosom* is less notable as a novel than it is as a picture. But notwithstanding the novel's "blemishes," "it remains in the mind a wonderfully large and vital picture" of life before the Civil War in a "small, isolated, backwoods community of men and women bred to pioneer hardship."[6]

Although to reduce *Lamb in His Bosom* to yet another example of regional historical realism would be to slight important aspects of its power and appeal, the reviewers who emphasized its historical realism were not wrong. If anything, even the most enthusiastic may have underestimated Miller's accomplishment. The yeoman farmers of the antebellum South left very few first-hand accounts of their experience, the poorer whites virtually none. In the absence of such personal testimonies, historians have been forced to reconstruct the everyday lives and beliefs of this most numerous portion of antebellum southern whites from impersonal statistics on population, size of holdings, crop production, church membership, or political participation. Here and there references to nonslaveholding whites in the papers of the slaveholders and the recollections of former slaves help to flesh out the story. But the nonslaveholding whites were, overwhelmingly, a people who lacked the time—and frequently the education—to keep the diaries or write the letters that make the thoughts and feelings of the wealthier slaveholders come alive.

In *Lamb in His Bosom*, Miller makes that most elusive group of antebellum southerners, the poor whites, come as alive as if they had been keeping running accounts of their lives and feelings. Perhaps most important, she does so in a way that, so far as we can judge today, remains remarkably faithful to what their experience must have been. First, as many of her reviewers noted, she demonstrated an extraordinary fidelity to the language of those she was writing about. Doubtless her accomplishment in this regard was facilitated by the comparative isolation of Appling County, where

[ 350 ]

she lived, from the social and economic changes that were creating the New South. When she drove into the countryside around Baxley, she was likely to have met people who still spoke and thought much as their antebellum forebears would have spoken and thought. And, like Elizabeth Maddox Roberts, with whom she resisted comparison, she had a gift—I am tempted to say a genius—for capturing the voices of plain folks in a literary language that never descended to condescension or reduced them to curiosities.

Second and no less important, Miller understood the context of the lives of those she was writing about. Her accounts of the business of everyday life—how children were birthed, how the crops were planted and brought in, what people ate, how they furnished their houses, the rare store-bought object they might possess and value—conform in extraordinary detail to what we know about the Old South from a myriad of sources. It is difficult to think of a single other text that could give students of antebellum southern history as complete or accurate an account of the lives of nonslaveholding whites.

Even as Miller understood the material context of plain folks' lives, so did she, almost uncannily, understand their mental universes. Her accounts, toward the end of the novel, of Cean's visions of heaven ring true, as do her accounts of Cean's understanding of and attitudes toward black slaves. Thus Cean knows that "never would she care to strive for heaven if once there, she could not stroke Dermid's very cheek (and Lonzo's beard, but she said nothing of that to Dermid), if there she would not see the white scar in Maggie's hand where Maggie had sliced it through once, long ago, as she helped her Ma cook breakfast" (328–29). Cean has no comprehension of or use for a heaven in which she would only meet those she had loved on earth as spirits: In her heaven, they would be as she had known them on earth, but without the marks of pain or toil; in her heaven, those she had loved on earth would live amidst morning-glories and clear green fountains.

Black slaves, whom Miller has Cean call "niggers," have no place in the world of Appling County as perceived by its white inhabitants, just as, for Cean and her family, proslavery and antislavery arguments have no bearing on their lives. Slaves are for folks on the coast. When the outbreak of the Civil War threatens to demand that her menfolk fight, she storms and rages. "A fool thing it was for Cal to go yonder and fight a war over a black nigger. If the nigger wanted to be free, let him fight his own self!" (330). And she comes to hate the elite white men who had made the war. Yet Cean, who throughout her married life has occasionally fantasized what it might be like to have a slave to do her work, is not antislavery. She shares the attitudes of the poor, rural southerners who simultaneously resented and coveted the fabulous and poorly understood luxuries that wealthy whites were said to enjoy. Cean knows that she "could work her fingers to the bone in the field beside Lonzo and she'd never live like the Coast ladies; they were diked out in silk cloth and breastpins; they could have a black lashed twenty-five times because maybe he didn't bend low enough when they passed by in shining carioles" (190). And when Cean's children fantasize about what they would bring back from the coast, were they able to go, Cean's son Cal outdoes the rest, announcing, "I'll fotch back a hundred niggers fer Ma to beat on'" (196).

From language to plot to the detailed descriptions of everyday life, Miller shows the intricate ways in which the lives and minds of Cean Smith and her family focus on their own microcosmic rural world, occasionally intersecting with strands of the larger culture within which it is set: Their lilting dialectic bears traces of the English of the days of Shakespeare and the King James version of the Bible; each year the men of the community travel the eighty miles to the coast to trade their small agricultural surplus for such exotic town goods as the clock that Lonzo brings Cean; the preacher, Dermid O'Connor, arrives to give ritual and language to their inchoate faith and rudimentary education to their children; vague news of the California gold rush draws Lias away in quest of adventure and fortune; Cean recalls that in Carolina, from where her parents had migrated, there were fruits called apples, although she has never seen one. Like so many rural, frontier settlements, they are at once in the larger world and yet not of it. The clock, which Cean lovingly polishes, captures the in-but-not-of-ness. It keeps perfect time, methodically marking the minutes and hours of their lives. But they live their lives by the rhythms of pregnancies and childbirth, the sequence of crops, and the cycle of seasons—not by the ticking of the clock.

Caroline Miller took her novel's title from the Bible, Isaiah 40:11. "He shall feed His flock like a shepherd; He shall gather the lambs with His arm, and carry them in His bosom." Seen, Cean's aged mother, has a Bible and insists on family prayers at which she sings a psalm and reads a chapter from the Bible. Above all others, Seen loves "How Firm a Foundation," which promises those who keep faith with the Lord that "'when hoary hairs shall their temples adorn / Like lambs in My bosom they shall be born'" (208). Seen, in her dotage, seems almost to be throwing that promise back in the face of the Lord. The harsh conditions of Cean's own life frequently leave reason to challenge it. Yet through the pain, the losses, and the unremitting toil of keeping on, these people, Miller suggests, are indeed God's own.

Throughout the novel, Miller shows the ways in which faith and respect for human culture wrestle with nature in order to forge meaning out of the recurrence of seasons and life. Her exquisite skill colors almost every page, but especially graces her evocations of Cean's relation to her husbands, her children, and her own body. For Cean's is a body that bears children as naturally as a tree bears fruit. Some women, she knows, have trouble conceiving; others bear only a few children. But she seems to become pregnant each time she weans the baby at her breast, bearing thirteen for Lonzo and another for Dirmid, when her hair is turning white. In mid-life she comes to resent her constant pregnancies, and she believes that she lost the two male twins she had been carrying because in her heart she had not welcomed them. But as the years pass, her flutter of rebelliousness dissipates, and she, wordlessly, accepts the pregnancies as natural extensions of her own body.

Caroline Miller's Cean grows from a shy girl into a strong, resourceful, and vibrantly attractive woman. Yet she could not be more different from the model of the southern belle as captured in Mitchell's Scarlett O'Hara. For Cean's greatest beauty comes after,

[ 353 ]

not before, the birth of her children and seems to grow throughout her life. And her attractiveness to men grows out of her membership in a community of women, not out of her competition with them, just as it grows out of her acceptance of the relations between women and men in a rural household. Thus Miller shows Cean as simultaneously delighting in her own strength and accepting her own weakness, alternately working beside Lonzo in the fields or, debilitated by another pregnancy, struggling simply to care for the children and get the meals on the table. Significantly, her moment of supreme strength comes when, exhausted from having delivered her most recent baby alone and too weak even to wash it, she kills the "painter" who has been drawn by the smell of her and the infant's blood. In that moment, Miller, with fierce understatement, represents Cean as the embodiment of human will in confrontation with the most dangerous forces of nature. Thus Cean, at her most "natural," is most at war with the nature that threatens to engulf her.

Louis Kronenberger reproached Miller, above all, for allowing the plot of *Lamb in His Bosom* to dry up during the second half. He felt that the sap and poetry collapsed into prosaic details. "The births, the deaths, the marriages are no longer rich chunks out of a unique world, but mere jottings in a parish register.[7] Yet Jane Judge, writing in the *Savannah Morning News*, thought differently, insisting that the scope of *Lamb in His Bosom* transcended a regional conception. "The types, the experiences, are in the deep sense universal, and even the setting, distinctive and local as it is, assumes a certain universality."[8] Judge, who was especially concerned to defend Miller against possible dismissal as a mere historical realist or regionalist, wanted readers to understand that the characters of *Lamb in His Bosom* should invite identification rather than be dismissed as curiosities. We are, she argued, more like the novel's characters than we are different from them. And what we share with them is what makes us human. From the vantage point of the New York literary scene, Kronenberger had difficulty in recognizing those commonalities, which he might well have found threatening. But had he been able to see them, he might also have seen that the plot of *Lamb in His Bosom* never falters. For unlike the novels of

[ 354 ]

self-conscious self-discovery and becoming of which Kronenberger presumably approved, *Lamb in His Bosom* is a novel of completion and, ultimately, continuity.

Thus Miller's decision to conclude with Lias's death amidst Spanish Catholics on the west coast simultaneously acknowledges that the daring, rebellious adventurer ends just like those he has left behind, and that even the separation of a continent cannot break his ties to them. "'I want 'em always expectin' me,' he said." And, at the end, "he turned back to his mother's God," begging for mercy (343). It might, Miller tells us, have comforted Cean, who knows nothing of his death, to know that his head has not one thread of white, but is all "the color of topazes and autumn-flowering saffron and gold leaf made of beaten gold" (345). In this perspective, Cean's story may be understood as the story of a community whose values she embodies. And the narrative's gradual shift from emphasis on specific events—her marriage to Lonzo, the birth of her first child—to absorption of events into a more general, less differential pattern may be seen as a faithful, and highly crafted, representation of the changing consciousness of this one woman—perhaps all women—as she moves through the cycle of her life.

*Elizabeth Fox-Genovese*

# Footnotes

1. Frank Daniel, in his review, "Lamb in His Bosom," for the *Atlanta Journal* ( 10 September 1933) claims that the play had been written in conjunction with King Bowden. It was produced in Savannah.

2. Caroline Miller to Frank Daniel of 1 May 1934, 2 June 1934, 23 April 1935, all in the Daniel Collection, Special Collections, Woodruff Library.

3. Letters from Caroline Miller to Frank Daniel of 1 May 1934, 2 June 1934, 23 April 1935, all in the Daniel Collection, Special Collections, Woodruff Library.

4. David M. Graig, "Caroline Miller," *Dictionary of Literary Biography*, v. 9, part 2, American Novelists, 1910–1945 (Gale Research Company, 1981), 208–10.

5. Frank Daniel, "Lamb in His Bosom," for the *Atlanta Journal* (10 September 1933).

6. Louis Kronenberger, "A First Novel of Distinguished Quality," *New York Times Book Review* (17 September 1933).

7. Louis Kronenberger, "A First Novel of Distinguished Quality," *New York Times Book Review* (17 September 1933).

8. Jane Judge, "Lamb in His Bosom: A Novel of Georgia Pioneers," *Savannah Morning News* (17 September 1933).

CAROLINE MILLER was born in Waycross, Georgia, in 1904, and lived in Baxley, Georgia, until 1934. Shortly after graduating from high school, she married William D. Miller, her high school English teacher, and had three children. She began traveling through rural south Georgia, interviewing the people she met and planning a novel; as she had not attended college, her husband taught her about literature. "He was my college," she said.

The success of *Lamb in His Bosom* and her resulting celebrity after winning the Pulitzer Prize in 1934 made it difficult for her to resume her former life in Baxley. She and her husband divorced, and she moved to Biloxi, Mississippi, and then to Waynesville, North Carolina. She remarried and had two more children. Her second novel, *Lebanon*, was published in 1944.

Caroline Miller died in Waynesville in 1992. Until her death, she wrote every day, leaving numerous unpublished manuscripts.

ELIZABETH FOX-GENOVESE is the Eleonore Raoul Professor of the Humanities and Professor of History at Emory University, where she is also an associate member of the English Department. Her most recent publications include *Within the Plantation Household: Black and White Women of the Old South* and *Feminism Without Illusion: A Critique of Individualism*, as well as an edition of Augusta Jane Evans' novel *Beulah*. She has published widely on women's issues and culture in scholarly journals and in the popular press.

CAROLINE MILLER was born in Waycross, Georgia, in 1904, and lived in Baxley, Georgia, until 1934. Shortly after graduating from high school, she married William D. Miller, her high school English teacher, and had three children. She began traveling through rural south Georgia, interviewing the people she met and planning a novel; as she had not attended college, her husband taught her about literature. "He was my college," she said.

The success of *Lamb in His Bosom* and her resulting celebrity after winning the Pulitzer Prize in 1934 made it difficult for her to resume her former life in Baxley. She and her husband divorced, and she moved to Biloxi, Mississippi, and then to Waynesville, North Carolina. She remarried and had two more children. Her second novel, *Lebanon*, was published in 1944.

Caroline Miller died in Waynesville in 1992. Until her death, she wrote every day, leaving numerous unpublished manuscripts.

ELIZABETH FOX-GENOVESE is the Eleonore Raoul Professor of the Humanities and Professor of History at Emory University, where she is also an associate member of the English Department. Her most recent publications include *Within the Plantation Household: Black and White Women of the Old South* and *Feminism Without Illusion: A Critique of Individualism*, as well as an edition of Augusta Jane Evans' novel *Beulah*. She has published widely on women's issues and culture in scholarly journals and in the popular press.